Gumnil's Deception

The Tol Chronicles, Book III

by Robert G. Ferrell

ISBN 978-01927384-31-2
Published by Zetabella Publishing
Toronto Canada, 2016
Printed in the US.
zetabella.com

Cover art by Jamie Noble Frier

For Ady

Chapter One

His Majesty Tragacanth sat in the Royal Situation Room with his Ministers for International Relations and National Defense, Eqbo Dehsz and Senrit Paqraq, respectively, as well as the ubiquitous Boogla, his wife and Magineer Liaison. They were discussing the recent sighting by the Tragacanth Coastal Patrol of a corvet crewed by orcs fleeing from the orc enclave near Balom in Galanga, just south of their border with Tragacanth. As sovereign of the nation spotting the activity, it was Aspet's responsibility under the Treaty of Mutual Containment to report it to the international community.

"No assumptions or speculations, please," Aspet instructed them, "Just report the facts. We don't know what the orcs are planning and I don't want to trigger some massive military response. This could be something as simple as a pleasure cruise by desperately bored people who basically are confined to prison for life simply because they were born orcs."

"Why is it, again, that we are so cringingly afraid of orcs as a race?" asked Boogla.

"They are mentally unstable and responsible for numerous massacres over the ages," replied Paqraq.

"Such as?"

"I haven't got the dates and locations committed to memory. The historical record is quite clear on that point, however. You *should* have learned all this in schola."

"Who would know those details?" Boogla persisted, ignoring that last remark.

Everyone shrugged. Aspet pushed a button on his desk, "Please ask Lofam to step in here." Lofam Kyriab was Interior Affairs Minister. One of her concerns was education, and she knew quite a bit about the scholarly research areas of universitas professors within the kingdom. She could not answer Boogla's question, either, but she did know who could.

"Azine Reoksa's doctoral disquisition concerned orcs and their relationship to the other races, as I recall," Kyriab told them, "She is on the faculty at Universitas Oria in Lumbos. I strongly suspect she will be able to offer insight into your question."

"We've met," replied Aspet, "She was working on the Qillopot dig when Boogla and I were resident at Saltchitterington during the palace renovations."

"I think I'll pay her a visit," Boogla said, adding "With Your Majesty's approval, of course."

Aspet shrugged. "I wouldn't dream of standing in the way of my cabinet members' inquiries. Please be careful, as usual."

"I promise." She stood and headed for the door. "Comm me later," Aspet called after her. "I wouldn't dream of doing otherwise," she answered sweetly.

Aspet turned back to the remaining ministers. "So, let's get on with discharging our duty. Eqbo, start the formal notifications. Senrit, I want to review the defense posture as it pertains to orc irruption scenarios. Do we have a good grasp of orc strategy in these uprisings?"

The Defense Minister looked a little uncomfortable. "We've done our best based on the historical record, Your Majesty, but hard data on the orcs as a military force is very difficult to come by."

"I'm a little confused by that," the King replied, "If these people periodically go on murderous rampages, surely someone would have thought to document precisely how they went about them."

"I agree, Your Majesty. However, that does not appear to be the case, for whatever reasons."

"When I was in schola at Mernalview minoring in cultural history they gave us the same vague assurances that the orcs were bipolar and both extremely violent and unpredictable. Most of the accounts seem to date to almost a millennium ago. Why haven't they gone on any rampages in recent centums?"

"The presumption is that the forced enclave system, combined perhaps with a dying out of whatever mental aberrations were prompting the outbursts, has been the controlling factor," replied Eqbo.

"Given that premise, then, what could have triggered the sudden irruption—if that is indeed what we're witnessing?" Aspet inquired, "What recent events or other factors might have contributed to it?"

"We have scholars from several fields working on that problem as we speak, Your Majesty."

"I see. Well, keep me posted, especially if there are any new developments."

"Certainly, Your Majesty."

Aspet walked to the door, accompanied by two RPC agents. He paused at the intercom panel, entering a code and pressing the transmit button. "Captain Jywi, please ask Sir Tol-u-ol to meet me in the bubble as soon as practical."

"As you command, Majesty."

Tol was staring out his office window at two barkwrats chasing each other back and forth along a ledge when he heard his comm unit beeping.

"Who is that, Petey?" He said in the direction of his overjack pocket.

"Signals trace indicates Royal Protection Corps Communications Center," the pen answered. "I recommend you answer it."

Tol sighed. "Probably a good idea," he agreed.

He fished the comm out of another pocket and clicked the green button.

"Tol here. Yeah. Acknowledged. Tell him I'm on my way."

He chucked the comm back into his overjack and grabbed his EE helmet.

"Family calls," he sighed, heading for the door.

"Look at it this way," said the voice from his pocket, "It is a superior experience to observing rodent reproductive rituals."

Tol cocked his head as he walked. "Yeah, you got a point. Watchin' them just makes me hungry for spicy wrat stew."

"There are many, many times I am thankful for not having been created a biological organism. This is one of them."

"You don't know what you're missin', Petey."

"I am entirely satisfied with that condition."

They proceeded in silence across the enclosed bridge that connected Justice Hall with the Royal Palace Complex. As Tol passed the first security checkpoint he recognized the guard on duty: one of the RPC officers he'd encountered on his way to see Aspet the day of his knighting. The officer looked vaguely uncomfortable; he knew the tables were turned this time. Tol smirked just a little.

"How's it going, fancy doodle?"

"It's...going well, Sir Tol-u-ol."

"Still got your white gloves, I see."

"They're part of the uniform for palace troops, Sir Tol-u-ol."

"Hope ya don't mind if I come this way. They'd just mopped the floor in the commoner entrance and it was still sort of slick."

"By order of His Majesty you have unrestricted access to the palace and the Royal Presence, Sir Tol-u-ol."

Tol was about to rib the poor gob further, but then paused and smiled at him.

"You're doing a fine job, officer. We all appreciate you and your colleagues."

With that he strolled on past, leaving the guard somewhat dumbstruck. In the midst of the encounter Tol had remembered the severe embarrassment suffered by the RPC during the attack on Boogla and relented. They didn't deserve any further harassment... right now.

"I'm really goin' soft in my old age," Tol muttered.

When he and the King were seated in the 'bubble,' as the high-security conference room near the Royal office suite was known to staff, Aspet wasted no time getting to the point.

"Tol, I want you to investigate the organization behind the assault on Boogla. They dismantled my security apparatus far too easily; they are obviously a threat we cannot ignore."

"How did Frem fit in with that?" Tol asked.

"She hired them, but contrary to what I told you earlier we now don't think she was actually part of their organization. Our sources say she's been manipulating trade agreements to supply her black market businesses for some years now. The Solemadrinan and Rublosqi authorities found multiple significant caches of weapons and high-value trade goods scattered around Turmia."

"Okay, so what do I have to work with?"

"The would-be assassins were true professionals—they didn't leave much in the way of physical evidence behind. I had the RPC bring all of it we did find here. It's in that crate on the table, along with the analysts' remarks. I haven't had time to look at it in any detail, but in my briefing they told me that they have intelligence which suggests that the overall 'corporate' entity is known as the 'Lycan Brotherhood'."

Tol nodded, riffling through the stack of analyst reports. "Looks like one nexus of the activity is somewhere in Solemadrina."

"Agreed. Most of my folks think the likely headquarters location is in or near Woklopen."

"Makes sense," agreed Tol, "Fair-sized city, good port facilities, relaxed government oversight due to tourism. I think that will be my first stop."

"Be careful, Tol. These people are not amateurs. They are very, very dangerous."

"Understood. I'll keep my eyes open."

"We've already notified Solemadrina EE via diplomatic channels. You can expect their full cooperation."

Tol grunted and headed for the door, taking along the thin leather case containing the reports. As he was about to pass through Aspet called after him.

"Come back to me in one piece, brother."

"That's the plan, Your Majesty."

Tol met with Selpla for lunch in the bistro on the lower level of the palace complex. He told her he was headed out on an international assignment. She, of course, wanted to come along.

"We've been over this, sweetie. This is a dangerous mission and I can't be worried about saving both our skins."

She sighed. "And I suppose you can't even tell me where you're going?"

"No. I'm heading out from Cladimil, if that helps."

"Since the Arctal current is in strong clockwise flow right now, that really only narrows it down to 'probably not Esmia,' which I already figured. How long will you be gone this time?"

"Hard to say, probably at least a fortnight."

"I'm going to miss you."

"I hope so. I'll make it up to you, though, don't worry."

They kissed for rather a while. Finally Tol disengaged.

"My carriage leaves in an hour; gotta get to the station. Please stay sweet for me."

"Request granted. Watch your rear end, Tol, since sadly I won't be there to do it."

"That's one of those very few things in life I'm pretty good at."

"I can think of at least one other," Selpla said, smiling slyly.

Tol blushed a deep blue-green despite himself.

On this journey Tol had a berth on a military vessel, the deepwater clipper-destroyer *Surfrider*. It was heading out to take part in an annual mutual defense exercise with Solemadrina. Tol would make his way to a smaller ship off the east coast of the allied nation that would then take him the rest of the way into Woklopen.

The Arctal current was near its cyclical midpoint and thus at its swiftest. Their ocean voyage was over just about the time Tol was getting his sea legs and settling down into shipboard routine. The swift frigate *Fjeeriam* intercepted the *Surfrider* about twenty kilometers east of Woklopen and Tol transferred to it via a dinghy

"Huh. Well, good luck with that," replied Tol, "What I'm looking for here specifically is how they were able to disable our entire Royal Protective Corps apparatus and gain access to the Royal Consort directly *in her secure residence*. I've reviewed the RPC's procedures and they're sound. You seen any 'training camps' that might explain something like that?"

Hanx looked thoughtful. "No, not as such. The Lycanics are frightfully clever, however. Some of the smartest people on the planet are involved with them, because they fund a number of 'legitimate' concerns that employ folks who wouldn't be collaborating with criminals ordinarily. They farm their schemes out one little piece at a time, so that no one 'research' outfit is responsible for anything actually contrary to edict. The shady stuff is carried out solely by the home office, as it were."

Tol nodded. "Thanks. That gives me some stuff to think about."

There was a fairly upscale restaurant and pub on Tallarbor Boulevard in uptown Woklopen called Kleggo's that Hanx had told him was a primary meeting place for the Lycanics and their various suppliers. Tol decided to have lunch there. It was a bit above his departmental per diem, but he'd figure that out later. He scanned the serving floor and paid the Table Master to seat him near the center, at a spot he judged would allow him maximum aural access. He pulled Petey out and set him inconspicuously near his silverware with instructions to scan for potentially significant keywords in nearby conversations employing an acoustic booster he'd had installed recently. Not an approved accessory, but smek that. He needed all the help he could get.

While he waited for his order to be taken, Tol mused over the way his relationship with the little metallic AI had evolved. Far from the irritant he'd once considered the electronic pen, Petey had now made full partner in Tol's eyes and he had grudgingly grown rather fond of the annoying thing along the way. There were times, such as this one, where he was downright useful.

At first he didn't encounter anything at all interesting. The diners he could overhear were mostly business types talking about their supply chains or recent acquisitions or how hard it was to find good people willing to work out in the warehouse these days. After about half an hour, however, three hobs in suits came in and sat together at a table just at the edge of Tol's hearing range. He was only casually listening until he caught the Higglin word "dazhkik," meaning, roughly, 'beating the rap.' Tol was not fluent at Higglin by a long shot, but decades of associating with hobs had given him a working vocabulary of the more common words connected with unsavory activities.

"Petey," he said quietly, "Concentrate on the conversation at my eight o'clock position." The pen flashed a brief tiny green light in affirmation. Tol listened as closely as he could without looking obvious about it. He could only understand every fourth or fifth word; he was unable to construct anything really coherent from them. He didn't want people to become suspicious of him by staying too long, so reluctantly he paid his check and left.

"What were you able to make of that?" Tol asked Petey out in his rented pram.

"They seemed to be using code words, but with a bit of cross-referencing against various EE and linguistics databases I have made a first-order analysis. They were discussing strategies for accomplishing some manner of large-scale transfer of funds. From the pains they took to obfuscate the language, I would presume this activity was not entirely within edicts."

"Anything unusual or unexpected in that language?" Tol asked, sucking on a piece of hard candy that came with his meal.

"Only one translatable phrase I could not cross-reference," replied Petey, "*Umbral mage*. The closest cognate was the Umber mages, a mage guild out of Zuum in Tantatku."

"Umbral mage? Hmm. Never heard that one before, either. Let's head back to Greenshield HQ and make inquiries there."

The Umbral mages, it turned out, were a very poorly-known

organization; semi-mythical, in fact. Local EE had only a thin dossier on them and nothing in it was based on more than speculation or anecdotal references. Tol realized he was going to have to do some serious digging if he wanted to find out more. But, was it worth it? While understanding the Umbral mages better might help solve crimes here in Solemadrina, was the organization relevant to Tol's mission? Logic suggested that it was not, but as Petey was fond of pointing out, Tol and rigorous logic were only casually acquainted.

At first Tol decided the Umbral mages were a red herring, but the more he thought about it, the more his gut instinct told him that was not the case. He finally gave in to his intestinal insight and headed for the local Mages' Guild to find out what they knew.

"The 'Umbral mages' are nothing more than a smear campaign," explained the Guildmaster, a Magus Arcanis who went by Triz'lo'K, "By forces who wish to obscure their own illicit activities."

"How does that work, exactly?" Tol asked.

"Basically, whenever a criminal group comes up with a new means for committing their crimes that they don't want made known, they attribute whatever it is to the 'Umbral mages.' In this way they can simply ascribe to magic a technique which may or may not be arcane in nature."

"So, you're saying that the conversation I overheard in the restaurant made use of that reference as a smokescreen? Who were they expecting to fool?"

"Perhaps they realized you were eavesdropping. Perhaps they simply made it a practice to invoke the Umbrals in any public discourse for security's sake. It is not possible to know for sure based on your limited information."

"I see. Thank you for your time and willingness to talk, Magus Triz'lo'K."

Back in the pram Tol talked it over with Petey.

"Something about that guy doesn't ring true," Tol said.

"I have experienced great difficulty in attempting to analyze the verbal and visual clues you employ to reach your conclusions regarding trustworthiness," the pen replied.

"Understood. Intuition is a crazy thing sometimes. I can't really tell you why I feel this way, and I'm not always right when I do. But I'm right often enough to warrant giving it serious consideration. At any rate, I can't ignore it, and that's usually a sign that I shouldn't."

Tol stayed in Woklopen two more days, talking to Shields, ordinary citizens, and shopkeepers, whom he'd always found to be excellent sources for intelligence as they were exposed to the everyday workings of their society most intimately. In the end, however, he had very little to go on but speculations and surmises.

On his way to the pier his luck turned. There was a whispered conversation being carried out in the shadows right around the corner from the ship terminal from which Tol was embarking. He was walking past when he heard Petey tell him through bone induction to stop and remain very quiet. He slipped as near them as he could without being seen and held his breath. When they finally moved off, Tol headed for the boarding ramp as Petey filled him in on the results of their surveillance.

"The conversation was not very audible even with the enhancement module. However, I did pick up what you will most likely consider a significant correlation. There was another mention of the Umbral mages, but this time I heard repeated references to Juymiz in connection with them. While I cannot guarantee the correlation is meaningful, it is certainly worth taking into consideration."

Tol considered this. "Yeah, I have to agree. If there's any chance of a bona fide connection between the Umbrals and Juymiz, then I need to investigate it." He went to the ticket office and changed his passage from Cladimil to Koppra, the only commercial port in Azlymosh. From there it was about three hours' drive into Juymiz.

"Wonder why Juymiz?" Tol mused out loud as they set sail in a coastal transport toward Port Jool, the first stop.

"Proximal analysis suggests its isolation and the Azlymosh

reputation for minimal edict enforcement presence might supply an answer," Petey said.

Tol grunted. "Yep, I suspect you have an excellent point. Not many people there to interfere with you, and those that are probably will keep to themselves. It's that kind of place."

Tol sent an encrypted message to Aspet announcing his attentions and then called Selpla.

"I'm sorry, doll, but it looks like I'll be a few days late gettin' home. I have a hot lead in Juymiz."

"Juymiz?" Selpla said, incredulously, "There's nothing there but social pariahs, cons in hiding, and drug dealers."

"And I'm an EE officer on the hunt for...what?" Tol replied.

"Oh, yeah. Please, please be careful, Tol. That's a real snake pit out there."

"You been there?"

"Once. On assignment. I was afraid to get out of the smekking pram. Did my interviews from the hotel lobby."

"Heh. What hotel?"

"Let me think...Oasis something...Oasis of the Sands."

"Did you like it?"

"It wasn't bad. No long-term scars on my psyche that I recall, anyway. This was about ten years ago, though."

"Thanks. I'll check that one out. Gotta run. Love you."

Chapter Two

"We should be entering the Gulf of Shadows any time now. Those cliffs off to starboard are Cape Farsight on the northeast tip of Tantatku. The only natural harbor in Azlymosh is Koppra, which is halfway down the coast."

Jovsox stood on the prow of the barquentine *Phyta Lotos* on which he and Hinyak had made the voyage across the Noorprid Sea from Galanga. "That's even more contrast than I expected," he observed, comparing the arbor-crested cliffs on the right and the sparse scrub grading down to barren sand dunes on the left.

"Yeah, it's dramatic, all right," replied Hinyak, "But don't worry. There are several major oases in the desert, and Juymiz is built around one of them. The photos I've seen, it's actually pretty, in fact."

"I hope so. I don't want to live in no sand dune."

"We ain't gonna be in no sand dune, Juvvy. Juymiz is a nice little city."

They entered the Gulf of Shadows just after dawn, but even at full sail it wasn't until the following morning they halted to allow the Koppra harbor pilot to board. The channel leading into the harbor at Koppra was narrow and treacherous; the Harbormaster therefore required all ships coming in to be steered by a certificated pilot to avoid potential navigation hazard-causing accidents.

Hinyak and Jovsox didn't pay a lot of attention as the pilot climbed the ladder headed for the bridge. They were speculating on what sort of home they would be able to buy in Juymiz. Once the *Phyta Lotos* was tied to the pier they were among the first to bring their luggage to the disembarkation ramp and were standing there when the pilot came down to leave the ship. Hinyak was looking at something on the dock when Jovsox nudged him.

"That gob is staring at us," he said. Hinyak looked back to see the pilot examining them closely. They made eye contact for a few seconds before the goblin continued along the gangway.

"What was that all about?" Jovsox asked.

"Not sure. Maybe one of us looked like someone he knew."

"It gave me the creeps."

"Don't worry about it. We have better things to do," Hinyak reassured him.

They announced their intention to settle in Azlymosh at the Citizen Services Station in Koppra. The clerk didn't even ask why. He just stamped the papers and sent them on their way. *Another couple of losers looking for someplace to duck the heat*, he thought, grinning at the joke. It was plenty hot no matter where in his nation you chose to live.

They hopped an express road carriage for Juymiz. It was more expensive, but it didn't stop at the half-dozen or so hamlets along the way, which would almost double the trip length. This one had mechanically cooled air, as well. Spending five hours in a non-cooled carriage in the desert was the way a lot of people got introduced to Juymiz; Hinyak decided it was not the way for him and Juvvy. Besides, they had a tidy sum from the loot he'd dug up in Galanga. Hinyak was too smart to start waving it around under people's faces, but he wasn't above springing a little to get a comfortable ride.

Their first view of Juymiz was a little underwhelming. There really wasn't much there, other than a few ramshackle buildings and some tired-looking tropical globenut arbors. Jovsox looked to be on the verge of panic.

"This don't look like it has several thousand people livin' in it. It don't even look like it has a hundert," he said with evident consternation.

"Yeah, I know what you mean," Hinyak agreed, "But that's what all the maps say. I guess we better figure out what's going on here."

"I...I'm not sure I want to stay in a place like this," Jovsox muttered.

"Just hang tight until we get the whole scoop, Juvvy."

They got off at the carriage station and walked around for a while. It was just beginning to get dark when they came across a sign for an inn. "Oasis of the Sands," Hinyak read out loud. "Sounds good enough for tonight."

"It's so *small*, though," Jovsox complained.

"I think I'm starting to figure somethin' out," Hinyak replied, "Because it's so smekking hot here, most of the buildings are underground. That's why it don't look like there's much here."

The goblin brightened up. "I never thought of that. Makes sense, now that you say it like that."

The above-ground portion of the hotel was little more than a concrete pie wedge housing a broad staircase that led down to a surprisingly elegant and expansive lobby. Hinyak had surmised correctly that the vast majority of construction in Juymiz, and Azlymosh in general, was underground. While the vista on the surface was bleak, even desolate, below ground was a very different world.

The companions discovered that the Oasis had rooms for long-term residency and decided to rent one. It was nicely furnished and felt like home almost immediately. Living underground for so long had given the inhabitants a special skillset: simulating sunlight and daytime in places where those things never happened naturally.

Essentially the entire city of Juymiz was carved one building at a time from the sandstone bedrock, which was quite stable seismically and extended in most places at least a hundred meters down from the surface. There were avenues and boulevards underground that connected commercial, municipal, and private spaces as with any city. The streets were lit not only by soft light from innumerable lamps, but during the day by sunlight directed down by a system of mirrors.

Two permanent magical 'suns' that rose and set in synchrony with the real ones were the centerpieces of the town square. Their

17

enchanting had cost an enormous sum, donated by a consortium of the wealthiest Juymizians to make subterranean life a little more bearable. The street lamps within a six-block radius of the square were programmed to brighten and dim in concert with the suns, heightening the effect. Watching these 'suns' rise and set from benches lining the square was a popular local pastime.

Once they were established in their room at the Oasis, Hinyak and Jovsox began to explore the city, scouting for a more permanent home. There were always domiciles for rent or sale in the city or nearby suburbs. Some of the outlying communities were connected to Juymiz proper by tunnels; some could only be reached via aboveground roads.

They returned to the Oasis at the end of each day. The *Thirsty Troll* pub located adjacent to the hotel lobby had established itself as their chosen hangout. One evening they were sitting at a table near the door leading to the lobby engaging in one of their own favorite pastimes: watching people come and go from the front desk. Suddenly Hinyak put down the razzle he was holding and stared hard at something in the lobby. Jovsox noticed and followed his gaze. He saw a burly goblin with an overnight bag waiting to check in, but nothing else.

"What ya lookin' at?" he asked, finally.

"That gob over there," growled Hinyak, "Is the same smekker who roughed us up back on the *Grollnash*."

"Nah. It can't be. The odds are just too big. It must just look like him."

"I'm tellin' ya, that's the same gob. I'd recognize his ugly mug anywhere."

"So, what're we gonna do about it? Jump him?"

"He'd just smack us down again. No, we need to plan something more...effective."

Hinyak rubbed his hands and grinned. "I *knew* fate would bring us back together. I will come up with some appropriate vengeance, that I promise."

"I dunno, Hin, let's just drop the whole thing. We're fugitives, you know. No sense in wavin' a flag tellin' everybody where we are."

"Have no fear, Juvvy. I will plan this such that no one but the victim knows who was responsible. Him, I want to be fully aware."

"You talkin' about plantin' him?" Jovsox asked, incredulous, "Ain't we got enough troubles without bringing down a murder rap on our heads? Let's just live life as rich people and let everything else go."

"He's just some gob," Hinyak replied, "The fuss will die down real quick."

"I got a bad feelin' about this, Hin."

"Relax. Everything will be fine. I got us this far, didn't I? Let's have another pitcher and forget about it for now."

*   *   *   *   *

The eastern coast of Solemadrina was quite scenic. Near Woklopen there were white cliffs dotted with scrub and brownish clumps of sticks from large sea-avian nests, but as they steamed south the landscape graded to larger and larger arboreal manifestations. By the time they were abreast of Dollo in Tantatku the western horizon was dominated by huge arbors that seemed to brush the very sky. This was the far northeastern periphery of the vast forest and savannah biomes where sentience first appeared on N'plork; it gave Tol an unconscious shiver to behold it for the first time.

As they turned the corner around Cape Farsight southeast of Dollo and headed into the Gulf of Shadows, the continent of Bazgush became visible on the port side. The leftmost vantage was Nerr and to its right, Azlymosh. Nerr had copses of smaller arbors and rolling hills; most of Azlymosh sat directly in the rain shadow of the gargantuan Folmnissi mountain range and exhibited nothing but sand dunes and vast expanses of salt flat. Tol shook his head.

"Would *not* want to live there. I hope it's a decent enough place to visit, though."

Another by-product of the rain and wind barrier provided by the Folmnissis was that the Gulf of Shadows possessed some of the more consistently calm seas of any marine environment on the planet. At night when at least one of the moons was up the glassy water reflected it like an enormous mirror, lending a surrealistic aspect to travel by ship. Tol enjoyed his time on deck and wished Selpla was there to enjoy it with him.

The docks in Koppra were a far cry from the bustling ports of Cladimil, Woklopen, or Port Jool, but they had a charm all their own. The pace of life and commerce was much slower here, much more ancient. This natural harbor had seen ships landing and launching for well over six thousand years. Galleys had been plying the rich waters of the Gulf of Shadows and the shallow coastal shelf surrounding Bazgush for as long as fishers had existed on N'plork. Rather than the paved concrete quays that were typical of the larger commercial ports, Koppra still featured a series of old-fashioned wooden piers, some of them extending out a full kilometer to reach water deep enough for safe docking.

Tol was not undercover for this trip. He was on a military transport as a VIP, berthed in the Commodore's cabin, in fact. He was a little embarrassed about this treatment, but not as much as he would have been even a year earlier. The trappings of his new responsibilities were gradually becoming more comfortable for him. Tol was reflecting on the strange twists and turns people take on their journey through life when the call came to disembark.

Azlymosh had no military to speak of, nor much of a diplomatic corps. Tol was left to his own devices once ashore, which is the way he liked it. He caught a carriage headed to Juymiz and stared out the windows. He'd never seen so much sand. Horizon to horizon, there was nothing but sand and dunes composed thereof. It was like being transported to a universe where everything except the sky was made entirely of sand. Even the non-sand sky was periodically invaded by huge clouds of...sand.

Protocol had demanded that Tol dine each night on board ship in the officers' mess at the Captain's table. That had proved a rewarding experience for him, though, because the officers at that table had been to Azlymosh on several occasions and gave him a great deal of useful information regarding life here. He knew, for example, that most of the habitations and businesses, not to mention government offices, were constructed underground to escape the oppressive heat, as well as the abrasive sandstorms that were all too frequent visitors.

He also knew that edict enforcement in the nation was lax for a variety of reasons, most of which centered on a shortage of people willing to take on that role and a paucity of political will amongst the residents to support such services. The natives were highly tribal socially and the tribes tended to police themselves rather effectively. Consequently, formal edict enforcement bureaus simply were not seen as needed. There was no central legislative body charged with creating edicts, anyway.

In point of fact, Tol reasoned, this simplified things for him. He didn't need to cooperate with local EE; he didn't even have to check in. Azlymosh had been notified of his presence and mission through diplomatic channels. The response of the office of the supreme ruler of Azlymosh was, in essence, "Good luck with that." Elected by the tribal chieftains, his name and title were *Lormix Aklika Azlymoshok*; literally, 'Lormix, in whom is vested supreme authority over Azlymosh.' It was primarily an honorific; no one paid him much attention.

They actually did have a tiny diplomatic corps, consisting almost entirely of ambassadors and a foreign affairs minister, but apart from international diplomacy the executive branch of government in Azlymosh confined itself mostly to arbitrating disagreements among tribes and overseeing other inter-tribal business. The capitol, such as it existed, was located in an elaborate and ancient underground complex built around the Stendi Oasis in the north of the country.

Stendi was a marvel of nature. In the midst of one of the otherwise driest places on N'plork, a breathtakingly spectacular spring fully fifty meters across bubbled energetically from an enormous reservoir deep beneath the broiling sands. The Azlymoshians had built a huge rock dome carved with intricate geometric patterns and zoomorphics that covered the oasis itself. The periphery was lined with globe-nut arbors whose whorled trunks gave the impression of thin orange vortices snaking down from clouds of red leaves and brown globes.

The waters of Stendi were crystal-clear, filtered by many meters of sandstone, and had an almost indescribable—not to mention incongruous—taste, with overtones of damp forest, spring rain, and mountain air. It took some getting used to, but once accustomed was accounted by many the finest water available on N'plork; so much so that the wealthier expatriates paid sizeable sums for bottles or better, barrels, from the homeland.

A fair percentage of what wealth Azlymosh had was derived from glassworks. Most of N'plork's glass and glassware, from simple water tumblers to complex laboratory and architectural pieces, was made in dozens of glass foundries dotted along the coast, stretching in both directions with Koppra at their center. Sand and heat were the principal components of glass, after all, along with pigments for tinting which were abundant in the mineral-laden sandstone formations of the interior as well as in neighboring Nerr.

By the time Tol drove up to the Oasis of the Sands hotel in Juymiz, he was relatively well briefed on what to expect, both architecturally and culturally. The hotel lobby was down a flight of steps and much nicer than one might expect given the sparse exterior aspect of the establishment. Tol noted with some satisfaction that the hotel had a serviceable pub adjacent to the lobby, which seemed fairly well-patronized, even in the middle of the day. That was usually a good indicator of razzle quality.

The next morning bright and early he met with the local Dotliq or tribal liaison, an ogre named Hu'laf. The Dotliq was not an easy nut to crack, being reluctant to talk to any outsider about tribal business, until Tol mentioned the Umbral mages. This name opened the floodgates.

"These shadow mages, they are not good. They cast curses on our livestock, sully our water, and bring storms upon our heads that are not of a natural form. They steal herbs and rare plants from our greenhouses for their potions and wreak all manner of havoc with our people. If you are here to eliminate them, the gods be praised."

"Eliminate might be a little strong," Tol replied, "But I am here to investigate their potential involvement in a very serious crime in Tragacanth. I'm going to need to find them first, though."

"Are you an archmage yourself, then?" asked Hu'laf.

Tol chuckled. "Not by a very, very long shot. I can barely work simple amulets like the one that unlocks my pram."

"In that case I would not suggest 'investigating' the Umbrals too closely. They are not good citizens and will no doubt take unkindly to your suggestion that their organization is involved in anything nefarious, be it true no matter."

"Appreciate the warning, Dotliq, but my job entails taking those sorts of risks. Do they have a history, from your experience, of assaulting edict enforcement?"

"They have a history of assaulting just about everyone," Hu'laf replied.

"You've witnessed these assaults?"

"Not personally. But I've heard many tales. As I said, they are not model citizens. The tribes detest them and will not abide their presence. Well, all but one."

"All but one?"

"Yes. The Juji'i, a small but exceedingly ancient tribe who live around a series of tiny oases in the center of the high desert along the western edge of the Walaba hills. It is rumored that in times of conflict the Umbrals take refuge there and are tolerated, if not welcomed, by the tribe and their chieftain, Aqyiar."

"Good to know. Thank you, um, Excellent One. Your

assistance has been most valuable and I honor you for sharing your wisdom," Tol said, using language from EE Protocol Unit's helpful phrase book for Azlymosh, which he'd laboriously memorized on the trip over. It had the desired effect.

"You are versed in the discourse of civil society, Sir Tol-u-ol, and this I find refreshing coming from a foreigner, especially one of your...professional persuasion," said Hu'laf, "I and my office will assist you where we may. I will begin by giving you a list of the known locations frequented by Umbrals in Juymiz. Most can be reached from tunnels accessible from the lobby of your hotel. Here is the latest official map of the city, as well."

There were six locales on the list; Tol circled each on the map and started hitting them. The first three yielded nothing in the way of information. They were local businesses who catered little to tourists and regarded Tol with obvious suspicion and some derision. Since EE investigations were so rare as to be almost unknown in Juymiz, he did not get even the grudging semi-cooperation he could expect from EE-averse concerns back in Goblinopolis.

By the time he visited the fourth place, Tol was beginning to wonder if his tried and true methods were going to get him anywhere at all here. The next spot was a *Fiw'o*: literally, a watering-hole. In addition to being along a well-travelled underground passage, it had a small surface entrance as well that allowed those passing by the tiny hut on an ancient nomad's path above to descend and refill their waterskins.

Fiw'os were apparently popular places for business transactions. While there were pubs here and there, they were quiet about their existence in a society that generally frowned on liquid intoxicants (those with various other routes of administration were, oddly, perfectly acceptable). Since access to water played such a central role in desert life, it was quite natural that watering holes enjoyed great practical and symbolic importance in Azlymosh.

The list Tol had been given featured minimal commentary. For the Fiw'o it simply read *Information exchange point*. Tol bought a traditional water gourd from a small shop and a belt from which to hang it so he could sit among the others occupying the benches surrounding the well without looking too outrageously conspicuous.

The predominant languages in Juymiz were Ogrish and a creole of Goblish and Higglin. He heard one of the dwarven dialects and some Gnomish, as well. Fortunately, he had an excellent linguist hidden in his overjack pocket who piped near-flawless translations directly to his inner ear via bone and skin induction.

"That one is bemoaning the fact that a fungal infestation has reduced his sakk'a grain yields this season to the point he will not be able to excavate the new addition to his processing mill he had hoped to build for at least another year," Petey related in his running commentary on nearby conversations. "The ogre at your one o'clock position is telling the other two about his search for a suitable mate to help in operating his dry goods mercantile. The only additional conversation I can hear is two half-ogres arguing over which one will...wait a moment. Those two who just sat down beyond the sakk'a ogre—can you get me a little closer to them?"

Tol stood up and drew a little more water before relocating to the other end of the bench. Almost immediately Petey began feeding dialogue to him. "They are speaking in barely audible tones about a meeting that is to take place at...I cannot make out the word well but it sounds like 'ril'lir,' which would be 'gaming parlor' in Ogrish."

Tol blinked. He looked down at the list and saw that one of the entries was *Ril'lir Mika*.

Was it the same place? He didn't much believe in pure coincidence where edict enforcement was concerned.

"I guess we'll head there next, then," he told Petey, "It's the only 'ril'lir' on my list and something tells me there's a good reason for that."

"Data on Juymiz is surprisingly hard to come by, but I did manage to scan a municipal database of sorts as we left the hotel. I see only three establishments that call themselves 'ril'lir,' and two of them are not within the limits of Juymiz proper. I would assess, therefore, that your surmise on the identity of the ril'lir in question has a reasonable expectation of being correct."

"You mean it's a good guess," Tol chuckled.

"As I said."

Ril'lir Mika proved to be a gaming parlor, indeed. Traditional gambling, like razzle, ran contrary to tribal custom, but that did not stop people from engaging in it under the guise of worship. The 'bets' were offerings to the ogre deity Imo that were collected before every 'service,' which happened once an hour around the clock. One quarter of the offerings was taken by the 'temple' to fund their 'good works,' while the balance was distributed as 'alms' to those who had prayed hardest and been rewarded by Imo for their piety with the best hand of 'holy cards.' Once a month those who had exhibited the most consistent piety during the preceding month came together for a special service, from which one of them went away with a considerable 'blessing.'

It didn't take Tol long to suss the setup at Mika. There was a gallery for those awaiting their turn to worship, as the 'altar' could only accommodate eight supplicants at once. Tol sat there and, while he did observe the proceedings, he was more interested in the other worshippers. Most of them appeared quite anxious to get in on the services, but there were two who entered shortly after Tol and sat in the gallery across from him, talking quietly and paying little attention to the rest of the occupants. They were the same two he'd seen in the Fiw'o.

Tol stood up as though to get a better look at the services currently being conducted and when he sat down once again had moved much closer to his objects of interest. One of them looked up with mild suspicion, but when he saw that Tol seemed intensely focused on the card-playing he returned to his conversation. Petey picked up bits and pieces of their speech, but something more important as well. As they walked back along the subterranean corridor, the pen reported its findings.

"Most of their discussion seemed, again, to be conducted in some manner of code. I caught linguistic elements from several endemic languages but their use was unorthodox and did not map in linear fashion to any known phonemic clusters. However, one word that corresponds to local topography was *Hiffa*, a small oasis reported to be claimed by the Juji'i tribe and therefore of some potential relevance."

"Great work, Petey. Can you tell me how to get to Hiffa?"

"That oasis is located in the deep desert near the geographic center of the country, roughly 270 kilometers as the avian navigates on a bearing of 040 degrees true north. It is embedded in a large dune field known as *Muti'i Maka* or 'hills of death'. Access would appear to be limited to extremely long-range all-terrain dray fitted with sand tires, pack animal caravan, or teleportation."

"Lovely. Since we're purportedly dealing with mages here, I would assume that last option is the one the Umbrals will be using."

"That is the most logical presumption, yes—especially since one of the participants in that conversation had a distinct persistent arcane aura."

"Yeah, I sparked a whiff of magic on the guy, too. I doubt I will be in a position to employ that means of transport personally, so where would I go to rent an appropriate dray?"

"Fortunately, a nearby place of business just activated a wireless network broadcast, the poorly-implemented authentication mechanism of which I was able to compromise, and via that pathway I have discovered and downloaded not only a list of vehicle rental locations but additionally a fairly comprehensive mapping utility for the entire nation. It shows routes to over thirty unique oases, including Hiffa, in significant detail. The route to Hiffa as indicated is approximately 365 kilometers and will require just under eight hours of driving time, presuming no obstructions or mechanical issues."

"Eight hours? Isn't that a little...slow?"

"Given the terrain, it would be unreasonable to expect an average velocity in excess of fifty kilometers per hour. Fifty would be somewhat optimistic, in point of fact."

Tol sighed. "Why am I not surprised? Nothing is ever easy."

"'Easy' is a highly subjective measure. By my calculations, 86.7 percent of the tasks you perform on a daily basis fall within the 'trivially simple to minimally challenging' zone along the difficulty continuum. Your statement therefore has little basis in fact."

Tol sighed again. "The hardest thing I do on a daily basis is avoid dropping you in the garbage disposal."

"Considering your accustomed level of manual dexterity, I can see how that would present a challenge."

The dray Tol managed to rent for the trip was not exactly in showroom condition. It had six huge mismatched balloon tires, an interior that resembled a failed secondary schola metal fabrication shop class project, and an engine that appeared cobbled together using objects scrounged from a domestic appliance salvage lot. "Looks like some of the junk I had to drive back in the precinct," Tol chuckled grimly.

For the first hundred kilometers the trip was relatively smooth. The paved road surface gave out only twenty kilometers north of Juymiz, but the sand tracks were well-worn and not difficult to follow or negotiate. For all its junkyard appearance, the dray ran just fine and was quite well-adapted to the sandy environment. The cockpit cooling system worked sufficiently to prevent out-and-out heat stroke, although it was a little above optimum temperature for Tol.

"How hot is it, Petey?" he asked, wiping the sweat that had flowed down around his supraorbital ridges and into his eyes.

"Internal temperature is 35.1 degrees. External is 46.3 degrees and climbing."

"Holy Gammag. Why would anyone want to *live* here?"

"Demographics suggest that virtually everyone who resides in Azlymosh is either a native who knows no other life or someone seeking to avoid contact with the rest of society, probably as a result of some illicit activity."

"I don't have *any* trouble believing that."

A little over halfway into the voyage the path Tol was following began to snake up into a seemingly endless sea of dunes, some towering as high as a hundred meters above the desert plain. The track was obscured in places by the constantly evolving topography of the sand. It became increasingly difficult to avoid being tossed around as the dunes shifted beneath the laboring pram. He was doing his best to stay in the center of a narrow dune ridge when without warning another vehicle darted across in front of them from left to right.

Tol had no time to think about his reaction: he just swerved hard and hoped for the best. The pram remained upright for a few moments, but then its weight shifted the supporting sand and the vehicle rolled over on its side, continuing through one and a half complete turns. There were no seat belts in the dray, but padded metal bars slid over the occupants when the doors were shut and kept them in position during an accident.

After the dray stopped moving, Tol managed with considerable difficulty to extricate himself from the bent tangle of restraining bars—which had fortunately proven quite effective. He was shaken and bruised, but nothing seemed broken.

"You make it through all right, Petey?" he said into his overjack pocket.

"Some minor damage, but nothing I can't work around for now. My sensors indicate a similar status for you. I would recommend applying pressure to your lower right leg, however. There is a subdermal hematoma there that might lead to incapacitation if left untreated."

Tol grabbed at the leg. "Yeah. Thanks. I feel that. I'll wrap a constriction bandage around it."

Tol was surveying the battered dray, lying on its side, when he heard an engine noise. "Vehicle approaching from the west," Petey reported, "Acoustic profile matches the one that ran us off the track."

Tol leapt up on the frame of the dray to give himself a little better strategic position. The other vehicle, a smaller dray with less voluminous tires, slid to a halt beside him, spraying a tsunami of sand. The two occupants popped up over the roll cage of the buggy. The driver was a half-ogre, the passenger a goblin. They looked vaguely familiar to Tol as he shaded his eyes from the brilliant afternoon suns.

"Hey, hotshot. Don't they teach you how to drive at cop school?" the driver yelled. Tol finally recognized him then.

"You just don't learn very well, do you?" Tol answered, "How many times do I have to knock you down before you figure out I'm not someone you want to mess with?"

"You ain't knocking anyone else down, smekker," replied Hinyak. "Me and Juvvy got a little present for ya."

With that the goblin in the passenger seat fiddled with something in his hand and then tossed it toward the disabled dray. Tol suddenly heard Petey say "incoming grenade!" through bone induction and threw himself off the dray in the opposite direction, hitting the ground running and diving behind the downsloping end of a nearby dune. The grenade blew the dray almost in half, catapulting metal parts in every direction.

Hinyak drove near Tol and shouted, "Good luck on foot, smekker!" Tol heard the half-ogre laughing as he sped away. He surveyed what was left of the dray and sighed.

"This contraption is history. Guess I won't get my deposit back, either." He pulled out his comm unit and rolled his eyes when he saw that it, too, was mangled.

"Petey, is this comm gone for good?"

There was a brief pause while Petey scanned the device. "I am afraid so. The transmit and receive circuits were both shorted on impact with the restraining cage and they've exceeded thermal tolerances as a result. It is, to use language more familiar to you, 'fried'."

"What did I say about things not being easy? So, we—or rather I—don't have any choice but to hoof it. Which way is the nearest residence or settlement of any size at all?"

"From the data I possess, the oasis of Hiffa would appear to be the closest. It is still over 120 kilometers away, unfortunately. At this temperature you would need in the vicinity of ten liters of water to have any chance of surviving a walk of that distance, even traveling only at night. I am transmitting a maximum power distress signal using arcane heterodyning with these coordinates. It will require that I shut down for several hours to recharge, however. I would suggest in the meantime that you construct a makeshift shelter from the remains of the dray and get out of the direct sunlight. If you start walking and leave this place, the odds that you will survive are considerably less than 2% by my estimation."

"Fifty to one, eh? I don't think any betting gob would accept that spread. I'll take your advice, Petey. Have a good rest. I'm not inclined to go anywhere until you're back up and running."

Tol ripped a sizeable piece of sheet metal from the exposed side of the dray and positioned it over a section of the roll cage to make a small but relatively comfortable shaded area. He cut off some wiring with his utility knife and employed it to attach the sheeting to the frame so that the sudden violent wind gusts to which the area seemed prone would not carry it away. Then he gathered up all the water that was left to him after the explosion, which wasn't a lot, and sat down to wait. There wasn't much else he could do.

Chapter Three

The faculty mess of Universitas Oria was an elaborate affair. It boasted all manner of carvings, bas reliefs, gilt statuary, and even one entire wall of frescoes depicting life over a thousand years ago, when the current structure (still known formally as the 'New Faculty Dining Hall,' even though the former one had been destroyed in a fire ten centums prior) was being built. Boogla walked in and motioned for her RPC detail to eat while she marveled at the artwork. The captain allowed one agent at a time to go through the line and get food.

She had arrived there half an hour in advance of her appointment with Dr. Reoksa specifically to allow her guards an opportunity to grab some lunch. The Magineer Liaison was very thoughtful that way, which was one of the reasons being on her detail was considered a prime assignment. She sat at a table with a good view of the entrance and waited.

Dr. Reoksa was a few minutes late; the result, she apologized, of a student who needed a little extra help in preparing for an upcoming examination. Boogla was in no hurry and told her not to worry about it. She wanted to make Dr. Reoksa as comfortable about the visit as possible.

"I'm here, as I said in the message, to talk about the orcs. Specifically, their history: what we know about their origins and psychology. Why they are so unpredictable and violent."

"That is a very long story," Reoksa replied after a moment's hesitation, "But at the same time there's not a great deal of meat to it." She paused to collect her thoughts. "When I began preparing my disquisition I expected to find evidence—a lot of it, in fact—of curious behavioral extremes and their violent consequences throughout the historical record. What I found was a lot of conjecture and mythmaking, but precious little in the way of hard facts."

Boogla was fascinated. "Surely these periodic rampages are documented. In schola we had to memorize, what, five or six different dates and places where orcs had run amok?"

"That was and still is the conventional history lesson plan; however, it has more to do with force of habit than actual historical record. I was not able to document in any rigorous fashion a single orc irruption, in fact. The evidence simply isn't there."

"Then how on N'plork did we get to where we are? Why has the international community spent untold money on these enclaves and the guarding thereof? What, for that matter, *are* orcs, exactly?"

"The answers to those questions are buried in a morass of academic pride, bigotry, and one influential historian's ancient vendetta. The first mention of the orcs in our historical records occurs in a census document from 835 years ago that mentions a small cluster of strange smooth-skinned 'elf-goblins' living near what is now Jessmirto in Asmagon, having emigrated from 'the sea.' These are almost certainly orcs. All contemporary accounts refer in one manner or another to the smoothness of the skin, which feature has presumably been at least partially bred out of them over the generations. The origins of these 'smooth-skins,' these 'elf-goblins,' are very hazy." She paused to take a sip of her thirra-leaf infusion and stare out at the courtyard for a few seconds.

"So, they truly are not one of the ancient races?" Boogla took the opportunity to ask.

"There's no evidence of them, either physical or cultural, until nine centums ago. They seem to have appeared here from out of nowhere. Dropped down from the sky, as it were. The first detailed information concerning them, and the first manuscript that names them as 'orcs,' is a treatise by the famous historian Winfaz Hidn. He was engaged in interviewing and observing the primarily goblin fishers of the Paradiddle Isles, which at that time were a part of the Merto Empire which comprised the southern half of Esmia. There were passing references in their conversations of a tiny band of people with what Hidn surmised from the accounts to be some manner of congenital skin disorder. They were reported to be small of frame, pinkish or dark brownish of skin, with almost no ridges, scales, or other normal dermatology. Their most striking feature was fur of various lengths that erupted from their scalps, under the arms, the pubic region, and on the males often from the face as well, somewhat in the manner of elderly bugbears. They were reportedly quite repulsive in appearance, but for the most part congenial and non-threatening."

"There is really no information on their origins? Are they a reproductively isolated group who mutated or something?" Boogla asked.

"Unclear. There were no genetic testing technologies then and we of course have no extant samples from the original population. They did eventually interbreed with local goblins and at least some of the offspring were fertile. That has always militated against the rather crackpot theory that they were some sort of alien visitors, because the odds that a totally alien species would be able to interbreed with goblins and produce not only viable children but fertile ones are extremely, extremely remote. However," she added after a moment, "I have some...reservations in that area."

"What sort of reservations?"

"I don't think the genetic incompatibility argument is quite so cut-and-dried. That a truly alien species would be able to interbreed and produce viable children naturally I agree is virtually impossible. However, it is also reasonable to conjecture that an alien species that had developed interstellar space travel might also be highly sophisticated in terms of genetics."

"Are you suggesting they are aliens who manipulated their own genome to become genetically compatible with goblins?" Boogla asked with some skepticism evident in her voice.

"Maybe. It has crossed my mind, at least. I must admit that it answers some rather vexing questions."

"And raises more."

"Most hypotheses of any profundity do."

"So, what did Winfaz Hidn say about these 'orcs'?"

"Hidn himself actually wrote relatively little concerning them. It was his student and successor as Merto Imperial Historian Gumnil Ke-juq who provided most of what we know about their early history. It was also Dr. Ke-juq who first details their violent tendencies. Curiously, his is the only contemporaneous account of this behavior. No one else who writes about the orcs mentions it all. From this point on, however, it becomes part and parcel of the accepted historical record due to Ke-juq's status as the most prestigious and unimpeachable historian of his age."

"You don't sound convinced," Boogla observed.

"I'm not."

"Based on what?"

"Based on almost six years of intensive research leading up to and immediately following my doctoral degree. Based on dozens of personal interviews and hundreds of hours spent poring over old journals, diaries, and other documents from that period. Every *single* account of the orcs being irrational and violent can be traced back to *one* monograph written by Ke-juq. For the next two hundred years *any* unexplained death—including those *clearly* attributable to contagions and in some instances even natural disasters—was blamed automatically on the orcs, with little to no dissent registered by anyone except the orcs themselves. By the time the enclaves were built and all orcs forced into them, their periodic bouts of unwarranted violence were an accepted 'fact,' despite no credible evidence *at all* of this tendency. In my opinion the orcs have been made the biggest blamebeasts in social history."

"So, why haven't you circulated this theory among the scholarly community?"

"Oh, I have. I'll let you read the first draft of my disquisition, if you like. I very nearly got ejected from schola for it. I was told in no uncertain terms that any challenge to something so firmly engrained in the historical record would need the strongest possible evidence to substantiate, evidence I have tried and failed for over twenty years now to produce. I had to remove any such intimation from my disquisition before my examinations committee would accept it. There appears to be a deep need to hold the orcs in contempt—as monsters, if you will. I have not been able to understand this irrational compulsion to any meaningful extent."

"Interesting. Absorbing, actually. Thank you very much, Dr. Reoksa. You've been incalculably helpful in my investigation. I will of course let you know if I discover anything further of interest."

"I would be most grateful for that."

Back in the palace, Boogla started making inquiries. She was deeply intrigued by the orc question and pursued it tirelessly, officially on the grounds that Tragacanth was poised to spend a lot of money on the military mission to contain any potential orc irruption, but privately because she shared Reoksa's distrust of the motives and scholarly objectivity of Gumnil Ke-juq. Why, precisely, she cared so much was something of a puzzle even to her, but there was no denying it.

One thing that seemed clear concerning the orcs is that they started out in or near the Paradiddle Islands. Even today that was a remote area, lying off the coast of Asmagon in the wild and unpredictable southern reaches of the vast Noorprid Sea. The only real exports were fish and globe-nuts; the tiny nation was consistently dead last in the rankings of world economies. But for all that, the inhabitants seemed content with their lot. They enjoyed simple, uncluttered lives, little changed from the way their ancestors had lived for the past several millennia.

Boogla had never been to the islands; she'd never been further south in Esmia than Nar Braylov in northern Ovinis, in fact. She'd love to go investigate this further, but how to justify that to Aspet? Since the attempt on her life he'd been extremely protective; she doubted there was any way he would authorize her to travel outside Tragacanth without an overwhelmingly compelling reason.

After a fair amount of searching she uncovered the first grain of that reason. There was a conference coming up in Jessmirto, the nearest Asmagonian city to the Paradiddle Islands, titled "Economic and Technical Considerations of Magic Use in Esmia." While ordinarily a meeting of that nature would be attended by one of the Magineer Apprentices or a SagMag officer along with perhaps a high-ranking member of the Finance Minister's staff, the presence of the Magineer Liaison and Royal Consort would certainly be within protocol; in fact it would signal a more serious interest by Tragacanth in the aims of the conference. That might be a bit misleading, but it did not represent any actual malfeasance.

For her next step, Boogla began to research the conference: its organizers, the results of past investments in such meetings, and as many other relevant aspects as she could in order to bolster her rationale for attending. She had little competition when it came to research, especially concerning a topic in which she was deeply invested. Three days later she walked into Aspet's office with a veritable mountain of documents. Aspet looked up from his desk and smiled.

"You'll be sailing on the Great Frigate *Hevvli* under the command of Commodore Smuklo. I've had the admiral's suite designated for your use on board, along with a small conference room if you need such. The *Hevvli* will remain docked in Jessmirto; I expect you to operate from that base. There will also be a naval sloop accompanying that can negotiate the smaller harbor facilities on the Paradiddle Islands when that becomes necessary, as I know it will. Your RPC detail will be doubled for the duration, and Asmagon will provide two additional agents while you are in their sovereign territory."

Boogla stopped in her tracks and stared at him. She set the bundle of documents down on a table and replied simply, "I love you."

Aspet smiled again. "And I, you. Which is why I've done all of this. It's obvious to me that you're quite interested in the orc question, and I must admit since you've started down this path you have piqued my curiosity concerning it, as well. I consider this not only an issue of academic historical interest, but a matter of national, even international, security. If we're wrong about the orcs—if there's something germane we're not seeing—it is very important that we correct that deficiency, for our sake and that of the orcs themselves."

She stared past him out a window overlooking the enormous public square. "I have a nagging feeling we've misjudged something here, something fundamental. There are aspects to this problem no one seems to have addressed. We've just swept the whole issue under the rug as a society. The more research I do, the worse that nagging feeling grows. That's why I *have* to do this." She shifted her gaze to his face. "I'm so very happy and proud that you understand this, and me, so well. I really made the right choice marrying you."

"I heartily agree. Speaking of marriage, since you'll be gone for a few days, I'd like an advance on certain...commodities basic to that contract."

Boogla grinned and flipped a switch on the wall that illuminated a 'Do Not Disturb' lamp outside the door.

"I am yours to command, Majesty."

*   *   *   *   *

The conference was somewhat less than absorbing, but Boogla did learn a few things about employing hybrid teleport spells for mass rivet insertion and using focused heat phylacteries for spot welding. She dutifully sat through the entire thing, went to breakout sessions, attended workshops, and took copious notes for dissemination to the mage community back in Tragacanth. After the closing remarks, however, she did not stick around for the final mixer. She headed back to the *Hevvli* and told the Commodore she was ready to board the sloop, a smaller, faster ship christened the *Aqukk*.

She used the voyage over to Kod on the isle of Pataflafla, the capitol and only real city of the Paradiddle Islands, to establish precisely what approach she would take, as well as reviewing some sociocultural information on the Paradiddlers themselves. They were fishers; most of them from families who had been engaged in that trade for two dozen generations or more. They plied some of the roughest and least predictable waters on N'plork, dealing with storms that could occur at any time during any season. They faced gigantic waves, sudden intense squalls, and treacherous eddies—in boats made entirely of globe-nut wood and pitch boiled down from oilgum sprouts that dotted the ancient volcanic hillsides.

The Paradiddlers were taciturn, even laconic, with an economy of speech that reflected their way of life and the often noisy environment on working fisher boats that made verbal communication less effective. Getting information from them was rather a challenge as a result. They were polite and friendly, but in a quiet sort of way. Predictably, they had little to say about orcs, but what they did convey exhibited no trace of the customary fear or intolerance. That in itself was very telling.

After a full day of interviews, diplomacy, and wheedling in Kod and the surrounding communities on Pataflafla, Boogla finally moved on to Flam, the next island to the south. She was running more or less on instinct now, based on a few fragmentary clues she'd pieced together from her portfolio of mostly fruitless conversations.

She spent the morning encountering much the same reticence. After lunch she decided to take a break and walk along the beach on the western side of Flam. The beach was flat with fine-grained light yellow sand that felt especially good between her toes. She walked down the beach for a couple of miles, her RPC detail sweating as they accompanied her.

"Your folks can at least take the overjacks off," she told the detail captain.

He shook his head. "That's where most of the hardware lives," he replied.

She shrugged. "Sad to be you, I guess. I do appreciate it, though."

A savage sea storm had ravaged that section of the coast only last week: the worst reported in some tens of years. The coast was therefore strewn with seaweed, carcasses of stranded and battered sea creatures, and bits of flotsam. As she made her way along the sandy shoreline she became quite accustomed to the way the sand responded to her weight, subtly compressing with each step. As a result she was instantly aware when something beneath her feet changed. With a puzzled frown she stopped a few steps beyond the anomaly and backed up. Her RPC detail obligingly followed. She walked forward again, troops in tow. She knelt down and brushed away the sand, which revealed an odd flat stonework edifice buried just below the surface.

"Help me, please."

Two of her guards got down and helped her sweep while the others stood watch. After ten minutes or so they had revealed a stone circle with a triangular tail that pointed off into the ocean. It seemed quite ancient. There were characters and symbols of a sort she did not recognize inscribed into the stone, so she got a notepad and copied them.

In the nearest fisher village they were aware of the stone marker. They said it was built by the 'fish people' many centums ago. When she asked what was meant by 'fish people,' the little bit of explanation she got was less than helpful. "They came out of the sea and called themselves fish, but they were really people."

Boogla decided to drop the 'fish people' mystery to return to her purpose in coming here to begin with: the orcs. She had tried every approach she could think of to squeeze more information out of the fishers when at last a pint of razzle at a dockside pub brought her the results she had sought for so long. A young goblin who'd overheard her asking questions approached and offered a tidbit in exchange for a gourd of the pub's best. She complied and so did he.

"If yer rilly needin' to find out about th' arcs, you oughta go to the south coast o' Drag," he drawled between draughts, "There be a cave carved into the hillside wi' a buncha arcs livin' thar as monks. It's them as can teel ya what ya want t' know, I'll be wagerin'."

Boogla scribbled this down with barely suppressed glee. She thanked the fisher and handed the startled barkeep fifty billmes, a frankly enormous sum in these parts. "Give this young gob as much razzle as he wants on me, and keep the change."

They docked off the south coast of Drag the next morning. Boogla, her RPC contingent, and a naval ensign took a dinghy to the beach near the spot indicated by her informant. At first there was no cave visible, but after a few seconds of scanning she saw a small but well-kept gravel path leading off into the hills. She followed it with her retinue as always tromping along behind. It terminated at a small cave opening with more of the strange characters she'd seen on the Flam beach stone carved around the door.

Her RPC captain sent an agent in first as a precaution; after about a minute he came back out and pronounced it safe to proceed. Boogla walked through the entrance and was immediately struck by how much cooler and drier it seemed in the vestibule. A robed figure came to meet her and introduced herself as the "Abbess of Eithmorg." Boogla was unsure whether that appellation was meant to be a name or a title, so she took the path of polite caution. "Honored to make your acquaintance."

The abbess was quite definitely of pure orcish extraction: she had very abbreviated eye ridges, her scales were almost invisible, she had long fur of black sprouting from her head and her skin was the color of fermented globe-nut pulp. Her Goblish was excellent, but tinged by an accent Boogla could not place.

"We are pleased that one of your high station would go to the effort to seek out our humble abbey," the abbess said, "And would wish to make your visit as profitable as we might. How may we be of service?"

Boogla was both stunned and immeasurably pleased that she'd actually found orcs not living in a forced enclave. This was due primarily to two factors: the Paradiddle Islands were not signatories to the Treaty of Mutual Containment; and they had the broadest religious tolerance policies on the planet. So long as the orcs presented themselves in a religious context and remained good neighbors, they were allowed complete freedom to conduct their lives.

The abbess led them to a simple but elegant room with a central round table where they were seated and given quite good infusion. The abbess poured all cups from the same pot, allowed Boogla to choose from among them, and drank first to show that there was no poison. An RPC agent drank before Boogla and reinforced the claim. As they sipped, Boogla struggled to frame her questions in a suitable manner. She decided to be direct.

"I seek to understand why your people are regarded by all other races as such a threat," she said gently.

The abbess stared at her cup for a long while. Finally she spoke.

"Our race has a...different history from the others. Our legends speak of an event called the 'First-Arrival,' which of course has clear implications of coming from somewhere else. Some of our scholars believe that references our coming to these islands, as our oldest records are here; others some other, less clear occurrence. What that something else truly is, we can only guess. What we do know is that at some point not long after that arrival, the ancestors who had been welcomed or at least tolerated at first began to be ostracized; even hunted down. The archives are not at all clear on what event precipitated this. We name it the Great Sadness and tried to combat it for centuries, to little avail. Most of our race, as you know, is confined to a small group of enclaves scattered in distant lands. We are the only freehold remaining."

"What is this place, exactly?" Boogla asked.

"This is Eithmorg Abbey, the orcs' most sacred site. Here is where we celebrate and preserve the artifacts and knowledge unique to our race. We are the caretakers of those sacred relics."

"I noticed the symbols carved into your door. Tell me about those."

"Those are letters from the alphabet of the language spoken by the First-Arrival ancestors, who created this sanctuary. Their meaning has been lost to us, or at least corrupted to the point that no meaningful translation can be derived."

Boogla steeled herself for what she was afraid would be a difficult question.

"Our accepted history names the orcs as wildly unpredictable and prone to murderous outbursts. Is this true?"

The abbess—Huld'gart, she called herself—sat with eyes closed for a moment. When she spoke her voice was weak and breaking.

"For centums we have heard this accusation over and over. It is burned into our collective consciousness like a vivid, ugly scar. Yet I will tell you this: not once have I seen an orc murder anyone of any race, nor have any such accounts been brought to me or passed down in Abbey records. There are lurid tellings of our own people being hunted and slaughtered, but none where orcs were killers, even in self-defense. Why we have been saddled with this reputation is beyond knowing. We call it simply The Curse."

Boogla was intrigued and disturbed. "I, too, have been unable to document any actual killings perpetrated by orcs. I do not understand where such a misconception could have come from, or why it would be perpetuated without any factual basis. I have one more question for you, if you are willing to answer it."

The abbess nodded her assent.

"On the island of Flam I saw a large edifice made from rock on the beach that consisted of a circle with a long thin triangle issuing from it. On that edifice were carved what appeared to me to be symbols of the same sort as those on your doorway. Do you know if there is any connection?"

Huld'gart's head jerked up and her eyes got wide.

"You...you've seen the Stone Beacon? It has been lost for many generations. We thought it destroyed."

She noticed Boogla waiting patiently for an explanation and took a few deep breaths to calm herself.

"The Stone Beacon, if that is what you have indeed rediscovered, marks the spot where the First-Arrivals came ashore in these islands. It is perhaps the single most important geographical location and symbol in our cultural history."

"Why would that be so critically important?"

The abbess seemed taken aback by the query.

"Because...because it *is*. I've never really questioned why before. Without exception our histories call it such and tell us that this spot must never be forgotten or lost. There was, we believe, a great sea storm centums ago that obliterated it and killed the caretakers who lived in a small hut built nearby. Since that time the exact location has been unknown. Can you give me that?"

Boogla shrugged and pulled out a map of the islands, circling the spot where she saw the stone marker in red. She handed it to Huld'gart, who took it as though it were a precious work of art. When she looked back at Boogla she had tears in her eyes.

"Thank you, Your Excellency: thank you from the entire race of orcs. We are unaccustomed even to small kindnesses from the other races, although the Paradiddlers have always treated with us fairly. This gift from you is beyond reckoning. From this day forward the orcs will consider the nation of Tragacanth to be a friend."

Boogla was impressed and faintly bemused.

"Tragacanth has no reason to consider the orcs other than as friends, as well. We have two enclaves within our borders and when I return I will review the steps necessary to, if possible, integrate their inhabitants back into mainstream society. There will be strong opposition, for we know little of the orcs save their apparently unwarranted reputation, and ignorance frequently breeds fear and mistrust. Nevertheless, I believe that with time and judicious handling that goal may eventually be brought to fruition. Farewell, and may your long Curse be coming to a close."

The abbess sniffed, teary-eyed, and nodded goodbye, clutching the map to her bosom.

The southern passage around the bottom of Asmagon was rather longer than the more direct route up the west coast to Cladimil for the return voyage, but it would put Boogla in at Lumbos. The carriage ride back to Goblinopolis from there was much briefer and more pleasant, and from the RPC's perspective posed a little less risk. The journey home gave Boogla plenty of opportunity to think.

She was trying to put together the puzzle pieces she'd so far managed to find concerning the orcs, but there were yet too many gaps to construct a coherent scene. What were the orcs, precisely? Where did they actually come from? What was the origin of the anti-orc rhetoric that had been accepted as fact for so many centums? Her biggest concern right now, however, was the nature of her next step in this investigation.

Back in the Royal Palace, Boogla sat in her office with all of the documents she'd gathered pertinent to this problem spread out on a large table. She couldn't stop thinking about the stone maker on the beach in Flam. Why would the spot where you came ashore—presumably simply where your boat happened to land—be judged important enough to go to all that trouble? The nearest raw stone source was several kilometers away. It would have to be quarried, brought back, shaped, and then placed in holes dug with considerable effort in beach sand that was going to have a strong tendency to fill in as soon as the openings were created. It was not at all a trivial exercise, especially for a people who landed presumably with only the tools they could carry in their small boats. They *had* to be marking more than a simple disembarkation point.

This new idea intrigued her. What could be there on the edge of the beach or in the water that they felt compelled to flag so permanently? Answering that question, she decided, would be her next goal. She went in to talk to Aspet about it and found him in the company of the EE High Commissioner and several members of the

EE leadership team. Aspet looked worried. Boogla sat down near him wearing her 'what's going on?' face. He sighed.

"Tol's on a mission in Azlymosh. He hasn't checked in for some time, but worse, our embassy in Uzplenq picked up a short arcane-mode distress signal with coordinates in the deep desert that was identified as coming from Tol's PDWA."

"What can we do?" Boogla asked.

"At this point, not a lot. We don't have any people nearby, and even if we did we can't violate Azlymosh's sovereignty by sending in a team without their consent. The best we can do immediately is relay the reported position to the government of Azlymosh and ask for their cooperation via diplomatic channels. While it isn't any sort of clandestine action, Tol's mission is not being conducted with the official consent and participation of their government—although they are aware of his presence—so his status there is the same as any ordinary citizen: for all practical purposes he's just another tourist."

"Can't he contact that transcendent mage or something?"

"That's what I'm hoping he does. What I'm worried about is that he might not be in a position to do so. He could be unconscious or otherwise unable to use the amulet."

"Or he might just forget he even has it," Boogla said.

"That's always a possibility with Tol," replied Aspet, nodding, "Magic doesn't enter into his thinking very often."

"I'm sure he'll be fine. It's not as though he hasn't ever done this sort of thing before," said Boogla reassuringly.

"I hope you're right." The king turned to the High Commissioner. "I want status updates absolutely as soon as they happen."

"Assuredly, Your Majesty," replied the official.

Chapter Four

After the suns went down the seemingly sterile desert came alive. Crawlers, hoppers, buzzers, night-avians with mournful, other-worldly vocalizations; all manner of things that creep, slither, and skitter their way across the sands turned the arid landscape into a beehive of activity. Tol was rationing his water one drop at a time, but he knew he wouldn't last more than 44 more hours at the outside. Just after midnight Petey came out of hibernation. Tol was surprisingly glad to hear his tiny operative status chirp through bone induction.

"Welcome back to the land of the conscious, Petey," Tol said through cracked lips.

"You are dehydrating, Tol-u-ol. My sensors show your circulatory viscosity has increased alarmingly."

"Yeah, I'm aware of that. I don't have much water left, though. I'm rationing it as best I can. Have you gotten any response from your distress signal?"

"Yes. It was only an automated beacon, but at least it indicates the signal was received."

"Wonder if that means rescue is on the way?"

"Difficult to estimate. Tragacanth and Azlymosh do not have mutual aid treaties, nor is Azlymosh a signatory to the *International Accord on Edict Enforcement*," Petey replied, "Any response would most likely need to come from local authorities and such are practically non-existent."

"So, who were you expecting might come get me, then?"

"I never said I expected you to be rescued; I only said I was transmitting a distress signal. It will make locating your corpse somewhat less problematic, at the very least."

"You're always a great comfort to me, you know that?" Tol crammed all the sarcasm he could into his whispered, broken voice.

"Contrary to your apparent belief, I do not stand to benefit in the least from your demise. It could be years before anyone comes along and by that time even I might have ceased to function. I have been analyzing your—*our*—plight constantly since the accident occurred. The best alternative I have developed is that you use your amulet to contact the transcended mage Oloi. He would be in a position to offer the greatest aid here."

"Already thought of that," Tol said, dejected. "I must have left it on the bureau in the hotel room when I took a bath last night: at your prompting, I might add. I always knew bathing was a bad idea."

"As your personal assistant, it is my responsibility to notify you when your lack of hygiene constitutes a threat to the public. You had reached that status. I will continue to work on a viable rescue plan."

Tol decided to take advantage of the cooler temperatures and absence of direct sunlight to do some scouting of the immediate area. He moved slowly, to conserve water, in a spiral with the wrecked dray at its origin. What had seemed almost totally featureless in the harsh light of day proved much more topologically diverse by the soft radiance of two of N'plork's three satellites. The occasional seemingly dead stalks of various heights and diameters showed themselves to be anything but, as elaborate pods glistening with nectar to lure in pollinators emerged all over their surfaces. The air was filled with the buzzes and hums of flying creatures living their lives under the cover of darkness, fleeing the oppressive heat and glare of day.

He heard a scritching off to his left and noticed sand sliding down a dune. As he walked over to investigate, a large object suddenly burst from the side of the dune and exploded into the air. It was an avian of some kind, with dark wings and breast and long legs terminated by toes sporting respectable talons. It circled him once as if showing off before flapping away silently, a passing spirit in the moonlight. Tol felt his heart beating rapidly: partly from being startled and partly from the sheer majesty of the encounter. A little more than half an hour later he saw presumably the same avian fly past once more, this time with some small squeaking animal in the grip of those talons.

In the course of his exploration he came across a truly impressive desert plant fully a meter in diameter and at least five tall. It had a number of small branches or arms curving up and away from the trunk at intervals, each dotted with sweet-smelling blooms. The petals of these flowers glistened with wet invitation. It suddenly occurred to Tol that since this moisture had obviously been secreted by the plant itself, there must be a reservoir of sorts somewhere inside. If he could extract it, he would increase his odds of surviving a little longer out here. He also reasoned that if he took only enough to sustain him for one day, the plant might be able to regenerate it and provide him with a longer-term resource.

As was the custom with most EE officers, Tol carried his department-issued survival knife in a reinforced sheath sewed into the thigh of his pants. He pulled it out and tried to figure the best place to make an incision. He decided to go with the base, just above ground surface. He slipped the knife carefully into the plant tissue, perpendicular to the ground to make collection easier. The desert-dweller obliged by squirting liquid into his cupped palm.

Excited, Tol raised the precious handful to his nose and sniffed. Didn't smell absolutely identical to water, but didn't smell like poison, either. He took a drop on his tongue: faintly sweet with a subtle bitterness. He waited a while to see if there would be any noticeable adverse effects. After only five minutes he realized he was developing an odd craving for more of the liquid. He shrugged and downed the entire handful.

Imagine you're a desert plant. There's almost no rainfall—ever—so you have to harvest what little moisture you can from the air, or by plunging your roots deep to seek out any ground water that exists. Whatever hydration you manage to accumulate is a precious resource that means the difference between life and death. If you don't protect such a valuable commodity in a place where every creature has to fight hard to survive, you will most assuredly lose it.

On Earth, cacti that store water in their flesh generally protect it using barbs and spines, some of them several centimeters long and sharp as needles. On N'plork that protective function is more often assumed by chemical means: putting stuff in your water that renders it less palatable to roving thieves while still allowing your own cells to make use of it.

You can make your water outright toxic, of course, but lethal toxins are metabolically expensive to synthesize and dead animals do not pass that learned behavior of avoidance to their offspring. Animals cannot afford to lose situational awareness, however, especially in highly competitive environments like deserts. If you ingest something that interferes with your senses and instincts, you might not last very long. This particular species of plant had therefore hit upon producing a toxin that mimics certain animal neurotransmitters and renders the imbiber somewhat less than fully aware of the rest of the universe for a time. Not necessarily fatal, but definitely something to be avoided in the future if you're a wild desert animal. If you're a goblin, though...

Ten minutes after drinking that few ounces from his cupped hand, Tol was beginning to feel a little weird. The dimensions of his surroundings were not playing by the rules he'd come to know and respect. Height, width, and depth were no longer static parameters for any given object. When Tol shifted his gaze, the thing he'd been looking at previously often seemed to shift along with his line of sight, as though it were anchored not to the ground, but to his visual field.

At first it was a bit frightening, or at least disconcerting, but Tol had some experience in this area due to having lived his entire life in Sebacea, where the gourds used for drinking contain hallucinogens if not prepared properly—or, in some establishments, *if* prepared properly. He knew more or less what was coming, so he made his unsteady way back to the dray and propped up against it to watch the show.

The experience ran the predictable gamut of spatial distortion, acoustic hallucinations, and seeming heightened awareness. He leaned back and closed his eyes, allowing the euphoria to wash over him. If he was going to die in the desert, at least he could go out high. After a few minutes he stretched and ran his hands along his thighs. There was an unexpected sensation associated with that motion, which after some puzzling he resolved to wetness.

Tol put the affected hand in front of his face and wondered whether the rocking motion was real or just part of the trip. Whichever cause, it finally settled down and he was able to focus to some degree on his supinated palm. It was dotted with something bluish-green, something that looked familiar. What that something was suddenly permeated his addled consciousness: goblin blood. He felt all along his thigh and brought back more; much more than he expected. He'd been injured worse than he thought in the crash. The hematoma was no longer subdermal.

The drug in his system tempered his reaction to this bad news, however. He still felt pretty good about life. As his glazed gaze passed over the moonlit sands, another anomalous sensation made itself known. He saw little globs of luminescence floating a couple meters off the desert floor, forming a straight line leading away from near his position. Tol shook his head and rubbed his eyes, but the glowing orbs were still there and had even grown a little more intense.

He got to his feet in a somewhat less than gracile maneuver and limped a little closer to the floating manifestations. Their appearance was consistent from multiple angles; this puzzled him, as he'd expected them to be mere hallucinations. Hallucinations, though, had a tendency to fail the 'close examination' test, in his experience, and these did not. Even somewhat mentally impaired, Tol could discern that these floating blobs spaced every ten meters or so seemed to lead somewhere deliberately. He shrugged and followed them, now favoring his injured leg.

The last blob in the line hung serenely over an almost invisible wooden post to which was attached a tin cup via a long chain. Tol picked it up and turned it over in his hands. He looked up at the light blob and then down at the apparently perfectly ordinary sand directly beneath it. He got down on his hands and knees and put his ear to the sand's surface. After a few seconds of holding his breath he heard a faint but distinct gurgling that was not, on this occasion, coming from his own gastrointestinal tract.

Glancing back at the wooden post, Tol noticed another chain attached to it that disappeared beneath the sand. He pulled on it and extracted a long-handled spade. Putting two and two together and deciding, after some fuzzy debate, that the sum was indeed four, he found the gurgling spot again and began to dig. His first excavation encountered a hard sandstone layer no more than twenty centimeters down, but on his second try he hit a small metal handle. Digging out around it enough to prevent sand from immediately backfilling the hole, Tol carefully pulled on said handle and found it attached to a metal lid set into a five-centimeter lip to discourage sand entry. The portal protected by the lid was just big enough, he noticed almost immediately, to admit the tin cup. An unmistakable scent of fresh, cool water wafted up from the opening.

Once raised, the cup held possibly the best water Tol had ever drunk. He downed cup after cup greedily, until he was satiated and saturated. He drew one final draught and washed his bleeding wound as well as he could. He started to walk away—more a waddle, actually—when the pale blue blob above the well began to blink red, insistently. Tol stopped and scratched his head before realizing that he'd forgotten to replace the lid. He did so and the beacon resumed its calm bluish luminescence.

Now that he had a presumably reliable water supply, Tol's survival odds increased dramatically—although he could still starve eventually or contract an infection in his lacerated thigh and die of...pus or something. He could also be flattened by a space rock, he reminded himself. No point in worrying too much about any of it. What he really needed to do now was figure out how best to make it through the next day's intense heat.

He spent the remainder of the relatively cool night expanding and improving his makeshift shelter. Using his survival knife he managed to remove a variety of materials from the wrecked dray, including insulation and enough shiny surfaces to make a decent roof panel for reflecting back some of the solar radiation. As the first sun rose above a horizon splashed with deep carmine wash, Tol sat in his cozy lean-to futzing with his comm unit. He knew he had no chance of repairing it, but it made him feel as though he were contributing in some small way to not dying.

Petey was monitoring his physical status and reporting periodically.

"Hemorrhaging is down 84% since nightfall. Your hydration state and blood viscosity are within norms now, as well."

"Glad to hear it. Last night got pretty trippy for a while."

"Yes. You were under the influence of a psychotropic moiety produced by that succulent to guard its water supply. Incidentally, now that you have returned to relative sobriety, I have some potentially useful information that you were apparently too fixated on your construction goals last night to hear me telling you. I detected persistent arcane harmonics in the vicinity of the dray."

"Lovely. Which means what?"

"Which means that something in or near that dray is giving off a magical aura. That is not a normal accessory in most vehicles. I suggest you carry me around so that I can pinpoint the source more accurately by triangulation."

"Exactly why should I lug you around out in the hot suns like a scholagob lookin' for pond jumpers to take back for biology lab?"

"Because whatever it is that is broadcasting on magical frequencies could potentially be employed to rescue us."

Tol shrugged and stood up. "Right. Let's do this."

He held Petey out in front of him and walked slowly around

and through the wreckage of the blasted dray. At one point Petey suddenly commanded him to halt.

"The nexus of the harmonics is 1.2 meters directly below me."

Tol reached down and fished around with his hand until it closed on something small and hard buried in the sand between two pieces of metal framework. He brushed it off and grinned. It was his Talisman of Summoning for Oloi.

"Guess I didn't leave it in the hotel, after all. Must have broke the chain and dropped off in the accident."

He held it in his palm and uttered the activation phrase Oloi had taught him. After a few seconds there was a shimmering a couple meters away that rapidly solidified into a thinnish biped with white fur on its head and face and a light brownish-pink skin. Tol never quite got accustomed to Oloi's odd appearance, but he was very glad to be observing it right now.

Oloi smiled at Tol and then looked around.

"Greetings, Tol-u-ol. Whatever are you doing in the middle of a desert?"

"Not much," Tol replied.

"Looks like you had a transportation failure," Oloi said, surveying the wrecked dray behind Tol.

"You could say that. A couple of little smekkers whose life span is now limited tried to off me with a grenade."

"Not very neighborly of them."

"Nope. Hey, listen archmage, I need a favor. I'm trying to make it to an oasis called Hiffa also in the middle of this desert."

"Whatever would you need to go to Hiffa for?"

"I need to introduce myself to the chief of some nomadic tribe called the *Juji'i* who lives there."

"Going into the camel business?"

Tol scratched behind his ear, "I don't know what a...*camel* is, but I'm trying to track down the Umbral mages, and they reportedly hang out there sometimes."

Oloi suddenly got serious. "Why do you want to find them?

They are dangerous people."

"You might have noticed that finding dangerous people is my job," Tol said, shrugging, 'We have good reason to believe they were involved in the infiltration and dismantling of RPC security at the Royal Palace. At any rate, the king wants them investigated, so here I am."

Oloi exhaled in a peculiar manner unique to transcendents, possessing no actual lungs.

"The shadow mages are amoral mercenaries of the worst sort, Tol, and they have developed an extraordinarily dangerous and powerful apparatus known as the *Rete Arcanis*. It is a network—a web—composed of all the members tied together by some very powerful magic. It allows each of them to draw upon the manna reservoirs of all the others, so that the spells they cast are potentially many times more potent than any single mage could manage. Many of them, including their leader Zizmziz, are at the bottom rung of the magus ladder: Magus Incipius. Once in the Rete, however, they are each equivalent in some ways to an archmage. Do not rile them."

"Dangerous or not, I have to find out if and to what extent they were involved. That's my job. I'll try not to rile them, but I'm not historically very good at tiptoeing around criminals."

"Hmm. Where do you envision me fitting in?"

"I just wanted to ask you to drop in somewhere and tell local EE (if you can find any) where I was, so they can come get me. I don't think I can walk all the way to Hiffa."

"What are you planning to do when you get to Hiffa?" Oloi asked, frowning.

"I have this letter of introduction from another tribal chief," Tol replied, patting his overjack pocket, "I am going to use to meet the Juji'i chief and ask him a few questions. Questions concerning the Umbrals."

"If the chief does implicate the shadow mages, what then?"

"Then I'll head back to Goblinopolis and report in. After that,

I suspect I will be returning to Woklopen."

Oloi shook his head. "I strongly advise against confronting the shadow mages in Woklopen. That is one of the centers of their power. Even I personally as an archmage, were I still corporeal, would be very cautious approaching such an encounter."

Tol shrugged. "Whatta ya want me to do? Go back to Aspet and tell him it's just too dangerous to investigate the people who almost killed his wife? That definitely will not fly. I really don't have a lot of choice here."

"You may not have a choice in the ultimate goal, but you do have options as to the approach you take," said Oloi, patiently, "Make discreet inquiries and keep the threatening rhetoric to a minimum. When you do finally go in to confront the alleged perpetrators, take your forensic mages with you. You cannot accomplish this without magical counterstrike support. This is one situation where being physically tough won't save you."

"I don't think it will be a drawback, though," replied Tol, grinning.

"Being tough? No. Being cocky about it? Quite possibly."

"I'm just yankin' ya. Being cocky will get you killed on the street, too. I don't plan to confront them, at least not yet, but I do want to get to the bottom of this thing. Anything you can do to help?"

"What makes you think the shadow mages were involved?"

"Two things: one, I overheard a conversation between two jloks with connections to the group that actually paid for the attack; and two, a mage told me they were mythical."

"Really? What mage was that?"

"Guildmaster in Woklopen. Name was…Triz'lo'K, I think."

Oloi thought for a moment. "Ah, yes. He's an Arcanis, I believe. As to the shadow mages being mythical, that's certainly what they want people to think. This Triz'lo'K has either bought into that or is covering something up."

"I'd bet solid billmes on the latter," Tol replied, "His body language just screamed 'liar'."

"How did a prevaricating magus contribute to your belief that the shadow mages played a role in the attack on the Palace?"

"Well, those really aren't directly connected. It's just that an organization which someone who should know better claims doesn't exist is in a really good position to carry out activities that fall in the, um, less-than-fully-legitimate category. In some convoluted way I don't know how to express very well, that makes perfect sense to me."

The archmage nodded. "I think I can follow your reasoning. I need to return to The Slice now, but I will think about your problem and help if I can. I will alert the authorities to your position, too."

"Thanks, your mageness."

About ten hours later, just as the last sun was hitting the horizon like a glowing red sapon bubble, a dray with more wheels than to which one might expect a single dray to claim ownership came rolling up. The occupants seemed impressed with Tol's ingenuity and knowledge of deep desert survival. He didn't tell them about Petey or the weird glowing orbs that led him to water, of course.

They took him into Hiffa and even graciously agreed to wait around (some distance away) to take him back to Juymiz when his business was completed. The Juji'i were not very receptive to any sort of government presence, which is why the agents were waiting at a respectable distance. Tol had spent the drive studying and memorizing the protocol stuff he'd been supplied, hoping to avoid any serious gaffes in that area.

He had expected tents or some other portable structures since these people were reportedly nomadic, but the Juji'i *Dhom Uy* or 'stationary house' in Hiffa was quite elaborate, with arches and domes covered with geometric patterns and stylized animals. Also rather contrary to what he was expecting, Tol was treated as an honored guest and carried before the chieftain in a richly upholstered chair borne by four kobolds dressed in identical flowing golden robes and headdresses. He decided to play it very, very smooth and show mutual respect.

"I am humbled in your presence, Great One, and my ancestors join me in praising you..." He paused for a moment, trying to remember the proper wording, "...in one chorus."

The Juji'i potentate regarded him with a stone face for a moment and then broke into laughter. He dried his eyes after a few seconds and, still chuckling, spoke.

"Forgive me, Sir Tol-u-ol. I did not expect such courtesy from a foreigner. But I must tell you, we have not spoken in like manner in this court for several generations. You have used the formal greeting of my great-great-grandsire's time, which I have not heard since I was very young. Do not think it unappreciated, however. Now, what brings such a silver-tongued goblin all the way to our little desert nation?"

"Well, noble Chieftain, I am investigating a very serious attack on the Royal Family of Tragacanth. I have reason to suspect that the organization known as the Umbral mages may have knowledge relevant to the case. It is my duty to follow each and every lead no matter what effort that may entail. I am told your tribe is on friendly terms with at least some of the members of this group, so I was hoping you might give me information as to where I might find and speak with them."

The potentate chose his words carefully. Tol could see him struggling to keep a cool demeanor.

"Sir Tol-u-ol, we in Azlymosh are tribal societies. Tribes maintain cohesion mostly through familial ties and an often complex web of interrelationships. Those born into one of the families which form the backbone of these social frameworks are accepted as integral members of the tribe regardless of whatever additional associations they may cultivate, although yet subject to the edicts and customs of the tribe itself. One of the senior members of the Umbral mages is close to a member of my immediate family, and so by association that organization is considered a *Pomos,* or auxiliary house."

"Understand, great Chieftain, I am not leveling any sort of accusation at this point. Their name came up in the course of the investigation and I simply want to ask what they know."

"I am aware of the somewhat unsavory reputation of the Umbral mages," Aqyiar replied, "But I can only say they have never betrayed this house or its customs to my knowledge."

He paused for a moment before seeming to make up his mind about something.

"I must admit that I knew of your impending visit and of your interest in the Umbral mages. Prior to your arrival I had determined that I would simply send you away. However, your courtesy and something...some simplistic honesty inherent to your nature...has convinced me otherwise. There is a mage who styles himself as the leader of the Umbrals—he goes by the name *Zizmziz*—who I very much suspect is the primary instigator of those events which cause the rest of the world to hold them in such low regard. From my experience most every questionable action committed in the name of their organization can be traced to him. He has made enemies even here in my own household, although officially he is still tolerated as the chief of that Pomos."

"Thank you, Great Chieftain. Have you any idea where I might find him?"

"He never comes here. From what I've been able to gather, he seldom leaves his home over in Zuum. But I have to ask, Sir Tol-u-ol, are you yourself a mage?"

"No, Great One. I'm just a cop."

"Then I would advise employing a great deal of caution and circumspection when dealing with Zizmziz. He is, from all accounts, accomplished at the use of both offensive and defensive magic. His specialties, one might say."

"So people keep telling me. I thank you once more for your extremely helpful information, great Chieftain. I promise to use whatever means are available to protect myself. Farewell."

"Farewell, Knight of the Crimson. May that Spirit who sustains us all watch over you."

Tol sat in his cabin on board the Tragacanthan transport, having checked out of the hotel after conducting a few sweeps looking for his erstwhile assailants, and studied the communiqués that had come in during his absence. By now Aspet knew he was all right; that took care of the most urgent one. He contacted Selpla and talked with her for a while also, because he was supposed to call her every night and of course that hadn't happened recently.

Once the compulsory notifications were out of the way, Tol started planning in earnest how he was going to approach the Zizmziz problem. He'd confronted hundreds of suspects in his career; the urge to treat this one as just another perp was strong. He knew that urge might get him in trouble this time, though. The criminals with whom he'd dealt in Goblinopolis, even the deadliest, were not mages. SagMag tended to police itself rather well, so the rare mage who was involved in criminal activities usually got taken care of by them. That begged the question: why hadn't they done anything about Zizmziz?

It was very tempting to sail directly to Zuum. It was just across the Gulf of Shadows and up the coast in Tantatku, more or less on the way home. On this rare occasion, Tol mused, he had decided to let common sense rule and instead headed back to Tragacanth—but only because he needed advice from a magineer.

Tol's first stop back in Goblinopolis was not the Royal Complex or his own apartment: it was Tropsalla, specifically Selpla's house. Through the haze of hyperactive hormones Tol realized that he was really hooked on this lady in a way he'd never remembered being before. He wondered if there was anything he should do about it. Eh, time to worry about that later. For now he had other pressing business to attend to.

Having achieved one quite pleasant goal, Tol then headed over to the Royal Palace to check in with Aspet. It was Boogla he most wanted to talk to, however.

"Hi, sis. I'm on the trail of the scumsuckers who attacked you, but I've run into a little magical roadblock. Specifically, a powerful mage by the name of Zizmziz who belongs to an outfit that calls itself the 'Umbral mages.' Before I just go waltzin' into his home turf, I'd like to discuss the case with the Loca Magineer. I figure you're the go-to person for that."

"Sounds reasonable. Hold on for just a moment." She pulled up a screen and scrolled down. "How about...two o'clock on Fourday?"

Tol nodded. "That'll work just fine."

Boogla typed for a few seconds. "Done," she announced, "Two o'clock in Loca Conference Room Three."

"You're an amazing gob," Tol said, "You're like the sister I, um...never had..." He tailed off and Boogla saw a brief but intense pang of sadness pass cross his face.

"What's wrong, Tol?" she asked, concern evident in her voice.

"Ah...it's nothin.' I'm fine. Listen, I got some errands to run. I'll meet you in the Loca lobby a little before two on Fourday." He didn't so much leave the room as flee.

Boogla stood there for a moment, lost in thought. She turned to Aspet, who had come in from the adjacent suite just after Tol arrived.

"What was that all about?" she asked.

Aspet hesitated before answering. "It's something I guess I've never told you. Tol and I had two sisters, once: Vesu and Resu. Twins. They...died young."

"How can you not have told me something like that?" Boogla asked, hands on hips.

"Unintentional oversight, I promise. It's just that I was also very young at the time and I don't really remember them, except as bundles in a crib. Tol knew them better. After they died we were never allowed to talk about them. I mean, not at all. It was as though they had never existed. I guess I just forgot about them, really. I know that sounds awful, but they really didn't make nearly as much impression on me as they did on Tol. As you can see he still thinks about them from time to time. Misses them. I can't honestly say I do, because as I said, I never actually knew them."

"That's very sad," Boogla said, "Thanks for telling me. I will try to avoid the subject around Tol."

"He's a tough gob. He'll get over it."

"Tol has enough to worry about without family adding to his burdens," Boogla replied, firmly.

Aspet chuckled. "That's one of things that makes Tol who he is. He doesn't worry about anything. He's always just lived in the moment. He makes up his mind what he's going to do about something and then does it. He doesn't over-analyze and he doesn't debate about whether his course of action is the best one he could have chosen. He just does what he does and then takes the consequences, good or bad. Most all of them are good, because if it looks like something is going wrong Tol fixes it, then and there, on the fly, as it were. I've always admired him for that, although I don't understand how he does it. He's a lot like our mom in that way. I never heard her worrying about the future, at least not where Tol and I could overhear. Dad was always figuring and planning and arguing how to make this or that scheme come to pass; mom just let him do his thing and tried to support him when she could. Once he left the feed store and became a cop the nature of his schemes changed, but they never went away. He was still looking for that get-rich formula right up to the day he...passed on."

Aspet hung his head and went suddenly silent; Boogla put her hand on his shoulder in a mute gesture of comfort. They stood this way for a long instant, a tableau of wife consoling husband, until one of the king's aides came to the door and asked for him. The poignant moment dissolved under the insistent barrage of the workaday world and they returned to their respective roles as monarch and advisor.

Chapter Five

"How are the manifestation practical exercises proceeding?" Ballop'ril asked, munching on his ogrecress rolls at the midday meal.

Prond swallowed the bite he was working on and nodded. "I got all the way to irregulars of the second platform during morning recitations. I'm having a little difficulty with asymmetric axials, but I think I'm starting to get the hang of them."

The archmage nodded in turn. "Yes, they can be difficult in the early stages, but as the recitations progress you will find the neural pathways growing better-established. After a time even the most complex of the manifestives will come as second nature to you. If you continue to advance at your current rate, I anticipate your Apotropaic Trial for Magus Incipius will occur around midsummer."

Prond's hand shook a little, but he did not quail. "I will do my best to be ready."

"Of course you will," Ballop'ril beamed. "Once you have achieved Magus, I want you to take a break before you study for the next level and complete your doctorate. I would like to schedule your oral examination for that degree by year's end. I've arranged for the exam to be conducted on the campus of Sutha Arts Collegium in Tillimil, where I hold an extramural professorship. You will submit your disquisition to them, as well, and your degree will be granted by that institution."

"Guess that means I'll need to dig out my notes on the Rebrugge Event."

"Yes, it does, but don't get too involved in them until after your Incipius trial. I don't want your attention divided. As I have warned you in the past, the Magus trials are both demanding and potentially hazardous."

Fleet Commodore Derra Bisylan turned to his Exec. "Bring

her around to the cross-pattern leg and we'll sweep one more time."

"Aye, aye, Commodore," replied the executive officer before relaying those orders to the rest of the bridge crew.

Commodore Bisylan and his tactical flotilla were patrolling the north-central Noorprid Sea, an immense area composed of nine sectors of over 3.5 million square kilometers. Ordinarily the Tragacanthan navy stuck to shore patrols within 100 kilometers of the Tragacanth coast, but since the sighting of the stolen corvet carrying orcs the king had ordered increased patrols of the established sea lanes leading to and from ports on all ocean-facing sides of the nation. Bisylan was charged with overseeing the patrols of the western coast, from Cladimil up around to Dresmak.

"Topper reports four smaller vessels approaching, Commodore," announced the Officer of the Deck. "Range four thousand meters and closing obliquely, zero-two-zero, vee ee 23 knots." 'Topper' referred to the four lookouts posted in the uppermost observation capsule fifty meters above the deck, facing each of the cardinal points relative to the ships' trajectory. They were supplied with high-powered optics and the Navy's best speedolites for determining range, velocity, and course.

"Plot probables," Bisylan ordered.

It took about three minutes for the answers to come back from the Navigation section.

"Destination has a greater than 84% probability of Uzplenq, Clewq, or Koppra. Origin, based on class of vessel and propulsion systems, has approximately equal chance of Cobloft or Xovcastra, with a slightly smaller probability of Jessmirto. All other origins are 10% or lower, Commodore."

"Identification?"

"Obvious national markings are absent but best guess is fisher fleet from Nerr or Asmagon. Behavior seems consistent with that analysis. Current course would take them near the mid-ocean shoals with their rich fisher grounds within the next two days. Commodore, there is one...rather odd thing about this fleet."

"What is it, Mr. Fek?"

"Several greater sea-avians have been observed coming and going. Not in the manner of avians simply following the fleet to scavenge scraps, but as though they had some specific alternative purpose."

"Ah, so? Well, avians and fishers are both sometimes inscrutable. They are probably being fed intentionally. Perhaps they serve as fish scouts. Carry on."

"Aye, Commodore."

"Missives have been dispatched to all enclaves."

"It is well. If this half-breed is the Uul, he will reveal this soon."

"And if he is not?"

"Then we resume waiting, as we have done for centums."

"May Providence guide us on the Valtir."

"Ammin."

Tol took Midweeksday off and spent it, as usual, at Selpla's house. After breakfast they were lounging in her leisure room when Tol reached down for something to read and found an old wooden crate on the floor near her divan.

"What's this stuff?" he asked.

Selpla glanced over. "Oh, it's got those documents the fishers hauled up near what used to be Morianella. You remember: it had that city council order that partially exonerated Plåk."

Tol grunted. "Oh yeah, I do remember. There was other stuff?"

"Yes. Several more documents. I never did get around to looking at them. I suppose I should. Might get another story or two out of it."

He reached into the box and hauled out a small ledger with ragged edges, flipping it open carefully. He couldn't understand a word. There were several similar documents in there that were equally inaccessible to him. At the bottom was an odd wood and metal slipcase of some sort. Tol pried it off the bottom—it was semi-fused from long years of being under tremendous pressure in the ocean depths, albeit sealed away from the salt water itself.

He turned it over and over. Although it looked like a slipcase, it did not seem to have an opening into which to insert a document. He shrugged and was about to disregard it when a small metal strip he hadn't noticed before caught his eye. He inserted a talon under it and carefully worked it back and forth until it popped loose. He pulled on the exposed tab and the end of the box suddenly folded back on a hidden hinge. A single thin but exceedingly tough vellum sheet slid smoothly out and glowed with an unmistakable arcane aura. Tol held it up for Selpla to see.

"This thing looks magical. Wonder what it is?"

Selpla came over to him and examined the parchment.

"No idea. Guess we'd have to ask a mage."

"Think your ex-camera gob would know?"

"Prond? Maybe. If not, I'll bet Ballop'ril will."

"Yeah, that little bugbear knows just about everything. He's amazing. I've got an appointment to keep tomorrow; I'm not sure where that will lead me. As soon as I get a chance, I'll drop in on Ballop'ril and ask him about this stuff." Tol said.

"I'll be more than happy to do it for you," Selpla replied, kissing him. "I haven't seen Prond in a while, anyway. I miss him from time to time."

"You don't like the new jlok?"

"Fob? He's all right. He's technically quite good, in fact. But he doesn't have as much personality as Prond. Mostly all he talks about is cinematography. Prond almost never mentioned it at all."

"Everybody's a geek about something," Tol observed.

Selpla smiled. "So, what's your 'geek' trigger?"

"You."

For most of the rest of that day, Tol proved his point.

The next morning Selpla went into the station to retrieve her news assignments and leads, then took off immediately for Cartlug, with the translocation amulet Ballop'ril had given her on a chain around her neck next to Tol's lifeforce talisman. She took note of the considerable progress that had been made all along the way toward rebuilding after the devastating hurrarcane and quakes. In many places the damage was completely erased; in others nearly so.

This time Selpla was prepared for the transfer and took it rather nonchalantly: at least she *hoped* it appeared that way. She stood there in Ballop'ril's chambers trying not to hyperventilate, clutching the satchel full of documents to her chest. The archmage regarded her placidly. Prond was nowhere in evidence.

"Always delightful to see you, Selpla," he said after a few moments, "To what do we owe the honor of your visit on this occasion? Sir Tol-u-ol is not missing again, I hope?"

Selpla took a deep breath to reinforce her composure.

"No. Well, he was for a while, in fact, but I saw him just this morning. I actually have a question about magic. I have here a piece of parchment that looks as though it may have been cut out of a spell book or something similar. I was wondering if you could identify it. It comes, we believe, from ancient Morianella."

Ballop'ril's eye ridges shot up.

"Morianella? I was not aware we had extant manuscripts from there."

"These were dredged up off the ocean floor near there by some deep-sea fishers. The capsule was sealed well enough that salt water had not invaded even after all these centums. I had one of the non-magical manuscripts translated already, but this one was obviously of arcane origin so I decided to bring it to you." She handed the slipcase with the parchment in it to him. He took it and extracted the contents carefully, setting the manuscript on a small table and examining it with a magnifying glass. He studied the document in silence for a full five minutes.

At last Ballop'ril looked up. "This," he announced, "Is indeed a page excised very carefully from an ancient spell tome: the *Codex Lapidismotus*, I would strongly suspect based on the symbology and context. It is curious that someone would remove just this one page, however, as by itself it provides no functional incantation. Additionally, whatever spell this represents would be rendered useless without it."

A little bell started ringing in Selpla's head. "*Codex Lapidismotus*? That name sounds really familiar." She pulled out her reporter's notebook and flipped through the pages.

"Yes! That's the same book that Plåk was using when he screwed up the spell that sank Morianella 900 years ago."

Ballop'ril frowned and looked back at the parchment page. He began to move his mouth as he pronounced the symbols under his breath. At length he seemed to come to a conclusion.

"This page is taken from a suite of spells designed specifically to transport large quantities of rock. If it was removed from the *Codex* prior to Plåk's use of it, that may well explain the disaster. Except...were this page missing, the spell would more than likely fail altogether. Odd."

"I happen to know that *Codex* is in the CoME library at Loca Duber in Goblinopolis," Selpla said, "Could you accompany me, or at least send a mage along who would be able to verify this page came from there?"

Ballop'ril smiled. "As it happens, my apprentice needs some library time to work on his disquisition." He drew a figure in the air with his fingers that left a visible glowing circular outline. He spoke into it. "Prond, please come here."

The Mage of the First Tier walked in and immediately brightened.

"Selpla! Great to see you."

Selpla smiled warmly at him. "You, too. You're looking really well."

"The young lady here needs a mage to accompany her to the CoME library at Loca Duber," Ballop'ril inserted, "I thought you could do the honors and get some research in for your disquisition at the same time. One day will not interfere with your magus studies too onerously."

Prond bowed slightly. "As you wish, my Master, so shall it be."

Selpla grinned at his obedient tone. "Kurg would be *so* jealous right now."

Prond chuckled. "Haven't thought about that old smekker in a while. How's he doin'?"

"Same as ever: ornery, judgmental, and impatient."

"Some things never change."

Prond rode to Goblinopolis with Selpla so they could catch up. He would simply translocate back to the Arcanium when he was through at the library. Prond told her about all the magic he'd learned and how his entire world had changed; how he felt far more confident and as though he had a real chance to contribute to society now. Not that being on a news team wasn't contributing to society, he hastened to clarify, worried that she might have taken offense. Selpla just laughed in response. He relayed the Rebrugge incident and expressed his uncertainty about the magical trial to advance from mage to magus. She was fascinated by the sudden and unexpected turn his life had taken.

For her part, Selpla mostly talked about Tol and his adventures. She spent so much time talking about him, in fact, that Prond felt compelled to ask when the wedding was. Selpla was taken aback; she blushed and told him that they hadn't really discussed that. Prond smirked but said nothing in reply.

Once in the CoME archives, they located the rare tomes room and asked the librarian for the *Codex Lapidismotus*. Prond had brought a missive from Ballop'ril as head of his schola and an established academic, so they had no difficulty accessing the requested resource. She brought the book out and gave them, or Prond at least, the standard safety lecture supplied with powerful spell books. Prond carefully inspected the *Codex* page by page until he found very subtle evidence of a leaf that had been meticulously sewn in with very fine magically obscured stitches. To anyone not looking for it specifically they were virtually invisible. He then compared the page Selpla had brought with the replaced one and verified that they were almost identical, with the exception of two small substitutions at different locations in the written incantation stream.

Working from the beginning of that specific spell, Prond created a little magical 'sandbox' in which to test the effects of the original and substituted incantations. He formed a three-dimensional wireframe model in the air over the table and read the incantations into it. About an hour of this provided all the proof he needed to conclude that the changes rendered the spell unstable and its results unpredictable. If this was the incantation Plåk used in Morianella, the quake may not have been his fault at all.

This discovery led to a slew of new questions. Who made the substitution? Why? Was Plåk aware? Why wasn't the original page destroyed to hide the evidence? All these questions and more were tumbling through Selpla's head as she left Prond and drove home to Tropsalla. Tol would almost certainly be interested in her findings. She wanted to talk to Plåk now, as well; the only way she knew of to contact him was indirectly through Tol. She left a message for Tol to come see her immediately after work.

Back home Selpla brewed a pot of her favorite infusion and thought about what she'd discovered from an investigative reporter's perspective. A massive quake nine centums ago had destroyed an island nation and killed almost all of its citizens. The proximate cause, according to the historical record, was a botched magical spell intended to rid the island's deepwater port of debris that interfered with movement of the large cargo vessels of the time. She now had strong evidence that the spell might not have been botched at all: Plåk may have completed the incantation perfectly accurately. It was beginning to look as though someone might have set him up, for an unknown reason.

As she sat at the table contemplating these questions, Selpla idly reached into the recovered document satchel and extracted a thin binder. It had a symbol on the front she'd never seen before and appeared to be a list of people's names; although that was purely a guess, as not only could she not read the strange characters, she didn't even know what *language* that was. She sighed and dropped the bound manuscript on the tabletop.

"How we doin' for time, Petey?"

"Your meeting is scheduled to begin in sixteen minutes. That means you have six minutes until your planned rendezvous with the Magineer Liaison. At your mean gait velocity and presuming no unexpected obstacles you are five minutes and eight seconds away."

"Good. I hate bein' late."

"Punctuality is indeed an important trait, especially for one in your position."

Tol climbed the elegant shellstone staircase leading to the executive offices of the Loca Duber and walked up to the pre-arranged meeting point just as Boogla approached down the hallway from the opposite direction. She smiled at him.

"Are you ready to do this?"

"Yeah. I sure hope he doesn't get too far into the weeds, though. These mage types lose me pretty quick, and sometimes engineers are even worse. The thought of talkin' to somebody who's both turns my stomach a little."

"I think you'll be pleasantly surprised by old Cromalin. He sizes up his audience quite effectively. At any rate, I will be there to translate if need be."

"I appreciate that, sis...er, Your Excellency."

They went in and were met by one of the Loca Magineer's assistants.

"Welcome to the office of the Loca Magineer Cromalin II, gentlegoblins. The Magineer is expecting your visit and will receive you shortly. May we offer you spring water or any of a variety of infusions?"

They were led through a brace of magnificently appointed

doors set with glowing magical runes into the office of the Loca Magineer. Cromalin was seated in an immense wooden chair, the arms and back of which were expertly carved such that the occupant appeared to be sitting in the bosom of a huge predator avian. It was a dramatic effect; Tol couldn't seem to stop staring.

"Welcome to you both," Cromalin said, rising with less apparent difficulty than one might expect for a goblin of his advanced years. "I am quite looking forward to our conversation. From what little Her Excellency here has told me, it should prove most illuminating."

Boogla looked pointedly at Tol. She was obviously expecting him to reply. Tol adjusted the neck of his overjack and cleared his throat.

"I deeply appreciate your having taken the time to meet with us today," Tol began, rather more lucidly than he anticipated. "Hopefully answering my questions will be worth the interruption to your busy schedule."

Cromalin nodded. "Of that I harbor little doubt, Sir Tol-u-ol. Now pray, what assistance may I provide to the EE community?"

Tol laid out everything that had happened regarding the attack on Boogla and the palace, his tracking of Frem to Erolossma, and the clues that led him first to Woklopen, then Hiffa and the Umbral mages. He segued at last into a specific discussion of Zizmziz.

"The sources I talked to were all agreed that the rotten fruit in the Umbral mage barrel is this Zizmziz. I need to understand just who he is and what he wants if I really hope to make progress in this investigation."

Cromalin had been once again seated during Tol's exposition, listening calmly and attentively. He exhaled slowly and stood up to face the burly goblin.

"Zizmziz represents perhaps the greatest perversion of magic ever to manifest on N'plork. His body is that of some hybrid— possibly even orcish in origin—but I strongly doubt the soul within is part of a matched set, as you might say colloquially."

"I'm not sure I follow you," Tol replied, frowning.

Cromalin paced behind his desk for a few moments before answering.

"As a mage develops his arcane skills, his physical body and neural patterning template evolve concurrently. It is impossible to speak of or consider one without reference to the other. With each level of advancement the unique arcane fingerprint, as it were, of the mage becomes increasingly apparent to educated observers. With most mages there is an intrinsic harmony between the body and spirit: they reinforce and augment one another in myriad ways. I have encountered this Zizmziz on several occasions and his very physical presence is an abomination to me."

"What you seem to be saying," Boogla clarified for Tol's benefit, "Is that Zizmziz did not follow the traditional path in his magical training."

"Yes, but it's much more than that. I don't believe Zizmziz is... *biologically normal*, for lack of a better term. His arcane aura does not match his physical shell in the least. I am frankly uncomfortable simply being in his vicinity."

Tol nodded. "Sounds like you're not a fan of the gob. If I have to go up against him, what would be your advice?"

The Loca Magineer looked him dead in the eye. "Get your affairs in order beforehand. This...person shows no evidence of possessing anything resembling normal morality, compassion, or even a rudimentary conscience. He is both psychologically and physically a monster."

"If this Zizmziz is truly involved in the plot to kill members of my family, not to mention the King to whom I have sworn fealty, taking me out entirely will be the only chance he has. I will excuse myself now and allow you to return to your important work. My most sincere thanks to you for your insight, Magineer." Tol turned and walked briskly out the door.

"He is quite the confident fellow," Cromalin remarked.

"That confidence is well-founded," answered Boogla. "While I don't know if he could survive a direct head-to-head matchup with a high-level mage, that's not the way it will happen. He's much, much smarter than he lets on. I know: I married his brother."

"If he has even a significant fraction of the intelligence of His Majesty," the Magineer replied after a moment, "The contest will be an interesting one. At any rate, I wish him the very best. N'plork would be a better place without Zizmziz polluting its magical pool."

Chapter Six

Tol had summoned Oloi and asked him to arrange a meeting with Plåk at Selpla's home. She wanted to know more about the Codex page and Tol just needed to get as much information on Zizmziz as possible in order to plan his next move. The archmage showed up when he said he would, which told Tol he expected entertainment, if nothing else. Plåk did what he pleased when he pleased, so cooperation of this sort almost certainly meant there was something in it for him.

"Thanks for showing up, your mageness," said Tol. "The lady here has something you might find interesting."

"I always find both of you quite interesting," replied Plåk with a grin, turning to Selpla. "Let's see what you've got for me."

Selpla showed him the parchment page with no explanation. He immediately noticed the arcane aura and examined it closely. After a full minute of scrutiny, he looked up at them, confusion evident in his countenance.

"This is a page from a very old spell book. It appears to have been removed from the book many centums ago. I do not understand. Where did you get it?"

Selpla explained the origin. She also told him about comparing it to the *Codex Lapidismotus* in the archives. Plåk looked from her to Tol and then sat down, stunned.

"Somebody set you up," Tol said, simply. The archmage nodded weakly.

Selpla continued, "This means you may be *completely* blameless for Morianella's destruction. After 900 years that's bound to be something of a relief."

Plåk stared fixedly into space for a few moments. When he allowed his gaze to wander a bit, it happened to fall on the binder Selpla had dropped on the table. He stared at it without taking it in for a moment, and then suddenly jumped for it.

"What...where did you get this?" he sputtered.

"Dredged up by fishers off Morianella. Same time as the Codex page," Selpla replied, intrigued by his reaction.

Visibly interested, Plåk used some of his manna pool to solidify fingers enough to flip through the book. "It's a class roster for the Morianella Arcane Academy. That's where I first learned magic."

"You can read that stuff?" Tol asked.

"What *language* is that?" asked Selpla.

Plåk shook his head. "One that has been extinct on this planet for many centums."

Tol frowned. "Whatta ya mean 'on this planet'?"

The transcendent archmage sighed and sat down heavily, or at least as heavily as someone without solid corporeal form can manage.

"You may have noticed that I don't look like you, or anyone else on N'plork."

"Not many of us are translucent, it's true," Selpla giggled.

"Hah. I mean that my skin tone and morphology are very different from any of the native races. Without boring you with too much detail, Morianella was colonized by, well, by people from another planet, difficult though that is to believe. We—I was one of them—had to abandon our deep space vessel in orbit because the systems we were using to produce breathing air were catastrophically damaged in an accident. N'plork was the closest habitable planet. We landed in a smaller craft specifically designed to serve as both transport and shelter and chose the island that became known as Morianella because it was uninhabited at the time. N'plork was not our intended destination—we were colonizers, not invaders—but our only chance for survival was a quick landing on a planet that could support our kind of life."

Tol and Selpla were fascinated and skeptical in equal parts but neither wanted to interrupt, knowing that Plåk could not stay on this plane indefinitely.

"When we started making contact with other races we found out about magic. Although we knew that N'plork was embedded in the Dark Energetic Continuum, we were not aware of the implications of that fact. We imported some academic mages and started a magic academy. I was in the initial class and in fact the only student who made it past Incipius."

While Tol was just trying to take all this in, Selpla's journalistic instincts were buzzing.

"What planet are you from, then?"

Plåk hesitated a bit before answering.

"I was actually born in deep space, as were the three generations prior to mine. The ship we were traveling on originated from a large spaceport in orbit around a planet known as Terra, or to the locals, Earth. It is clear around on the other side of this galaxy, so far away that even my mind can't comfortably contemplate the distance."

"That still leaves the question of who would stand to gain from substituting a fake page into that spell book," Tol said, cutting back to the topic, "There are only a few minor-looking differences; whoever did it must have been aware of the damage it would cause."

Plåk shook his head. "It was a long time ago. I don't remember having any enemies, really. I mean, there was another student who sort of competed with me at first, but I actually spent a lot of time trying to help him out. He could never make it past Incipius, as I said. Always choked during the Arcanis Trial."

"What was his name? Is he on this list?"

The archmage ran his finger down a page.

"Here it is: Philmon Iwo. He tried hard, but he just wasn't good advanced Magus material."

"Which one of these is your name?" Tol asked, looking over his shoulder.

Plåk pointed to a line.

"That says '*Plåk*'?" Selpla asked, amused, "Obviously not a one-to-one correlation with Goblish characters."

"No," Plåk admitted, "It doesn't say Plåk. It says Dennis Blass.

That was my birth name."

"Dennisblass?" asked Tol, "What kind of name is that?"

"It's two words: the given name 'Dennis' and the family name 'Blass.' That's how we traditionally named people. Everyone from a family had the same second name, but each person's first name was different. There are a few societies here on N'plork that employ this same convention: the old Merton Empire and some of its descendants, for example."

Selpla frowned. "Where did you get 'Plåk,' then?"

"I have to go soon, so I'll make this quick: my species has teeth that need a lot of cleaning and maintenance. They are not self-regenerative like yours. The medical professionals—physics—who specialize in teeth are called *dentists*. Dennis sounds a lot like dentist. One of the things dentists did routinely was scraping off a thin layer of gunk known as *plaque* that accumulated on our teeth, so I took a form of that name as a sort of inside joke. It's also a play on words in another way. My species exhibits a range of skin tones, depending on how much pigmentation the epidermis has, which is related to the amount and intensity of sunlight to which our ancestors were exposed. Mine came from a location near our equator, which meant that they needed more protection from ultraviolet radiation, and so my skin when I was corporeal was dark. Our word for that color was pronounced 'black' even though it was really sort of dark brown. So, *Plåk* sounds like *black*. It's humor you'd probably have to be from my species to appreciate. Gotta split; I'll be back."

With that, archmage Plåk dissolved into a sparkling shower that drifted lazily to Selpla's library floor.

Selpla whistled through her teeth. "Wow. That was a lot to take in."

"I just can't get over this feelin' that all of this stuff—the Umbral mages, Zizmziz, Morianella—is somehow connected," Tol said sometime later, "It's one of those gut instincts." He paused, apparently waiting for something.

"Well?" he said into his overjack pocket. A thin metallic voice came out in reply.

"Sorry, was that interrogative directed at me?"

"Interrogative?" interjected Selpla, "Something in your pocket uses words like interrogative? What is it, a vocabulary builder unit?"

Tol chuckled. "You might say that. It's Petey, my PDA pen. He's certainly had an effect on my vocabulary: in more ways than one."

"And in turn you have vastly improved my understanding of colloquialisms and profane expression," said Petey. "Returning to the interrogative, to what were you expecting me to respond?"

"I mentioned my gut instinct. I expected a remark concerning my employment of an alternate organ system for cogitation."

"See? *Right there* is why I made no such remark. The progress you have exhibited insofar as clarity of spoken communication is concerned is sufficiently impressive that witty pejoratives no longer seem appropriate as often. I do not want to discourage you, in other words."

"I guess I'm grateful. I sort of miss our repartee, though."

"Not to put too fine a point on it, but what we had was *not* repartee. It was witty commentary on my end versus largely monosyllabic verbal abuse on yours. That is not the same as repartee."

"Heh. So, what did you think of archmage Plåk's little revelation?"

Petey paused. "He withheld some information, according to his voice stress patterns, but overall he seemed more truthful than previous encounters would have led me to expect. I believe you caught him off guard; a condition in which nine hundred year-old transcendent archmages are seldom likely to find themselves."

Tol hiked his supraorbital ridge. "I had no idea Plåk was such an interesting character. Being an alien explains a lot, though." A thought struck him. "It's always been pretty obvious to me that he and Oloi are, if not the same species, at least closely related. I guess that means Oloi is an alien, too."

"That is almost certainly the case," agreed Petey. "The harmonic overlay patterns of their arcane auras match to three standard deviations. They are very different from those of other archmages in whose presence I have been. Some of this is no doubt related to the fact that they share transcendence, but that cannot account for all of it."

Plåk did return a couple of hours later, and he brought with him a lot of laboriously excavated memories.

"The only person with motive and opportunity was Philmon. It *had* to be him."

"What became of him?" Selpla asked.

"I always assumed he died in Morianella. Thinking back on it, though, I did not see him at all for a few days prior to the disaster. He was bitter because he failed to pass the Arcanis trial yet again, although why any of that bitterness would be directed at me is hard to fathom. It's possible he altered the *Codex* and then fled to avoid the inevitable outcome."

"What did you do between the time you teleported those people to Woklopen and your transcendence?"

"Mostly I kicked around Solemadrina and Rublosq, which back then was still part of a larger empire. It took me about ten years, give or take, to accomplish the rituals necessary to transcend. It's a demanding process that has to be performed slowly, in careful, rigidly-defined stages."

"How well do you know Oloi?" Tol asked, changing tack.

Plåk shrugged. "He's another transcended archmage. The new kid on the block from my perspective, although he's been around for a couple centuries now. We see each other in The Slice from time to time, and even 'socialize' there, if you want to call it that. I consider him a friend, at any rate."

Tol pressed on. "Is he the same species as you?"

The archmage seemed taken aback by this. "Um...yes, he is.

82

That is, his ancestors and mine came from the same planet. We were both starship crew, although his ship was far more advanced than the one I lived on. Mine was intended simply to colonize other worlds; his was built for exploration and interacting with sentient, spacefaring civilizations. My ship, the TCV *Isomer*, was essentially without defenses other than running away; his was quite capable of defending itself. His ship made use of wormholes something like the ones mages use to translocate—only on a far, far larger scale. They could get from one side of the galaxy to the other in the shipboard time it would take the *Isomer* to go from one star system to the next one over. A very, very fast ship, in other words."

"You know, it occurs to me that there are large segments of the population of N'plork who don't really believe any other intelligent life exists in the universe. You and Oloi are living—or whatever it is you are now—proof that they are mistaken. Maybe we ought to educate them."

Plåk laughed. "Those in authority already know, believe me. Ask your brother. The bottom line is that we present neither a threat nor an advantage to the regimes, so they simply ignore us. That is always the way of governments: while the common people share wild theories and talk of deep, dark conspiracies, those in power adjudge whatever is the topic of discussion to be of no consequence to them and disregard it. Allowing the people their fantasies is a tried and true technique of governing. All you have to do to maintain control is interject a small pulse of doubt from time to time, so that the thought leaders amongst the conspiracy theorists are seen as potential crackpots. People want to believe whatever reinforces their pre-existing philosophies; they will glam onto any accommodating straw proffered them as a result. If you provide those straws in a variety of shapes and sizes, you keep everyone happy."

"Dark," Selpla observed. "Cynical."

"Not really. It's just the nature of sentience to seek to explain everything it sees, or thinks it sees. People want to feel important:

as though they matter. One way to do this in a social system where you don't have any temporal authority is to get with other similarly impotent people and complain about the government. No matter what problems you propose fixing, as soon as they are fixed you will find others. It isn't a solution that you actually want; it's the social solidarity inherent to the act of protesting. People enjoy theorizing. They don't want that entertainment besmudged by facts. Facts are ugly, stark; utilitarian. Theories and hypotheses can be elegant, soaring things that expand your mind and take over your imagination. To paraphrase a philosopher from my planet, many centuries ago: 'What's the point of staying up half the night arguing whether there is or is not a god when someone just goes and gives you his bleeding phone number the next morning'?"

"What's a 'phone number'?" Tol asked.

"It's like a comm circuit. The point is, people ask a lot of questions they don't really want answered. It's just part of being intelligent. A smart government nurtures that curiosity and allows it to free-range as much as possible without breaking through the fence, to take the farmyard metaphor to its logical extreme."

Selpla decided to pursue a potential story she'd thought of earlier.

"You said you came to N'plork on a spaceship. Where did it land? Is it still there?"

Plåk shook his head. "No. The *Isomer* was abandoned in orbit. Once the fuel for its boosters ran out the orbit would have decayed and the ship burned up in the atmosphere. That had to have taken place at least 850 years ago. Somewhere there might be a contemporary account of strange lights in the sky, and possibly a high-altitude explosion or two as the ship broke up. I did not witness the event, however, so presumably it happened on the other side of the world from Morianella."

"So, how did you get down to the surface? Teleport?"

"We had two small vessels called lifeboats. They served as both shuttle and shelter once landed. They were also built to withstand high seas and rough weather if they set down in the ocean, which both presumably did. We lived out of ours while we constructed our first permanent buildings. The last time I saw it was a couple of years before the disaster. It was docked on the west end of the island, in use as a museum of sorts. I presume it was destroyed, or at least cast adrift and eventually sank, when Morianella did."

"What happened to the other one?"

"I don't really know. We lost contact with it during the descent. I heard rumors of another population of us in southern Esmia, but we never confirmed that."

"The people you rescued from Morianella—you said you took them to Woklopen. What happened to them after that?"

"They all lived pretty much together in the same neighborhood on the north side of the city along the estuaries; I guess for moral support. Since they weren't the same species as everyone else, they didn't blend in very well. The other residents called them 'the smooth people' or 'the wraiths' because they were so much less sturdily built and seemed thin and insubstantial next to the goblins, ogres, and trolls, especially."

"What did you species call itself?" asked Tol.

"We were called 'humans' or 'mankind'."

"I've never heard either of those terms before. Did they still call themselves that in Woklopen?"

"As far as I can remember. As an archmage I got involved immediately in the mages' guild there and lost track of the others. I believe they died out after a few generations, mostly due to inbreeding."

"You mean you more or less ignored your entire race until they died out?" Tol asked.

"When you put it like that it sounds positively dreadful, but the reality is that I didn't know most of those people to begin with; I lived in Woklopen pretty much the same way I had in Morianella: in the mages' guild scholaterion. Plus, I thought I had just destroyed their entire nation with one spell. I didn't really want to be reminded of that."

Selpla and Tol were silent, both trying to grasp such an extraordinary way of life. Plåk seemed about to continue, but appeared to change his mind.

"Time for me to leave. I will not be back this time."

He dissolved in a sparkle. They stared at the spot where he'd been standing, but still held their tongues. Finally the heavy silence was broken by Petey.

"Proximate analysis suggests that Plåk and the orcs share a common ancestor."

"How is that possible?" asked Selpla, coming back from the mental voyage she'd been on, "He said he was from another planet."

"While much of orc genetic material is of N'plorkian origin, a significant proportion cannot be attributed to any known ancestral race. If the orcs were originally a totally alien species that was able to hybridize with goblins, as the genome suggests, that would explain the discrepancy."

"A completely alien species not only able to interbreed with us but produce reproductively viable offspring?" Selpla asked, incredulous. "What are the odds of that?"

"Admittedly quite remote," replied Petey, "If the reproductive process were left to its own devices. However, were scholars to have artificially manipulated the genetic material via a theoretical procedure known as gene splicing, the probability increases dramatically."

"Gene splicing?" said Tol, "900 years ago? We can't even do that *today* very well, as far as I know."

"Correct. But remember that these people were many centums if not millennia ahead of us technologically. They were interstellar explorers, for example, with the ability to traverse unimaginable distances in vessels of whose construction techniques and propulsion systems we can only dimly conceive. The likelihood that they were capable of genetic manipulation of the sophistication necessary to achieve this is quite high."

"But if Plåk and the orcs are related, that means that we should be able to trace all existing orcs back to those people, the 'humans,' Plåk rescued from Morianella. There should be a strong connection between Woklopen and orc history. How come I've never heard of one?" Tol asked.

"Good question," Selpla agreed.

Tol sighed. "Well, I have to go back to Woklopen to follow the Umbral trail, anyway. Guess I'll ask around while I'm there."

On a ship heading once more across the Noorprid, Tol was putting pieces together. The Umbral mages, the Lycan Brotherhood, the Morianella survivors: Woklopen seemed to be the central point from which all of this radiated—the commonality. This just *couldn't* be a coincidence. He was still trying to wrap his mind around the connection between orcs and Morianella, but it wasn't his primary goal. He knew Boogla was on that case, anyway. She had been very excited when he related everything Plåk had told them about their history.

Tol figured the mages' guild in Woklopen would be a good place to start. He had a little better idea where he was going this time, so he didn't need to spend as much time orienting himself. Woklopen was actually a very pretty city: well-manicured and thoughtfully laid out, with plenty of public spaces and greenery. It was an easy walk from the passenger piers to the mages' guild compound, so Tol decided to hoof it.

He was no more than fifty meters from the ornate cast iron gate of the compound when a cargo dray drew alongside and disgorged three kobolds who leapt onto the sidewalk in front of him wielding wicked clubs with multiply-knobbed heads. One of them shouted in rather broken Goblish something to the effect that he would be wise to go back to Tragacanth and mind his own business before swinging the weapon at Tol's head. Tol caught the club in mid-swing and ripped it from the surprised kobold's grasp.

The other two kobs closed on him simultaneously. He blocked one of their swings with the commandeered club and ducked out of the other, grabbing the one who swung first by the jack and shoving him sideways hard into the second assailant. The kob who'd started the attack now came at him with some sort of knife. Tol punched him right in the face, so hard that blood squirted from his nostrils and both ears. The other two ran for the dray. Tol hauled the stunned leader up by the jack and growled at him.

"Hey, cupcake: you tell whoever sent you that I was just doin' my job before. Now you've gone and made it personal. I'm not such a nice gob when things get personal. The next time I won't be so friendly. Understand?" The kob nodded dazedly. Tol tossed him a full two meters out into the street with one arm. The kob staggered back to the dray and it sped off. Tol shook his head.

"Pathetic."

Triz'lo'K was not in on this occasion, so Tol met with his assistant Guildmaster Fivcan. The Magus Arcanis was cordial, if not actually pleasant.

"How may I assist you, Sir Knight?"

"I just have a hypothetical question, and I understand that it's not going to be something you've probably ever considered before. Imagine you are a member of a criminal organization who has need for a high-level mage willing to commit an unsavory act on your behalf, or at least assist you in the commission thereof. Where would you go to find such a mage?"

Fivcan knotted up his brow and thought hard for a few moments.

"While the public believe mages to be, at best, amoral, the truth is that the vast majority of us have strong ethical underpinnings. We just don't always convey that because we approach most topics from a scholarly, detached perspective that people confuse with amorality. Consequently, that would be a difficult challenge. I would more than likely make inquiries with the Umbral mages, I believe."

"I was told the Umbral mages were just an empty label created to take the blame for any unethical acts committed by mages anywhere."

Fivcan looked surprised. "No, I assure you, they exist. They began as the Umber mages, after the Umber forest south of Zuum in Tantatku where they were first formed, but over time the name was corrupted to Umbral, perhaps in part as a result of the fact that some of their members were willing to take on the type of jobs to which you alluded, those eschewed by the mainstream magical community. I would hesitate to assert that their principal announced focus was anything other than legitimate arcane research and practice, but they are...less strict about member activities than are most guilds."

Triz'lo'K was lying, as I suspected, Tol thought.

"Presuming you were not a mage yourself, how would you go about contacting the Umbral mages?"

Fivcan frowned. "Precisely what are you trying to accomplish here, Sir Tol?"

"I am trying to establish one possible mechanism by which a mage was engaged to help circumvent some very tough security measures. That's all I can say."

"The Umbral mages have a small business office of sorts on Teylli Circle in west town," Fivcan answered, a little reluctantly it seemed to Tol, "Beyond that, I can suggest nothing other than traveling to Zuum itself. Be warned that certain elements within that group are likely to take a dim view of your investigation. It could present some...significant hazard to your person."

Tol chuckled. "Just about everything I do in my line of work involves hazard to my person. I appreciate the warning, though."

The western end of Woklopen was the poster child for architectural eclecticism. There were artist's studios adjacent to financial firms down the block from wholesale grocers and around the corner from industrial factories. Nestled smugly in the midst of all this commercial diversity was a narrow three-story brownstone with iron railings on either side of the steps. It looked out of place, as though it had been wrested bodily from some densely urban city like Relem or Xovcastra and deposited unceremoniously here in a tiny gap between two 'conventional' buildings. Above the door there was a small sign showing a black arc over the silhouette of a many-branched arbor.

Tol rang the bell and waited. After a few seconds the door opened and a curiously-attired dwarf stood there, regarding Tol inscrutably. Tol looked at him for a long moment, expecting some form of communication, but the dwarf stood there motionlessly, almost as though he were the product of mostly successful taxidermy. Finally Tol broke the silence.

"I'm here to talk to whoever is in charge. My name is Tol-u-ol; I come from Tragacanth."

The dwarf reacted precisely the same way a deceased wrat would react to happy birthday wishes. Tol repeated his introduction, and then did so a third time.

"The 'dwarf' is not alive," Petey said from Tol's overjack pocket. "There is no point in continuing along these lines."

Tol reached out and poked said dwarf. It felt stiff and rocked back and forth a little. A banner that had been rolled tightly beneath the figure's chin suddenly unrolled. It read:

We are Closed
Go Away
This Means You

He started to shove the mannequin out of his path when Petey sounded the warning tone.

"There are magical traps all over the place. Be very, very cautious."

"Understood. Guide me, then."

"Do not move the mannequin. Step to the right, but not too far. There is a body impedance-triggered electrical trap there. You will have just enough room to squeeze between the mannequin and the trigger boundary. Good. Now, look to your left. You should see a faint pattern of crisscrossing lines in the air. I shall broadcast a signal that should make them more visible. Do not come into contact with any of them."

Tol wriggled and ducked his way through various snares under Petey's guidance until at last they emerged into a small room at the rear of the building; *really more of a closet*, Tol thought. There was a raised platform along the back wall that glowed with a faint golden radiance. Tol frowned at it.

"Another trap?"

Petey didn't answer for a moment.

"Not a trap, as such, but definitely very energetic. It appears to be a static translocator."

"Leading where?"

"The nature of arcane translocators is such that calculating their termination point is virtually impossible from the portal terminus. In essence you step first into The Slice and then out a 'door' located there back onto the physical plane. You would have to be in The Slice itself to tell which further path that spell was programmed to follow."

"So, the only way to find out where it leads is to step on it?"

"The risk inherent in that activity is incalculable. Literally. I strongly advise against it."

"Look, all of these traps are guarding *something*. You don't go to that much trouble just to keep people out of what is otherwise an apparently empty building. This teleportal most likely leads to someplace the Umbral mages don't want people to find; hence the security. If it's a static portal, even more reason to keep unauthorized people out of it. At any rate, it's the only lead I've got. If I walk away now, even presuming I get out of the building alive, I'm right back where I started. Taking risk is what I get paid to do."

"I do not believe the potential benefits outweigh the risks here. However, I am only an advisor. It is my experience that you will do as you will regardless of the intelligence or logic underlying those actions."

"Ah, now you're just being mean. On the bright side you'll probably survive whatever happens to me."

"Survival does me little good without someone to serve. My reason for existence is not, as seems to be the case with most biological organisms, merely to survive long enough to reproduce. I exist to provide assistance to one or more edict enforcement officers. Existence itself is pointless without someone for whom *to* exist."

Tol blinked. "Wow, that's deep and sorta depressing, Petey." He took a deep breath. "Here we go."

Tol stepped onto the platform. He caught a momentary glimpse of a fantastic landscape he'd seen when teleporting before—The Slice—and then the world around him erupted in fire.

Chapter Seven

Boogla sat at the table in her breakfast nook, nibbling on buttered ogrecress scones and planning out her day. She was growing more and more intrigued with the orc issue as new information kept coming in. The revelations Plåk had provided via Tol and Selpla were nothing short of astonishing. She wasn't entirely able to accept the talk about aliens and starships quite yet, but she had to admit it did provide explanations for some otherwise inexplicable aspects of the ever-widening puzzle.

If the orc race was indeed based on the survivors of Morianella transported to Woklopen, there should be some clear genetic markers to that effect. The small breeding population should show up as specific haplotypes in the orc genome, even though it had been diluted by many generations of allospecies breeding. She didn't fully understand how that had been made possible, either. She had an appointment to speak with perhaps Tragacanth's foremost genetics scholar at Tropsalla Tech later in the day.

Gnawing at the edge of her mind was the apparent discrepancy between the Woklopen origin story and what she'd seen in the Paradiddle Islands. Did the Woklopen orcs, or at least a sizeable contingent of them, emigrate from Solemadrina and land on Flam? The Arctal Current wouldn't take them anywhere near those southern islands, no matter which way it was flowing when such an expedition set out. It would require an experienced sailor and navigator to make the trip from Woklopen to Flam before onboard food supplies would run out for a colony-founding sized group.

The oral traditions of Eithmorg, or at least the ones Boogla had heard recounted, made no mention of Woklopen or indeed of any other orcs at all. Another thing that bothered her is that so far as she knew 'orc' was not related to any existent language on N'plork. If those people were originally known as 'humans,' where did 'orc' come from?

Dr. Hellis Breqal was a life mechanics scholar and expert on the genetics of N'plorkian sentients. He had only limited profile information available for orcs, as they were not very cooperative in such matters, but he thought he could come to at least some preliminary conclusions based on her new information. He did have swabs taken from orcs in every official enclave and they showed remarkable genetic marker similarity.

"I can safely say with very little margin of error that every one of these individuals is related to a small group of ancestors. The genetic drift as the hybridization progressed is quite mathematically predictable. You hypothesis that all orcs are descended from a very small population is undoubtedly correct. We've known, or at least suspected, that for some time now, however. What we haven't been able to figure out is why that would be the case. In terms of evolution, the orc race just popped up out of nowhere. It's not there one day, historically speaking, and there the next. No credible explanation that fits the available facts has been put forth by the scholarly community. Do you have one?"

Boogla started to reply, but then thought better of it. This might not be the best time to drop something as outlandish as alien life into the discussion.

"I...have some ideas, but nothing I'm prepared to share at this juncture. Once I've done some more investigation I promise to fill you in on them."

As her RPC squad drove her away from Tropsalla, Boogla came to a decision. She needed to talk to 'wild' orcs in an enclave; preferably some form of history scholar if such a thing existed in orc society. Achieving this would not be easy, though: the relentless persecution of orcs for their supposed bipolar violence had resulted in a deep-seated xenophobia. Boogla was a goblin; orcs hated goblins worst of all. She needed to find some way to connect with them.

Back in the palace, Boogla set Tragacanth's formidable

intelligence machine to work trying to come up with some common ground that would allow her to approach the orcs without raising too many hackles. It was a difficult assignment. The orcs had been forcibly divorced almost entirely from the rest of the world centums ago and now had no particular desire to reconcile.

The next morning a courier from the Tragacanth Intelligence Bureau delivered a hard drive with thousands of documents related to the orcs on it. Intelligence data was never placed on even the most locked-down portions of the Arnoc for security reasons: it was always hand-carried to wherever it needed to go on robustly encrypted storage media. Boogla had a dedicated workstation into which the hot-swappable drive fit snugly. She sat down and started reading.

Three hours later it was glaringly apparent to Boogla that everything Dr. Reoksa had told her was spot on. There was absolutely no reliable solid physical evidence that the orcs had ever attacked anyone at all. But their bipolar, unpredictable violent natures were an accepted fact. What was going on here? Boogla decided to start from the beginning.

The earliest mention of Morianella at all was simply as an island nation that traded with various other seafaring peoples of that era. Prior to its abrupt disappearance, it was largely ignored by the major civilizations of N'plork. Even the cataclysmic destruction of the island and its people itself barely merited a few passing mentions in contemporary chronicles. The orcs and their ancestors seemed marginalized from the very start.

Every account of the orcs' tendencies to violence led back inexorably to a few papers written by the famous middle-period historian Gumnil Ke-juq, who had studied under the legendary Winfaz Hidn at the Neripa Arts Institute in Lardonica. Curiously, despite his celebrity there wasn't a lot of biographical information to be had concerning Gumnil, although Dr. Hidn's life was thoroughly chronicled by three different biographers.

Gumnil first appears on the scene as a student in the history schola of Neripa Arts, where he is obviously one of the older enrollees. He self-identifies as goblin, although there seems to have been a little confusion regarding his origins in the schola's records. One of his fellow students, in a letter home, calls him 'creepy and decidedly artificial,' although there is no explanation for these designations included.

Gumnil struggles academically at first, but eventually begins to excel as a historian and is finally offered a scholastic stipend to study with Dr. Hidn—a most rarified accomplishment. He completes his doctoral disquisition in only three years and assumes a junior post in the same department. When Dr. Hidn retires some years later, Gumnil takes his place.

His disquisition was surprisingly difficult to locate, but Boogla finally found a copy of parts of it in an old archive of influential middle-period scholars. It was boring and pedantic, at least the parts she could find, but it did contain several references to a 'race so singularly unable to control its profoundly violent tendencies that in truth it represented a threat to all the civilized peoples of N'plork.' It seemed that whatever Gumnil's grudge against the orcs, it predated his professorship.

Boogla realized the only way she was likely to get to the bottom of this was to delve into Gumnil's earlier life. That topic seemed to be a giant box full of empty, however. She sighed when it became apparent that the only real course of action she had here was to go to Neripa herself and hope that some records from that far-off time remained.

Lardonica was a smallish, sleepy tropical nation that occupied the center of the continent of Esmia. Other than a range of moderate-sized mountains along its border with Ovinis in the southeast, it was mostly lowland rainforest. A series of rivers, streams, and creeks formed a complex network that drained into both coasts: the vast Noorprid Sea and the Gulf of Wollu.

Located on the Wollu side, Neripa was a port city known principally for its fruits, nuts, and exotic wildlife. It was supported by a bustling tourist trade, a goodly portion of which constituted expeditions to a range of nearby ruins from the first settlements fifteen centums ago. Native stone had been transported both overland and in coastwise barges from the mountains a hundred kilometers to the southeast and used to construct a series of curiously-shaped buildings that radiated in a large semi-circle with Neripa at its center.

The abundance of local archaeological sites resulted in a thriving scholarly community headquartered at Neripa Arts Institute, founded twelve centums ago to train masons, brickworkers, glassblowers, smiths, and other like artisans. Over the years this artisan enclave grew into a respected universitas from whose hallowed halls some of the world's most renowned art, history, and archaeology scholars had sprung. One of them was Gumnil Ke-juq.

Even though Boogla was on a mission, she took her usual time out to do some sightseeing, being particularly drawn to tropical locales. She joined a tour of some of the more popular nearby ruins and took a glass-bottomed boat voyage over the famous reefs in a sheltered cove just south of the main harbor.

The next day she started to work bright and early. The enrollment records for Neripa Arts from nine centums ago were spotty at best. She did after a morning's work finally locate Gumnil's application and associated information, however, but the useful data contained in these records was minimal. Gumnil listed his home as Nar Braylov in Ovinis; that claim had been investigated by numerous historians over the years and thoroughly discredited. So, where was he actually from, and why did he feel compelled to lie about it?

Since Gumnil had apparently come to Neripa with his negative opinions about orcs already established, the logical presumption would be that he had encountered them earlier in his life. The problem was that the records of orcs themselves started about that same time. It's entirely possible that Gumnil knew something about the orc's origins, in fact. Given the considerable value of such knowledge to the scholarly community, it seemed rather odd that he would not have written about this at some length, or at least in passing, if so.

Gumnil could not establish Lardonican residency and therefore his eligibility for lower tuition rates; ipso facto he must have immigrated. That being the case, either the immigration authority or the Harbormaster's office (better: both) should have some record of his entry into the country. They would be next on her visitation list.

The Lardonican Immigration Bureau was minimally staffed. While the country got a lot of tourists, very few people actually wanted to *live* there. The economy was as sluggish as most of the residents. There were a few relatively affluent retiree communities dotted here and there, but most of the people subsisted at the poverty level and seemed disinclined to change that.

The archives of the LIB were so musty, dusty, and fungus-ridden that they could serve as the ultimate archetype for such places. Boogla actually went out to a hardware retailer and purchased respiration filter masks for herself and her RPC detail to minimize the chance of inhaling something noxious while in the basement repository. They spent the better part of two days rooting around in that unpleasant cellar before Boogla finally concluded that she wasn't getting anywhere. The only piece of the puzzle she'd managed to retrieve here was Gumnil's National Citizen's Identifier Code, or NCIC.

A little despondent, she reluctantly decided to abandon the quest because she'd already spent enough kingdom funds on what was looking more and more like a futile venture. While she was waiting for her ship to be brought into dock from its deepwater berth—the piers in Neripa were not large enough to accommodate very many ships at once so vessels not actively loading or unloading were anchored offshore—she wandered into the Harbormaster's office just to say she'd looked there.

In stark contrast to the Immigration Bureau, the records of

people coming in and out of Neripa as passengers were meticulous and well-organized. While there weren't a lot of archives from 900 years ago, there *was* one with Gumnil's NCIC. She pulled every document with that number attached to it and spread them out on a table. They didn't reveal much she didn't already know, except for one arresting detail: the first use of that NCIC was on a record for someone named 'P. Iwo' who had sailed from Nar Braylov. That name sounded vaguely familiar, but she couldn't put her finger on precisely why.

Only the very first mention, chronologically, had this name associated with it. All the others said *Gumnil Ke-Juq*. She wondered if it was some sort of error. No way to tell at this point. She made copies of all the relevant documents and carefully put the originals back into their archival boxes under the watchful eyes of the Harbormaster Librarian.

On the voyage back to Lumbos Boogla struggled to connect the dots she'd so far managed to accumulate:

- A person who may or may not be a goblin enters the country and immediately changes his name. He has an intense dislike for orcs, who nevertheless are an almost completely unknown race at the time.
- He enrolls as a history student and struggles at first, but then miraculously converts to a brilliant academic performer who graduates with honors and continues on to postgraduate studies.
- He establishes early on the idea that orcs are dangerously unstable and prone to extreme violence. Bizarrely, no one seems willing even to debate his assertions to that effect, despite no physical evidence or contemporary corroborating accounts of these supposed incidents.
- He builds an entire much-vaunted career around the single idea that orcs are a danger to society and must be contained. He publishes over forty academic papers

in which this concept plays a pivotal or at least highly significant role. No one in the usually contentious historical academic community challenges any of them.

- At the height of his preeminence, Gumnil suddenly just drops off the face of N'plork. He is teaching one day and no longer exists the next. No trace is ever found, no explanation with a rational basis ever tendered. It remains to this day one of history's greatest mysteries.

On the carriage from Lumbos to Goblinopolis, the Magineer Liaison put in a call to Selpla.

"Hello, Selpla. This is Boogla."

"Greetings, Your Excellency. I know you don't have a lot of time for social calls. What can I do for you?"

Boogla chuckled. "You're practically family, Selpla. You may very well get a social call from me occasionally—but in this case you're correct. I've been down in Neripa 'chasing down leads,' as you might say, and I'd just like you to jog my memory about something."

"Happy to help, Your Excellency."

"Save the title stuff for formal occasions, all right?"

"Fair enough, Boogla. What is it you wanted help with?"

"When you were relaying the story told to you and Tol by Plåk, I think you mentioned some names. Can you tell me if one of them was...she consulted her notes...*Iwo*?"

Selpla thought for a moment. "Ah, yes. Yes, it was. Philmon Iwo was the name of the arcane academy student there in Morianella who kept failing his Magus Arcanis trial. Plåk seemed to think it was possible he was the one who altered the *Codex Lapidismotus* and indirectly caused the death of nearly everyone in Morianella."

"Did Plåk mention whatever became of Iwo?"

"He said Iwo disappeared a short time before the disaster."

"Thanks. That makes perfect sense."

"What did you figure out?" Selpla asked, her journalistic

instincts triggered.

"I'll tell you about it over infusion later. I have a few more details to work out first."

"Looking forward to it."

Boogla now thought she had pretty well divined the 'who' and 'how' in this drama, but she still didn't know for sure 'why.' She was getting closer, though. Disgruntled mage who disappears days before a calamity of his own making is knowingly triggered—taking revenge on someone or just a psychopath who snapped? Difficult question to answer nine hundred years after the fact. Somewhere out there, someone had the information that would allow her to put all these pieces together. She just had to find them.

*   *   *   *   *

Selpla winced. Her assignments list for the week looked like a new intern's busy work activity sheet: three ground-breakings, a couple of interviews with candidates for minor offices, an 'investigative report' into why speed limits were so low in certain neighborhoods of Goblinopolis, and a segment responding to viewers' questions about the best place to get a decent ogrecress smoothie. She hated weeks like this.

The best way out of this waste of air time was a breaking story. Since she didn't have any of those lined up, she would have to manufacture one. She sat at her desk in the newsroom and remembered something Tol had mentioned about how odd it was that there was no apparent connection in the historical record between Woklopen and the orcs. Making one of her infamous snap decisions, she grabbed her 'go bag' and headed for the door. When she passed the receptionist, she said, "Tell Kurg I'm on a hot story. It will take a few days. Get one of the undies to fill in for me. I'll check back when I can."

On the carriage to Cladimil, Selpla left a voice message for Tol telling him where she was headed and why. She figured what

101

this mystery really needed was an investigative reporter not afraid to get her hands dirty. Presuming Plåk was telling the truth, there had to be *some* trace of the rescued Morianellans in Woklopen, and *some* form of oral tradition concerning them preserved by the residents. It would just be too weird otherwise, even though it had been nine centums. N'plorkians by and large loved to tell each other about their past, particularly when something out of the ordinary characterized it. A community of slender smooth-skinned people who had suddenly materialized out of thin air would make for some pretty entertaining tales, after all.

She was taken aback momentarily in the Customs office in Woklopen Harbor when the officer looked at her passport. "Oh! I've seen your newscasts on the delayed international circuit. Love your work." She recovered quickly, though. It wasn't exactly the first time she'd been the object of adulation.

"Thanks. I really enjoy what I do."

"Will you be doing a story here in Solemadrina, then?"

Selpla put on her mysterious face. "That depends on what I find, I suppose. Have any hot tips for me?"

The officer laughed. "Not that I could relay without endangering my job."

Selpla handed her a business card. "I can be very discrete. 'Unnamed sources' pass me juicy tidbits all the time. Just something to think about if you are ever looking to effect positive change."

Her first stop was the local tax office. If there's one entity that keeps track of people and their movements in every city, it's the tax collector. Other governmental organizations may misplace your address, or forget about you entirely, but not the people who collect the revenue that pays everyone's salaries. They know where you are and who you are and precisely how much you owe, at all times.

The tax office was going to make Selpla file a Request for Examination of Tax Accounting Records and Deposits and wait two weeks—until she showed them her press credentials. That bought her instant access. Apparently the Solemadrinans, or those in the

Woklopen Tax Office at any rate, had been burned by frustrated/bored journalists before.

It was therefore with something akin to preferential status that Selpla got to work in the voluminous archives located in a crypt-like cellar beneath the quaint old municipal tax building with its carved stone pillars and vaulted ceilings. It was musty and possessed of a rather indefinable odor beyond simply that of old paper, but she couldn't really call it unpleasant. Scents of this nature were like perfume to an investigative reporter.

She found the relevant historical data fairly rapidly, as the organization was quite excellent, but matching any of the records to the Morianellan refuges specifically was quite another matter. There were no hard references to an influx of strange-looking people, per se, probably because tax collectors don't care about appearance, only assessment and payment.

Selpla concentrated on sudden jumps in tax revenue numbers around that time. The data formats were a little difficult to decode, but finally she stumbled across some figures that looked promising. They were associated with a neighborhood northeast of the city proper called Nuvinis, built at the confluence of two rivers. The land on which the settlement was constructed was marshy and tended to flood; for that reason the entire village had been floated on wooden platforms supported by a network of stone pillars that elevated all structures above the 100-year flood line. While the pillars themselves were stone, all of the other structures were made of local timber.

The tax records showed virtually everyone in the enclave employed as fishers, shipwrights, or fishmongers. The few accounts she was able to find with details beyond occupation and tax payments indicated that the residents were highly insular and not well regarded by the remainder of Woklopenites. They referred to them as the sea-people, or 'Moreani.'

The community existed for about twenty years, so far as Selpla could ascertain from the tax records, until suddenly one year no tax money was collected at all. She wrote down the date and went back upstairs to talk to the tax officer.

"Thank you so much for allowing me to access your records. I tried to make sure everything was properly re-filed. One last question: centums ago there was a little village known as 'Nuvinis' up on the north side where the rivers come together. Do you know anything about it?"

The officer pondered for a few moments. "Up where all those old stone columns are? I heard a few things about it growing up. The ones who lived there were said to be spirits or something like that, although that seems absurd now, of course. They spent a lot of time out to sea on their boats. They were supposed to be master mariners and had boats that could they make disappear at will. One day a massive fire supposedly destroyed the entire village and the people sailed out on their boats and never returned. Of course this is all just legend passed down from generation to generation. I have no idea what, if any, of that is factual."

Selpla was busy scribbling in her reporter's pad. "Thank you. Thank you *so* much. This is enormously helpful, even if it is mostly legend."

Her next stop was Nuvinis itself, or what was left of it. After nine centums the stone pillars were barely visible under an exuberant panoply of foliage. Only a few seemed intact; the rest were broken off at various heights. None of the wood from the superstructure had survived the fire and the intervening long years. The pillars were home to a respectable variety of animal life.

Selpla had stopped at a sporting supplies store in town and bought herself a pair of chest waders just to be on the safe side in these wetlands. She was, as a consequence, able to reach areas that would have been inaccessible otherwise. There was something about the ancient stonework that drew her in, as though the stones themselves stored energy from those who had built and lived near them.

She wandered among the monoliths for some time, marveling

at how closely fitted they were using only whatever primitive tools had been available to the Moreani 900 years ago. Even if they were spacefaring aliens with advanced technology to begin with, she doubted Plåk had teleported heavy construction machinery along with the survivors from Morianella. This line of reasoning brought her to the remark the tax clerk had made about disappearing boats. While it was probably just part of the Moreani myth built up over the centums, it could contain a grain of truth. The most persistent myths often do.

Selpla noticed a loose stone in one of the columns. That was hardly unusual; there were loose or missing stones in almost all of them. This one seemed different somehow, although she could not have told anyone precisely why. She waded over and put her hand around it. At first it seemed stuck, but a little determined tugging was rewarded with the stone—more like a brick in terms of shape and size—rotated outward as though hinged vertically in the center.

The movement revealed a small compartment, from which Selpla extracted a dark irregular blob. She scraped off centums of lichen and mold to reveal a rectangular metallic object with no obvious joints. She turned it over in her hands but once cleaned it was uniform from every angle. She dropped it in her bag and continued exploring.

Having satisfied her curiosity at last, Selpla returned to Woklopen and booked her passage home. She had a hunch the object she'd found was magically sealed; she'd need a mage to deal with that. Before she left, though, she called Tol. The last she'd heard he was also in Woklopen; it would be nice to meet up and maybe do a little sightseeing together.

Tol's circuit went straight to messaging. She frowned and switched the comm unit over to arcane heterodyning mode for maximum signal boost. You could generally reach any point on the globe that way if magical propagation was favorable. Still no connection. Selpla rolled her eyes and muttered, "Only Tol can figure out some way to be incommunicado with a comm that never runs out of power or turns off." She tried several more times while waiting to board the ship for Cladimil, with no luck.

On the return voyage she read through her copious notes and thought about the story she was going to write, while trying not to worry about Tol. It wasn't as though he'd never been out of touch before: impressed into a ship's crew, in a prison cell far underground, on a variety of top secret international missions... Still, as a journalist she was adept at thinking up all sorts of horrifying calamities in which he could be entangled.

She called Tol from the harbor in Cladimil, and again on the carriage back to Goblinopolis. Frustration, annoyance, and creeping fear made a jittery cocktail of her emotions, but Selpla had dealt with all of those before, albeit not often simultaneously. She thought back to what Tol had told her on their first morning-after together about the price one has to pay for having an edict enforcement officer for a mate. She realized she was thinking of the big goblin as her mate now and blushed.

Back home, Selpla went immediately to the palace to see Boogla. After relaying all the information she had uncovered in Woklopen she showed her the mystery box. Boogla summoned the senior RPC mage to provide opening assistance. The container was not magically locked, however, or if it was, the spell holding it closed was not one the mage had ever before encountered. They sat and puzzled over it for a while.

"Well," Boogla said finally, "If it isn't magical, it must be mechanical. We probably need a gnome for that."

"Oh," Selpla exclaimed, "I have an idea. There's a gnome professor of engineering mechanics at Tropsalla Tech who is an old friend of my father's: Dr. Huthut. I'll bet he'd help us out."

Tropsalla Tech was one of the most elite colleges on N'plork. Most of its student body were of upper-class origins, although occasional scholarship recipients could be seen wending their rather conspicuous way across campus. The buildings were elegant and beautiful, as befit one of the world's premier architectural training grounds. The pathways and streets were marvelously constructed and lavishly landscaped. Graduates were almost guaranteed to be leaders in their fields.

The faculty dining hall where they arranged to meet with Dr. Huthut consistently received three stars from most every culinary review magazine. It had a grand foyer with a ten meter diameter gold and crystal chandelier suspended from a high arched ceiling that opened into a cavernous interior studded with carvings, murals, and gleaming appointments in every direction. A major carriage terminal could easily be housed here.

Dr. Huthut was an elderly gnome who in all ways typified the eccentric professor, curious haberdashery not excepted. He sat with the visitors in awkward silence for some time, until Selpla reminded him who they were and why he had agreed to meet them over luncheon.

Huthut examined the box. He turned it over in his hands and sighted along its edges with one eye closed. He squeezed it with both thumbs and forefingers at once. He produced a strange pair of magnifying spectacles from a pocket that appeared too small to contain them and pored over the box intently. Finally he removed the glasses and set the box down on the table.

"This container is a data storage unit of a type I've never before seen up close." He slid open a virtually invisible panel along one edge, "These tiny holes here," he said, pointing, "Are receptacles for an electrical connection to a reading device." He looked at Boogla. "Your Excellency probably has the best chance of extracting these data of anyone I know. I can give you what little theoretical information I have on the electrical and digital characteristics of such devices."

Back in the palace, Boogla led Selpla to her private laboratory in the Royal Residence. It had just about every tool and system available on N'plork installed on rows of benches: enough to make most academic researchers jealous. Boogla sat on one of the padded stools and started to work with Selpla looking on.

The first order of business was to fabricate a plug that would fit in the receptacles. She shined pinpoint light sources on the tiny holes and swung a huge lighted magnifying lens over to peer into them. She had a sketchpad to draw what she observed. It looked as though there were five separate receptacles. She guessed two for power, two for data input/output, and the last probably for something like error correction.

The most demanding task would be determining the precise power requirements for the unit. Too much or the wrong kind of power could destroy whatever data may have survived nine centums of sitting in a rocky tomb. Boogla went about this by injecting extremely brief pulses of current into the holes and analyzing the results. The aggregate of hundreds of injections allowed her to determine the most likely power requirements.

The next step was to energize the unit and determine what format the data signals exhibited. Since Boogla had no idea what sort of technology this was, the odds were actually against her here. She tried a lot of different approaches, a few of which yielded potentially useful results, but she didn't know how to convert the resulting bitstreams into language because she didn't know what language they started out as or the encoding method. Trial and error might take years or even centums to hit upon the right algorithms.

Much later they sat sharing a pot of infusion and brainstorming. Selpla had left earlier in the day but came back after her broadcast because she still had not been able to contact Tol and frankly needed the company to avoid obsessing on worst-case scenarios.

"I have succeeded in dumping the entire contents of the archive; at least, I think I have," Boogla said, "And it's staggeringly huge. It would take a roomful of our equipment to store that much information with anything resembling reasonable error correction. Trouble is, I don't know how to convert that binary data into anything I can interpret. I wrote some data parsing and analysis algorithms and I believe that based on those I can sort numerical data from characters representing language, but I have no idea what that language may be."

Selpla chewed on her scone thoughtfully. "If the Moreani are truly the same people teleported to Woklopen by Plåk, it's logical to assume he speaks their language. He's already demonstrated that, in fact. Let's just ask him."

"I thought of that, but there are two problems I can see right off the bat: one, he didn't seem very happy with us when he left last time; and two, the only person I know who can get in touch with him is Tol. Neither you nor Aspet have been able to contact Tol. If he's not communicating with his king or significant other, he's not communicating at all. I know Tol well enough to be certain of that."

Selpla fought back tears. "He's all right. I *know* he is. He just gets in these…situations that don't lend themselves very well to comm unit operation." She fingered the crystal hung on a fine but exceedingly strong chain around her neck and peered down. It was glowing reassuringly. She sniffled, despite herself. Boogla put one hand gently over hers.

"Tol is fine. I am also sure of it. But he's not going to be able to help us with this problem right now, wherever he is. Any other ideas?"

Selpla calmed herself and thought.

"Plåk said that he and Oloi were the same species," she said after a few moments, "There's a possibility that Oloi might be able to help. Actually, come to think of it, Oloi is from a period several hundred years more recent in that planet's history. He might have more knowledge concerning their data storage systems than even Plåk."

"Perhaps. These systems are presumably from Plåk's ship, though. Either way, we need Tol to get to Oloi *or* Plåk."

Chapter Eight

"The half-breed and the goblin have landed in Koppra; so say the Moreani."

"Have they informed the Fullians?"

"Yes. Elder Yiplas has people monitoring their movements. They seem to be taking up residence in Juymiz."

"No one relocates to Juymiz unless they are avoiding the authorities. They must be criminals."

"The Chieftain's casket may have contained ill-gotten goods, then."

"Quite likely. However, the contents of the casket are irrelevant to the Valtir quest. The prophecies merely state that the Uul will enter our lands from the outside and by his actions begin the quest. From this point forward we are committed to finding the Valtir and returning it to Eithmorg."

"It is time we address the actual identity of the Valtir. What is it, precisely?"

"The prophecies do not make that clear. Discovery of this is intrinsic to the quest itself."

"How will we know when we have found it?"

"We will know."

"We must convene the Round Table. Send the notifications."

"We have not conducted a full-scale deployment of QuEST-Link in some years. If all nodes are not charged and in receive mode it will not be effective."

"All nodes must report back upon receipt of the transmission. We will see any that fail to do so and send alternative messages if necessary. Once as many of the noble blood as can be reached are notified, we shall call a full Council of Elders and convene the Round Table in accordance with prophecy and the ancient teachings."

"They will try to interfere. They may even wage war against

us."

"It is of no consequence. Our course and our duty are clear. We must face whatever hardships the goblins impose upon us for the sake of the Valtir and the legacy it represents. All opposed speak now." No voices were raised in opposition. "Then, let it be done."

The ceremony for the Round Table was ancient and elaborate. Multiple elements were required to be put into place in the correct sequence and at very specific times. It was necessary to draft very nearly the entire population of the Balom Enclave in order to conduct it properly. The ceremony was, in essence, a 'calling down': accessing a single mental projection amplified by a large number of simultaneous broadcasts. The goal was to tap into a biological engram embedded in the collective orc consciousness long ago. The orc gene pool had been sufficiently diluted over time such that a fair number of participants were now necessary in order to activate the engram, the purpose of which was to 'download' an elaborate memory stored offline, as it were, in the architecture of the engram itself.

The Round Table engram incorporated elements of legend and philosophy derived from a period so ancient in orc history that it considerably predated even the presence of their race on N'plork. No one alive truly understood the entire basis for the engram's structure, but once elucidated its meaning was unambiguous to those elders indoctrinated into its mysteries. Perpetuating that indoctrination was the sacred mission of a tiny, elite group of intellectuals known as the *Punditi*.

The Punditi were fanatics. Chosen at a young age based on the intellect they displayed, these orcs were charged with safeguarding the mystical history of their race—kept secret in the putative fear it could spark rabid xenophobia amongst the native peoples of N'plork. The Punditi chose to believe that they accepted and encouraged the myth that orcs were violent and unpredictable as the only viable alternative to potential extermination. Being isolated in guarded enclaves was deemed preferable to extinction. This was, of course, fundamentally a rationalization to justify acceptance of something over which they had no control.

Once the minimum number of orc participants had been assembled, the carefully-constructed ritual that would generate the intact engram was begun. The incantation incorporated acoustic, magical, and electromagnetic elements orchestrated according to a formula passed along orally for over two dozen generations. The first elders—*Anciens*—who originated the ritual felt that it should only be undertaken in times of greatest need, so they constructed such a complex procedure that casual employment was effectively out of the question.

The reason the Anciens felt it necessary to protect the Round Table ritual so stringently was that it provided a direct link to the very heart of the orc identity. The orcs had maintained the lowest possible profile for centums in order to protect their fabricated origin; only a select few were even fully aware of these details. During the Round Table ritual orc society was at its most vulnerable—any carelessness could reveal their secret and doom them utterly, at least in the eyes of the Anciens.

The modern-day elders were not quite so paranoid, but the need for absolute discretion was deeply rooted in their psyches. The ritual was as much a part of their psychological makeup now as language or the urge to reproduce; violating even the tiniest aspect of it was, simply put, unthinkable.

While the ritual itself would take place in Balom, every orc enclave worldwide was required to be represented remotely via a sophisticated, albeit extremely old, system known as QuEST-Link, for QUantum Encrypted Signals Transmission. It used quantum encryption over a form of wireless data transfer unknown to traditional N'plorkian technical scholars. As such, the communications were effectively one hundred percent secure.

The transceivers, or nodes, in each enclave were equipped with alert signals to notify those monitoring them that a network-wide broadcast was being scheduled, but of course for such notifications to be received the node had to be powered up and operational. It was standard practice for nodes to be kept available at all times, but since the network was subject to testing so infrequently—and had never in fact been used for actual live message transmission before—the ultimate reliability of the system was questionable.

While ideally all enclaves would participate in the ceremony, given the urgency of the situation the elders were prepared to forge ahead even if one or more nodes failed to report. They had rehearsed for this moment on paper for generations, but never seriously expected it to fall within their own lifetimes. This was in many ways the most important event in orc history, if it was genuinely taking place. The problem was that the orcs as a society, or at least the elders, all had to agree that the Valtir quest had been initiated. There was no unequivocal trigger. The Round Table ritual would decide.

*   *   *   *   *

Phaeon Timeskin sat in his carved seat a mile below the Nile Valley pondering the form Fontaric and his brethren would take on this new world he'd chosen to call home for at least the next eon or so. There were effectively infinite morphologies from which to select, but he wanted something that would resonate with the native life forms if glimpsed. After all, he sometimes sent his minions on errands that took them to points quite distant from his residence here in this latest iteration of Dzilidonia.

The dominant sentients on this planet were smooth-skinned bipeds descended from tree-dwellers. They were quite intelligent, but frequently irrational and occasionally violently so. A little research led him to the conclusion that a fair number of them believed in semi-divine creatures they called 'angels' that looked like themselves only with wings. Seemed like a good fit.

Fontaric served as the prototype, as always. Phaeon made him tall, with majestic wings that resembled a feathered cocoon when closed and wrapped to a breathtaking halo of alar glory when spread wide. Satisfied with the appearance and functionality of this new form, Phaeon then created a host of lesser creatures to act as servants and companions in his deep lair. He dubbed them the *Angelorum* and gave them the ability not only to fly but to pass through solid objects by temporal molecular shifting, so that this time they did not need to construct tunnels in order to come and go from Dzilidonia. That would prevent the natives from stumbling in uninvited, as well.

Over time Phaeon grew quite fond of the little planet: its oceans, land masses, climate, and biosphere, not to mention its considerable distance from the troublesome Dark Energetic Continuum. He could see a very real threat to this idyllic setting coming from the dominant sentient species, however. Even in their current primitive state the potential they exhibited for eventual ecological catastrophe was pronounced and disturbing. They could not or would not see the deleterious effects their lack of respect for the planet's natural systems was generating. He therefore decided to provide them gentle nudges along the path to developing interstellar travel so that they could disperse. Once the species was guaranteed survival off-world, he would not feel so bad when his host planet's potential for sustaining life was compromised. He could always restart it himself and prevent the same sequence of events from taking place next time.

He began by placing subtle representations of flying craft all over the globe: hieroglyphics, temple carvings, and so on. He injected elaborate dreams into the minds of scribes and religious leaders that suggested the possibility of huge ships propelled through the sky by fire. He also planted representations of beings and vessels from another world in various guises and bearing a variety of names such as *Bep-Kororoti*, in accounts which were incorporated into the *Popol Vuh* and *Chilam Balaam* of the Mayans, the Indian

Mahabharata, and many other ancient texts.

Individually these drawings and accounts were little more than curiosities, dismissed by academics as the product of vivid imagination or attempts to illustrate some fanciful mythological construct, but collectively they very subtly got the natives thinking about the possibility of life beyond their little blue bubble. This primed them to pursue space exploration and travel when their technological development had reached the proper level. They might have reached that same point eventually on their own, but Phaeon's 'clues' had at the very least accelerated the process.

The pièce de résistance of his plan was the monolith. Phaeon traveled to the nearest easily explorable body in the local system and in the floor of a large crater buried a deep black slab on which was detailed the plans for a functional wormhole drive that enabled faster-than-light travel not only between stars, but even galaxies. He chose that planet, the second nearest body, because the surface temperature would encourage exploration; the closest planet was too hot to be an attractive candidate. By the time the inhabitants were technologically advanced enough to begin investigating the other planets in their system, they would be able to comprehend the wormhole drive well enough to construct it after some trial and error. Phaeon's last bit of encouragement would be, when the time was right, to plant the buried monolith idea in the mind of a prominent fiction author and futurist whose subsequent literary creations cemented the concept in the popular consciousness.

Now all Timeskin had to do was to wait. He figured three, maybe four thousand years, tops. In the meantime he could amuse himself by manipulating the spiritual environment of his adopted planet's sentients. There were so many possibilities: appearing to the occasional astonished traveler as a divine presence, sending his 'angels' to deliver cryptic messages about people and events, inducing slight modifications to various theologically-related timelines, and performing witnessed 'miracles' from time to time. After all, Phaeon figured, he was the closest thing to a god these creatures were ever likely to experience. He had never decided if the widespread sentient need to believe in divinity was a product of their fundamental insecurity or a latent megalomania in aspiring to godhood themselves. It didn't really matter to him one way or the other, to be truthful. They were primed for faith and faith was entertaining.

Chapter Nine

Tol dropped to his knees and instinctively held his breath to avoid inhaling the superheated air enveloping him. Petey was saying something to him at maximum volume but even with the benefit of bone induction he couldn't make out the words over the extremely loud hissing and screaming sounds penetrating his flesh like physical weapons. He crawled painfully along on his stomach toward the only part of the immediate area that did not seem to be actively combusting. As he crossed over some invisible threshold the flames suddenly ceased, along with the accompanying tumult.

He sat up and rubbed the soot from his singed scales. He appeared to be deep in a forest now, surrounded by arbor species unfamiliar to him. The undergrowth was lush and thick; the dense canopy allowed only occasional streaks and spatters of sunlight to penetrate. The air was full of sounds and redolent with heavy scents of the forest floor: leaf litter, decaying vegetation, and the collective musk from dozens of different animals.

Tol got to his feet. "Petey! You all right?" he said into his overjack pocket.

There was no answer for a moment, but then a faint, somewhat squeaky voice replied, "Yes, other than my primary voice circuit experiencing reversible thermal degradation. You appear to have emerged from the inferno relatively unscathed, as well."

The goblin shook off a layer of soot from his overjack and looked around. "Any idea where we are?"

"I have not established sufficient external reference points to make that determination. Based on the polarization of the little sunlight we are receiving, I would say we are considerably south of our prior position. Once I have had opportunity to map the local magnetic and geophysical environment I shall be able to establish a more precise location."

Tol nodded. "Fair enough. I guess a little exploring is on the menu, meanwhile." He surveyed the area. They were on a narrow, well-worn path that picked its way among the majestic arbors in two directions. He examined the ground and began to follow the faint traces of recent passage. Suddenly he stopped dead, staring intently at the arbors framing the path directly ahead.

"I'm no kinda mage, but I'd be willin' to bet magic has somethin' to do with these little threads goin' up here on each side," he said, indicating two barely visible filaments that crossed over the path at chest level. "They sure spark like it, anyway."

After a pause, Petey chimed in. "You are undoubtedly correct. The arcane signature is unmistakable. Given the topology and latent energetic profile, I would conclude that it constitutes a component of a trap or a trigger for a warning signal."

"I have to agree. The fact that we just teleported here, wherever 'here' is, from a building in Woklopen makes it all the more likely. This is probably here to warn somebody—maybe Zizmziz himself— if someone manages to find the teleportal and survive that warm welcome. The question is, how do we deactivate it?"

"Or is that necessary at all?" added Petey. "Perhaps there is a way around for those who use the portal regularly. While most magical traps of this nature are persistent spells, they require some effort to re-arm after activation and so avoiding triggering them in the first place is the easiest course. My scans indicate that the residual arcane field is weakest near the base of that large arbor to your left. I suggest examining that area more closely."

Tol shrugged and knelt down near the arbor's roots. He scoured the area, crawling back and forth numerous times.

"Have you found any tracks?" Petey finally asked.

"None," Tol answered, "Not even from buzzers, crawlers, or avians. It's as though the ground near the arbor has been swept cle..." He stopped in mid-word as he saw the footprints he had just left disappear before his eyes. He made a gouge in the soil with his boot and watched it vanish as well in a matter of seconds. His brow went up.

"Obviously there's some kind of permanent track-removal spell goin' on here. That tells me I'm definitely in the right place. You don't go to the trouble of casting a spell like this unless you want to hide something of significance." He began backtracking along the path, trying to pinpoint the spell's range of effect. At length he grunted.

"Found it. There've been quite a few folks coming and going through here lately, it seems. And they're all heading for that arbor. Time to figure out why."

Tol returned to the trunk of the huge arbor and began examining it in minute detail. After ten minutes of silent concentration he stepped back, cocked his head, and ran his fingers lightly along the rough texture of the orange-rust bark. He halted at one point and backtracked very slowly, holding his breath.

"Petey, the place where my hands are right now: does it show anything unusual on your sensors? Magic or EMF stuff, I mean."

There was a slight pause while Petey ran scans. "Yes, as a matter of fact. Your carpal digits are framing a clever arcane manifestation known as a Multiple Overlay Anchor Point, or MOAP. The purpose of the MOAP is to allow spells to be laid one atop the other in a semi-permanent configuration while minimizing artifacts resulting from interference or unintended synergies. In this case the arcane components present appear to be a topological dissimulation matrix, a local dimensional gateway, and some form of temporal magic. The most probable result of that specific ensemble would be a doorway to an area augmented by magic, hidden from casual view, and not subject to degradation or visible alteration within biologically-relevant time scales."

"How do I open this doorway?"

"There should be a trigger nearby. Wave me around the doorway perimeter slowly. Now reverse the direction so I can eliminate outliers."

After two full times around in opposing orbits, Petey paused for a few seconds.

"Look on the left side of the trunk, barely more than a meter from the ground. There should be some form of protrusion."

"Well, there's a growth or boll or something about there."

"That is more than likely your target. Try pulling it down or otherwise manipulating it. Gently—you do not want to remove it from the bark surface."

Tol followed these instructions; after a few false starts he rotated the gall towards himself and pulled it out from the trunk a centimeter or so. The arbor's bark suddenly melted away to reveal a neatly navigable opening.

"Nice," he said, "I gotta get me one of these to hide my laundry."

"I do not believe olfactory obfuscation is a component of this particular MOAP," Petey retorted. "Such functionality would seem obligatory for any installation in your abode."

Tol snorted with laughter. "Yeah, you might have a point there. All right, let's do this."

He put one foot through the opening tentatively. There was a faint, transient tingling, but otherwise no ill effects seemed forthcoming. He took a deep breath and stepped through the gateway bodily. The impression that he was stepping into the trunk of an arbor surprisingly did not vanish entirely on the inside. There was a tight corridor that proceeded perhaps five meters before turning sharply to the right. The walls and ceiling all seemed to be made of wonderfully intertwined wood so tightly woven that it left no visible gaps. The air smelled of all the best things about that biome: water, aromatic foliage, and the faint but readily-identifiable scents of forest flowers.

The interior was multileveled, with steps formed from the same intertwined branches. The corridors were just wide enough for two goblin-sized creatures to pass abreast. They wound back and forth and up and down in no discernible pattern. Tol realized that it would be almost impossible to navigate in here without some form of external reference. Often other hallways or rooms could not be seen until you were standing literally at the intersection; sometimes even then it was challenging.

He moved cautiously along the corridor, trusting Petey to map their progress. Tol had no idea what, or who, he would find in this ligneous labyrinth, although he harbored suspicions. For the time being, however, he was just going to take in the scenery, such as it was.

"Someone is just around this next corner," Petey announced via bone induction. "By the signature I would guess hobgoblin or possibly kobold, moving this way."

Tol nodded and squeezed himself behind a nearby braid of leg-sized vines serving as some form of structural support. He held his breath as the hob walked past. He appeared to be engrossed in some reading material. Tol chuckled silently and muttered to himself: *didn't know they could read; must be a racing form.* He noticed that the hob was wearing a uniform consisting of a dark blue unitard with silver stripes and a belt on which hung a pistol of some type he didn't immediately recognize. There was a large circular embroidered patch on the breast he couldn't make out, either. The whole outfit looked faintly comical to his eyes, like some kid's comic book character.

"What's with the pajamas?" he asked Petey after the hob was out of hearing range.

"Analysis of the design shows no similarities to any known organizational uniform. It may be simply a personal fashion choice, albeit an unusual one."

To shrugged. "Whatever floats your boat, I guess. He looked armed, at any rate. That means he's probably guarding something or someone. Wonder what or who?"

"The probability that a mage or multiple mages are ultimately responsible for this structure is quite high. Logic would suggest, therefore, that he may be providing security for said mages or their interests."

"Why would mages need security in the first place? Why not

just set traps?"

"Traps are, as you have yourself recently demonstrated, not very dependable as obstacles when the adversary is equipped to detect and avoid or disable them. Mages demonstrate consistently high intellectual capacity; providing guards as backups is a predictable and intelligent move. Speaking of guards, two more are approaching: larger and moving more rapidly than the first."

Tol had been creeping forward along the twisting corridor as they conversed; he ducked into a nearby gap in the wall to avoid the new threat. The gap proved in actuality to be a small chamber just slightly larger than a goblin. It was relatively dark in there, but sufficient light remained for Tol to see that he was in an unusual place. The texture here was different: smooth and featureless, rather than possessing knots and irregularities as a result of the material's biological origins. It seemed intended for something beyond simple storage.

The two goblins Petey had detected passed him by without incident, but Tol was so intrigued by his new location he scarcely noticed. The very air seemed to be charged with some kind of electrical field; he could feel himself buzzing gently as he stood there.

"What is this place?" he whispered to Petey.

"It is a teleportal node, triggered by some key carried by the user. I am analyzing the properties of the expected key now; hopefully I can simulate it closely enough to allow you to activate it if desired."

"Where does the portal lead? I might not *want* to go there," Tol replied, "It's not like I've had a lot of luck with those things recently."

"Curiously, the portal is not statically linked to any location. There are no lines of force burned into the arcane matrix that would indicate a set destination."

"What does that mean, practically speaking?"

"It means that rather than the chamber serving as a portal

to some predefined place, the user can choose any destination for which coordinates configured in the correct template format are supplied. An anchored teleport spell, in other words. I have no other closely similar examples in my database. This appears to be unique among contemporary teleport magic."

"Huh. Well, I'm sure CoME or SagMag will eat up whatever data you can provide for them concerning it. The real question for me is: where would I go if you manage to activate it?"

"Without a template, it is not possible to predict with any reliability. The likelihood is that there are a number of potential termini, any one of which might be the default choice. There is also a possibility that you would go nowhere at all, or even be trapped in the arcanic interstice."

Tol scratched his head. "That doesn't sound like something I'd enjoy, either. Maybe I'd better just give this one a pass." He stepped back out into the corridor and was met by a surprised yelp followed instantly by an energy bolt that tore a nice chunk out of his elbow. He heard more running footsteps approaching and ducked back into the chamber, drawing his own disruptor.

"You made any progress on figurin' out that key?" he said to Petey.

"Yes. But not on deciphering the proper format for destination coordinates."

"I'm sort of trapped in here. Wherever it is, the destination's probably going to be less hazardous than staying here." He dodged as a barrage of energy pulses left scars in the walls on either side of the doorway to his little cubbyhole.

"Agreed. Hang on."

The entire cubicle flashed a dull orange and everything changed. For a few moments Tol couldn't seem to focus his eyes. When at last the world around him resolved, his first impression was that he'd somehow fallen asleep and was dreaming. The landscape was far beyond anything in his experience. He stood staring in stunned amazement at the nightmarish scenery for a long while. Finally he mustered enough neural control to speak, albeit weakly.

"Petey, what...what the smek *is* this place?"

There was no answer.

Concerned, Tol fished the pen from the overjack pocket he'd had specially modified to provide a secure resting place for it and held his little companion up. Neither of the status lights was visible, meaning that Petey was completely turned off. A total shutdown had happened only twice in the number of years Tol had been carrying Petey, both times initiated by Precinct equipment techs for maintenance activities. Tol racked his brain trying to remember the cold start procedure. He hadn't been called upon to initiate it since training.

As he fiddled with the mechanism, cursing his technical ignorance and wishing he were more like Aspet, Tol suddenly sensed that he was being watched. He whipped around to see a tall creature or apparition—he wasn't quite sure what to call the thing—regarding him placidly. It had about a meter on Tol, height-wise, but was so thin as to appear almost emaciated—or at least had it normal body morphology. Rather than a person, however, to Tol it more resembled the living manifestation of a troll's funhouse mirror image. Goblin and troll-thing stared at one another until Tol decided this had gone on long enough.

"I don't suppose," Tol started, holding Petey up, "You know how to work one of these things?"

The creature gave him something that might have been a benevolent smile but otherwise made no move or sound. He didn't detect any overt threat from it, so Tol shrugged and went back to what he was doing. A few more minutes slid by before he began to feel a source of heat on his upper chest. He dismissed it as imagination at first, but before too long it grew impossible to ignore. The source of the discomfort? Oloi's summoning amulet.

Tol pulled the cast metal figure away from his body and noticed that the creature seemed to be intently interested. He removed the thin chain from around his neck and held the amulet up, waving it back and forth and watching the creature's eyes. They followed the motion precisely. Tol wondered what it was about the talisman that seemed to attract the strange being. The fact that he was probably not on N'plork at the moment suddenly dawned on him. He slipped the inert Petey back into his pocket and began to examine his surroundings in detail once again.

He knew that his having been through a teleportal meant that magic was involved. Since he started on N'plork and did not seem to be there now, the only logical conclusion he could manufacture was that he had somehow gotten stuck halfway, in The Slice, as he had been told that one passed through there on the way. He had some fairly vivid descriptions of the terrain in that exotic realm from both Oloi and Plåk. Trouble was, this landscape didn't match them very well. Oh, it was bizarre enough—undulating land masses sporting a range of ridiculously incongruous colors, sounds more appropriate to an insane asylum embedded in a zoo, and phantom architecture that appeared and disappeared without warning—but many of the defining characteristics as relayed by both transcended mages seemed wrong to him.

To begin with, while the scenery was phantasmagorical, it was too fluid. No given manifestation seemed to persist for more than a minute. Oloi had stories of favorite spires, curtains, and other formations that had been in place for centa, as time was measured in The Slice, anyway. Secondly, there were no floating tendril-bearers or other animate creatures, apart from the skinny troll, in evidence. Those were also always mentioned by both mages as being ubiquitous in that magical realm.

All this thinking about The Slice triggered a sudden anxiety in Tol. He remembered Oloi telling him that visitors who had not transcended had only a limited time before they became unable to return to Primus. If they remained too long they effectively starved, as there was nothing to eat in The Slice that a living creature such as a goblin could digest. If that was where he had indeed been transported, he needed to get back to N'plork as soon as possible.

He turned his full attention to Petey as his best potential source of information.

About ten tries into the reboot saga, Tol had to stop and rub his eyes. That was weird; he didn't usually have any trouble with them. Must be a lot of pollen in the air here. There must be *air* here, right? He was breathing *something*. Not only was the air affecting his focus, it was beginning to make him a little drowsy, too. Tol realized with a start that something was wrong; he was losing consciousness. He tried to fight it, but he had no weapons for that battle. He was abruptly too weak to move. He wondered how anyone could starve to death in the short amount of time he'd been here, but then remembered something Oloi had told him about time passing very differently in The Slice. He looked up at a blurry scene of the giant gaunt creature leaning over him. The situation suddenly triggered another memory. "Aren't you a little tall for an alfar?" he whispered.

Tol awoke in his own bed in Sebacea. He lay there for a while staring at his old familiar ceiling, trying to sort through recent events. He sat up and rolled off the edge of the bed.

"That was one smekking vivid dream," he muttered, "Better lay off whatever it was I had for supper last night."

Dream notwithstanding, there were decided discrepancies to be dealt with here. He called Selpla and surprised her.

"Hi, honey."

"Hi, babe! How's the mission going? Seeing the sights in Woklopen? Did you go to that little bistro I told you about?"

"Um, I sort of need to talk to you about all of that. Can we meet somewhere soon?"

"I'm back in Goblinopolis now, sweetie."

"So am I."

There was a pause while Selpla did some math. "I don't see how that's possible, unless you got a mage involved."

"I'll...I'll explain in person." Tol hoped he could fulfill this pledge.

On the way to the *Midtown BariStation* Tol heard Petey's boot-up self-test routine signal coming from his pocket. He pulled the pen out and saw the little lights flashing. "This oughta be interesting," he chuckled.

Petey came back on line with no problem, but when Tol asked him for a recap of events over the past 48 hours he was uncharacteristically vague.

"Please stand by while I correlate those data points," was the only reply he would give. Tol shrugged and kept driving.

At the BariStation Selpla couldn't stop staring at Tol.

"There's something different about you," she observed more than once.

Tol rolled his eyes. "Yeah. I'm here when I should be somewhere else." He recounted all of his recent adventures he could be sure of. He left out the weird tall creature, though, because of all of it that seemed the most dream-like aspect.

"So, you were in an arbor-based building of some kind somewhere and then you what...fell asleep?" Selpla sounded a little doubtful.

"I honestly don't know. If what happened next is not a dream, I haven't really got an explanation for it. It was smekkin' bizarre, in any case."

"What is your last clear memory, again?"

"I found a teleportal in a building on the western edge of Woklopen. It was trapped, but I managed to avoid getting fried by it and came out in a woods full of arbors I didn't recognize. I found a hidden door that led into a trunk and then to a bunch of tunnels or something formed from twisted vines and roots, or at least that's what it looked like. I got pinned down in a very small room by some armed goons. Petey said it was a locked teleport node that needed a template, or something like that. I didn't have a template, but I *did* need to make a smekking quick getaway before I got hit again, so when he broke the key we just took off."

"What do mean, 'hit again'?" Selpla asked, concerned.

Tol slid up the sleeve of his overjack and showed her the nice burnt lesion on his elbow.

"Ow!" she cried, touching the area just above the wound gingerly. "I don't like it when you come back to me damaged."

He grinned. "The parts that really matter are still in great shape, I promise."

Selpla blushed a little for Tol's benefit.

"So, that mostly leaves the question of how you got from... wherever the strange forest was located back to Goblinopolis."

"More specifically, how I got back to my own bed in my own house."

"I would almost guarantee that magic was involved," Selpla said, taking a sip of her infusion.

"In ways you might not expect," came a voice from Tol's pocket. He pulled out the pen and set it on the table between them.

"Petey!" Tol exclaimed, "Welcome back. You shut down for some reason and I couldn't remember how to start you up again."

"It has been a very atypical diurnal period for me. My shutdown was initiated by the teleport process; it has never affected me in that manner before. Something quite unusual took place during teleportation that has no equivalent events in any archive I can access."

"What happened to you, Petey?" Selpla asked.

"My logs show an abrupt cessation of power—referred to by those who designed me as an 'ungraceful shutdown'—thirteen point one seven seconds after I submitted the teleport key to the gateway daemon. It was not a failure of my internal batteries or a circuit glitch: I have run full diagnostics on all of those subsystems and found no errors or even transient faults. The preponderance of the evidence, paltry though it is, suggests that my electronics failed because Tol and I were teleported to a place where electron transport via metallic conductors simply does not work. The standard laws of physics, in other words, are at least partially invalid there."

Selpla scrunched up her face. "Does such a place actually exist, to our knowledge?"

"There are theories that small bubbles of alternate reality may be possible as extrusions from the Dark Energetic Continuum," replied Petey, "But there are no empirical data concerning such a place, nor is there any real conceptual framework for what physical laws may prevail within those spaces. However, if my timeline and system data are accurate, the existence of at least one of these extrusions may have been confirmed. I have shared those data and will report any further germane analysis as it is received."

"So, I really was in The Slice?" Tol asked quietly.

"I cannot be certain, as my sensors were inactivated for most of that period, but first-order analysis suggests that a very real possibility exists you—we—were."

"Eh, I don't believe it. I think the teleport in that arbor, wherever we were, sent me back to Goblinopolis somehow. The rest was a dream while I was unconscious."

Selpla was about to argue with him but saw the expression on his face and decided against it. Whatever really happened, Tol did not seem to want to confront it right now and she could see no reason to force the issue. She needed to change the subject and Petey obliged.

"I have calculated the terminus of the Woklopen teleportal," the pen announced, apropos of nothing, or at least nothing immediately obvious.

Tol grunted. "Really? Where were we?"

"Tantatku. A few kilometers south of Zuum."

"I guess that's not really surprising. The forest near Zuum is where they told us the Umbral mages were headquartered. They sure didn't want unauthorized people using that teleportal, that's for certain. Now," he sighed, "I guess I get to go back there the hard way."

"Do you get frequent traveler points for all these ocean voyages?" Selpla asked, smirking.

Tol shook his head. "I wish. All of that stuff goes to the

department, not me personally."

"Too bad. I want to take this opportunity to remind you that my birthday is in two days. *I* think fate just wanted you back here in time for that. You are planning to be here, right?"

Tol grinned. "Wouldn't miss it for the world. The bad guys can wait."

Chapter Ten

"The rangers pursued the Woklopen Gate interloper, by accounts a goblin, into a Transit Bulb and he did not exit. He must have had a key and a template ring."

"Where did he go?"

"The Bulb log had no entries for that day."

"That's impossible. Transit far points are logged before the template is even activated. He must have tampered with the log somehow."

"With all due respect, Your Magnificence, he didn't have time for that. He was in the bulb no more than a minute before the teleportation took place."

"Then he must have brought some device or talisman with him that did the tampering automatically. There is no other possibility. Check the logs of all the other bulbs during the same time for an incoming transit."

"We have, Your Magnificence, and there is no corresponding event."

"The guards at the Transit Bulb were hallucinating, then. Remind the rank and file that use of mind-altering substances while on duty will not go well for them if impairment results."

"As you command, Magnificence."

Zizmziz sat in his enormous throne carved from a solid block of extremely rare fluorescing flowstone highlighted with hides from a variety of animals and brooded darkly. He didn't like it when his demesne was violated by outsiders. He would have to review the protections he'd placed on the teleportal network nodes and adjust their security where possible.

His office, really more akin to a lair, was a veritable storage closet of magical artifacts and cryptic reminders of his centums on N'plork. There were talismans, phylacteries, reliquaries, amulets, and sundry other arcane objects on shelves lining every wall. Zizmziz had done everything he could to give the impression of being one of the great mages of legend. His household members and close advisors were all deeply indoctrinated into this belief: in their eyes he was the greatest mage who had ever lived.

Although he referred to himself as an archmage, from the perspective of SagMag he was only a Magus Incipius—at least he had at one time borne this distinction. That physical body, however, was long dead. Zizmziz was now in a very real sense a golem rather than a biological entity, although one of a sophistication and type unique to himself. He had researched the specific set of spells that resulted in the creation of his golem body for nearly a quarter-centum. For this reason alone he felt justified in claiming the title archmage. None of the 'true' archmages had prolonged their lives significantly by any means but transcending. They were thereby tied eternally to The Slice; he was not. He was, to his way of thinking, superior to them all.

He had subjected himself and those around him to this faulty logic for such a long time that he and they believed it without reservation now. The mere notion that a more powerful mage might exist no longer even made any sense to him. Zizmziz surrounded himself with lesser mages and drove off (or otherwise disposed of) any that showed promise of surpassing him. In this way he was able to maintain the illusion of his greatness indefinitely. Misperceptions of this nature are often self-correcting over time, however.

Today's agenda included a visit to the Umbral Academy, where student mages were trained using the Zizmziz method. This consisted primarily of fundamental lessons from well-known arcane textbooks liberally sprinkled with propaganda and indoctrination in the "Umbral Way of Magic." It was Zizmziz's custom to visit the classrooms periodically to inspire/intimidate the students. He was careful not to allow any of them to get too good a look at him, however, so he wore an elaborately embroidered floor-length golden robe featuring a jet black hood that curved around to hide most of his face. Ironically, the perpetual golem body he had enchanted for himself was by far his most impressive achievement as a mage, but it was also the one he did not wish anyone to examine closely.

Zizmziz had not started the mage enclave here. The Umber mages, as they were originally known, were founded by two brothers named Lerma and Drazmul, both Magi Superior. They hailed from the city of Foryaqra on the southern coast of Tantatku. Foryaqra was in fact the southernmost point on the continent of Turmia, and served as an important shipping center. Tantatku's vast forests supplied much of the world's hardwood lumber, in fact—lumber being one of that nation's principal exports.

The densely-forested lowlands in the southeast were known as *Aboriginia*. They were widely believed to constitute the epicenter from which the ancestors of all sentients on N'plork migrated to form the reproductively isolated populations that evolved into the races present today. The aboriginal race itself seems to have died out not long after the dispersion event, although scholars could not agree on precisely why this had been the case. Most suspected an epidemic of some sort, or perhaps a natural disaster. Whatever killed them off, the archaeological evidence for the aboriginals' existence was to be found in abundance by those who knew where to look.

Zizmziz joined the Umber collective about five years after its inception and eventually ended up being the senior mage by simple dint of outliving the founders. He knew that his claim to be an archmage and therefore undisputed leader of the guild would be ineffective without some fancy illusion-making because archmages have a specific aura any mage can easily read. The way he solved this problem was as ingenious as it was macabre.

Archmage Hio-hiu was killed in a freak, tragic accident involving an advanced class in levitation and a student who suffered an unexpected seizure at just the wrong time. Zizmziz had been sitting in on the class and was the first Umber member to reach Hio-hiu after the debris was cleared away. He noticed that the fatal injury had involved a major skull fracture with consequent expulsion of cerebral contents. On a mad impulse he scooped up a palm full of archmage brains and secreted it on his person.

An archmage's distinctive aura derives from profound changes wrought in his neural architecture during study for and execution of the archmage trial. All mages possess arcane auras, but archmages exhibit peculiar resonances that mark their status unmistakably for anyone tuned into their arcane frequency. What Zizmziz did was to extract sufficient material from Hio-hiu's neocortex to overlay on the components of his own aura he had incorporated into the golem to give a passable appearance of archmage. Anyone intimately familiar with Hio-hiu's aura might have been able to recognize parts of it in Zizmziz's, but most all of those mages were now deceased. He was, in effect, carrying the archmage masquerade all the way down to his brain tissue.

Having the apparent aura of an archmage did nothing to increase your arcane prowess, however. Zizmziz maintained the illusion by never allowing himself to be placed in a position where archmage-level magic was required. He could do enough magic on his own or using one of his considerable collection of enchanted items to keep up the charade the vast majority of the time. In those instances where the illusion was threatened he simply ducked into one of his cleverly designed sanctuaries, one of which Tol stumbled on via the teleportal in Woklopen.

Zizmziz shared his own origins with no one. He just appeared at the door of the Umber guildhall in Zuum one day and never left. Various people had tried unsuccessfully to engage him in conversations concerning his earlier life but Zizmziz was wholly uncommunicative on this subject. They didn't even know how old he was.

As time went on Zizmziz's influence grew to the point of autocracy, while the focus of the guild gradually slid down the ethical continuum until the name evolved by popular mandate from *Umber* to *Umbral*, denoting the organization's willingness to take on tasks deemed too morally questionable for more traditional magical societies. That is not to say that the majority of the members did not adhere to the widely-adopted Mages' Code of Ethics—only a very few mages disregarded these—but that the leadership; i.e., Zizmziz, did not forbid members from taking on commissions that, well, blurred the ethical line.

*   *   *   *   *

"So, Boogla and I made a discovery that we need your help deciphering," Selpla told Tol as they snuggled on her sofa that evening.

"Yeah? What kind of help could I give you two?"

"We need to get in touch with Oloi."

"I can arrange that. What's up?"

"We need something translated, and Boogla thinks it's a language that only Oloi and Plåk can read."

"All right. Let me pull out my amulet thingy."

He felt around his neck. "Oops. Think I took it off after I got back from Woklopen. It was acting sort of weird when I was... wherever I was during all that stuff. I can run home and get it right now, if you want."

"It's not that critical. If you would just bring it to work tomorrow that would be soon enough."

"Good, 'cause I had other plans for this evening."

"I really admire your skill at planning."

The next day Tol got a message asking him to come to the Royal Residence to meet Boogla, Selpla, and Aspet for lunch. He fingered the amulet of summoning and thought back to the dream or whatever it was. The amulet had grown very warm then: too warm to touch. It was nice and cool now, but something about it had changed. The light hit it differently, maybe.

Sequestered in a private restaurant, the others waited while Tol uttered the activation phrase. Instead of glowing a brilliant

137

white as usual, the amulet remained inert. He tried again, with the same result. Tol scratched his neck, embarrassed.

"I guess it got burned out or something. Sorry." He sat down and sighed with frustration. "I wish I had some other way to contact Oloi for you."

Suddenly everything in the room seemed to shift, a displacement right at the far range of perception. A wavy blob in front of Tol resolved itself after a few seconds into a rather surprised-looking Oloi.

"Hi, Oloi. Guess the amulet worked, after all." Tol said in greeting.

"Amulet?" Oloi replied, somewhat shaken, "That was no amulet. The amulet simply notifies me that my presence is requested. This was an active translocate spell. Only an archmage could have cast it."

Tol shrugged and swept his hand around in an arc. "Have a look. No archmages here."

Boogla frowned. "The Loca Magineer, perhaps?"

"Not his signature," Oloi responded.

"Whose signature is it, then?" Aspet asked.

Oloi eyebrows went up. "That's the truly puzzling part. It isn't the signature of an archmage, at all. More like some sort of... elemental."

"An elemental?" said Boogla, "What kind of elemental could it be?"

"I'm not at all certain. Moreover, I can't think of any reason an elemental would want to return a transcendent to Primus. Doesn't make a lot of sense."

It was Selpla's turn. "Well, since you're here, could you take a look at some writing we've found and tell us if you can read the language?"

Oloi seemed lost in thought for a moment, but then came out of it. "Of course. I'd be happy to."

Boogla took him over to a table and pulled a spiral-bound

138

manuscript from her satchel.

"This," she explained, "Is part of a data dump from a very odd storage device Selpla discovered near Woklopen in Solemadrina. There are actually over a thousand pages, all told; this is just a sample. We were hoping you might be able to decipher it for us."

Oloi opened the cover and gave a little gasp. He sat down and read for a solid five minutes before looking up.

"This is a language that no longer exists on N'plork. It is a tongue endemic to my own species, native to a planet almost incomprehensibly far from here. What you have here is a logbook of the Moreani, the orcs who survived the destruction of Morianella when Plåk teleported them to Woklopen."

"Plåk already told us some of that story, and hinted at the origin of that language, also," Selpla said.

Boogla was fixated on something else Oloi had said.

"What exactly did you mean by 'the *orcs* who survived'?"

Oloi bit his lip. "Just a slip of the tongue."

Tol wasn't buying it. "You don't make those. Archmages are very, very careful about what they say. Ask Plåk what happens if they aren't."

Oloi nodded. "You are correct. All right, I meant what I said: the inhabitants of Morianella were orcs. Or, rather, *became* orcs later. I have to return to The Slice now. I was not prepared for this transfer and my manna stores are consequently quite low."

Tol detected a very faint suggestion of duplicity, but decided not to make an issue of it.

"Thanks for your help, archmage. Hope you figure out whatever it was that dragged you out of your living room, as it were." He fished around for his summoning amulet and handed it to Oloi.

"Guess you can have this back now. I think it got busted."

Oloi regarded the talisman with surprise and concern.

"Thank you. It shouldn't be possible for it to get...busted. I'll try to repair it and return it to you."

"That would be swell."

"Farewell, for the present, to you all."

Those who remained looked at one another without speaking for a few seconds. Finally Aspet broke the silence.

"I have to get back to work. Interesting little project you've got going here. Please keep me posted on its progress." With that he and his RPC shadow left the room.

Boogla looked at the clock on the wall and headed for the door also. "I have a meeting in 15 minutes, too."

That left Tol and Selpla alone at the table.

"Does that mean," asked Selpla, more of herself than Tol, "That Oloi and Plåk are *orcs*? They don't look much like orcs."

"How many orcs have you seen up close and personal?" Tol inquired.

"Not many," she admitted, "But none of them have looked much like Oloi."

"He said the Morianellans became orcs later. I wonder what he meant by that?"

"I suppose he'll tell us, or at least you, eventually."

Back in his abode in The Slice, Oloi was wrestling with a far more pressing issue from his perspective: the elemental 'fingerprint' he'd seen in the translocation enchantment that dragged him forcibly to Primus. He had not encountered anything similar before; the event simultaneously intrigued and disturbed him. He'd experienced no warning, no transition period, nothing. He was in The Slice one moment and Goblinopolis the next. There *had* to be an explanation, but what was it?

Translocation was a balanced combination of two types of spells: kinesis and fabric manipulation. Fabric manipulation spells opened gateways or anastomoses between topologically distinct (and often widely separated) sections of the spacetime matrix. Kinesis spells controlled the motion of one or more objects. While even third-tier mages were conversant with kinetic magic, fabric manipulation was the exclusive territory of the highest arcane echelons.

Even an archmage, Oloi reasoned, would have to know not only precisely where Oloi was but even his direction of travel and momentum at the instant of translocation to cast that spell successfully from the Royal Palace. Of course he already knew an archmage was not responsible, because of the telltale signature— but an elemental? The only elementals in this vicinity of the universe were titans: they were actually demi-elementals, with only limited magical abilities that did not include translocation.

There was one other possibility, but it seemed so remote that Oloi had great difficulty envisioning it. The arcanelementals were true elementals in that they were actually components of The Slice itself. They did not need any external power source or mechanical assistance in order to manipulate the dark energetic matrix; it came as natural to them as breathing did to creatures on Primus. Such a creature could have performed the translocation, but why? Oloi had only seen and interacted with an arcanelemental once since he'd transcended.

He nonetheless felt a kinship of sorts to these primordial keepers of magic. One of their functions in the organism that N'plorkians called 'The Slice' was to ensure that sentients residing on planets embedded therein were taught how to make use of magic in order to drain some of the excess manna that constantly accumulated throughout its ten billion-light year expanse. Without that bleed-off the dark energetic continuum would eventually tear itself apart and disperse.

The arcanelementals also served as the 'recruitment' arm of The Slice, itself a form of sentience. They contacted and recruited certain select transcendentals into an uber-elite group known as the Noils, whose mandate was to oversee and protect the various mechanisms in place for maintaining the health and stability of The Slice. They were, in effect, the white blood cells of The Slice as a living system. Oloi was a Noil, as had been the transcended archmage Namni—

until he forsook his oath for personal gain. Namni's life energy was now broadcast over a large area like defunct grass seed.

Given their dedicated mission, Oloi felt it very improbable that an arcanelemental was involved in his mystery translocation. He could see no way that such an action would contribute to the overall stability of The Slice. He brooded over the incident for hours, but came to no satisfactory conclusion. There was a mystery here that would require more than simple reasoning to solve.

Chapter Eleven

Captain Ekkot climbed the rickety stairs to the pilot dispatch office overlooking Koppra harbor. He paid little attention to the other two pilots sitting there, but went straight to his own desk and fished a beat-up comm unit from a drawer. He flipped open a greasy leather-bound journal and paged over to his comm circuit list. Locating the number he was after, he punched it into the comm.

"Hey Breqq, it's Deril. Makin' it; you? Glad to hear it. You remember those two twankers what deserted back when we was both still active duty? Yeah, them. I found 'em. No kiddin.' They're here in Azlymosh. I piloted their tub into Koppra harbor. Report it? That's a good one. Azlymosh ain't got extradition treaties with nobody: not even Nerr. If we want to bring these twankers in, we'll have to do it ourselves. I'm pretty sure they're livin' in Juymiz. I seen some freight come in for 'em not long ago that went there. I'll find out more. All right. I'll be waitin' for you."

Ekkot switched off the comm and glanced around the room. No one else seemed in the least interested in his conversation. Good. What he was arranging was technically in violation of international edict, although that sort of thing really didn't matter much here. He had discovered the whereabouts of two fugitives from Frespiolan justice and getting them back to face trial was a personal matter for him. Of course, if they resisted arrest they might accidentally be injured, perhaps even fatally, but that was a risk he was willing to take.

Ekkot had been a Senior Petty Officer-Master's Mate in the Frespiolan Marines. One of his responsibilities was assessing enlisted sailors for their suitability as officer candidates and making recommendations to Recruiting Command. Most officers actually came up this way. While Frespiola did have a Marine Academy in Melaman on the southwest coast of the island nation, its matriculating classes were small and infrequent, producing fewer officers than were needed for staffing purposes.

The file for a promising Sextant Sergeant named Hinyak came across Ekkot's desk one morning. He was bright, industrious, and a fine deckhand. He had no universitas diploma, but his aptitude scores showed he wouldn't have had any difficulty obtaining one had he been so inclined. Diplomas meant nothing to the Marines anyway, other than proving you were capable of devoting yourself to a long-term goal and absorbing a body of knowledge successfully. You would get trained the Marine way no matter what sort of background you came in with.

Ekkot took an interest in Hinyak and started compiling the documentation necessary to submit a formal officer candidate recommendation. It was a lengthy, involved process. SPOMM Ekkot took his job and his responsibility seriously; he put a lot of effort into researching Hinyak's performance and highlighting his strong points for the Officer Candidate Review Board.

The Board was suitably impressed with Hinyak—and Ekkot's efforts—voting to interview the Sergeant. Ekkot notified Hinyak's commanding officer, who passed the information along. The morning of the scheduled interview Ekkot brought his extensive portfolio on Sgt. Hinyak and spent an hour preparing the way for him with the interview panel. Time for the interview came and went. Ekkot's frantic communications to Hïnyak were met with silence. Finally the personnel officer of Hinyak's patrol unit reported that he and another Marine had been classified as AWOL.

When it became apparent at last that Hinyak had deserted, the resulting scorn and professional backlash was too much for Ekkot. He retired—earlier than he'd planned. The grudge he held against Hinyak for cutting short his career was deep and abiding. Now he had found the instigator of all that personal grief and the price he intended to extract from him would be great, indeed—but not, from his perspective, disproportionate.

"You think that cop is dead?"

"Unless some kinda miracle happened, yeah."

"I hope you're right. He didn't look like the 'forgive and forget' type, to me."

"You can forget about it. He ain't gonna be interferin' with us anymore."

"You think he was here lookin' for us?"

"Nah. I checked around; he was askin' about mages and such. Ain't nobody knew we was comin' here, and he ain't in no shape to tell anybody he saw us, neither. With him outta the way we're home free."

"I hope you're right."

"I'm always right. That's why you hang with me."

"I guess you're right."

"Let's head down to the *Troll* and get a drink.

Just into their second gourd of razzle a scruffy-looking hobgoblin sat down on the stool next to Hinyak and ordered his own libation. After a few sips he said, still facing straight forward, "Anybody lookin' ta score?" The guys couldn't help but notice that there was no one else within hearing distance of the hob but themselves. The question was repeated about two minutes later. Finally Hinyak sighed and took the bait.

"Depends on what ya got."

Still staring straight ahead and sipping from his gourd, the hob replied, "Exotic stuff. Highest quality. Comes from all the way from Litria."

At the mention of their home continent both Hinyak and Jovsox stopped in mid-quaff. Hinyak finished his gourd and then grunted.

"We might be interested in the *right* stuff."

The hob reached into a pocket of his overjack and extracted a small pouch containing a couple of leaves. He slid it over to Hinyak; the half-ogre sniffed cautiously. His expression registered just the tiniest trace of surprise and excitement, which he quickly suppressed. The hob, who called himself Vitto, noticed it and nodded.

"You want it, or not?"

"Maybe," replied Hinyak. "I need price, location, and quality."

"Price is cheap. There ain't much market in this part of the world. Location is close enough. Quality you can judge for yourself." He tossed over a wrapped bundle of dried leaves.

"We'll get back to you," Hinyak said. "Leave a comm circuit."

The hob slid a rectangle of parchment across the table.

"Don't take too long. The supplier will be moving on soon if he doesn't get some business here."

Klikka, the street name for those leaves, is harvested from a plant found only in the Frespiolan highlands, between Correq and Terimpu. It is a versatile intoxicant that can be chewed, smoked, boiled, or eaten. While it is virtually unknown to the outside world, many native Frespiolans grow up pleasantly addicted to it. Expats will often pay a hefty sum to procure even raw leaves, as exports of the plant and its derivatives are contrary to Frespiolan edict.

"I ain't had klikka since I was a Marine," Jovsox said, wistfully.

Hinyak frowned at him. "You did klikka on active duty? Didn't you know gettin' caught was an automatic Board of Ejection?"

"Yeah, I knew. But I didn't care. Most of the guys in my unit did klikka, too: even some of the officers. We paid a civvy that lived there on base to supply us with clean pee for the tests. I found where my sergeant kept the test schedules in his office so we was always ready for them."

The half-ogre chuckled. "Well, I guess it don't matter now, anyways. Havin' been high on duty would be the least of your worries if they get hold of us."

"That ain't gonna happen, is it?"

"No, it ain't. We're safe here. Nobody knows us and nobody here cares."

That evening in the privacy of their leased suite they sampled the product. Jovsox dug around in his sea trunk and brought out a little metal and wood device. Hinyak stared at it, puzzled, for a moment before his eyes lit up in recognition.

"A *k-juicer*! I can't believe you still *have* one of these things."

"Yep. Been carrying it around since we left home."

The 'k-juicer' was a device specifically designed to extract and concentrate the active ingredient from klikka leaves. It allowed users to experience the maximum effect from the psychotropic substances in the leaves with minimal effort. It crushed the leaves and mixed them with a volatile solvent, which it then evaporated with a little heat and presented the resultant concentrate in the user's choice of liquid, paste, or powder form for consumption.

With the assistance of the k-juicer Hinyak and Jovsox were soon drifting in a euphoric haze of endorphin neurotransmitters coaxed beyond their normal cerebral concentrations. The pharmacologically active components of klikka had both euphoric and soporific effects, depending on dose size and delivery mechanism. They were also potent mood mediators. By the next morning they were both pretty well convinced that this was indeed the good stuff and deserved their further attention.

Hinyak called the number the hob had left to arrange the buy. They didn't know any other Frespiolans in the area—and few outside the island nation had any knowledge of or use for klikka—but they were rather wealthy now and decided that having a near-lifetime supply of something that reminded them so much of home was a good personal investment.

Vitto agreed to meet them on the outskirts of town at the Juymiz West Agricultural Waystation, which was really just a raised platform covered in tarps where area farmers could deposit their waste plant material for credits. The waste product was picked up by recyclers and put to a variety of uses, including containers, cleaning pads, and wafers for religious ceremonies worldwide. Hinyak rented a commercial dray and they headed out to the rendezvous point with high anticipation.

When they were a few minutes away and chatting about what

they would do with the klikka, Jovsox frowned and bit his lip. Hinyak noticed.

"What ya thinkin', Juvvy?"

"I've never seen klikka outside Frespiola before, at any port we've ever hit. It just seems sorta impressive to me that Vitto figured out the only two guys in Juymiz who would even know what he was sellin.' He must be real smart."

Hinyak chuckled. "I asked him about that. He said he has a friend in Citizen Services who let him look at the immigration list. He saw we were Frespiolan."

Juvvy's frown deepened. "I thought you said you put down we was from Grosyem to throw the cops off."

Hinyak's eyes got wide and he slammed on the brakes. He turned the dray around and sped back the way they'd come.

"What're ya doin?" Jovsox asked after recovering from being slammed against first the dashboard, then the door of the dray.

"You're right. This doesn't add up. I think it's some kinda setup. That was good thinkin', Juvvy. You may have saved our butts."

"*I* saved our butts? Wow."

"Looks like they ain't gonna show," Vitto said into the comm. "Sorry about that. I don't know who or what tipped them off. It wasn't me, I swear."

"Smek. *So close.* Eh, it don't matter: we'll nab the twankers yet. I got another, better plan. It'll take some time and work to set up, though."

"You want I should tail 'em, boss?"

"Nah. We know where they live. They just got spooked by somethin' and backed out of the deal is all. Don't give 'em any more reason to think they did the right thing. Let 'em stew in their own misgivings."

In truth what precious few misgivings existed for Hinyak were connected with his own temporary insanity at almost falling into that trap—and he harbored no doubt whatever that a trap is what it had been. Looking back the signs were quite obvious, but of course we all know what they say about hindsight. Hinyak vowed never to be taken in like that again.

*　　*　　*　　*　　*

Oloi, as a Noil Emissary, reported to the rather nebulous and indistinct entities known as the *Lumeniles* who represented themselves as corporeal manifestations of The Slice's sentience. While they were theoretically omnipresent within The Slice, Oloi most often communicated with them in an area shaped to resemble an elaborate geyser that cascaded down a set of concentric deep blue bowls. Set all around this centerpiece were carved benches of vibrant multicolored material resembling stone. The archmage sat on one of these and meditated in order to commune directly with the Lumeniles.

"I seek to understand a thing," he began. "I was translocated to Primus with no warning, through a closed dark energy conduit. The signature was not directive."

"Was the outcome of advantage to you?" the ethereal voice in his head inquired.

He thought for a moment. "Yes, it was. I appeared in a place where I could be of assistance to a friend."

"Your friend is an archmage, then?"

"No, it was Tol-u-ol, the one chosen to rid N'plork of the fallen Namni."

"You are correct in saying he is not an archmage. However, it was the Chosen One who summoned you to Primus."

Oloi was confused. "How can this be? His amulet of summoning was not even functional."

"The amulet played no part in it. Our appendage Ix was dispatched to heal a bleb created by a poorly-executed teleportal and encountered the Chosen One there. A tangential manna

149

imbalance was increasing geometrically at that locus and Ix found it necessary to return the Chosen One immediately to Primus to stanch it before reversing the eversion. Our appendages, however, are not themselves mages. In order to accomplish the transfer an infrangible apotropaic implantation was required."

Oloi was silent for some time before replying.

"I am...grateful for the enlightenment, Masters." He stood and bowed before walking away. As he reached the perimeter of the fountain plaza he heard one final voice.

"He will need your assistance to grow into the implantation. It cannot be removed or reversed. You will reveal to him the path he must tread in this matter."

Oloi stopped. "I am ever your servant," he replied without turning, and was gone.

Chapter Twelve

Selpla's birthday dawned foggy and drizzling in Tropsalla, but the weather was fighting a losing battle if its goal was to dampen her spirits. She leapt out of bed before the first sun crested the horizon to complete the party preparations she'd begun three days prior. This would be her first birthday with Tol and he'd promised to be there no matter what. Even Prond had agreed to make the trip up from the Southern Reaches. She had gone to great lengths to ensure this birthday bash was an epic one.

The theme she'd chosen was Morianella, in honor of the topic that first brought her and Tol together one-on-one. Every bit of history she could locate concerning that ancient island was reflected somewhere in her choice of decorations. There wasn't much in the way of surviving artifacts, as the entire nation was destroyed in a matter of hours, but she filled in the multitude of gaps with articles from her own fancy. Never allow a paucity of facts to get in the way of telling a story.

Morianella was, first and foremost, an island. She found a plethora of sea-themed drapes and objects, choosing those specific to the Ustrad Sea preferentially when possible. The Morianellans had been known historically for their intricate glasswork and rare minerals. She hung little glass or simulated glass objects from curtain rods, lines strung across the room, and dangling from any available protrusion. Celebrating rare minerals was a bit more challenging from a decorator's standpoint; she finally decided on posters and objets d'art representing rock strata, rough gems, and the like.

The party was well-attended; virtually everyone she invited showed up. Selpla was, after all, a media personality who lived in a ritzy neighborhood. The temptation to mingle with famous and important people in a well-heeled setting was too strong for most to resist. There was also the fact that Selpla was a genuinely likeable sort with a large number of friends.

Tol was not the first one there, although he'd meant to be. The EE High Commissioner had stepped into his office just as he was packing up to leave; naturally he'd been forced to stand there and look attentive while the boss prattled on about something that would have much better expressed in a written memo. There were still only a handful of party-goers there when Tol arrived. One of them was Prond. He smiled as Tol walked over.

"Hello, Sir Tol-u-ol. Great to see you again."

"Hi, Prond. You, too. How's the mage lessons goin'?"

"Intense. Archmage Ballop'ril wants me to undergo the trial for Magus Incipius soon, and then finish and submit my disquisition as soon as practical after that."

"Sounds like a lot of work. Hope everything turns out all right for you. I know Selpla is very proud of you: she's told me so enough times."

Tol noticed Prond was staring at him with a puzzled look.

"What? Do I have bitterseed paste on my face again?" Tol asked, scraping at his cheeks self-consciously.

Prond blinked and shook his head. "No, no. It's nothing. I was just...I saw something I don't understand. It's my problem, not yours. I'll...uh...talk to you later." He moved away, but Tol noticed him staring on and off for the rest of the evening. He shrugged. These mage types were hard to figure sometimes.

The party was lively; the guests full of wit and sparkle. After the Tragacanthan tradition where each guest in turn offered a specific wish for the celebrant's good fortune in the coming year, Selpla asked Prond to do a little magic for their entertainment. He was visibly embarrassed by her request, but there was an undercurrent of eagerness to show off his skills for an audience that was apparent to Tol. They crowded around Prond in an approximate circle and waited while he came up with an impromptu demonstration.

He started with a little ballet of colored shapes and liquid-like streams of light. They moved simply at first, but the choreography increased in complexity and sophistication until the final act, where they moved inwards toward the center and one by one merged into a swirling sculpture of pulsing luminescence.

While the audience applauded, Prond set up his next trick. This one would involve creating what mages referred to as 'arcane blossoms.' These were little bursts of concentrated dark energy that exploded from precisely-placed microscopic pinholes poked in the spacetime matrix. They were actually tiny wormholes to The Slice, and the 'blossoms' extrusions of the fabric of the Dark Energetic Continuum itself. Done correctly, the effect was stunning. It was a favorite among first tiers, and Prond was pretty good at it.

For the pièce de résistance, Prond settled on one of the exercises he'd been preparing for his Magus trial. It was a risky choice—not only because he was far from polished at executing it, but also in that it involved transmutational invocation: creating matter from energy. That is a very exacting discipline with the potential for catastrophe if not executed with precision. He was forbidden from practicing outside the controlled environment of the academy until he had achieved Magus Incipius, but Prond figured one little illicit demonstration wouldn't hurt anything.

In honor of Selpla's theme, he had decided to invoke a scale model of the island, complete with buildings and roads, floating in the ocean. To accomplish this he had to establish a temporary conduit to The Slice that would act as both energy donor and sink. Without this persistent connection any excess energy created by the invocation would be dispersed in the local area, with undesirable results. The Slice, in contrast, was so unimaginably large that energies many orders of magnitude greater than those required for such spells could be absorbed or emitted with no appreciable effect.

The tricky and dangerous aspect of this process was maintaining tight control over the transmutation. A mage cannot simply convert energy to whatever elements are necessary for the object directly: it must pass through an orderly series of transmutations along the way. Each of these transmutational events requires that a very precise energy balance sheet be kept. Any deviations from entropic steady-state can lead to cataclysmic explosions or their functional opposite, known as entropy sponges. In these events a large amount of energy is suddenly withdrawn from the surrounding environment, effectively freezing both matter and ambient space.

While explosions are far more visually violent, energy sponges have in fact greater destructive potential. Whereas explosions result from instantaneous releases of energy that restore entropic balance almost immediately, entropy sponges trigger a localized violation of the laws of thermodynamics. Nature may abhor a vacuum, but she absolutely detests lawbreakers. Entropy sponges don't just freeze all the surrounding matter to near absolute zero: they actually in some cases introduce wildly unpredictable anomalies into the spacetime continuum itself.

He built the island first, carefully converting the raw energy into matter and then transmuting it to the elements he needed to form the appearance of beach, mountain, grass, soil, and buildings. At first the process demanded every particle of his concentration, but after a couple of minutes it felt more familiar and in concert with the positive feedback from the crowd's admiring oohs and ahhs he began to relax a bit. As a Mage of the First Tier, unfortunately, Prond had nowhere near enough experience at transmutational magic to be able to afford any such relaxation.

The water was filling in quite nicely; he had saved it for last because its constituent elements were some of the easiest to create and control. As he began to shape the waves and the interface between tide and beach, however, he failed to notice that one side of the table where he was building his little diorama was growing colder. It was subtle at first, but when he opened another microchannel to The Slice to pull in some more energy for raw material he suddenly lost control.

In a flash the water on that side froze solid; the freeze propagated within a few seconds to the rest of his creation and spilled out over the table. "Smek!" he yelled, "Everyone get out of the room—now!" As the suddenly panicked crowd ran for the exit, Tol, who had been on the back patio talking to one of Selpla's father's business associates who shared his disinterest in magic tricks, saw some of the partygoers spill out the kitchen door and asked what was going on.

"Don't know. The mage suddenly told everyone to get out. He sounded pretty scared."

Tol ran back into the room looking for Selpla. She was standing by the front door trying to facilitate the evacuation. "What the smek is going on?" he huffed as he skidded to a halt in front of her.

"I'm not sure. Prond was doing some pretty impressive magic and then all of a sudden he told everyone to get out. I guess something went wrong."

"What kinda magic?" Tol asked, although he didn't intend to.

"He was sucking energy in from somewhere and forming it into a representation of Morianella, I think."

"Sucking energy in from...smek me." Tol sprinted for the table where Prond was.

"Wait, Tol! There's nothing you can do to help! He needs to fix this himself. It's mage stuff."

Tol ignored her. She was too busy dealing with her guests to argue further.

Prond was desperately trying to halt and reverse the transmutational chain reaction he'd inadvertently triggered. He wasn't having much success. The best he'd been able to do was slow the progress of the runaway entropy sponge temporarily; he knew he couldn't hold it for long. Tol stood there watching him growing rapidly fatigued as he struggled and all at once he felt a bizarre compulsion that he was unable to fight.

He walked calmly over to the table directly opposite Prond and placed both hands on the surface. "Concentrate on stabilizing the lateral anchors," he heard himself say. Prond looked over at him, surprised. "I'll terminate the flux and dampen the harmonics.

As soon as the flux has stopped slam those anchor streams together and into the gap. That won't close the hole completely, but I'll take care of the residual."

"I...I don't think that..." Prond began, doubtfully.

"Just do it!" Tol snapped.

Prond shrugged and took a deep breath. He pulled his hands apart a few centimeters while rotating them outward and four streams of energy picked themselves out in glowing red. Tol stuck his hands right into the middle of the angry blue-white mass of swirling ice crystals in the center of the maelstrom. He grimaced and began to perspire profusely despite the cold; his fingers curled forward as though he were grasping something very heavy. The muscles on his beefy arms stood out like steel bridge cables. He let out a mighty grunt and then shoved upward with incredible force. A veritable tsunami of golden magical energy rushed into him from the surrounding air and swept the frozen diorama along with it, disappearing into a pinprick floating about a meter above the center of the table.

"Now!" he shouted.

Prond clapped his hands and the four red streams crashed into one another and then themselves flowed into the pinprick. Tol gave a final shove with his hands and the hole evaporated with a loud pop. A moment later the room was silent; the table empty except for a thin coating of rime ice. Prond and Tol exhaled in unison.

Tol stood there motionless, so thoroughly shocked and confused by what had just taken place that he simply couldn't cope. After Prond had regulated his hyperventilation and was breathing more or less normally again he walked over to Tol.

"That was *incredible*, Sir Tol. You literally saved all of us. I had lost control of that whole situation: it might have taken out the whole block. How...how did you do that? Even archmage Ballop'ril couldn't have reversed an entropic sponge that quickly. I don't understand."

Tol exhaled slowly and shook his head. "That makes two

of us, kid," he muttered before turning and walking away a bit unsteadily.

That night as Tol and Selpla lay in bed together (it was her birthday, after all), she decided to broach the subject she'd been avoiding all evening because Tol seemed genuinely uncomfortable with it.

"Tol," she began gently, "What exactly happened out there today?"

"Your mage kid got in over his head and nearly froze everyone to death," Tol replied.

"And you stopped him."

"Yeah, apparently I did. Good thing, too."

"How did you do that?"

"I really didn't do much, at least that I can remember. I just sort of stood there."

"Oh, no. Prond was babbling like a schoolboy with a crush. According to him you did a lot more than just stand there. He said you reversed his entire spell, or something like that."

"I...I don't know what I did, or how. It was almost like I was in a dream or something. Can we talk about something else?"

Selpla giggled and snuggled into him. "We don't really need to talk, at all."

"That's my favorite topic."

As soon as he got home, Prond put himself in what was known in the Arcanium as "corrective isolation." Ballop'ril paid him a visit only after the first twenty-two hours, as was standard Academy practice. Any mage could institute corrective isolation and expect not to be bothered for at least a full day. The purpose was to review a serious error and try to understand not only the error itself, but the underlying toxic or otherwise dysfunctional thought process.

He relayed the events surrounding the near-disastrous entropy sponge in as much detail as he could muster, including

157

Tol's involvement. Ballop'ril listened without comment. Prond had violated the rules of the Academy, but the archmage expected each advanced student to establish the roadmap for their own corrective measure and follow through on them. Since no one was injured and no property damaged, there would be no additional censure from the Academy itself.

"There as one further...oddity, Master," Prond added.

"Oddity?"

"Yes. Earlier in the evening, when Sir Tol-u-ol and I first came into contact, I noticed his aura. It was...different."

"Different in what way?"

"It was...golden, like a speculum, but surmounted by a thin bright silver radiance. I have never seen anything like it, even in books."

"Are you certain it was not some form of optical distortion?"

"Yes, Master. No matter what angle or distance I was at, it looked the same."

"I see. Thank you for the report, Apprentice. Return to your meditation now."

Ballop'ril went immediately to his library and began searching for a book in its voluminous shelves. Contrary to his usual tendency to get sidetracked and spend all day reading material not related to his original question, on this occasion the archmage kept his focus and ignored everything else until the object of his quest was finally located. The tome was a slim one, covered in dust from many years without use. It was a technical monograph with the cumbersome title *Intervention from Above: Hypothetical Manipulation of Sentients by the Dark Energetic Continuum*. In it were three historical case studies in which the best evidence available pointed to some form of direct contact between sentients on N'plork and creatures originating in The Slice. The first and most widely-known of these was of course the putative inculcation of the parasciencers with advanced arcane skills and knowledge over four thousand years ago by the creatures that came to be known as the Arcanelementals.

There were two additional documented instances, however. One was roughly four and a half centums ago and involved the supposed overnight advancement of what was then known as an 'undermage' (approximately equivalent to a Mage of the First Tier) to 'tradesmage' (somewhere between Magus Arcanis and Magus Superior). The details surrounding that near-miraculous occurrence were sparse, but scholars of the history of magic had reached a consensus that only the intervention of a creature born to magic could have accomplished it.

The other anomaly took place about two centums later during the *Stillo Event*. A Magus Superior named Stillo at the Arcanical Guild in Ovinis was designing a new form of energy conduit that he hoped would permit higher manna transfer rates from The Slice to the guildhall for the mages' use. After several months of preparation and spell-casting Stillo decided it was time to test the gateway at full flow capacity. He had made a miscalculation in his stream containment equations, however—or perhaps it was simply an artifact of the fundamentally chaotic nature of magic.

Whatever the reason, as the manna transfer reached its maximum the conduit began to contract and collapse in on itself. Ordinarily this would simply have terminated the manna flow with nothing damaged beyond the mage's ego, but the exceptionally high energy of the stream induced a feedback resonance within the collapsing structure that began to destabilize the surrounding fabric. As the crisis worsened actual chunks of the matrix that constitutes The Slice came tumbling through the mangled conduit.

Suddenly the flow stabilized and, a few seconds later, terminated altogether. Once such a feedback loop has been established it is almost impossible to halt it via traditional magic; the only rational conclusion scholars could reach as a result is that some entity acting on behalf of and residing in The Slice was responsible. Stillo always maintained that he'd been able to avert the catastrophe himself, but the archmages of the time, and those since, were not convinced.

Archmage Ballop'ril closed the tome and pondered in the hushed solitude of his library for some time. At last he stood and made his way to the academy office. Once there he opened a magical channel to the Loca Duber.

"Ballop'ril!" said the miniature holographic version of Cromalin that floated in the air above the invoking table, "It's been some time. How may I assist you, archmage?"

"Thank you for taking my call, Magineer Cromalin. I know you've a great many duties to which to attend so I'll be succinct: I am seriously considering calling for a convocation."

"A convocation?" Cromalin answered, stroking his chin, "We've not had one of those in decans. What could have happened to warrant such a drastic move?"

"I have strong reason to believe an intercession has taken place. Moreover, this event has created an elemental naïf."

Cromalin was silent for a few moments. "Such a person has never been documented with certainty, apart from the parasciencers, and even they are largely circumstantial. What evidence have you?"

"Stabilization and reversal of an uncontrolled manna flux by a non-mage with a distinctive elemental aura. Witnessed by my apprentice and at least a dozen others."

"Difficult to believe. How came about the flux in the first place?"

Ballop'ril sighed. "My apprentice, dabbling in invocations while still at First Tier. He has placed himself in corrective isolation and I think will learn this lesson from the pain he has caused himself."

"Was there injury or destruction?"

"None, but only because the intervention took place, it seems."

"A non-mage performed elemental magic, you say? What was his name?"

Ballop'ril told him. The Loca Magineer was once again silent for a while.

"You have my support for the convocation. I will notify the Magineer's Circle immediately."

Chapter Thirteen

Boogla pushed back from the desk in her office in the Royal Palace and stretched. She'd been reading the Moreani logbook translation supplied by Oloi (via Selpla) for two solid days, taking copious notes. The more she read, the more Oloi's connection between orcs, Morianella, and aliens made sense. Even the most mundane, trivial references in the logs were more relatable in the context of alien anatomy and thought processes. Diverting though such thoughts were, Boogla's real purpose was still to understand who the orcs were and how they came to be globally reviled.

The Moreani logs made only occasional references to the 'before times' on Morianella, but a careful analysis with benefit of hindsight left no real doubt of that singular origin. Now that she knew Plåk's name in Morianella had been Dennis Blass, she found at least one solid mention of him as the mage who teleported them to safety. Curiously, they seemed to be unaware that he was in any way connected with the disaster. They regarded him as an eccentric whose singular contribution was a well-timed and much-appreciated teleportative rescue. It seemed likely that only the Council who'd hired him were aware of his role.

Boogla's chief research interest at present was the transition from Morianellan refugees based in Nuvinis to orcs scattered around the globe in forced enclaves. Although the Moreani were master coastwise mariners, from the logs she possessed it seemed that they did not venture into the deep ocean often. Was the orc dispersion planned, therefore, or a reaction to specific circumstances? To have any chance of solving this riddle she would need to gather as much information as possible on every known orc settlement first.

Dr. Reoksa was once again enormously helpful here, as she had accumulated a great deal of data on orc demographics, but studying her collection it struck Boogla how much they *didn't* know. The orc enclaves were instituted as concentration camps centums ago, into which all orcs in a geographic area were herded and confined. She wanted to visit an enclave and talk to them about their history, but the orcs' justifiable dislike for the other races, goblins most of all, made cooperation rather unlikely. She had to befriend an orc somehow.

The abbess at Eithmorg had been friendly, but Boogla felt she'd already mined that vein. That orc had been nothing like the stereotype, however—she wondered if any of them truly deserved the reputation with which they'd been saddled. She stared out the window at her rooftop garden, thinking. Those thoughts kept leading her back to the marker on the beach at Flam. Even the Abbess didn't know what it meant, but they wouldn't have gone to all that trouble without a good reason. She looked up at the clock: it was time to interrupt her ruminations for the evening meal, her last with Aspet for a while.

The next morning Boogla left to return to the Paradiddle Islands. She headed straight to Flam and had the captain dock off the coast. Once on shore she discovered that the orcs from Eithmorg had carefully uncovered the stone marker and built drift fences on either side to keep blowing sand and tidal debris to a minimum. She stood on the marker and stared out at the surf in the direction it pointed.

"Do we have divers on board?" she asked the young ensign assigned as her Naval escort.

"Yes, Your Excellency. We have a detachment of Search and Rescue Marines who are certified as both free and suited divers."

"Excellent. Let's head back to the ship. I want to talk to the Captain."

Three hours later the divers had all made it back aboard and were gathered in the galley to give their report.

"It looks like there was a rock-strewn reef here at one time that has since collapsed, possibly due to the passage of a strong cyclone," said the squad leader. "We did sight a strange object—a capsule of some sort, perhaps—at about sixty meters down, but that's deeper than we are equipped to stay for any reasonable length of time."

"Do we have any way of exploring something at that depth?" Boogla asked.

"We have diving globes that allow us to see things in deep water, but we have no means of manipulating them."

"Couldn't you build some sort of suit that a diver could wear to keep him safe at that depth?"

"Hmm. That might be possible. We never had any real reason to pursue that before, to be honest."

"Well, thank you all, anyway. At least now I know for sure there's *something* down there."

Boogla stopped by the Paradiddle government offices in the capitol of Kod on Pataflafla to enquire about the official stance on the potential sunken artifact. The Chancellor was not present at the moment, but her aides relayed that any such object would be considered property of the orcs of Eithmorg on Drag, who were full citizens of the Islands, unless proven otherwise.

Back in Goblinopolis Boogla told Aspet about her latest discovery as they lay in bed.

"There has to be some way of exploring that capsule or whatever it is," she said.

"Sounds like a job for magic, to me," Aspet replied after a moment's thought. "Why don't you ask Ballop'ril if he has any ideas?"

The next morning bright and early Boogla was on the comm circuit to Ballop'ril.

"Yes, archmage. They say it's about sixty meters down. I don't have any idea what is in it, or how to gain entry."

"Interesting problem, Your Excellency. Let me put some of my students to work on it and I'll get back to you."

"Thank you, archmage. I'm trying to solve a puzzle that may have global implications here."

*　　*　　*　　*　　*

Tol stared at the message on his screen. It had been delivered via the EE Net using an encryption scheme common to Turmia but little-used in Tragacanth, so cracking the code had taken a few extra minutes and some searching around on the closed network. Finally there were words he could read staring back at him, though.

The missive was from the Greenshields; it said that they'd intercepted comm traffic relating to movement of a large shipment of what was most likely stolen equipment, including in all probability some of the proscribed material from Tragacanth. It also included an attachment of a bunch of gobbledygook that was intended to be used by a mage as teleport coordinates for Tol to get to Solemadrina in time to be part of the bust, if he so desired. Tol very much *did* so desire; with that goal in mind he contacted the SagMag EE liaison.

"I don't know exactly where it leads. Somewhere in Solemadrina, I guess. It's just a buncha numbers and symbols from one of their mages. Yeah, I'm forwarding it now."

Tol packed his field kit and called Selpla.

"Hi, babe. I'm heading out to Solemadrina soon. No, by teleport. I don't have time to take conventional transport. Of course I'll be careful—well, once I'm there. I can't do much about being careful during the teleport, I guess. I'll call as soon as I can. Love you."

A few minutes later he got a call back from SagMag.

"Sir Tol-u-ol, we're ready to conduct the teleport. It would best if you came here; we'd have more control and resources available if something goes wrong."

"What do you think might 'go wrong'?" Tol asked.

"Hopefully, nothing, of course. But we don't like to take chances, especially where a member of the Royal Family is concerned."

"Yeah, I can see where a mistake there might put a crimp in future operations. I'll be there in fifteen minutes."

Be on site at coordinates in about 30, he wrote to Greenshield.

Waiting for you. We won't have much time to spare, they replied.

Tol chuckled. *I'll be ready to roll.*

On the way he picked up some lunch: a particularly aromatic spumefish and aged olak-curd sandwich. Tol grinned as he walked into Sage Hall and saw people wrinkling their noses or closing office doors.

"Understand that we have not had time to test these coordinates for accuracy," the Magus Superior warned Tol, "And so we cannot guarantee you won't end up in...well, someplace you don't want to be. They appear, however, to be pointed at a clear spot along the beach east of Erolossma."

"Understood and noted," Tol replied. "I officially absolve SagMag of any liability if these coordinates are faulty. They came from an EE Magus in Solemadrina, however, so I'm pretty confident they're valid."

"I sincerely hope you are correct, for everyone's sake. Are you prepared?"

"Let 'er rip."

The Magus initiated the teleport spell after some puzzling over Tol's unusual aura and Tol found himself standing on a platform facing some boulders. He could smell the sea nearby. Perhaps five meters away was a group of Greenshields. One of them noticed Tol and walked over.

"Glad you could make it, Sir Tol. The Lycanics are loading a lot of equipment onto a cargo ship at a fabricated dock the other side of these rocks. We've seen at least two crates containing what we know to be proscribed material."

"Super. So, are we gonna bust 'em now, or what?" Tol asked.

"There's a complication. They anticipated our attention and

they've taken hostages, whom they've threatened to kill if we try to interfere."

"What's the plan, then?"

"We have a specially-trained commando unit on the way, but they're coming over from Aspolia by ship. We'll just shadow the Lycanic vessel and keep tabs on it so we can direct the commandos to intercept at sea."

"Not exactly what I came for, but fine. I'm ready."

"Good. We'll board a fast patrol cruiser and give chase as soon as they're gone. It's parked down the coast right now, out of sight."

"Can I borrow some glasses?" Tol asked. The officer handed him a pair. Tol wedged himself between two rocks and stared at the loading operation.

"Looks like they're just about ready to shove off," Tol reported. "I count six visible: a mix of gobs, hob, and ogres. How many are we talkin' total?"

"We estimate about thirty. That ship requires twenty-four crew, at minimum, for deepwater voyages. That leaves two hostages and four dedicated guards. Plus or minus a couple."

"Got any details on the hostages?"

"One is the daughter of the Lord Mayor of Erolossma; the other is a friend of hers."

"Sounds pretty high-profile."

"Yes. If anything happens to either of them the political repercussions will be considerable."

"How old are they?"

"Late adolescence. Last year of secondary schola."

"Good. Old enough to follow instructions well. How did they end up as hostages?"

"One of the Lycanics had apparently been surveilling the daughter for weeks and picked up on her patterns. He snatched her and the friend between the main schola building and the natatorium where they were headed for swim team practice. Narrow dark culvert that came right up to the walkway. Perfect timing, perfect execution. These jloks are good, I'll give them that."

"I like the ones who show meticulous planning. They're more likely to leave nothing to chance, which means that they don't expect 'bad luck' to happen. Me and bad luck are old pals."

The Greenshield frowned. "Not sure I follow your logic there, but whatever works for you."

Tol chuckled. "I'll illustrate later."

"Hopefully you won't need to. We'll let the commandos take care of the rescue."

"Never underestimate the power of bad luck."

The cruiser sent a skiff to pick them up as soon as it could do so without being seen from the Lycanic vessel. On board the Solemadrinan cruiser *Kell-Joma* Tol sat in a conference room with the Greenshields, discussing their plan for rescue of the hostages and subsequent takedown of the Lycanic perps.

"Once the commando unit has signaled that the hostages are secure, we'll deploy drag harpoons to slow the Lycanic vessel and board her here and here." He pointed to areas on both starboard and port sides of an illustration of the target. Noticing Tol's unspoken question, he explained further.

"Drag harpoons are anchor-like devices launched at a vessel we want to keep from running. They strike the hull and weld themselves on with a chemical reaction, then a very strong cable unspools and an attached multi-lobed shell unfolds in the current stream, greatly increasing the drag forces on the ship and slowing its forward movement."

"Smart gadget," Tol said, nodding.

"After we board we'll deploy two primary fire teams and two support squads. They will insert at these locations. Blue team and their support squad will head for the bridge and Red team for the engine room. Comms will be on local encrypted channel 2, subfilter 88."

There was definitely an art to following a ship at sea without being seen. Tol was fascinated by the process and, with the captain's permission, spent as much time as possible on the bridge learning about it. He was a bona fide expert at tracking people on land, but the marine environment was a very different kettle of fish. A combination of residual wakes, dead reckoning, and something called 'sailor's vision' that as far as Tol could tell was just guesswork and a certain amount of superstition rolled into one pseudo-scholarly package. He didn't care if it involved astrology and fortune tellers so long as it resulted in them not losing their quarry.

The Lycanics must have known they were going to be followed, of course; otherwise the hostages would not have been necessary. Tol felt a little sorry for Uffa, the Greenshield officer in charge, as the Lord Mayor or his aide called him at least once an hour around the clock for status updates. "*I* would 'accidentally' turn off my comm, or at least leave it in my bunk," he muttered.

The third day out Tol and said officer were standing at the foredeck railing straining to catch a glimpse of the target ship's masts through powerful glasses.

"Have we got any idea where these jloks are headed?" he asked.

"The Lycanics have a global network established," Uffa replied, "It could be just about anywhere. They have a warehouse of sorts on the outskirts of Erolossma where they store and periodically ship black market goods. This appears to be one of their larger movements of product. They might even be relocating all or part of the operation to some other area."

Tol scratched his neck. "So, you know who they are and where they are and that they have contraband stored there. Why wasn't the bust conducted back in Solemadrina?"

Uffa shook his head. "The Lycanics are experts at laundering both cash and goods. If we bust them and can't prove conclusively that any of that stuff was stolen and/or proscribed, their barristers and public relations machine will be all over us and whichever justice issued the search warrant. They'll be very, very reluctant to grant warrants in the future. Remember, Solemadrina is a pure democracy. Every official is subject to personal recall and every action taken by any official can be reviewed or even reversed by popular vote. It's a very different EE environment than the one you have in Tragacanth."

Tol blinked. "Wow. That would be really hard to cope with. How do you ever get anything done? I mean, every EE action's going to piss *someone* off, by definition."

"Well, there are rules in place about thresholds for reviews and that sort of thing—it isn't as big a deal as all that. It does mean that we have to stay squeaky clean and document every step we take very thoroughly, though."

A naval officer walked up at this juncture. "Commando ship should intercept this afternoon," he announced. "Weather section says relative humidity is climbing, too. There might be some fog later if the breeze slacks off."

"Great," Tol replied, "Perfect cover for being sneaky."

The plan was that the commandos would approach and board the Lycanic vessel under cover of darkness in an inflatable swiftboat. Their transport pulled alongside the *Kell-Joma* at around 1430 local time and the commandos came aboard. The ship that brought them would now steam on ahead and act as a diversion, sailing in full sight of the Lycanics while the commandos made their approach.

The rescue attempt was set for 0100 hours the next morning. Just after sunset the predicted fog rolled in with a vengeance and grew increasingly thicker as the night wore on. By midnight visibility was only a few meters. They were now sailing blind, relying solely on the navigational mages to detect nearby vessels and obstacles by magic. The metal hull of the Lycanic ship distorted the local fabric sufficiently that its unique fingerprint could be read by experienced nav mages.

Tol was restless. "You have the perfect cover for this operation! You couldn't have designed this thing better if you wanted to. Why are you still here?"

Major Miglu, the Marine commando unit leader, was dismissive.

"We cannot accurately plot a stealthy course to the enemy vessel in this fog. We will wait until tomorrow night, when the weather is forecast to be more cooperative."

"By which time a lot of stuff could have changed. They *know* we're here; they won't be expecting us to take any action in this fog. You would have an almost guaranteed element of surprise if you go tonight."

Miglu shook his head. "We would be taking too many unacceptable risks with zero visibility. We will wait."

It was Tol's turn to shake his head. "A Marine unit that won't take risks. I thought I'd seen everything," he muttered with derision as he walked away.

"Who is that...person, exactly?" Miglu asked.

"His name is Tol-u-ol. *Sir* Tol-u-ol," Uffa replied, "He's a Tragacanthan Special Investigator and Knight of the Crimson. He's also brother to the King of Tragacanth."

"Seems reckless to me."

"That, he may be," Uffa said after a moment, "But he's accomplished some pretty astounding things despite, or perhaps because of, it."

"He does realize that he's only an observer here, right?" Miglu sniffed.

"I doubt he sees it that way. Tol has reason to believe the Lycanics were involved in the near-assassination of the Royal Consort in Tragacanth, who would be his sister-in-law. This is very personal for him."

"Cops who take missions personally are very dangerous to have around, you know."

Uffa stared off into the enveloping mist. "I'm counting on that."

Tol was not happy. It seemed to him they were wasting a

veritable gift from Providence in waiting for the fog to dissipate. He sought out the mages who were tracking the Lycanic ship. It was holding steady at about 1,800 meters on a bearing of 300°. Tol did a little math in his head—not his strong suit, but he got through it—and calculated the best route given what they knew about the layout of the other vessel. Now he just needed some transportation.

He wandered below decks until he found the Quartermaster Depot. He walked up to the window.

"May I help you...sir?" The Quartermaster's Mate asked.

"Yeah. I need a boat. Just a small one."

"Do you have orders from a command-grade officer for this requisition?"

"Sort of. I have this." He pulled out the Memorandum of Agreement between Aspet and the Secretary General of Solemadrina authorizing Tol to function with the equivalent rank of Brigadier while on official business in Solemadrinan territory. The Mate looked at it and blinked a couple times, then did some figuring.

"That makes you equal to a...Rear Admiral. That's definitely command grade. I'm not sure who to charge this to for accounting purposes, though."

Tol whipped out another piece of parchment.

"Got that one covered, too. I have an open Royal treasury writ that is accessed via this Solemadrinan requisition number." He handed the parchment over. "Anything charged to that account with my signature will be paid by Tragacanth."

The mate shrugged. "Looks good. What kind of boat do you want? We don't have too many in stock; they're a little, you know, bulky."

"Just something I can use to take a short trip. It needs some kinda motor, but it doesn't have to be real powerful."

The mate reached under his counter and got a key. "Come this way. We'll take a look in the large item lockers."

In the end Tol picked out an inflatable dinghy and a compact but powerful clip-on motor with a self-contained battery.

"This boat is certified to three-meter swells and thirty knot winds. The motor will give you about forty-five minutes at full power, or up to three hours at half velocity."

"That oughta be plenty," Tol replied.

"May I ask what you plan to do with this materiel?"

"I'm just goin'...fishing."

Tol borrowed a dolly from the Quartermaster and lugged his new acquisition to the hatch the Marines were planning to use for their deployment. Their boats were lined up there, lashed to the deck. Tol figured the little sentry wouldn't be too cooperative if he just waltzed up and wanted to launch his own boat. He needed a diversion: something that would make a loud noise down the hall and draw the sentry's attention. A split second after Tol had this thought an accommodating crash and clatter reverberated down the corridor. The sentry leapt up from his seat in alarm and tore off in that direction.

Tol shrugged, grinned, and dragged the boat he'd just finished inflating over to the hatchway. He spun the wheel and slid the hatch open, dropped the motor into the boat and then tossed both over the side, followed immediately by himself. He landed in the boat just as it touched the water and spread-eagled to stop it from rocking dangerously. Once the boat was stable he snapped the electric motor into place in its frame, turned it on, and lowered the propeller into the nicely calm sea. He looked at his compass, set his bearing, and tooled off into the fog.

When the sentry came back after being unable to discover the source of the noise, he was puzzled by the open hatch. It somehow must have come open on its own, he concluded, as there was no one else in evidence. He thought he heard a faint humming noise coming from somewhere out on the water, but having just been duped he was in no mood to trust his ears at the moment. He slid the hatch shut, secured it, and sat back down. Only an hour left in his shift. He was going to try to get a little extra sleep tonight in case he was coming down with something.

In order to catch up with the Lycanic vessel Tol had to run the little dinghy motor flat out; even then the rate of closure was very, very gradual. If they hadn't needed to slow substantially in the dense fog bank he probably couldn't have caught them at all, to be honest. He realized that the battery life may or may not be sufficient to get him where he needed to be.

"Petey! Can you tell how close we are to that other ship?"

"Extend your right arm."

That was a weird answer, but Tol did as he was told. His fingers brushed heavy steel plating.

"Holy smek. I almost rammed the thing."

"I doubt they would have been aware of it."

"*I* would have been aware of it. Probably painfully so."

"There is a high probability you are correct."

"Now I just have to figure out how to get aboard."

"Did you not bring a grappling line?"

"Yeah, but I don't see any railings to hook it to anywhere."

"There is one above you, but it is quite small and situated in such a way that hooking it would be very difficult from this position."

"Well, 'very difficult' is not the same as 'impossible.' Tell me when I'm aiming in the right direction."

"All right. Rotate about one degree to your right. No, too much. Back a small distance. There. The railing is twelve point three meters straight up. Get the hook as close to the hull as possible during its ascent."

After securing the free end of the line to an oarlock on the dinghy, Tol spun the hook four times, releasing on the final upswing. The grapple shot up into the dark fog. There was a clattering and the rope hung there limply.

"Unbelievable. You appear to have snagged it on the first throw. There is something not altogether normal about you. This phenomenon was apparent before, of course, but lately it has increased significantly. Something happened to you in The Slice." It was not phrased as a supposition, but a statement of fact.

Tol grunted. "Yeah, I got freaked with by the not-so-jolly green giant—although I still think that might have been a dream."

"It was no dream. All evidence points to the entity you encountered being an arcanelemental, improbable though that sounds."

By this point Tol was almost to the railing, climbing up the somewhat slippery hull of the Lycanic vessel. He wrapped one hand around the rail and pulled himself aboard. He left the grapple in place and hoped no one would notice it. Tol ducked into the first area that offered significant concealment.

"Petey, can you come up with some sort of layout for this ship?"

"I can give you a composite of three ships built by this same shipyard that share a number of external characteristics. However, the present owners may have made unregistered modifications that could render that estimation less accurate."

"Understood. I'm trying to take a guess about where might be a good place to hold hostages."

"Strategically, the optimum location would be on deck four near the center of the vessel. There is, or at least should be, a small suite there with toilet facilities that would be easily guarded on all approaches."

Tol stared at the holographic deck plan Petey was projecting. He nodded. "Yep, I agree. Now, the much more difficult question: how do I get in there and smuggle the hostages out?"

"It will be a difficult operation, presuming they have posted guards at the appropriate locations. If you have the element of surprise you may be able to infiltrate, but even were you to extract them successfully, what then? No one on the *Kell-Joma* even knows you are here."

"This is gonna sound seriously wacked out, but I *know* that once I get them out of there I will be able to rescue them."

"Is this more of your 'cop's intuition'?"

"No, it's not like that. It's just a solid conviction that I've got this. I can't explain it any better."

"You understand that your statements are irrational and identify you as potentially delusionary, correct?"

"I do, but I'm not. Something weird has been happening to me the past few days, as you noticed. This is not the first time I've had this feeling, and it's proven correct every time."

"Your corolla integumenta has been modified." Petey announced after a moment's silence. "I did not detect it previously because I do not possess a dedicated sensor for that attribute. I have to synthesize those data based on related telemetry."

"What the smek is a corolla inte...whatever?"

"The corolla integumenta is the aura that surrounds all biological creatures, detectable only to trained eyes. For most it is merely a thin monochromic luminescence. Mages, however, possess more complex corollas, ranging from different hues in the lower skill levels to multilayered presentations for higher magi and archmages. Yours is of a type that does not appear in any of the arcane reference databases. It is possible that your 'feelings' and this phenomenon are connected."

"You mean I've got *mage* all over me?" Tol sounded a little revolted.

"Corollas are indicative of what you are, not what you are wearing."

"I ain't no smekking mage."

"No, you are not. But you are...something beyond goblin now."

Tol grunted. "I'm the same goblin I've always been. One who needs to get moving."

He headed off down the corridor toward the aft stairs, which according to Petey's blueprints should be right around the corner. Suddenly he heard footsteps and threw himself into a dark alcove. Two Lycanic sailors carrying side arms came walking by.

This may be trickier than I thought.

Once the sailors were past, Tol slipped down the stairs to deck four. He knew he was getting close when the incidence of armed hobs increased dramatically. This would be quite a test of his stealth skills, but he'd handled worse. He wedged himself into a shadowy corner and observed for a while, watching for patterns.

The guards were not walking regular patrols, unfortunately. Their activity seemed more or less random to Tol. It was becoming increasingly apparent to him that he'd have to trust to luck on this one. As he was preparing himself mentally to make a dash for the door during the next gap between patrols, he heard the peculiar vibration that was Petey communicating via bone induction.

"Before you do anything rash, I think I may have found an alternate path to the hostages."

Tol grunted, and Petey continued. "At the rear of this recessed area there is a utility access panel that leads to a crawlway common to all of the interior staterooms on this deck. If the layout diagrams I have are accurate—and so far there has been a 97.4% correlation— you will be able to access the hostage cell, or at least the suite in which it is putatively contained, from there."

Tol grinned and whispered into his pocket. "You're all right, you know that?"

"I was aware, yes."

The access panel proved a bit of challenge to remove, as both the hinges and latch were rusted quite thoroughly, but Tol finally worked it off there in the darkness. He squeezed his bulk into what was rather obviously a long-disused crawlspace. Rust, dirt, and something that may have been a layer of fungus sloughed off the walls as he forced himself along the passage.

"How far do I have to travel through this?" he whispered to Petey.

"Approximately fourteen meters in total. Take the next right, then head left at the tee intersection. The passage should terminate at your target."

"If I'm not immobilized by gunk before then," Tol muttered.

When at last he reached the end of the line he could see by the dimmed light of his torch that the panel there would not come off without a fight. How to do battle with it quietly? He sat there in the darkened crawlway pondering this and wishing he had some oil and a few tools when suddenly light from the room beyond flooded the passage. He stared in alarm at the hole where the panel had been moments before.

"What the smek just happened?" he whispered to Petey.

"It would appear," the pen replied a little doubtfully, "That the panel has been sequestered."

"What does that mean?"

"It means that all of the molecules that constitute the panel were moved simultaneously into an alternate physical dimension."

"You mean teleported."

"Not precisely. Teleportation is the transfer of a physical object from one location on Primus to another via a wormhole that passes through The Slice. Sequestration involves transdimensional movement. Much more sophisticated and with considerably greater energy requirements."

"Why?"

"Presumably to solve the problem with which you were confronted."

"All right, then: who?"

"Improbable though it seems, all indications are that the answer is 'you'."

"There you go with that smek again. *I* didn't do anything at all."

"Perhaps not consciously. But evidence strongly suggests that you *did* do it."

Tol sighed. "Whatever. Doesn't matter right now." He slid quietly out of the passageway and into the room. He glanced back at the hole and was startled to see the panel apparently in place. He reached out to touch it and his hand passed through effortlessly. He shook his head in bewilderment and turned back to the task at hand.

He was only guessing that the hostages were nearby. Tol had no solid evidence to support that assertion; only cop's intuition. He stood very still and listened. There were some noises coming from the next room over. He padded over to the wall and put his ear to it. Definitely female voices.

"Petey. Can you tell me how many people are in that room?"

"My sensors show two in the room proper and one just outside the door, in the outer corridor."

"Hostages and guard. Check. Let's wait until the next check-in to make the move."

Tol peered around the corner and ducked back as he heard a door open.

"How accommodating," Petey said.

Tol waited until the male voice was no longer audible and the door had shut before slipping into the room. The two girls saw him and started to cry out but he held up a finger to silence them. He then pulled out his Special Investigator badge and waved it in front of them. They nodded and followed when he motioned them to do so. Tol led them back to the access panel and chuckled as their eyes got wide when he passed his hand through it. He crawled in and then indicated for them to join him. After a whispered discussion they disappeared into the narrow passageway, with Tol in the lead.

Rather than returning to where Tol had come in, Petey guided them to an exit that opened onto a balcony running around the outer perimeter of the vessel. Tol climbed out first to check the lay of the deck. The area seemed deserted, so he brought the girls on out as well.

"You've managed to extract the hostages: now what? Their absence will be noted any moment now, if it has not already. They will follow the utility passageway to this spot within a few minutes. Your dinghy is on the other side of the ship. I am finding it difficult to construct a scenario in which your intended outcome is viable."

"I told you, it will work out. I know it will."

"It had better begin 'to work out' immediately," Petey said, "I detect six persons converging on this spot."

"Time to go," Tol said to the hostages and urged them on. He was running on pure instinct now. They raced along the balcony until suddenly Tol veered off and kicked a nondescript section of sheet metal under a railing. It crumpled under his foot and he yanked it away from the adjoining panels, leaving a hole just big enough for them to fit through. He stuck his head out and looked down. The dinghy was positioned perfectly beneath them, as though it had been anchored there intentionally.

"Highly improbable. Verging on ridiculously so, in fact," Tol heard Petey say.

Tol chuckled. "It gets worse." He reached over to his left and pulled in a heavy-grade rope of sufficient length to reach the dinghy—already securely attached to the railing less than a meter from the grappling hook. Petey apparently found no further remark to make.

He lowered the girls individually and then rappelled down to join them. As they motored off at flank speed he heard a commotion behind them consisting of shouts and a loud splash.

"Sounds like they've launched," he said to the girls. "We're gonna need to pull some fancy evasive maneuvers, so hold on to the oarlocks."

He swung the outboard motor handle to the right and they slewed around to port. They straightened out and headed into the very thickest fog bank in sight. He kept going on the same course for a few seconds and then swung to starboard for another few before cutting the engine. They drifted in silence, listening to the approach of the Lycanic runabout. As Tol had suspected, their pursuers shot by them at no more than ten meters range following their previous course. In the thick fog they were completely invisible.

The Lycanics zagged back and forth in a desperate effort to locate the escapees, but they were off by over twenty meters now and getting further away. Tol grabbed the oars and began to row them on a course supplied by Petey back to the *Kell-Joma*. When the Lycanic search party could no longer be heard Tol put down the oars and fired up the outboard again. He pulled out his comm unit and punched in the *Kell-Joma* tactical channel.

"*Kell-Joma*, this is Tol-u-ol. I have the lost woolbeasts and am returning to the flock. Repeat: I have the lost woolbeasts and am returning to flock. Do you copy?"

There was a moment of crackly silence and then the deck officer replied.

"We copy you, Sir Tol. Present position?"

"We're in a dinghy at about 025 degrees bridge relative. Range is probably around..."

"235 meters," Petey supplied.

"...235 meters."

"We'll be waiting."

"Oh, there's a small Lycanic boat of some kind zippin' around out here looking for us. You might run into them."

"Copy. We actually already have. Or, rather, *they* ran into *us*."

Tol chuckled. "So, you've had an impact on their misspent lives. Good for you."

Miglu was deeply annoyed that this foreign goblin had stolen their primary mission, but Uffa reminded him that the overall mission was to stop the black market goods shipment and the commandos would be welcome to assist with that. Once the Lycanics realized their bargaining chips were gone for good, they poured on the speed in an attempt to outrun their pursuers. While the transport ship had been modified to increase its forward velocity, it was no match for either of the Solemadrinan vessels.

Uffa had orders to return the stolen equipment if at all possible; that meant boarding and taking control of the Lycanic ship without disabling her. His original plan was to move in at high speed under cover of darkness and overwhelm the defenders with superior numbers and firepower. That strategy would no longer be viable, he suspected, as the Lycanics were now on full alert and expecting their pursuers to attempt to board. The game was on.

Chapter Fourteen

The parties assembled on Flam's Ayu-minn beach were not exactly typical visitors to the island. They consisted of the Magineer Liaison/Royal Consort of Tragacanth, her security detail, a Mage of the First Tier from the Schola Arcanium, a representative from the Paradiddle Islands Historical Commission, and the Prefect of Flam, along with a few aides.

Boogla had not intended to generate such a crowd, but the Paradiddle government decided it wanted to know why a Tragacanthan high functionary had taken such an interest in their tiny country. She had asked for help from Ballop'ril, who had sent the inevitable Prond. She wanted a mage present because she was hoping magic could help to solve a problem that current marine exploration technology could not.

They stood beside the arrow pointing out to sea while Boogla explained the particulars of her quest.

"We know there is something out there, not very far offshore and located at a depth of about sixty meters. That's a little too deep for free diving and while we could send someone down in a diving suit, he more than likely wouldn't be able to gain entry to the capsule—if that's what it is—due to limitations of the suit itself. I would like to know if we can use magic as all or part of the solution here."

That last bit was pretty obviously aimed at Prond. He hemmed and hawed while he composed his answer.

"Um, there are...there are spells which provide a breathable air bubble, but I'm not certain of their pressure limitations. They also require a rather, um, robust subject because they aren't very stable. That's why magic has never been adopted widely in this area."

Boogla ruminated on this. "I guess we'll need to find someone suitable. I'll comm back the ship that brought me here and see if they can find me an appropriate volunteer."

"How about one of your RPC guys?" Prond asked.

"We've already used them as test subjects once. I don't want to make a habit of it," she replied with a smirk.

As she was dialing in the captain's circuit, one of the aides shouted, "There's something coming out of the surf!" The RPC snapped on guard and herded Boogla up off the beach until the threat was identified. As she watched the interloper come slogging up out of the water, Boogla realized he looked awfully familiar. The RPC supervisory agent went over to talk to the stranger and she saw him holster his weapon as soon as the two came into close proximity.

The RPC agent escorted the new person, a goblin, over to Boogla. By the time they were halfway up the beach there could be no doubt of the soggy goblin's identity: it was Tol. She stared at him in amazement.

"What on N'plork are you *doing* way out here? I thought you were in Solemadrina."

Tol grinned. "I was. For a little while."

"How did you end up here?"

"I fell off a boat. Well, to be more accurate, I got pushed."

"When did *that* happen?"

"Maybe an hour ago?"

Boogla turned to the RPC. "Do you folks see any ships out there?" The SA shook his head. "No, Your Excellency. The cruiser we came on reports no ships spotted or reporting within at least two hundred kilometers."

"Could a ship have come in close enough for someone to fall off and swim to shore in an hour without being seen?"

"Highly unlikely. At least, not one large enough to be classed as an ocean-going vessel."

Boogla turned to Tol and raised her eye ridges.

"Well, I am standing here, so that's a pretty solid indication that I'm telling the truth from my point of view. The fact that it's difficult to explain doesn't really surprise me; that's the way my life has been going lately." He pulled a pen out of his pocket. "Petey, please tell these folks where we were prior to my falling off that ship."

"Our last verifiable position was in the Ustrad Sea, 740 kilometers due south of Rillwe, Rublosq."

"That's on the other side of the planet from here. You are one fast swimmer, Sir Tol," the SA replied with a smile.

"Petey, how long ago did I fall in the water?"

"My chronometer says 74 minutes."

"So, you traveled halfway around N'plork in a little over an hour. That's a good clip," Boogla remarked. "Can you explain that?"

Prond had said nothing during this exchange but now piped up with, "I suspect it is somehow connected with his bizarre aura."

"What is bizarre about his...aura?" Boogla asked.

"It isn't normal. Not only is it not normal, it isn't like anyone else's *anywhere*, as far as I know."

"How would an unusual aura be connected with the ability to travel halfway around the world in an hour?"

"I don't have a solid answer for you. He has changed, and whatever caused him to change has given him some form of innate magical abilities. That's the best explanation I can offer."

"Is that true?" Boogla asked, turning back to Tol, "Are you able to do magic now?"

"No. I mean, no I can't *do* magic by casting spells or any of that stuff. The last few days some pretty smekkin' odd things have been happenin', though. Ever since that screwy teleport in Zuum..." He tailed off, shaking his head.

Boogla heard a small alert tone just then coming from her encrypted arcane-mode transceiver. She punched in her code, read the message, and chuckled.

"Says here you're missing at sea off the coast of Rublosq," she said to Tol.

"I told you."

"I guess I'd better let them know you're safe."

"How are you going to explain that I'm safe on the other side of the world?"

"I won't. I'll leave that up to you during the debrief back in Goblinopolis."

"Thanks a bunch, sis."

"Anything for family." A thought suddenly struck her. "Since you're here, I have a job for you, if you think you're up to it."

"What sort of job?"

"There's some kind of capsule or ship or something off the shore here that I want to have explored. It's too deep for free divers—about sixty meters—and people in diving suits probably couldn't gain access to it. Prond here, though, says he could create an air sphere with magic that would allow you to poke around down there for me."

Tol looked at her with the expression he usually reserved for perps who offered some insultingly ridiculous alibi.

"Did you just ask me to go sink down sixty meters in the ocean while relying on a magic bubble over my head for breathing?"

"Yes, that covers it, more or less," Boogla replied, sweetly.

Tol rolled his eyes. "I just spent an hour treading water and now you want me to go back out there and *not* tread water? What if Mister Wizard here screws up the spell?" He looked at Prond. "No offense, kid, but this is my *life* we're talking about here and I've seen what happens when mages screw up."

Prond nodded. "Understood. There is always a modicum of risk with these things, but something tells me I couldn't really endanger you even if I wanted to. You're...special."

Tol chuckled grimly. "I wish this was the first time that adjective has been applied to me." He returned his attention to Boogla. "What's in this capsule or whatever that's so smekking important, anyway?"

"I think," She replied, "It might hold the key to who the orcs really are and why we've always treated them like murderous maniacs."

"You mean they're not?"

"No. There's not a shred of hard evidence to back up that reputation."

"How did we get things that wrong?"

"We'll talk about that later. Right now I'd like to get on with the exploration."

Tol sighed. "Fine. What do I need to do, exactly?"

Half an hour later Boogla, Prond, Tol, and Boogla's RPC detachment were in a Navy runabout anchored over the sunken mystery object. Tol was wearing a diving skin that would help minimize effects from the increase in pressure at sixty meters depth. It sported numerous pockets filled with dense metal blocks for ballast that could be jettisoned to assist in returning to the surface.

"When you get down there look for some way into the capsule. If there's a doorway or hatch, try to figure out how it opens. It may not be possible to open it if it's sealed, because the pressure might be too great for you to remove the hatch, but do your best. If you find a way in, look around for something like this." She took out the data storage unit Selpla had discovered in Nuvinis. "They might not look exactly like this, but the things I'm most interested in will be probably be small rectangular metal boxes that at least resemble this one."

Tol took the little box and turned it over in his hands.

"What's so special about this doohickey?"

"It's an orc data storage unit. The orcs are...not from around here, originally."

"I'd always sorta wondered about that," replied Tol.

"I'm going to create a transparent shell around your head—an 'air helmet'," Prond explained, "It will have an integral feed from a couple of meters above the surface that will continuously suck in air and exchange it for the gases you expel when exhaling. That will ensure you have a steady supply of air to breathe."

Tol grunted skeptically. "How long will it last?"

"It won't really have a time limit. Once the gas exchange cycle is established it will continue until the enchantment is dispelled."

"This isn't going to turn out like that freeze fest at Selpla's birthday party, right?"

Prond blushed. "No, no. That was the result of a foolish mage experimenting with forces he didn't fully understand. This is an established, well-documented spell that even a mage of the second tier could cast successfully. Thank you again for your help with that...incident."

"You're welcome, I guess. I really don't know what it is I did, to be honest."

"That makes it all the more intriguing. Are you ready for the air helmet?"

"Ready as I'm gonna get. Let 'er rip."

Boogla handed him an oilskin bag containing some tools. "These are specially designed for underwater use. They might help you gain access to the capsule and remove the storage units, presuming they're still there. There is also a powerful waterproof torch."

"Thanks. I wasn't lookin' forward to doin' this with my bare hands."

"Good luck, Tol, and...take care, all right? Aspet and Selpla would not be happy with me if anything happened to you."

"No worries, sis. Surviving has always been what I do best."

Prond completed the spell and the air helmet formed around Tol's head. It looked like his head was lodged in the center of a giant transparent kickball.

"Are you able to breathe all right?" Prond asked.

Tol nodded and gave him a thumb up. He shouldered the tool bag and waded off into the surf. After about fifteen seconds the top of the bubble sank into the waves and Tol was gone.

He followed the gentle downslope for a few tens of meters until he reached an abrupt ledge that marked a near-vertical plunge into the dark depths. There didn't seem to be any means of climbing down, so he just shrugged and slid along the steep decline, doing his best to stay more or less upright during the rough descent. He reached into a pocket on his sleeve and folded out a depth meter positioned so he could read it easily with no hands. He knew he wasn't supposed to exceed 120 meters for any extended period. He had no idea just how far down the dropoff extended. If he started getting close to the maximum depth he would have to drop ballast.

Fortunately, his descent was arrested soon after by contact with a large dome of some kind covered with layers of coral and other sea life. The impact produced a resonant thunk that confirmed to Tol he'd landed on a hollow object. He felt his way around the top surface, continuing his exploration along the sides by hanging on to metal protrusions or marine growths. After a while he was beginning to think that the door, if there was one, must be located on the face of the capsule now embedded in the sand of the slope.

As he pondered what to do next, a long, thin toothfish swam up and after a brief but intense chase nabbed a small crustacean crawling on the capsule's surface. Tol was watching the action in bemusement when a narrow slot cut into the strange metal caught his eye. It was almost completely hidden under a crust of marine growth; he probably would never have noticed it without the focus lent by the predator fish's antics. He scraped off most of the material, forced his huge fingers as far into the opening as possible, and pulled.

Tol had just enough success with his first effort to encourage him to keep at it. Even with his considerable strength and tenacity, he was making very slow progress until he remembered the tool bag. Inside he found a little hydraulic pry bar that enabled him to get the outer hatch open far enough to squeeze into the small airlock. Once inside Tol realized that the hatch opening controls, even were they still operational after all these centums, would be interlocked such that they could not be operated with the outer hatch open. He broke out the torch and pulled the outer doorway closed. To his surprise and satisfaction it seated and sealed properly.

Tol was not prone to claustrophobia, but being in a very small enclosed area sixty meters underwater in total darkness was nevertheless quite uncomfortable for him. After a little searching he found a panel that slid back to reveal several buttons with strange characters above and below. He extracted Petey and held his tiny camera lens in front of them.

"I suppose," Petey said through bone induction, which sounded even weirder than usual at this depth, "That you want me to translate?"

Tol nodded, not realizing he could talk just fine with the air bubble around his head.

"These characters appear to match those on the manuscripts associated with the Morianellans. I have not been given sufficient data to translate from that language with any reasonable degree of accuracy, but based purely on semiotic conjecture I would hazard a guess that the top button's label says 'hold to open'."

"Good enough for me," Tol muttered, surprised that it came out so clearly. He held the button down and waited. After a few moments he heard a noise coming from somewhere deep inside. Against all odds, motors whirred to life and the door slid partially open, albeit slowly and with obvious reluctance.

Tol pushed the sliding hatch the rest of the way and stepped inside. He was quite obviously the first to enter the capsule since it sank beneath the waves so long ago; there were no footprints or other signs of occupation in the layers of dust covering every surface. At Petey's suggestion he pressed a small switch near the door and dim but revealing lighting illuminated the interior. He stood in the center and slowly made a complete 360 degree sweep, taking in as much of the view as possible while holding Petey up to get a video record of it all for Boogla.

During the visual assessment he noticed a narrow door in the part of the capsule furthest from the hatchway. There was no obvious way to open it. Tol knelt down and fished the pry bar back out. He was about to start trying to leverage his way in when Petey intervened.

"Unless you simply insist on a physical display of force, there may be an easier way to gain access."

Tol put down the tool. "I'm all ears."

There was a slight pause while Petey processed the idiom. "Ah. Quaint. Electromagnetic signatures show an active power circuit leading to a location near the edge of that door; presumably an actuator for the opening mechanism. The switch seems to be point six meters to the left of the door itself and one point two meters from the floor."

Tol walked over and hunted around for said switch. There was nothing at the indicated position but a child-sized handprint outline. He puzzled over it for a few seconds.

"Biometric," Petey explained after completing his own analysis, "A palm print reader designed for hands smaller than a goblin's. Such systems are generally intended as safeguards for particularly valuable equipment or data. They are also notoriously difficult to circumvent. Simple cross-circuiting is almost never effective."

"Which means...what?" Tol asked.

"It cannot be hot-wired."

"Oh. Got ya. So, what can we do?"

"I would suggest that we try an experiment. Place your hand on top of the palm reader. Center it as well as you are able. Now, imagine the door opening."

"What?" Tol said, frowning. "What kinda hokey experiment is that?"

"I have been observing and analyzing your arcane presence for some time. You are exhibiting evidence of peculiar abilities that I believe may be of some use here. Just do as I suggest."

Tol shrugged and followed Petey's instructions. For a few seconds nothing happened and he was about to give up. Petey sensed this.

"Stay your course," he instructed, "You are having an effect. Visualize the door sliding open."

Tol kept his hand in place and concentrated on the desired outcome. There was a faint click, a whirr that increased in pitch and volume as the motors strained, and with an unpleasant scraping noise the panel ground open. Tol blinked in surprise and shone his torch inside. There was a variety of derelict-looking electronic equipment, but he had eyes only for the storage blocks Boogla wanted to recover. After moving a fair amount of stuff around, Tol encountered a metal cube with a dial on the front. He puzzled over it for a while.

"It is a safe," Petey finally explained, "A strongbox for storing important items with some measure of security."

"Super. How do I get it open?"

"You have to turn that dial in different directions and stop on the correct numbers in the proper sequence."

"How am I meant to accomplish that?"

"*You* are not meant to accomplish it at all, of course. That is more or less the point of the mechanism. If you will position me to the right side of the dial and follow my instructions, I will attempt to 'crack' the combination for you."

Tol did as he was told.

"Start by turning the dial to the left through several complete rotations. Good. Now turn it very slowly the same direction while making as little extraneous noise as possible...stop! Now reverse the direction. Keep going. Keep going. Stop. Go back the other way...... stop. Push the dial assembly down until you hear a latch pop."

Tol did this and the door swung open.

"I think I've said this before, but sometimes you're pretty handy to have around, Petey."

"I rejoice in that affirmation. Truly."

Inside the safe lay a stack of precisely the things Tol had been sent to bring back. He felt around in the tool satchel and pulled out a waterproof bag to minimize any ill effects from the ascent. Once all of the storage blocks he could locate were securely packaged and the bag sealed, Tol took one last long look around the strange little alien grotto and stepped back into the airlock. He could not get the inner door to close fully due to debris in the tracks and frame, so the odds were good that the capsule preserved intact for so long would now be flooded with salt water when the outer hatch was opened. It had fulfilled its purpose, however,

Boogla was ecstatic at Tol's success. She carefully loaded the storage blocks into a heavy-duty case for transport back to Goblinopolis. Tol wanted to go back to the *Kell-Joma*, but he figured by the time he could return via conventional transport the operation would be a dim memory, so he just sailed along with Boogla. They were taking the long way around the tip of Esmia so they could dock at Port Zog and cut the carriage ride to a minimum. That meant five and a half days at sea even at flank speed.

The evening of the third day out from Flam found Tol sitting on a deck chair watching the last sunset. He was pondering what Petey had said about him being *something beyond goblin now*. He looked at his hands and stared out across the rolling blue Sea of Fleriz. He didn't perceive any differences, he told himself—yet something deep down disagreed. He felt anger boiling up at whatever twist of fate was responsible for changing him, yanking him out of the cocoon of familiarity and habit he'd built around his life.

Tol wasn't certain what aspect of this new and wholly unsolicited development made him the most leery, but he had a hunch it had to do with magic being way outside his comfort zone. He'd always regarded mages as people who fiddled around with invisible and dangerously unreliable forces he didn't even pretend to understand; Prond's near-disaster at Selpla's birthday party offered a prime example. Yet, he reluctantly admitted, he had somehow been responsible for averting that magical meltdown, or rather freeze-up, although he had no idea how he'd accomplished that. It was almost as though someone else had taken control over him for a few moments...

He realized in a flash of insight that this perceived loss of control was at the root of his misgivings. Tol had spent a lifetime maintaining exquisite direction over his body and mind, at least as far as he was concerned. Even imagining allowing another entity to act or speak through him put him in a cold sweat. The problem was, he had no idea how to stop it from happening again. He was not in control.

This line of reasoning was disturbing him too much, so Tol took a walk along the deck to clear his thoughts. Two of N'plork's three moons were up now, shimmering pastel orange and gold in calm pelagic reflection. They were making close to forty knots, which meant that any exposed areas of the deck were quite windy. He made his way to the foredeck rail above the prow and stood there with the brim of his 'civvy' hat pulled down low to ward off some of the strong breeze.

He started thinking about Selpla. That always calmed his mind and lifted his spirits. He began to have...fantasies about her that escalated in intensity with time. At one point he closed his eyes to heighten the sensation and when he opened them again he was quite literally in her bedroom. He noticed that a stuffed animal she'd had since childhood was on a settee near the window rather than in its accustomed position on her bed. He could smell the familiar cocktail of scents unique to that location was well. Even the temperature was right: considerably warmer than the cold deck of the ship. He was so shocked and disoriented by the unexpected transition that he closed his eyes again to escape it.

The temperature dropped and the smell of the ocean returned. When at last he felt prepared to open his eyes her bedroom was gone, replaced by waves and undulating moonlight. Tol immediately told himself sharply that it had simply been an unusually vivid daydream. Part of him did not believe this, but for the sake of his own sanity he suppressed that disbelief, burying it under a thick blanket of rationalizations and scorn.

Selpla was out on assignment somewhere when he got back to Goblinopolis, which was just as well. For some strange and discomfiting reason, he didn't want to see her just yet. He needed to understand what was going on, and the only person who could help him with that was Oloi. Getting to him would be problematic, though. He'd given his summoning talisman back and the transcendent mage had yet to return it. On a wild urge Tol hopped in his pram and drove to the empty lot where the pub in which he'd first encountered Oloi had materialized what now seemed ages ago.

There was a sign informing passersby that upscale apartments would soon be constructed here, part of an initiative to revitalize the economically-depressed district immediately south of downtown. He felt a certain sadness at reading this, although he knew the physical location had very little connection with the illusionary pub itself. He parked and got out to walk the vacant space one final time before progress rendered it merely a terse footnote in the long history of his city. Not even a footnote, really—it had no significance at all to anyone but him.

Somehow, his footprints were still readable. There had been rain and wind and ice on many occasions since that day, not to mention numerous other visitors to add their own tracks over his; there was little logic to be found in the discovery. He had no doubt they were his nonetheless. The prints were a perfect match with his boots, and led both to and away from his rendezvous point with Oloi with aching familiarity. He walked in them as closely as possible, as though by doing so he might call more of that event back into existence.

When Tol reached the spot that had hosted the table where he'd first conversed with Oloi he stopped and closed his eyes, conjuring up as many details of that meeting as he could pull from his memory. When the odor of fried wrats suddenly assailed his nostrils he was oddly reluctant to open his eyes; cognitive dissonance had become one of his most primal fears of late. So long as he kept his eyes shut he was in a superpositional state: both in the ghostly pub and a simple vacant lot. Once he allowed light back onto his optic nerves the waveform would collapse and it would be one or the other.

With a start Tol realized he was not thinking like himself. He had no idea what "superpositional state" or "waveform" meant. Something was using his brain for its own cogitative purposes. Bewildered, angry, and feeling emotionally violated, Tol stumbled as quickly as he could back to his pram, staring only at the ground in front of him the entire way. He no longer wanted the truth.

Chapter Fifteen

Oloi sat motionless in the habitation he'd built for himself, deep in fifth-level meditation. He had been here for a long while from his point of view—not that time had any objective meaning here. He was drawing upon the cumulative wisdom of the Exxus, the shared body of knowledge contributed by every sentience residing in The Slice. There were tens of billions of them, scattered along the twelve billion light year-long ribbon of the Dark Energetic Continuum like water droplets.

An arcanelemental known as Ix had created a problem that Oloi had been commanded to deal with; namely, a goblin on the planet N'plork with no training in or proven aptitude for magic had been unavoidably granted deity-like arcane abilities. Oloi's assignment was to indoctrinate the goblin into his new powers and provide him with the mental tools needed to handle them wisely. It was not a mission he looked forward to carrying out. The goblin in question had very little interest in or use for magic.

Still, Oloi had a certain fondness for him. He was honest to a fault, courageous, and possessed of a simple, pure dedication to doing the right thing. He had performed a great service for his planet and The Slice itself, which was undoubtedly why the Lumeniles were so interested in his welfare. Oloi sighed and stood up. He would not accomplish anything further here.

Mages who transcend are essentially immortal, drawing sustenance from the fabric of The Slice itself. They are able to return to Primus, the physical world, for short periods dependent on the amount of manna they stash away in a shell of their former bodies. In extraordinary circumstances a sort of 'pipeline' can be established from The Slice to the physical shell in order to extend that time. The process required a bit of preparation, however, which Oloi began now.

Performing magic on Primus involves siphoning off manna—dark energy—from The Slice. High-level mages can establish quite large conduits for this purpose, but even an archmage cannot extend the life of one for very long. Transcended mages have unlimited access to manna while in The Slice, but are subject to the same limitations when acting on Primus. An elemental such as Ix, however, experiences no such limitations because elementals are extrusions of The Slice itself and therefore draw manna through an interdimensional gateway intrinsic to their own structural makeup. They carry The Slice with them at all times, in other words.

For mages the practice of magic requires developing extensive neural and, to a lesser extent, musculoskeletal pathways. Physical and mental patterns tied to specific expressions of dark energy are impressed upon them through years of constant repetition and practice. To the uninitiated magic can seem to violate the laws of physics, but in fact all arcane activity is subject to the same rigid limitations and mathematical characterization as the non-magical universe. The difference is that dark energy allows the mage to manipulate the framework in which that activity is taking place—in effect blending additional spatial and temporal dimensions into the mix. It is the addition of those extra degrees of freedom not available to non-mages that results in the apparent disregard of magical practitioners for the physical laws that define the normal world or mundanosphere.

In the end, Oloi decided to lay everything out for Tol as simply and honestly as he could and let him absorb it at his own pace. By now it must be apparent to him that *something* had happened. Elementals could bring events to pass simply by willing them into existence. Tol had doubtless stumbled over that phenomenon in some manner, although he probably did not understand what was happening or the underlying mechanism. Oloi could see he had been exposed to his new abilities because the artifacts of those encounters were plainly visible in the arcane fabric to anyone who knew how and where to look.

Finding Tol on Primus had been simple when he wore Oloi's summoning amulet. Now that he'd given it back one might presume that he would be much more difficult to locate, but as noted above that was not the case. Oloi found him in less than what would have been a quarter-hour on N'plork. The archmage considered his options and decided to coordinate his appearance with Tol's presence in either his office or home. The goblin seemed to be moving at present; probably in a pram. Once he became stationary again Oloi dropped in on him in his little bachelor apartment in Sebacea.

"Hello, Tol-u-ol."

"Um, hi, Oloi. I was just thinking about you a while ago."

"Here I am. We need to talk."

Tol looked down at his feet and was silent for a moment.

"Yeah, I guess we do."

"You go first, then," Oloi said.

It was a further few seconds before Tol finally spoke.

"Something's...happened to me. I'm not really in control of what I do or even think anymore. At first it made me mad, but now I'm gettin' sorta scared about it. I'm almost afraid to even leave the house anymore."

Oloi regarded him. "What you've undergone is going to take some getting used to, but once you do there's no reason for it to change your life if you don't want it to."

"So, you *do* know something about all this. I figured you might. Can you explain it to me?"

"You were effectively in the wrong place at the wrong time. Or, you were in the right place at the right time. Incredibly so, I would say. However you choose to view it, you have been granted something I'm not aware of any other biological organism in the universe possessing; at least, not in this galactic neighborhood. You are now part elemental."

Tol looked at him blankly. "And I'm supposed to know what that means?"

"No, not yet. An elemental is an entity that is able to use magic naturally, without any training or external equipment such as talismans, specula, and so on. You were transported to The Slice by a poorly-configured teleport gateway and the result was a dangerous destabilization that could have had disastrous results for both The Slice and N'plork if not contained. The Slice has a group of creatures—I guess you could think of them as guardians—that serve to keep things running smoothly and correct imbalances that occur. Here on N'plork they are called arcanelementals. One of them came to take care of the problem caused when the teleport sent you into The Slice with no exit point. Since he needed to return you to the physical plane as soon as possible he chose to give you the power to do it yourself."

"Super. So I can...what, zap myself to The Slice and back now? When does it wear off?"

"It doesn't, I'm afraid. And your abilities go far beyond translocation. You have been the recipient of what we call an *implantation*. Remember the stories of the parasciencers, the first mages on N'plork? They were given a similar but much more limited form of implantation in order to allow them to engage in magic without any formal training. Using that 'head start' they were then able to develop their skills at a very accelerated pace until they reached archmage level in only a few years. You could do the same, if you wanted."

Tol huffed in annoyance. "I don't want magical powers at *any* level. I just want to be a plain, garden-variety goblin."

"Tol, listen to me. You don't have any say in the matter as far as your abilities are concerned. I have been sent to help you understand and use them wisely. If you'll work with me I can show you how to keep them suppressed, if that is what you desire. It will require discipline and concentration, however. You are essentially an extension of The Slice itself now, with power even I don't fully comprehend. Make no mistake: that power can overwhelm you if you don't control it."

Tol sank down on his sofa, feeling very tired. "Why does all this hocus-pocus smek keep happening to me? I never asked to be the 'Chosen One' and I never asked to be magical. I'm just a cop trying to do a job."

Oloi nodded sympathetically. "I know, Tol. As I told you before, there are forces at work in the universe that none of us will ever be able to understand fully. We all have to play the hand we're dealt and yours just happens to have a lot of high cards in it. You can feel sorry for yourself, sure, but if I were you I'd look on the bright side. Embracing your elemental side will allow you to be the best cop who ever lived. There's literally not a criminal on N'plork who would stand a chance against you, if you learn how to use your abilities."

The goblin stood back up. "Fine. Let's get it over with so I can stop feeling so smekking helpless."

"That's the Tol I know and respect."

"Wait...don't you have to go recharge soon?"

"Not on this occasion. I'm prepared for an extended stay because it's going to take some time to do this right and I don't want to keep being interrupted."

Tol sighed. "I'm all yours."

* * * * *

"This convocation is begun," Ballop'ril announced to the several dozen mages assembled virtually via either electronic or magical remote connection. "As most of you are aware, I have called this meeting with the concurrence of the Loca Magineer to discuss the ramifications of a most unusual event: the creation of a naïf."

There was an audible mumbling as the mages talked amongst themselves across side channels connecting two or more of them in small conversational groups. One of the Rublosq Magi Superior spoke up.

"What evidence have you of this, archmage? Extraordinary

claims require extraordinary proof."

"Agreed. The subject in question stabilized and reversed an uncontrolled manna flux in front of a number of witnesses. Moreover, he has acquired an arcanic aura overnight."

"What manner of aura?" asked another mage.

"My apprentice captured an impression. Here it is."

Ballop'ril pressed a button on his console and a holographic image appeared in the air next to him. It featured a generic head and shoulders silhouette seemingly backlit by a diffuse golden radiance terminated in a three-quarters circle by a brilliantly sharp silver band.

The murmur rose to a din as the gathered mages expressed their disbelief.

"What are the specifics of this naïf, if he truly exists?" asked Kryptoq, the Oria Magineer.

"He is a goblin with no magical training. He was instrumental in defeating the transcendent mage Namni, who did a great deal of damage in Tragacanth during an attempt to monopolize access to the dark energy reservoir. We do not as yet understand the precipitating event leading to his naïf status, but I have been in contact with the Noil Emissary Oloi and he is working with the goblin to help him transition more safely and effectively."

"How can we be certain that even with a Noil's assistance this naïf will not endanger anyone? Who is he, precisely?"

Ballop'ril drew a deep breath. "His name is Tol-u-ol. He is a Knight of the Crimson, an Edict Enforcement Special Investigator, and brother to the King of Tragacanth."

Several of the mages nodded, recognizing the name.

"Those of you who are familiar with Sir Tol," added Cromalin, "Will know that he is highly principled and shows remarkable restraint for one in his occupation...at least most of the time."

"Even a principled goblin can be overwhelmed by the temptations the sudden considerable power being a naïf will offer," said one of the Ovinis mages.

"Which is why Oloi was sent to educate him," replied Ballop'ril. "I, too, will keep a watchful eye on him, as he lives in my nation."

"We must be vigilant. If he shows any sign of malefaction we must act quickly and definitively or great suffering could result."

"Agreed."

After the convocation had dissolved, Cromalin remained connected to speak with Ballop'ril privately.

"Tol-u-ol has confided in me that he seeks to bring Zizmziz to justice. At the time I warned him of the great personal risk any hostile encounter with that mage would entail. Now, I fear the damage that may result from that meeting will be far worse: perhaps even catastrophic. Zizmziz is a monster, and although he is not officially recognized as an archmage he has devised some means by which the powers he does possess are greatly magnified; I do not fully understand that mechanism, although I have my doubts that the so-called 'rete arcanis' is truly the source. If Tol is in fact a naïf with the legendary arcane abilities attributed to such entities, a conflict between them could be devastating."

"Our best defense is educating Tol on precisely what he is and is not capable of doing," Ballop'ril replied, "I know him well enough to understand that he neither trusts nor has any love for magic; I believe this innate antipathy may serve us well. When Oloi feels confident his mission is complete I will speak with him and report back."

"The stability and harmonious balance of the magical community on N'plork may well depend upon it."

*   *   *   *   *

Boogla stared at the mountain of data she'd pulled from the storage disks in a mixture of awe, excitement, and triumph. Oloi had given her some basic reference information for translating the strange language of the Morianellans into Goblish. That translation process was slow and often perplexing—their language seemed to have more idiosyncrasies and exceptions than rigid rules—but gradually she was building up an idea of the impressive depth and breadth of the archives before her.

Quite a lot of what they chose to preserve seemed to be literature. That made sense, when she thought about it. If they were trying to chronicle an entire culture, literature told the story more eloquently than mere facts and figures could hope to. It would take a long time to sort through and catalog all of this information by herself. She decided to contact Dr. Reoksa for help.

The good professor was deeply interested in the news that Boogla had brought the salvaged data archives back to Goblinopolis and hopped the next carriage for the capitol. Together they sorted the data that Boogla had extracted into broad categories and then began to drill down, trying to understand the meaning of the often difficult content. The semantics and terminology of this language were quite abstruse to them.

Eventually they translated everything they could, assigning a confidence factor to each translation and compiling a list of words, phrases, and concepts they wanted to ask Oloi, as a native speaker and descendent of the same society, to explain to them. Even without these clarifications, however, they learned a lot of fascinating things from the archive. They were reading about an alien intelligence, after all. While the implications were only just beginning to be realized, the orcs represented concrete proof that sentience had evolved somewhere else in the universe: on the other side of the galaxy, even. Further, that sentience had developed interstellar space flight capability over ten centums ago.

The knowledge that other sentient life existed was not poised to be the philosophical bombshell on N'plork that it might be elsewhere; the fact that sentients lived in The Slice had been known to the magical community for millennia. True, most of the ones with whom N'plorkians came into contact were originally from their own planet and so not aliens per se, but the arcanelementals who reputedly trained the first generation of N'plork's mages were creations of The Slice itself. Aliens, in other words.

Literature was common on N'plork. All sentients who developed written language, which was the vast majority of them, had some form of it. It was a natural outgrowth of the intersection of the story-telling urge and the need to express societal instincts in abstract form. Naturally, every intelligence approached that primal impulse somewhat differently. On N'plork literature was more didactic overall than on Earth—somewhat akin to the works of ancient Greece. Pure expository forms were quite rare, so the literary novels in the orc archive were especially intriguing to them.

Most of the documents they'd examined up to now had been in the same general logical area of the archive. Boogla was poking around in other places when she came across a large file that she deduced was a ship's operational log. It was full of technical terms they could not translate, but the timestamps were obvious. One of the oddest aspects they noted was the apparent addition of two extra hours to each day. The orcs must be using a 24-, rather than the normal 22-, hour day length, they concluded.

"Perhaps it has something to do with the fact that they were in the artificial environment of a spacecraft," Reoksa speculated, "Adding the extra hours may have served some purpose under those circumstances." Another item added to the list for Oloi's attention.

While they couldn't make out most of the technical details of the log entries, they did possess enough information to perform rough translations of the more common words. Even with substantial portions of the text intellectually unavailable, they could use context to figure out quite a lot of the meaning. After a few days of hard work, they invited Selpla over to share in the effort, as she had been the one to start this ball rolling with her discoveries in Nuvinis.

Selpla was immediately taken by the ship's logs. Her reporter's instincts kicked into high gear at the sight of them because they told a story she wanted to hear: how humans who became orcs got to

N'plork to begin with. She spent all evening trying to understand the last few pages of the log leading up to the landing on N'plork. She realized that she needed an interpreter not only for the language itself, but also for the conventions used. All roads led to Oloi (or Plåk, but the former seemed more accessible).

Even without the archmage's help, Selpla figured a few things out. The ship—a multigenerational colonization mission—had suffered some form of catastrophic mechanical issue that disabled it. After exhausting every possible means of repair, the crew felt they had no choice but to abandon ship, which was their eventual intent anyway. The colonization capsule, now serving as their emergency escape pod, was stocked with everything they would need to start a settlement and preserve the legacy of their civilization.

The escape capsule was able to operate in space and on the ocean, providing its occupants with a range of survival options. It was also equipped with a variety of sophisticated sensors that allowed it to, among other things, map the sentient populations of the planet and choose an unpopulated location for landing. Morianella was that location, chosen for its unique suitability for colonization. It was an extinct volcanic mount with rich soil, two decent harbors, and mild climate, situated in a prime spot for trading and fishing. Why, in fact, it had remained uninhabited until then was something of a mystery, especially given that it was effectively the southernmost island in the chain that constituted the continent of Litria.

When Boogla got back to her office there was a communication from the Sisters of the Code waiting for her on one of their encrypted channels. It contained the results of a complex analysis she had asked them to perform to help out the RPC forensic mages investigating her near-assassination. The Sisters were very protective of their members and Boogla was in many ways the matriarch of that clan, having inherited the position along with her name.

She thanked them for the information and looked it over

before forwarding it to the RPC's Arcane Unit. It was a brilliant piece of data mining and pattern analysis that teased out the magical signature of a specific mage from the web of obfuscation and false leads in which it had been cleverly entangled. She doubted anyone else on N'plork could have extracted this signature so cleanly and unequivocally: not even CoME. Somewhere, hopefully, this arcane fingerprint was on file and that mage could be interrogated to reveal the means by which the Palace RPC apparatus was disassembled so thoroughly and effectively.

The forensic mages were extremely pleased with the new information and promised to match the signature to a known magic user as soon as possible. Boogla nodded in satisfaction and started plowing through the work that had piled up while she was in the Paradiddle Islands. Mostly she had to deal with the often convoluted politics of the relationship between the monarchy and the magineering community, with the occasional foray into rumor-quashing or public relations. It was not nearly as engaging as her extracurricular search for answers concerning the orcs, but it was her job.

Chapter Sixteen

"All nodes are present, Elder," the technician charged with overseeing the Balom QuEST-Link system reported. Igra, the Grandmaster of the Punditi and Principal Elder of the Balom Enclave, nodded.

"Thank you. That comes as something of a surprise, although most certainly a welcome one. Please initiate the two-way links." He waited until the technician gave him the 'go' signal.

"Brothers and sisters of the noble bloodline, it is my privilege to bid you welcome to the first full session of the Round Table. Today, if all goes well, we shall begin the greatest event of our lives, if not the greatest since the Before Times. The ritual we shall undertake will activate the engrams encoded deep within our collective psyche; it will require participation from each enclave to achieve the full manifestation. Are there any questions from the Table members before we begin?"

"How confident are you that the Valtir has been set into motion?" asked one of the remote participants.

"All of the principal signs are present," Igra replied, "Nothing that has happened since the first has run contrary to the prophecies. Ultimately, however, we are here today to reach a consensus on that point. As Grandmaster of the Punditi my job is to inform the Elder Synod that events have transpired which fulfill the signs set forth in the Vaticination of the Valtir. Only you, as a body, can declare the Valtir Quest truly underway. That is our first matter for consideration."

The ensuing debate was spirited, continuing into the evening. When he finally called recess, Igra was tired but elated. Although they yet lacked clear consensus, considerable progress had been made. Once they had agreed that the Valtir quest was in play, they had to decide on the next step. This was the purpose of the engram, the existence of which had never actually been confirmed in totality.

The orcs of Fullia were keeping close tabs on the half-breed and his goblin companion who had begun the events leading to the Round Table. Their latest reports seemed to indicate a distinct paucity of further evidence of quest-related activity. Igra was beginning to believe their only purpose in this was to trigger the Round Table. The Valtir prophecy was, after all, a bit vague about the role the Uul would play in the larger quest. The Grandmaster experienced some difficulty sleeping that night, considering all of this.

The next day bright and early the links were reestablished and the proceedings continued. As morning turned into afternoon it became apparent to Igra that they were almost there. All that remained on his agenda was, in effect, a history lesson.

"While it is true that we do not know the precise location of Eithmorg," he began, "The Moreani are constantly searching and they have several strong possibilities."

"Are we even certain this 'Eithmorg' literally exists?" asked one of the Elders from Qoplebarq. "Or is it some form of metaphor or allegory?"

"The Punditi believe it to be a real place, where our history is maintained in secret, hidden away from the goblins and their ilk. The Vaticination states that we are to find the Valtir and return it to Eithmorg. The prophecies were written by orcs who were planning for the long-term survival of our race; it is doubtful they would include too much abstraction without any guide for translating it into concrete concepts."

"If that be the case, why were we not told exactly what this 'Valtir' was?"

Igra was composing his answer when he felt a curious sensation behind him and turned to see a strange figure standing there. It was a little bit on the translucent side and resembled a smoother-skinned orc. He jumped involuntarily, startled.

"Who...who are you?" he stammered.

"My name is Plåk, but you might know of me as the archmage

Blass."

Igra stood there blinking with a blank look on his face for a few moments until one of the other Punditi spoke up.

"The archmage Blass lived almost a thousand years ago, according to our histories. He was of the Before Times. You cannot be him."

"You obviously know little of magic. I am transcended. I have only a temporary corporeal shell. I live in The Slice."

"Why are you come before us only now, then? Why do you not appear as an orc?"

"I am human, as were your ancestors—before the Coalescence."

"The Coalescence? Was that a real event? We thought it some form of metaphor."

"It was quite real. When your human ancestors fled the *Isomer* in lifeboats, one of those ships landed in the Paradiddle Islands. Those people ended up on the coast of what is now Asmagon, near modern-day Jessmirto. On board was a geneticist: a scholar who studies the processes that make us appear the way we do. She realized that there were too few humans to maintain a viable breeding population, so she changed your genetic makeup to allow you to interbreed with goblins and produce fertile offspring. That is why you look like a cross between me and a goblin—you are precisely that."

There was much shouting and bickering amongst the assembled orcs at this point, but Plåk calmly held his ground until the noise died down. Igra had compiled a list of questions sent to him from other Elders.

"What is this 'Isomer' of which you speak? What did you mean by our ancestors fled from it?"

"I don't have a lot of time left here before I must return, so I'm just going to lay everything out for you. Your ancestors were aliens. They themselves were born in deep space on a colonizing ship called the *TCV*, or 'Terran Colonizing Vessel,' *Isomer*. *Their* ancestors originated on a planet called Terra, or Earth, two thirds of the way out along a spiral band on the other side of our galaxy: so very far away from here that no one in this meeting other than me could possibly comprehend the distance. There was a serious accident on board this ship, so serious that it was decided to place the ship in orbit around the nearest habitable planet and abandon the vessel in two lifeboats to settle on it and start a colony. The lifeboats got separated during the descent. One—the boat carrying your ancestors—apparently landed near Flam. The other landed near what was then the uninhabited island of Morianella."

"Is that the one your ancestors were on?" asked Igra.

"Not my ancestors: me. *I* was born in deep space aboard the *Isomer*, which is why I know so much about it."

"This is a lot for us to take in at once. Why, exactly, did you choose this time and place to tell us all of this?"

"Because I know about the Valtir quest and I know what the rest of the world is going to think when they see you out roaming around conducting it. I also know that the stories about orc instability and aggression are complete fabrications. More to the point, someone else is figuring that out now, someone in a position to change everything about orc society for the better. Her name is Boogla; she is the wife of the King of Tragacanth and a goblin. When she comes to you for information—and she will—treat her with respect and hospitality, as a friend and not an enemy. She is the first goblin with any influence to realize that you have been persecuted unjustly for centums. She is vital to the betterment of the orc condition."

"You know that we are not violent and psychotic, then? Do you know why those not of the noble blood regard us as such?"

"Sadly, I do. And I'm beginning to think I understand how it came to be. I am actually involved in that saga, although not directly. I haven't put all the pieces together yet, but I felt compelled to come here today to make certain that you do not endanger the best chance the orcs have ever had for a normal life. Treat with Boogla fairly and openly and she will reciprocate. I must return to

The Slice now. I will monitor your progress and assist further where I may. Good fortune to you all and farewell."

He dissipated in a shower of fine silver sparkles. Igra stared at the spot in silence for a few moments before turning back to the Round Table members.

"I propose," he said after a further moment, "That we take a recess to absorb this new information and resume in two hours."

*   *   *   *   *

Plåk headed to Jessmirto as soon as he had recharged in The Slice. He had on his previous visit established the location of the ancient human colony; now he was looking for answers. Specifically, he was trying to track Iwo. He'd always presumed that he'd been lost with Morianella, since he was not among those he'd teleported to Woklopen, but he did now recall that the Magus Incipius had disappeared abruptly a few days before the disaster.

An Incipius would not be capable of teleporting himself the 2,500 km to the southern tip of Grosyem, the nearest landmass to Morianella, without a template, but it's just barely possible that he had a teleportation talisman or something similar at his disposal. The other possibility was that he left by conventional means. Either way, was the fact that he saved himself just in time coincidence, or something else? And where did he end up?

There were no written archives that Plåk could find in the sparse buried remains of that ancient settlement—at least at first. Everything was charred, whether by some wildfire that had swept in from the interior grasslands or a deliberate act was impossible to say. He stuck to it, though, and on the third visit finally hit something of interest. From a deep hole he levitated a metal box: the outer surface was a thick layer of rust and carbonized scorching, but once he got past all that he could see that the interior space was not similarly compromised. He peered inside and was rewarded with a thick sheaf of what appeared to be reports concerning the state of the colony, including supplies, foodstuffs, and other logistical records.

Being only semi-corporeal, Plåk couldn't actually manipulate the papers individually unless he was willing to invest more manna in solidity—but that would shorten the time he had on Primus, as he'd already used up quite a bit uncovering and opening the cache. He decided to teleport them out of the box and transfer the stack to someone who could go through it with the necessary dedication. A few seconds later the documents materialized on Boogla's desk, followed immediately by the appearance of the archmage himself.

While archmage Plåk was not subject to damage from any weapon in the RPC's arsenal, he was nevertheless careful to appear in a manner that minimalized their emotional trauma. In this case he announced himself before becoming visible, so that Boogla and her RPC contingent were expecting his sudden appearance.

"Welcome, archmage. To what do I owe the honor of your visit?" Boogla asked cordially.

"That pile of papers on the corner of your desk there," Plåk replied, pointing, "Is just about all I could find that's left of the lesser-known human colony just north of present-day Jessmirto in Asmagon. When you go through it you will more than likely find evidence, albeit perhaps indirect, of the genetic manipulation that turned humans into orcs. I have strong reason to believe this colony was composed of the people who escaped in the other lifeboat that launched from the *Isomer* at the same time as mine. I would very, very much appreciate an electronic version of the contents that I could upload into The Slice."

Boogla blinked. She hadn't noticed the papers until now. "You can...upload data into The Slice? How does that work?"

"I can't manipulate solid objects easily here on Primus. I can, however, convert electromagnetic impulses into a form I can access in The Slice. Essentially I can dump the data stream into a type of external storage that operates on a principle similar to binary mathematics, except in a nine-dimensional matrix. It's pretty esoteric. The important thing is that if you digitize data, I can use it."

"Wow. That's pretty exciting. I'll be happy to get it all converted for you. Is this just for historical curiosity, or are you looking for something specific?"

"Very specific. I'm looking for the missing piece of your puzzle: the connection between humans and the irrational prejudice against orcs. I'm pretty sure I know what it is, but I need some more concrete links to corroborate my suspicions."

"I don't suppose you'd be willing to let me in on the identity of your suspected culprit or culprits?"

"I already did. I just didn't realize it at the time. See ya."

After Plåk's shimmers had dissipated, Boogla picked up the pile of obviously very old parchments he'd left behind with something approaching reverence. This was not information she'd expected, which made it all the more interesting. She'd already made up her mind some time ago who the likely instigator of all this orc-centric mayhem was; being able to add another block to the platform of her investigation would nevertheless be most excellent—especially if it offered new evidence. She wondered if her perp and Plåk's were the same.

While she was still far from fluent, Boogla had a certain aptitude for languages and she was steadily becoming more conversant with the strange writing of the humans. Being a totally alien script, of course, meant it had no real cognates to speak of with Goblish. Even the most basic mechanics were quite foreign to a native of N'plork. It did give Boogla some insight into the myriad ways in which sentient species with similar vocal apparatus could create a complex system of semiotics and semantics, however.

Oloi and Plåk had both managed to master Goblish with human brains and vocal chords, although they had centums to practice and of course neither was constrained by anatomy any longer. She wondered about anatomical limitations, but since the Morianellans enjoyed a thriving trade with the native races long before electronic communications had been invented, it was obvious some form of verbal discourse must have been possible.

Once she'd scanned and converted the rather sizeable stack of documents, she sent them to a network address Plåk had provided that somehow interfaced with The Slice itself via a method she didn't understand very well. Magic was no doubt involved—or perhaps a human technology so far advanced of hers it appeared to be magic. It struck her that the distinction made little difference.

*   *   *   *   *

"As you can see, High Mage, construction on the complex is proceeding well. Your headquarters installation should be ready for occupancy by the end of next week. The central Arcanium is roughly half-completed; we expect it to be finished in approximately four months."

Zizmziz, smartly dressed in tight-fitting black punctuated by blue lightning bolts and sporting a long blue cape with the Umbral logo embroidered on it, was silent for a few moments as he surveyed the scene. Finally he nodded.

"You've made satisfactory progress so far. I caution you against complacency, however. My tolerance for unrealistic estimates of time or money is exceedingly limited."

"We understand, High Mage. Every effort has been made to present you with estimates based on the best information available. Unforeseen circumstances can arise, but we are prepared to handle them in the most expeditious manner possible."

"I sincerely hope so, for your sake. I don't believe in 'unforeseen circumstances.' An unforeseen event is indicative of poor planning, nothing more."

At this, Zizmziz turned and left the construction overseer standing there. As the mage walked away the rigid smile on the overseer's face snapped off like a light being extinguished and was replaced by something more akin to a scowl. He did not like the pretentious mage, but his job was to see to it that the construction firm by which he was employed did a job acceptable to the customer. Feeling affection or even basic respect for said customer was not required.

Zizmziz headed for the tower that housed his new headquarters. The cobblestone walkway was lined with exotic vegetation and immaculately sculpted topiaries, but he scarcely noticed them. He had eyes only for the tower itself; specifically, the rotunda-like penthouse suite surmounted by a narrow cylinder of stone that brought the total height of the structure to over a hundred meters. He circled around the base, staring intently up at the top level as he walked. Spaced evenly around the perimeter of the penthouse were rectangular openings about a half-meter tall and twenty centimeters wide. They appeared to be 'kill-holes:' slots cut to allow crossbows to fire through for defensive purposes. They were a little too narrow for that purpose, conventionally.

The mage knew the real reason for the holes' existence; they were not designed for crossbows. He had after centums of searching finally succeeded in locating the raw ingredients for a weapon that would change the face of N'plorkian society and place him in an unquestioned position of leadership. The citizenry of every nation would admire him; those that did not would fear him. He cared little which it was, so long as he garnered the respect and deference he felt was his due.

He had stored raw materials gathered laboriously by servants sent to the far corners of the world in separate highly secure rooms in the catacombs beneath his new complex. In the center of those underground spaces was a chamber he'd designed as a laboratory. Anticipating the potential 'energetic' nature of experiments he'd be conducting there, the walls were twice as thick as elsewhere and a series of vents to the surface were installed to help equalize pressure and vent off smoke or toxic gases.

Stacked on shelves on one end were casks of raw materials: charcoal from special furnaces in the next room over, sulfur, and nitron. A reliable source for this last had taken him many years of scouring the planet to locate. He found it at last in caves on the southern end of the Tellibon Mountains near Yiucrax in central Asmagon. The nitron itself was impure and had to be carefully leached with potash to extract the useful reagent. The sulfur he collected from volcanic vents on peaks in central Spleroste.

With these three substances he planned to change the balance of power on N'plork forever.

*   *   *   *   *

Prond woke suddenly from a dream of Rebrugge. Thoughts of that municipality, or at least the small corner of it that had been dramatically distorted by the rifting event, occupied virtually all of his waking and now even apparently nighttime hours. He had spent so much time either being there or writing about it that he sometimes had difficulty remembering what life had been like before 'The Event.'

Now he was back at the Schola Arcanium and spending twelve hours a day writing his disquisition. In less than a week he was to present and defend it to the panel of scholars at Sutha Arts Collegium. After that would come the trial for Magus Incipius, followed by the final oral examination for Doctor of Apotropaic Arts. Not the original timeline, to be sure, but he and Ballop'ril had agreed this was the best way to proceed now. Things were moving very fast in his life. Despite the heavy workload, Prond was happy with his lot. Ballop'ril's rigorous training and emphasis on deep self-awareness had instilled considerable confidence in his own abilities.

Once the Incipius trial was complete and he had passed the oral exam for DAA, Prond looked forward to a few years of relative quiet before he was ready to undergo the trial for Magus Arcanis/Academicus. While the intervals between lower-level trials and between Mage and Magus could be relatively short, depending on the acumen of the student and the judgment of the mentoring

216

Magus, Arcanis, Superior, and Archmage intervals were accounted in years or, for archmage particularly, even decades.

No one since the Council of Mages (later absorbed into CoME) had first been established over two millennia prior had ever advanced to Archmage in under twenty years, and for good reason. The power possessed by an Archmage is so great that it takes tremendous mental and physical discipline to control it. Those neural pathways require years of constant repetition to establish. Students typically attain Magus Incipius in three to five years of full-time study. The interval between Incipius and Arcanis is usually around three more years. Arcanis to Superior progression seldom occurs in fewer than five years; Superior to Archmage requires at least ten more.

Few Magi feel that advancement to Archmage was worth the effort; in fact, there were only twenty-five registered Archmages on the entire planet at present. Even the Tragacanthan Magineers were only Magi Superior, with the exception of Cromalin. Archmages were in effect irrevocably committed to magic, in that the constant influence of the arcane permanently modifies their physiology and psychology. Archmages can no more function without magic than they can without air or water. It becomes an indispensable part of their makeup. There is some evidence to suggest that metabolic pathways and even genetic material itself are altered by a lifetime of continuous magic use at the archmage level.

As he sat in his tiny, sparsely furnished cell with manuscripts and texts spread all around, Prond took a short break to reflect on his journey. It seemed an age ago now that he'd trained as a cinematographer and worked with Selpla, Drin, and Lom on the videoz news crew. Memories of his former life seemed more like some story he'd read than events that actually happened to him personally. He chuckled as he remembered clonking that chimera on the head to get him off the back of the news dray down in Dreadmost during that otherworldly magical flood. He also remembered that Selpla owed him a case of razzle, not that he really drank these days.

The monograph he'd written on the Rebrugge Event was the most intense effort Prond had ever put forth on anything in his life. He'd done his very best to cover every last detail as thoroughly as possible. Oloi's book had been extremely helpful; Prond was careful not to use any of the Archmage's research without full credit being given.

Ballop'ril had read and commented on every draft along the way and seemed convinced that the disquisition was both complete and well-written. Prond was more skeptical, but he had no prior experience for comparison. At any rate, he was to turn the final paper over tomorrow so that his examining committee could, presuming they accepted it, prepare an oral exam based on his research findings and conclusions. He rubbed his eyes and started wading through one more time.

Chapter Seventeen

Tol pushed the 'Do Not Disturb' button on his comm and offered Oloi a cup of stankabru out of social habit, even though he knew his guest would refuse. Eating or drinking used up manna and offered no nutritional benefit to a transcendent. Mostly he was just trying to prepare himself for what he expected would be the ordeal to come. Tol sighed and sat down at his little kitchen table.

"I'm going to start," Oloi said when Tol seemed comfortable and attentive, "By trying to explain what has happened to make you who you now are. To do that I need to give you a little bit of background concerning the way magic works. What we call 'magic' really isn't. There is nothing magical about the way magic works. Magic is manipulation of energy, pure and simple. It doesn't violate any laws of physics or thermodynamics. It's just that magic operates using forces that are not accessible in a manner native to the prime plane. You need some form of conduit to the Dark Energetic Continuum, The Slice, in order to acquire and channel the manna necessary to perform magic spells. New mages must rely on specula arcanis—manna reservoirs—but establish larger and longer-lasting conduits as they progress in skill. These reservoirs and conduits are necessary because the energy used by mages is of a type that does not exist here on Primus.

When mages employ magic, they use their own bodies as antennas to direct the flow of manna in such a way as to accomplish some task. They visualize what they want to see happen and construct a mental template of it. It requires very specific neural pathways built up over years of constant repetition to be successful. This is called *directive* magic.

There is, however, another means by which magical energies can be manipulated: elementalism. That path is not open to magic users under normal circumstances, but there are a few examples on

N'plork, most notably the titans. You can think of elemental magic as akin to that provided by phylacteries or talismans: 'canned' magic, if you like. Creatures of Primus who employ elemental magic are limited to a single spell or at best a small set of related ones, such as the storm titans' abilities to store and channel electrical energy from atmospheric disturbances. Titans are born with these templates already embedded in their neural cortex, although they must be shown by their elders how to make use of them most effectively.

The entity you encountered during your brief sojourn in The Slice was an arcanelemental known as Ix. He and his kind are manifestations of the dark energetic continuum itself. They are living creatures in most ways, but they rely entirely on The Slice for their metabolic requirements, you might say. For them magic use is no more difficult or extraordinary than is breathing. You, in many ways, are now one of them."

Tol stirred uneasily and Oloi hastened to continue.

"There are important differences between you and them; I want to emphasize this point. An arcanelemental really has no choice in the matter of magic use; magic is simply how they accomplish virtually everything. You, on the other hand, may choose to use magic or not, at least in most circumstances. One of my purposes in coming here today is to train you how to make that choice."

"What do you mean, 'at least in most circumstances'? Are you saying there will be times when I use magic whether I want to or not?" Tol asked, frowning.

"At your current level of awareness and control, most definitely," Oloi replied. "It's already happened on several occasions, as you are no doubt aware."

Tol sighed and nodded. "Yeah, I guess it has. So, what can I do about it?"

"We're going to indulge in a modified and greatly abbreviated version of some of the exercises we put young mages through when we teach them to access mental arcane templates. The first step is to identify your 'spell trigger.' That's a word, object, or phrase you use as the anchor point for reliably accessing the part of your brain that controls your magical abilities. You need to choose something that you can remember easily, but which has no pre-existing memory attached to it. You can't use a childhood pet you felt strongly for, as an example, or the name of a friend, because the memories associated with those things will divert you from the path you're trying to take. The best approach I've found is to make your trigger a word you've always found amusing or odd because of the way it sounds. Mine was 'aardvark,' which is a strange animal from my home planet."

"An odd word, eh?" Tol scratched under his left ear. "How about...human?"

Oloi seemed taken aback. "Oh. Well, all right. If that word is easy for you to remember, then we can work with that. Understand, though, that if someone starts using your trigger word in a conversation you will have to concentrate to avoid having it take you someplace you might not want to go."

"Not a problem. Other than you and Plåk, who on N'plork even knows it, at least that I'm ever likely to run into?"

"Point taken. Now, we're going to learn a little about meditation, after which we'll start exploring your arcane abilities and associating them with your trigger. If you need to use the facilities, this would be a great time."

When Tol returned, they got down to serious business. Oloi took Tol through the process of achieving a meditative state; once he had made satisfactory progress in that exercise they began to probe the depth and breadth of Tol's newfound magical talents.

"The arcane community refers to people such you as *naïfs*. A naïf is someone who has achieved arcane powers by higher intervention, rather than study and practice."

"Are there a lot of us around?" Tol asked, surprised.

"No. And most who were given that label throughout history had only one or two limited abilities, quite unlike your broad capacity. Nevertheless, it is the existing category in which you fit.

The reason the Council of Mages found it useful to invent that designation is that, while traditional mages are taught to channel their use of magic with tight control, naïfs have not the benefit of such education and are therefore often a danger to themselves and others. We're here to make certain that will not be the case with you."

"So long as you teach me how to avoid using magic at all, that won't be a problem," replied Tol.

"I will do what I can. But if your implantation is as deep as I suspect, that might be a very tall order. You will engage in magic in some instances when you have little to no conscious control over your actions."

Tol looked exasperated. "I didn't ask for any of this. Why does this stuff happen to me?"

"Fate," Oloi answered after a moment, "Never asks permission and it's not concerned with what *you* want. But I have observed over the centums that ultimately it always has a purpose. You were chosen to rid the world of Namni and I strongly suspect Fate has a further role for you now. At any rate, there's nothing I or even the Lumeniles can do to reverse this change. Like it or not, you are now a very powerful creature of elemental magic."

"But not powerful enough to *stop* being one."

"No. Not while you live, at any rate."

"Yeah, well, the alternative has never been an option that interested me much."

"Many people are quite happy about that, Tol."

"I can think of a few who probably aren't," Tol replied with a wry grin.

Once Oloi was satisfied Tol knew how to access his 'magical control center,' they moved on to an exploration of precisely what his arcane capabilities encompassed. They were impressive. He could essentially manipulate the flow of both time and space at will, albeit on a local scale, as well as transfer matter from place to place and even convert it from one state to another.

"The bottom line, Tol," Oloi summed up when they were approaching the expiration of his time on Primus, "Is that you are at least at the level of archmage—or beyond—in many respects. You must be extraordinarily careful not to allow this power to corrupt you, or to escape your firm control. Traditionally-trained archmages have two decades or more to learn these lessons; you have not been granted that luxury. There are very few people on N'plork who could handle this awesome responsibility, but I believe you to be one of them. I will always be there to help you whenever you feel you need me. This is, in fact, part of my 'job' these days, if you want to think of it that way."

Tol shook his head. "I'll do my best, but that's a lot to pile on my plate at once. My preference would be to ignore magic altogether. I've never had much liking for this hocus-pocus stuff. I prefer forces I can see and relate to."

"Understood and appreciated. With the tools you now have, you might be able to pull that off, at least for the most part. It is critically important if that is your goal to continue suppressing the arcane flow when you feel it beginning, as we practiced. Farewell for now, Tol, and again, don't hesitate to call on me if you feel the need. You will no longer require the talisman to do so; just concentrate on my name."

After Oloi vanished Tol sat in his living room for a long while, reflecting on life and fate. He could never have begun to guess that anything of this sort would befall him. He had seemed destined to finish out his career in EE and then retire, spending the remainder of his days sitting around playing cartes and dot blocks in the same Auld Fellows Club his grandfather had frequented at the corner of Berquin and Jiggla, across from the scrapyard. Now, who knew? Was there a home for retired naïfs? Were there any other naïfs *in* Tragacanth, for that matter? He shook his head and heaved his heaviest sigh.

Tol glanced at the clock on the wall and leapt to his feet. He was supposed to meet Selpla at the station where she worked in fifteen minutes! He threw on his overjack and bolted out the door to his pram. On the way Tol thought a lot about how his new handicap, as he thought of it, was going to affect his life and relationship with Selpla. He realized that Selpla was the real reason he did just about everything these days.

On the way to the station, Tol wondered how much about this naïf nonsense he should tell her. He didn't want to keep secrets from Selpla unnecessarily, but he also wasn't sure he could explain things with anything resembling lucidity. He finally decided simply to wing it, as usual. Selpla had spent the day doing interviews for an investigative report on a local labor dispute and she was tired. That worked in Tol's favor; when Selpla was tired she was not very inquisitive.

Selpla had semi-witnessed Tol's 'correction' of Prond's mistake and was aware of the extraordinary circumstances surrounding his transport from the Ustrad Sea to the Paradiddle Islands. She knew there was *something* going on with him, but Tol had gotten himself entangled with some powerful magic users of late; the fact that he was getting teleported all around the planet did not seem as unusual as it might have otherwise. The incident with Prond was anomalous, admittedly, but she was sure there was a rational, mundane explanation buried there somewhere. She was in love with the big guy, after all.

"How did your meeting with Oloi go?" she asked as they sat on her couch watching videoz later that evening.

Tol shrugged. "Fine. He explained some stuff about the magical hoo-hah that's been happening to me. I figure if I just ignore it, it will all go away eventually."

Selpla looked into his eyes for a long moment before replying. "You're a lot smarter than you let on, Tol; maybe even smarter than you yourself realize. I don't pretend to know what's going on with you, but one thing I do know is that you'll deal with it. Just remember that I love you and I'll do whatever it takes to make things easier for you."

Tol broke into a grin. "I love you, too. There ain't nothin' on N'plork or The Slice or anywhere else that can change that. This smek's only gonna be a problem if I let it be one. Let's watch that video you rented and snuggle." Selpla saw nothing in that suggestion to debate.

*　　*　　*　　*　　*

Plåk sat on a curious curved seat carved from a substance that resembled silver gelatin right down to the jiggling and stared in rapt concentration at numbers and letters floating before his face embedded in half-meter translucent cubes. He was crunching the Jessmirto colony data supplied by Boogla, looking for some very specific information. At long last he found it.

It was quite obvious to him now that *Isomer* lifeboat Bravo had in fact ended up disabled off the coast of Flam. The occupants decided that the island was not a good place to settle, for whatever reasons, and migrated over to the mainland of Asmagon, a dozen or so kilometers north of the modestly-sized city of Jessmirto, at that time the southern regional administrative center of the mighty Merton Empire. They established a small colony there. The records showed it to have been doing relatively well in most all respects until...something happened.

The events that precipitated the abrupt failure of the colony were not obvious in its surviving records. That wasn't too surprising: not that many civilizations comprehend and document what is killing them as it happens. Usually the culprit is a fatal medley of economic, social, and environmental woes that gradually whittle away at the settlement's resources, eroding its core values until there is not enough substance left to prevent it collapsing.

A careful researcher can, with sufficient data, track the telltale harbingers of this dissolution but the process is painstaking and difficult. Plåk was highly motivated here, though, and time was not an issue for a transcendent. He was determined to figure out what went wrong—not only because these were 'his people,' but also because he had a very strong suspicion concerning the root cause and if he was correct, it was personal.

He began by trying to construct a list of the actual members of the colony, which they apparently named 'Nusterton' after Alonse Nuster, the captain of the *Isomer*. The colonists had conducted censuses every five years, so that part was relatively simple. Looking at the manifest of names Plåk recognized a number of them. The old memories came flooding back, although in a different way than they did when he still possessed a neural cortex. The 'external storage' of The Slice was incorruptible itself, but it could only provide raw data of the same quality extracted from the organic brain during transcendence. Memories that were incomplete or hazy remained that way, but access to them was crystal clear and instantaneous; it was rather like watching a shaky old black-and-white film via an ultra-high definition video feed. Imperfect recollections notwithstanding, Plåk did find himself adrift on a sea of long-suppressed reminiscence. These were, however, people he had known a lifetime—make that many lifetimes—ago, in a very different existence.

The final data points in the Nusterton archive formed a tangled jumble of contradictory entries of concerns about the community's water supply and some mysterious malady that struck with no warning. Among the symptoms of that illness seemed to be confusion and degradation of motor skills; the last few days' worth of journal entries were increasingly difficult to decipher.

Plåk read and re-read the archives, looking for any clues whatever to the fate of the colonists. He had almost given up on solving the conundrum when he discovered a separate document chronicling the genetic experimentation that led to the creation of the first human-goblin hybrids that became known as orcs. While reasonably engaging in and of itself, the salient moment for Plåk came as he scanned the list of people assisting with the effort. Under 'Support Personnel' he found a single entry for 'Arcane Consultant:'

P. Iwo.

Since he had all of these records in digital format now, thanks to Boogla, it was a simple matter to search the entire archive for that name. It only turned up twice: once in the genetics account and again in port records. The colonists had brought the shipboard time-measuring system with them—it took Plåk a little while to remember how it worked—but finally he was able to match up their dates with the N'plorkian calendar.

From his best analysis it appeared that the colony had suffered its ignominious demise less than two months after the destruction of Morianella. Philmon Iwo had arrived in Nusterton almost simultaneous with that latter catastrophe, demonstrating that this is where he had fled after substituting the fateful page in the *Codex Lapidismotus*. This suggested that he knew about Nusterton beforehand, which Plåk found quite odd, since he had never heard any news concerning the fate of the other lifeboat. Had Iwo died there along with the rest of the original human inhabitants? Plåk's overwhelming intuitive feeling was that he had not. Whatever else he might be, the guy was a survivor.

Presuming he had indeed avoided whatever it was that wiped out the Nustertonians, Iwo must have moved on. Plåk's guess was that he had fled into Jessmirto, the nearest habitation of any significant size. That doesn't mean he stayed there for any length of time, of course. Tracking him after Nusterton was going to be a monumental undertaking. Then he remembered that Boogla had said something about having seen a reference to a *P. Iwo* in the immigration records of Neripa. Time to pay her another visit.

Plåk caught up with her eating lunch with Aspet. As usual, the archmage ignored the RPC's threatening response to his sudden materialization nearby. Aspet waved them off.

"Sorry to intrude, folks, but I have some new info to share with Her Excellency concerning Philmon Iwo. You said you found immigration records with that name on them in Lardonica, yes?"

Aspet grinned. "Nice to see you, too, Plåk."

"Correct," Boogla answered him, "He was listed as having sailed from Nar Braylov in Ovinis, although there was no other information besides that. What did you discover?"

"He arrived at the now-defunct human colony of Nusterton outside Jessmirto at approximately the same time that the Morianella disaster took place."

"What happened to Nusterton?" she asked.

"It was wiped out by some sort of disease or toxin. I presume Iwo traveled from there to Nar Braylov, although not necessarily directly."

"Odd how he seems to leave dead people in his wake, isn't it?" observed Aspet.

"Yes. Not to mention very, very suspicious. I am now committed to finding out where he ended up."

"Wherever it is, he's long dead by now."

"You would think so," Plåk replied grimly, "But I'm not so sure of that."

"How could a...human still be alive? What's the life expectancy of your species?" inquired Aspet.

"Certainly not this long. But I don't think Iwo has been human for some centums."

"What is he, then? Orc?"

"I don't know yet—but I *will* find out. And if he is still alive, he has a lot of accounting to do."

"As possibly the greatest mass-murderer in history, in fact."

"Thanks for the info," Plåk said. "I'm off to Nar Braylov now." He sparkled away.

"Sounds like he's got a definite agenda there," Aspet remarked.

"Well, if you had lived for nearly a thousand years with the idea you'd been inadvertently responsible for the destruction of an entire island civilization and then discovered that you'd actually been set up, you'd probably be pretty sore about it, too."

"I suppose I would. So, how about dessert?"

Chapter Eighteen

Nar Braylov sits on the northeast coast of Ovinis, roughly a thousand kilometers below the broad mouth of the Zongat River that forms the border between Tragacanth and Galanga. It is a tropical port city situated almost directly on the equator of N'plork and serves as a major shipping hub, as the Arctal and Austral oceanic currents are equally accessible from its deep-water harbor. It straddles one of the world's great estuaries, where the relatively short but exceedingly capacious Hyvvlik River meets the sea, carrying hundreds of thousands of tons of alluvium down from the Prablu Mountains. Lining the mouth of the river were numerous mining camps where this heavily-enriched silt is stripped of its valuable minerals.

The ships that cart away this geological bounty to industrial plants worldwide are forced to execute a sharp turn in order to dock at the terminus of the carriage line over which most of the ore is transported. This 'Hyvvlik Maneuver' requires the careful supervision of a specially-trained pilot, fewer than a dozen of which were authorized by the Nar Braylov Harbormaster.

Plåk knew that the odds were against him finding immigration records from nine centums ago, despite Boogla's unexpected successes in Neripa. He had an advantage that Boogla did not, however: magic. Even magic could not resurrect long-destroyed data, but it could help reveal hidden parchments and log books. He didn't have to ask permission to search through the records, either, as he could accomplish that by remote viewing.

Boogla had found a reference to Iwo in the Neripa immigration logs that indicated he'd sailed from Nar Braylov. Plåk felt compelled to fill in as many blanks in Iwo's path as possible. Partly he was trying to document the movements of an ancient criminal for historical reasons, but more important to him personally was a deep conviction that the threat Iwo posed was not yet ameliorated.

He didn't have any empirical reasoning for this feeling, but it was too strong to ignore.

He searched for several days, on and off, but could not locate any local immigration logs from that period. That could mean that Iwo simply passed through as a transit passenger and therefore did not declare as an immigrant. However, the timeline Plåk had constructed based on his own recollections and the data supplied by Boogla contained a significant discrepancy if Iwo had spent only enough time in Nar Braylov to book further passage to Neripa. Also, since the immigration logs from Neripa had indicated Nar Braylov as being Iwo's habitation of record, he must have attained some level of citizenship in Ovinis prior to boarding the ship for Lardonica. Even accomplished liars have to provide some minimal proof of their claims on occasion.

If he couldn't pinpoint Iwo's arrival in Nar Braylov, perhaps Plåk could find some trace of his residency in the town's official documents. Citizenship records seemed a logical place to begin that search. He headed over to the hall of municipal records.

When you're a semi-corporeal magus you have to take a somewhat unconventional approach to research where printed matter is concerned. You can't physically manipulate the books and ledgers unless you want to dedicate precious manna to creating temporary 'hands,' but you can scan the contents of written pages by projecting them in mid-air using a modified *scry* spell.

This method really wasn't any less tedious, however. It took several more visits before Plåk finally scored some useful information: Iwo's application for citizenship. The human had listed Jessmirto as his place of birth. "I guess *on board the TCV* Isomer *in deep space sector MW-9851-Z64* wouldn't fit in the blank," Plåk muttered. On the same page was a death notice for a mother, father, and infant son who perished in a structure fire in the city limits. The family name, a fairly common convention here although not on N'plork overall, was Ke-juq. Interesting coincidence.

Armed with this new data, Plåk was able at last to construct a reasonably complete chronology of Iwo's movements after fleeing from Morianella. He took ship from Jessmirto about the same time as the Nusterton colony's demise, sailing around the southern tip of Esmia and up the coast to Nar Braylov, where he applied for citizenship and lived for some months. After that he sailed over to Neripa, at which point his track disappeared utterly.

Plåk appeared to have milked Nar Braylov for all the information concerning Iwo he was going to get, but on a whim before he left he stopped by the cemetery where the luckless Ke-juq family was interred. He found their grave markers after a little searching. The nine centums-old engraving had eroded and the stones were chipped, but the names were still legible. He wondered idly if the famous historian were any relation.

As Plåk was about to return to The Slice, he noticed a nearby mausoleum flanked by elaborate winged creatures. Carved into the entrance was a manifest of the family members entombed therein. The first and oldest name caught his attention: *Gumnil*. Another interesting coincidence. He looked at the dates and did a little math. Gumnil's death preceded the demise of the Ke-juqs, which meant that both names would have been visible to anyone visiting the cemetery during Iwo's time. The coincidence escalated, but it still proved nothing.

Boogla, meanwhile, had made some more progress in her own quest to trace the life of Gumnil Ke-juq. The authorized biographies of him glossed over his childhood and early adult phases with vagaries that strongly suggested a paucity of real data. By a stroke of incredible luck, however, she met a dwarf who had years before chanced across a tome in a bookseller's stall near Neripa Arts Institute that had been bound in the wrong cover. It contained an unauthorized biography—really just a draft, editorial markup and all—of the famous historian.

While the chapters covering his education and career were fairly conventional, the author had engaged in some real investigative journalism where Ke-juq's pre-academic life was concerned. First she relayed the scholar's own account of those early days. She then provided a detailed point-by-point examination of each of those life events, illustrating that most of them were completely undocumentable. There was no evidence that Ke-juq was born or spent his childhood where he claimed. In fact, there was little evidence he existed at *all* until he enrolled in Neripa Arts Institute as an undergraduate student.

Boogla had been hoping to uncover some traumatic incident from his childhood that might help to explain Ke-juq's deep-seated hatred for orcs, but the more she pursued this goal the more obvious it became to her that Gumnil Ke-juq the adult was a manufactured persona. At last, after three visits to the Neripa Hall of Records, she hit paydirt in a musty subbasement file drawer: the Neripa Magistrate General's Daily Register of Charters and Transactions for the year Ke-juq enrolled at NAI. In it she found a stunning tidbit: Gumnil's name change petition. His birth name: Philmon Iwo.

This new discovery created a dilemma, however. Philmon Iwo was a human; Gumnil Ke-juq, by all accounts including the anonymous biographer's, a somewhat disfigured goblin. Was it possible that there were two Philmon Iwos? That name followed no known N'plorkian construction, but this alone did not prove its alien origin. Why would he choose to rename himself 'Gumnil Ke-juq?' The case for the murderer of Morianella being one of history's most respected scholars was far from airtight. She felt on the verge of an important breakthrough, but for now it was time to get back to being Magineer Liaison.

*   *   *   *   *

Tol was preparing to leave for the weekly EE senior leadership briefing in the conference room down the hall from his office when Boogla quite unexpectedly walked in the door. She had a folder with her, which she dropped on his desk.

"I found your perp."

Tol grunted. "And I didn't get you anything."

Boogla rolled her eyes. "I mean it. I found the mage who disabled the RPC. The Sisters of the Code analyzed his magical signature and the forensics guys matched it. He's a goblin named Weekax who resigned from the RPC Mage Unit the day before the attack."

"Good timing. How did a crooked mage manage to screw up the entire RPC?"

"Combining the Sisters' analysis results with Dolmax's internal security audit, I think I've worked that out, too. It's quite clever. The main thing Weekax accomplished was exfiltrating a lot of highly confidential technical data on security systems and protocols. He did this using teleportation."

"I thought the mages had teleportation of controlled documents in and out of the Royal Complex blocked."

"They do. And they have scanners that pick up magical watermarks embedded in all those documents. But those scanners are installed only at the entrances to places those docs are stored, not the employee portals. What Weekax did was teleport those docs into his gym locker, picking them up and carrying them out at the end of the day, copying them offsite and bringing them back in the same way. The teleport spell was allowed because it did not cross the barrier erected around the complex and since the docs never passed through the scanners, their temporary absence wasn't noted."

Tol nodded. "Yep. That was pretty sneaky, all right. I hope that hole got plugged."

"It did. His other contribution to the effort was to smuggle out credentials for a small crew who came in the morning of the attack and disabled most of the security systems under guise of maintenance. They triggered false alarms all over the underground stations on the opposite end of the complex to draw most of the RPC over there while the hob commando squad came in through an unlocked sewage grate."

"What *I* wanna know is how that hob made it into your private quarters," Tol said.

"Ironically, I may have let him in myself. The RPC said he had a device called a 'tandem interrupt key' that delayed the electromechanical door re-locking long enough to slip in behind me. He was obscured by a refractive camouflage spell so I wouldn't notice him following me in my somewhat panicked state. The dweomer from that spell was still faintly detectable on his body at the post-mortem."

"And all of this cloak-and-dagger rigmarole just to...what? Get some weapons and parts released for sale on the black market? Surely there was an easier way than compromising the security apparatus of an entire government."

"There had to be more to it than that," Boogla admitted, "But I don't have all the answers yet. Maybe if you can track down this Weekax person we might be able to get additional information out of him."

"Any idea where he ran off to?"

"Nothing certain, but there is some suggestion he might have fled to Tantatku based on port authority records from Lumbos."

Tol nodded grimly. "Makes sense to me. I'd bet he's in Zuum."

"Why Zuum?"

"There's an infestation of magic-using wrats there known as the Umbral mages, headed by a very large wrat who calls himself Zizmziz. I strongly suspect the perp is one of their members and scurried back to the nest once his treasonous assignment here was completed. How confident are the forensics guys that this Weekax is the guilty party?"

"The report calls it 'almost a certainty'."

"I can live with that. Better than most of my odds." He picked up the folder and grimaced. "Jlok looks like some kinda walkin' freak show. What's with the scars?"

"Apparently he was the victim of a rather spectacular spell

backfire in his youth. It seems to have altered not only his physical appearance, but even his genetic material. There is speculation that this singular modification may in fact be one of the reasons he was selected for the job, although precisely why that condition would be relevant is not known."

"I'm pretty sure he didn't charm the hiring supervisor with his roguish good looks," Tol chuckled. "I've known I was going to end up in Zuum eventually for a while. Guess now's as good a time as any."

"You can't just walk into a city in Tantatku and start arresting people. Not your jurisdiction," Boogla said.

"I'll simply be providing 'goodwill logistical assistance' to Tantatku EE. They're already on board with it."

"I'm afraid for you, Tol," Boogla said, wearing her serious face as she was headed out, "From what I've read on the Umbral mages and Zizmziz, these people are very, very dangerous."

"Yeah, so I've been told on several occasions," Tol said, walking her to the door. "But, apparently so am I."

On her way back to the Palace, Boogla kept replaying her brother-in-law's words. Was it bluster, self-confidence, or... something else? She'd never known him to be an egotist, but if that wasn't bragging, what was it? She decided not to let Selpla in on her misgivings for the time being. No sense alarming her over what might simply be an offhand remark.

Tol, meanwhile, sat in a departmental briefing mulling over his next move. He heard very little of whatever the High Commissioner was droning on about. He was wondering what to tell Selpla and whether or not he should try to convince Oloi and/or Ballop'ril to help. Tol wasn't accustomed to asking for assistance, there not being much available for most of his career, but he had a hunch he was going to be outgunned this time if he went in alone.

After the meeting he headed up to the third floor to talk to the forensic mages. He hadn't developed any close professional relations with them because he wasn't exactly a magic enthusiast, but he'd never gone after a criminal mage organization before, either. There was only one of those in existence, as far as he knew, and as they'd had no physical presence in Tragacanth prior to Weekax they had not been his problem. He was looking for anything that could give him an edge now, though.

Forensics knew about the Umbrals. "Those smekkers are just scum, pure and utter," one of them told Tol. "They have little regard for the ethics of magic and are simply available to anybody with sufficient funds, like common laborers. I'm glad to see EE finally going after them. No one's had the guts before, confidentially."

To shrugged. "If you violate edicts in Tragacanth and put the public at risk I'm coming after you. I just never had any personal reason to notice these jloks before now. What I'd like from you guys is whatever tools you can provide, defensive or offensive. I'm not a mage myself, of course."

The forensics mage stared at him for a few seconds with a puzzled look on his face and shrugged. "We have some stuff that might be useful. Better still, though, would be to take a couple high-level mages with you. There's no substitute for fighting fire with fire, as it were."

"I'm workin' on that. Mage-on-mage action is not so easy to arrange as all that. Mages have an acute sense of self-preservation, and they seem to be reluctant to take on their brethren."

"That's because there should never be a need to do so. It's programmed into us, you might say, to regard magic and mages as above the petty squabbles and ambitions of the kludgers."

"Kludgers?"

The mage looked embarrassed. "Um, that's our slang term for the non-magic using populace. It derives from the idea that many things are much easier to do with magic."

Tol smirked. "See, I've always felt just the opposite. It seems to me that picking up a crate and moving it to the next room by hand is a smekking lot easier than chanting and waving your hands just the right way."

The mage laughed in turn. "That's why mages and klu...non-mages work together so well. We complement each other's abilities and philosophies."

"Right. So, what kind of complementary help can I get from you?"

"We have phylacteries that are protective for a variety of magical attacks, shielding amulets, and this." He opened a locked drawer and extracted a small ring made of some light yellow metal—like a cross between gold and silver. He handed it to Tol. "Put it on. Any finger; it will adjust."

Tol slipped it on the middle finger of his right hand. It expanded to fit over the knuckles and then contracted again to precisely the correct diameter to rest comfortably but snugly around the digit. Tol admired its simple elegance.

"That is a grounding ring. It prevents anyone from making you the subject of telekinesis against your will. Can come in very handy during a magical battle. Since telekinesis is one component of teleportation, you can't be teleported, either."

"What happens if I need to teleport somewhere?"

"You have to concentrate on the ring and 'tell' it to allow the activity. It takes a little practice, but it isn't that difficult to master. The ring will give off a slight pulse you can feel and see in a darkened room when it's been temporarily disabled. You can practice releasing it in a place like that. If you want to remove it, twist all the way around once to the right and once to the left and it will expand enough to come off."

"Great. Thanks. What else you got?"

"Before I answer that, I need to know what sort of magical equipment you're already wearing: other than the ring, I mean."

Tol was taken aback a bit. "None. I don't routinely have any contact with magical stuff."

The mage gave Tol his most puzzled expression. "Forgive me, Sir Knight, but your aura says differently."

"Again with that smek," Tol replied in exasperation. "Look, I don't know anything about my 'aura,' but I'm telling you I ain't no kind of magic user."

"Profound apologies, Sir Tol. I didn't mean to upset you. I've just never seen an aura like yours before."

Tol took a deep breath. "No sweat, kid. Sorry I reacted that way. I guess I'm tired of hearing about my aura because I didn't ask for it and there's nothing I can do about it."

"I won't mention it again, Sir Knight. Here is a carrying case I've prepared with three of the most useful magic items we can provide you. Attached inside the lid are fold-out descriptions on the employment of each, along with any other information you'll need to take full advantage of their protective effects."

Tol smiled. "Thanks a lot. I'll bring these back as soon as I can."

"They are signed out to you indefinitely, Special Investigator. No need to return them. Best of fortune in your deployment, Sir Tol. You are a brave goblin and Tragacanth is extremely lucky to have one such as you fighting for us."

Tol shook his head. "I'm just a 'kludger' doing the job the taxpayers hired me to do, kid. Thanks again for the doohickeys."

After Tol had rounded the corner the mage turned back to what he'd been doing.

"Whatever else he may or may not be, he's definitely not a kludger," he muttered.

* * * * *

Selpla had figured out that something big was in the offing. All the signs were there, both at home and on the street. She wondered how much, if anything at all, Tol was planning to tell her concerning the Zizmziz takedown. Selpla was perfectly well aware that Tol's job was hazardous. He'd been going after dangerous criminals his entire career with EE. Up until now, though, he'd had very little interaction with perps who possessed significant magical abilities.

The presence of magic changed the edict enforcement tactical situation radically. Every squad had at least one mage, usually first tier, assigned to it to render assistance in these situations, but their role was by design more advisory than operational.

In the end Tol decided to give Selpla the broad picture but not the details. He wasn't sure about them, himself. This operation had so many deflection points where the planned track could become skewed that he probably couldn't have spelled them all out even if he wanted to. He'd prepared himself in every way he could figure; that would have to do for both of them.

Tol was not at all comfortable with the number of people who'd become involved in this mission. More accurately, he was unhappy with the crowd who were *obvious*. All EE work required people doing a lot of different jobs, but most of the time they remained in the background—out of sight, out of mind. This case seemed more like planning for a party than an investigation. He was much happier operating on his own. The more people who joined the team, the more chances that a weak link among them would break that entire chain apart. He had a sudden crazy impulse to ditch them all and strike out on his own. Just the thought made him smile.

Selpla was an investigative reporter, after all, with contacts and sources scattered across Tragacanth and beyond. By the time Tol got around to filling her in on his plans she already knew all about them. Despite the dark prognostications and dire warnings that Tol was about to head into the dragon's den, she was strangely complacent. It's not that she wasn't concerned or worried, of course, but something told her that Tol's self-confidence in this matter was not simple bluster. He was prepared for this mission in ways few understood. Still, she made certain their last evening together before he left was, well, epic—just in case.

Chapter Nineteen

The Round Table had concluded in some disarray. The sudden appearance of Plåk had completely changed the equation underlying the Valtir quest; none of the Elders really knew how best to proceed as a result. Igra had retired to the Elders' Sanctum in the Balom enclave to ponder their strategy in light of this new and disruptive information. The Valtir had been a symbol for orcs throughout their entire history—a history that had now taken a bizarre twist.

While most people on N'plork believed that the universe was likely populated by other sentient beings, there was no solid accepted evidence that any such aliens had ever visited this planet. If what Blass had told them was true, the orcs themselves were in fact that evidence. The very weirdest part of all this, from Igra's point of view, is that this colonization by an entirely alien race had been glossed over by everyone. One would think this would represent a civilization-changing moment worthy of at least *some* mention in the historical record.

Archmage Blass had intimated, however, that the orcs' ignominy and their curious absence from the chronicles of N'plorkian history—representing anything other than a scourge, at least—were closely related. It was well known in the orc community that a historian by the name of Gumnil Ke-juq had fabricated most of the pejorative rhetoric surrounding their people, but why he felt this way and who, exactly, he was had been lost to them. They had long ago given up collectively on ever clearing their names and just concentrated on survival as a race.

One of his aides came in just then, a brilliant young female named Marilka, carrying a stack of folder and documents.

"Honored Elder, here is the information you requested. I have compiled every fact, theory, and even marginally reasonable hypothesis we've generated concerning our origins and dispersion.

Here," she handed him a sheaf of parchments, "Is my summary of each; whatever substantiating evidence exists for them is annotated and the folders arranged in logical fashion accordingly."

Igra smiled for the first time in days. "Thank you, Marilka. Your assistance in this matter is most welcome and appreciated."

She smiled back at him. "All orcs owe you and the rest of the Council a great debt of gratitude, Elder Igra. Without your efforts we would no longer exist as a race. I am honored and humbled to be able to contribute."

"My dear daughter, so long as there are people such as you the noble bloodline will stand with heads unbowed, no matter the indignities heaped upon us by the outsiders. You are why we Elders devote ourselves to what has seemed at times a hopeless cause." Elders called all orcs who were not Elders themselves 'daughter' or 'son.'

"The Round Table has given all of us fresh hope," she replied.

"I can make no promises, the world being what it is, but my instinctive feeling here is that we may be on the cusp of a new era for the orcish race. Precisely what that will mean for our people remains to be seen."

Igra sat at the table in the Sanctum and read through each of the reports Marilka had supplied. He was looking for clues as to the nature of the Valtir itself, lost to orc oral tradition somewhere during their tumultuous and tragic history. He was also hoping to find some hint as to the irrational characterization of unpredictable violence to which the orcs had always been subject.

There were almost as many theories on orc origin as there were pundits to formulate them. Only one seemed to jive with what archmage Blass had told them, however. It was derived from the journal of an orc from the earliest period of their recorded history, even before the forced resettlement into enclaves. The journalist's name was Samil Derry and he was also the only one of the bunch to mention Morianella as a sister colony. His most telling statement in this regard was that orcs as a race should *look to the sky rather than the land to commune with their ancestors.* Subsequent researchers considered this to refer to ancestral spirits occupying the aethereal realm, but if the sky was indeed from whence the orcs had come his words took on an additional layer of meaning.

Igra was intrigued by Derry's vivid account of life in those distant days; approaching midnight found him still absorbed in the journal. He was not the first to study those accounts in depth, but he was perhaps the first in centums to do so with the proper context in mind. As he rubbed his tired eyes and prepared to head off to bed, the Elder came across this arresting entry:

Today packet boat arrived w/ fruits & root vegtibles from Morinela. Aboard also was the mage Filmon.

The timing of the entry corresponded to shortly after the historical date assigned to the Morianella disaster. Since it must have taken quite a few days to travel to mainland Asmagon where the orc colony, called in the journal "Nusterton," had been located at that time, this put the sailing of the boat a day or two prior to the subsea quake. Iwo, who seemed very likely to be the passenger indicated, had gotten out just in the nick of time. Good fortune... or something else? Igra was still mulling this over as he fell asleep.

The next day the Elder returned to his research immediately following the morning meal. His diligence was rewarded by additional references to 'the mage,' the most interesting and potentially revealing of which was a brief account of the chronicler's interactions with said mage. The mage was said to be *alternately sad, angry, and prideful, with occasional bouts of some deeply-felt remorse.* This matched closely with what archmage Blass had relayed of Philmon Iwo's character and mindset.

The last mention of 'the mage' in Derry's journal was cryptic:

Few have escaped the sickness. The mage is so far unaffected; he has done what he can for us and preparing to travel to Jessmirto to seek help

The final entry was incomplete and seemingly incoherent:

Sea has lost rumble and world has no longer color.
Finding it increasingly difficult to

There the journal ended. Igra puzzled over Derry's final words. Was this some form of allegorical statement? Was it intended to be poetic? The author had demonstrated an affinity for poetic language from time to time. It was impossible to know, he finally concluded. One thing was clear, though. In the case of both Morianella and Nusterton, Philmon Iwo had departed shortly before disaster struck. He was, it seemed, very, very lucky.

*   *   *   *   *

Tol walked down the gangplank in Dollo, the capitol city of Tantatku, and was met at the bottom by two detective-inspectors from their EE's elite apprehension unit or "Bashers," as they were known locally. Tol had gone through both EE and diplomatic channels this time, as he doubted Zizmziz could be taken down without a fight that might well spill out into 'civilian space.' He wanted to be sure all affected agencies were involved in order to minimize collateral damage and hurt feelings.

The Bashers were unsure what to think of their new colleague. On the one hand, he was a career EE operative with a vast amount of experience and connections all the way to the Royal Family of Tragacanth. However, he was going after a criminal they had previously considered essentially untouchable because of his immense defensive capabilities. No one in Tantatku EE would even have considered tackling that many-tentacled monster. They contented themselves with isolating him and the Umbral mages to the extent possible and monitoring their movements.

Still, they would lend the possibly insane Sir Tol-u-ol what assistance they could. Zizmziz had been a malignant presence in

244

their midst for many years now; the litany of crimes attributed to him personally or to his organization occupied a large amount of space on the criminal 'wall of shame' at Basher headquarters there in Dollo. While they considered the possibility that this Tragacanthan knight could have any significant negative impact on the Umbral organization rather remote, most of them were happy to give him a shot. At the very least he might shake things up.

Tol attended a briefing at Basher HQ where he was given all of the information Tantatku EE had developed on Zizmziz and the Umbrals. He listened patiently while the intelligence section briefers laid out a vast array of details large and small concerning habits, methods of operation, personnel, quirks, peeves, patterns, and more. It was overwhelming, to say the least.

"When do you guys have time to walk your beats?" Tol asked.

"Oh, we have officers to do that. This is from the intell shop. All they do is collect and collate data on known perps," his assigned escort replied.

"Must be nice to have a budget big enough for that."

"Don't you have intell guys in Tragacanth?"

"Yeah. Probably. I don't go to that floor very often. I read their briefings occasionally."

The detective-inspector blinked. "Must be hard to carry out EE operations without accurate, fresh intell."

"I get my intell on the street, with my own eyes and ears," Tol replied, "That's about as fresh as it comes."

The gob shrugged. "Whatever works."

From Dollo Tol traveled via EE pram to Zuum. The local EE did things a bit differently from the national EE organization, and Tol immediately felt more comfortable. They were very much cast from the same mold as Tol himself, maintaining a sizeable network of street operatives reporting to beat officers, who relayed that information back to their precincts for correlation. They got to know their beats and the people who lived along them intimately and so almost always had plenty of warning when something major was in the offing.

The Zuum EE branch actually had a surprisingly simple and effective plan for taking down Zizmziz that they'd held in reserve for years, waiting for the proper moment when their patient surveillance had amassed enough hard evidence to get a solid conviction. The takedown itself would be quite direct: Zizmziz came into town once every fortnight to visit a local apothecary and conduct some other business. He usually had no more than three bodyguards with him. EE had two drays outfitted with industrial null-magic devices and generators to power them that they would position on either side of said apothecary.

When Zizmziz emerged they would be waiting for him with enough muscle that his bodyguards would have no chance of winning in a firefight. The null-magic units would erase any magical defense he might have prepared. It would be quick, uncomplicated, and efficient. Tol heartily approved.

Unfortunately for simplicity and elegance, however, Tol's presence had spurred the Bashers into action. They converged en masse on the Umbral compound south of Zuum and immediately nixed the local EE plan as being too simplistic and naive to work. Tol rolled his eyes.

"Why can't you back off and let these guys do their jobs?" he said to the Agent in Charge of the Basher detachment, who had assumed control over the joint operation, "I think their plan will work just fine."

The AIC, a goblin named Akkla with troll or ogre genes and a head taller than Tol, looked down his nose and sniffed. "Ya, vell, I hev no doubt zat is ze vay such things are handled in Tragacanth, but here in ze fatherland ve conduct our operations in a more... structured manner. Ze plan as presented by local EE has serious shortcomings and is, quite frankly, slipshod from both strategic and tactical standpoints. Our approach vill be much more likely to accomplish ze goal as stated."

"If that goal is start a full-scale regional conflict, then yeah, I agree with you. All you're gonna do with that pile of hardware and people is force him into a deep dark hole. When he does come out, he'll be swingin' with everything he's got. From what I've heard, he and his magical army can put a smekkin' lot of hurt on us."

Akkla smiled. "Sir Tol-u-ol, ve have a great deal of experience with zese sorts of operations here in Tantatku. Everyzing will go as planned, I assure you. If you have mizgivings you are welcome to observe from the rearward command post."

It was Tol's turn to grin. "I didn't travel all the way here to sit in the back. Zizmziz and one of his mage goons were involved up to their eye ridges in a plot to assassinate members of the Tragacanthan Royal Family: *my* family. I have been charged by the King with taking them down and I intend to do just that."

"While I commend your sense of duty, Sir Tol-u-ol, I must caution you against interfering vith our operations. Zis is Tantatku sovereign territory and you hev no jurisdiction here."

Tol shook his head. "We're on the same team, mister high-and-mighty—and I was bustin' low-lifes while you were still crawlin' around on all fours. You stay outta my way and I'll stay outta yours." At this Tol walked away. The AIC turned to his lieutenant.

"Watch zat one. He is a potential troublemaker. If he interferes, lock him up. Ve vill deal vith ze international diplomacy later."

Tol had decided that his position on this team was on one flank. He had zero confidence in the Bashers' ability to conduct this arrest effectively. If they were so competent at this sort of thing, why were Zizmziz and other members of the Umbrals wanted on over a dozen outstanding local warrants for serious crimes? The official explanation that they hadn't had the budget to take them on until now fell flat. He knew a rationalization when he heard one. He concluded they were just embarrassed that a foreign cop was threatening to upstage them.

The plan now seemed to revolve around a belief that the Bashers could move a significant number of officers into position surrounding the Umbral mage headquarters compound south of

Zuum unseen by Zizmziz. Tol regarded this as pure fantasy. The Umbrals had proven themselves quite adept at surveillance and no doubt had a web of agents and informants spread over a wide radius centered on their bases of operations. They were probably aware of and observing this very muster, in fact.

Taking all of this into consideration, Tol decided he could either get there first or mop up afterwards. Neither alternative seemed very attractive, but it was really too late to get in and accomplish anything before the cavalry here came crashing through the hedges and obliterated any subtlety to the proceedings. He decided to stay back and watch, hoping the blunder boys would flush Zizmziz and Tol could catch him on the lam. He cursed himself for following protocol and notifying everyone and their pet lapspider of his intentions. He should have just gotten in and out before local EE even knew anything was up.

The operation was set to commence two hours prior to dawn the next morning. That was the time calculated by the Bashers at which the Umbrals' defenses were likely to be at their least effective. Tol didn't see anything wrong with this particular assertion, apart from Zizmziz being a megalomaniacal mage likely to have lots of magical traps and wards in place, none of which were subject to diminished efficacy simply because it was dark outside. Tol would have gone in during broad daylight, when he could at least see what he was doing.

One of the many reasons Tol was reluctant to be an integral part of this EE team effort is that he had no idea how the unwanted magical nonsense he'd been saddled with was going to affect things. If something happened that he was unable to control, he didn't want to endanger any fellow EE officers—no matter how annoying and antithetical to his personal approach they might be—as a result. He decided he would use the Basher operation as cover for his own infiltration.

At 0500 the signal was given to move into position. Tol accompanied the Bashers to the staging area, but then kept going and hid himself in a row of hedges to one side, with his back to the first rising sun for added cover. Now he would watch and wait for the proper moment.

*   *   *   *   *

When an archmage transcends, his entire memory is mapped one neural connection at a time to a lattice composed of discrete dark energy pulses frozen in n-dimensional space by a perpetual stasis field. Actually, even in The Slice nothing is truly permanent, but the half-life of these containment structures was on the order of four billion years, so it would be a while before dementia set in. One of the interesting and potentially useful aspects of this transference process is that any memory with even a few hundred former neurons devoted to it could be extracted and amplified with careful and patient effort.

Plåk sat in the 'estate' he'd carved from the malleable fabric of The Slice and accessed the older portions of his personal memory archive. He was trying to tease out all information relating to Philmon Iwo, the son of a life-support engineer and an agronomist on board the *Isomer* who had been educated in the social sciences before they'd abandoned ship for N'plork. In Morianella Philmon had taken on odd jobs before the founding of the Magical Arts Academy there prompted him to enroll as a student in the same class as Dennis Blass.

Dennis and Philmon had known each other on the *Isomer*, but were not actually friends there. Blass was a physics graduate student working on multidimensional quantum teleportation theory when the evacuation order came down. He'd gravitated to matters arcane on N'plork because there were no facilities for his sort of physics research available; magic seemed the next best thing. He had been the only academy graduate to make it to archmage before the disaster.

Blass and Iwo progressed side-by-side until the trial for Magus Academicus/Arcanis, at which point the latter repeatedly choked.

He could never seem to grasp the mechanics of arcanic vector mapping, an essential skill for mages executing precise manipulation of energy streams. He attempted and failed the trial a total of six times over a number of years. Meanwhile, Blass had progressed all the way to Magus Superior and was preparing for the archmage trial, one of the most difficult and exacting examinations of any type known to N'plorkian society.

The archmage trial was not a single event. It took place over a period of about ten days as a series of physically and mentally exhausting challenges leading up to a fiendishly difficult exercise known as the *Fait Accompli*, wherein essentially the archmage candidate travels back in time and gives himself a passing grade in a magically sealed envelope that is opened by the examination proctors during the trial. While abstruse and complex, the entire trial was designed to be sufficiently objective that it could be administered and evaluated by Magi Superior or Arcanis, in extreme cases, because archmages themselves were quite rare. Even the largest academies could boast no more than two; a fair proportion of both academies and universitas had access to one only as adjunct faculty, as was the case with Ballop'ril and the Sutha Arts Collegium.

The first few times Iwo had failed to progress, he'd seemed grounded in reality inasmuch as he'd laid the blame on his own lack of mastery. As the years wore on, though, his human capacity for rationalization took over—he began to assign the fault to a variety of people and processes connected with the magical academic community. As his paranoid delusional defense mechanisms came to dominate he arrived ultimately at the conclusion that everyone and everything had conspired against him. When all the world is against you, no action you can take in defense of this assault is immoral or unethical. Iwo in effect gave himself a blank check.

Of course, it wasn't that cut and dried, Plåk realized. Philmon hadn't simply sat down one day and decided to pursue a career of evil. Plåk remembered him as a fairly kind soul, with a seeming genuine interest at the outset in the welfare of his fellow

Morianellans. Having your inadequacies thrown in your face day after day for years, however, can corrupt even the most saintly demeanor. Eventually the psyche takes whatever face-saving path is open to it and builds a comfortable shell of rationalization around it in order to provide affirmation.

The events surrounding the act of replacing the *Codex* page probably represented the final nail in the coffin of Iwo's self-respect. Precisely to what extent he comprehended the effect his subterfuge would have on Morianella was impossible to say, but Plåk's gut told him that the Magus Incipius had only intended to prevent the spell from functioning. He'd probably expected to hear that the great Archmage Blass had failed to fulfill his contract, nothing more.

What had prompted him to flee Morianella beforehand was therefore also a matter for conjecture. More than likely he just suspected that Blass would figure out what had happened and come looking for Iwo—far better to be halfway around the world when an archmage has a bone to pick with you. There was no direct evidence he knew that Morianella itself would shortly cease to exist. Hearing about that disaster and coming to the realization that he had been responsible for the obliteration of an entire island full of people was probably the trigger that propelled his already unstable mentality over the precipice into the abyss of criminal insanity. The fact that he apparently knew about Nusterton was fascinating, but then Plåk hadn't really been aware of the international community much, sequestered in the mages' schola as he was.

The research conducted by Plåk and Boogla indicated that Iwo had sailed from Nusterton to Nar Braylov and then some months later to Neripa. Maybe he just liked towns that began with *N*, mused Plåk. Once in Neripa, it seemed, Iwo's trail went cold. Not just cold: frozen solid. The only clue they had was Boogla's discovery that the identifying number for Iwo and the historian Gumnil Ke-juq were identical. A clerical error...or something more significant?

Contemporary reports were unanimous in their assertion that everyone in Morianella had perished—the small group of survivors who established Nuvinis after being teleported to Woklopen by archmage Blass having apparently escaped the chroniclers' attention—so Iwo probably had little reason to fear being connected to that catastrophe if he dissociated himself totally from that place. Likewise with the mysterious fate of Nusterton, as its existence was probably largely unknown outside the local Jessmirto area. The only documentable connection between these two doomed human colonies was Iwo. Could that really be a coincidence?

Plåk returned his attention to the data archive uploaded by Boogla and concentrated on finding the last 'Iwo' reference and the first 'Ke-juq.' He then started scanning every activity documented as occurring between those two events. Nothing seemed obviously relevant: lots of shipping records, port authority permits for loading and unloading from relatively local destinations like Nar Braylov, Qoplebarq, and Moqip.

Something about 'Moqip' held significance for Plåk. He extracted that kernel from his memory archive and amplified it. While modern-day Moqip was little more than a tropical tourist hub for southern Galanga, with a smattering of gnomish high-tech engineering fabrication plants thrown into the mix, at one time the town was more or less the world epicenter of magical artifact creation, thanks largely to an archmage named Mybir who achieved notoriety chiefly for his ill-conceived Artifact of Instantiation.

The artifact was really just a blank template created during a spurt of febrile inspiration. Once the fever had subsided the archmage realized precisely what a dangerous item he'd enchanted, so he locked it away in its nascent form, to be forgotten when Mybir died without transcending. Several centums later a minor noble who considered himself a rapier duelist inherited an antique pedestal and stumbled across an odd mechanism while restoring it. He discovered that rather than a simple pillar he'd actually come into possession of a cabinet, inside which was a curious object that glowed with faint greenish radiance.

While he was not a trained mage, the noble—Rufka—dabbled

in magic and realized after some study and consultation that what he'd uncovered was an artifact which could be used for creating just about anything he wanted. He decided to bring into objective existence what had up to then been merely a philosophical concept employed by martial arts trainers: the duello golem.

His intention was that this golem, more accurately a spirit golem, could be called up at any time to serve as a training aid for sword fighting. It could be set to react to the user's skill level and ratchet up gradually as that faculty progressed. It was, in many ways, the perfect training tool.

Of course, spirit golems could be created using medium-level spells or much less sophisticated magic items. What distinguished the golems generated by the artifact was that they could employ weapons with real physical presence that could therefore inflict physical damage. If the person using the artifact was not explicit and careful, he could be seriously injured or even killed by his own training golem. With normal spirit golems this would be impossible, as the blades were weak energy manifestations that merely flashed when a 'hit' was registered. With this artifact, however, the energy containment matrix was powerful enough to generate blades that behaved in all meaningful ways like solid objects.

An artifact of instantiation is so named because it allows the potent magic contained in it to be directed to a physical manifestation of the abstract concept underlying the enchantment. The process involves two distinct phases: artifacture and commiture. Once the energies required are bound to the artifact itself, the final form of expression—the physical representation of those energies— is selected. This choice must be made with extreme care because it is irrevocable and the results for all practical purposes permanent, in that the pattern it creates is anchored directly into the quantum boundary between Primus and The Slice.

Unfortunately for everyone involved, Rufka was not sufficiently aware of the subtleties of this particular aspect of magic and so made two tragic mistakes in dictating the final form the artifact would take. The first was choosing to complete the enchantment at all, as this action was far beyond his competence or comprehension. The second, even graver, error was misunderstanding the mechanics of artifactive commiture.

He envisioned a training partner that would help him improve his dueling style by continually challenging him to do better, learning as it went. What he failed to grasp is that the end result of a true outrance duel is almost always the death of one party. The first encounter between a mage and his golem burns the underlying behavioral component into the template. Rufka expected the golem to perform similarly to spirit golems he'd encountered in the past: unable to do any real damage to its opponent. Since Rufka in his ignorance used genuine swords against the golem during their initial encounter, the golem responded in kind.

Rufka was an accomplished sword fighter and as such it was some time before the magnitude of his mistake became catastrophically apparent. One morning during an intense bout one of his servant girls came into the training suite to dust his trophy shelf. Rufka turned to talk to her without disengaging from the golem and it ran a saber through his ribcage. As the instantiator, Rufka was the only person who could deactivate the archetypical golem; when he expired without doing so the die was cast. The training golem became Duellomortu.

The artifact was left in an open-ended state by Rufka's demise; it would continue to generate these combat-seeking manifestations in perpetuity. Since they were programmed to learn from experience, each one was a little deadlier than the previous. The reactive intelligence component of the template fostered a slew of unintended consequences, among them the 'kill or be killed' mentality engendered by carelessness born of Rufka's paucity of knowledge concerning the precise nature of these extraordinarily powerful magic items.

Because the original Duellomortu was not given a clear set of instructions but was gifted with adaptive intelligence and a geas to duel at all costs, it developed its own internal rule set based in part on Rufka's displayed behavioral traits. One of these, alas, was impatience. This trait manifested itself in the golem's tendency to stalk and eventually slay any who refused to engage in battle with it using dark energy molded into 'spirit swords.'

In order for spirit swords to cause real damage, the creature to which they were applied must be temporarily relocated into an extrusion, or pocket, of The Slice, where in effect the swords become solid. The injuries sustained by living tissue in that milieu are then retained when the organism is returned to its native environment. During the period of translation the creature's manifestation on Primus is a mere shell; a persistent reflection of the actual organism currently residing in The Slice. Consequently, no actions applied to it on Primus during that period have any effect. If the creature is fatally wounded while translated, the life force remains behind in The Slice when the physical body reverts—the golem's victims killed in this manner haunted The Slice in perpetuity as semi-transparent spirits known as *wisps*.

All of this serves chiefly to illustrate what a skilled magical item enchanter Archmage Mybir really was. While the artifact was his most famous achievement, he produced dozens of additional phylacteries and talismans of a less notorious but still quite impressive variety. One of his specialties was reportedly an arcane subdiscipline known as *transmorphics*. He created talismans that gradually converted one race into another by magically altering the subject's genome. While magic was the driving force for the 'controlled mutations,' the process was otherwise totally organic and natural.

It was this aspect of Mybir's accomplishments, not the ill-fated artifact, that most intrigued Plåk. No one before or since had been as successful at transmorphics. Most mages, even archmages, contented themselves with merely creating the illusion of transmorphication, but Mybir's items actually went the whole biological distance. While pondering this, the germ of an idea began to grow in Plåk's mind. He charted a course for Moqip.

Chapter Twenty

In the case of a transcended archmage, 'charting a course' merely meant choosing the proper coordinates for reentry to Primus. Once at his destination, Plåk headed for the district that had for the past millennium served as the focal point for magical activities in Moqip. In most of his travels to N'plork he was somewhat cautious about where he manifested, semi-transparency being disconcerting to most people. In places like this, however, the sight of a wavering, translucent figure was, while perhaps not commonplace, at least unsurprising.

There were no archmages residing in that area at present. The mages' guildhall here was small and populated by a few aged magi arcanis who gave Plåk only a passing glance as he headed down the stairs to the archivium. Finding concrete evidence from so long ago promised to be a challenge, but Plåk's investigation enjoyed one advantage over those of Boogla, Selpla, and Tol: magical records were not subject to the same processes of degradation as normal archives.

For well over two millennia arcane archivists had been making use of a quirk in the underlying architecture of magic to preserve the legacies under their purview. Magic was expressed using a set of symbols infused with invocative dweomer. These symbols were entangled with energy quanta located in The Slice; as a result the parchment or other surface upon which they were inscribed was protected from environmental effects such as rot, oxidation, or abrasion. The practical upshot of this protective effect was that so long as at least one linked magic symbol was present on a page, it was effectively invulnerable to anything other than targeted magical destruction.

Since time immemorial, then, mages had been in the habit of putting an activated magical symbol, customarily *o-o*, at the top (or sometimes bottom) of all correspondence and research notes. Some of them do it quite unconsciously, in fact; most would have to make a concerted effort *not* to. Archivium research therefore tends not to exhibit the normal inverse relationship between age of document sought and quality of results obtained with nearly as much correlation. The downside of this is that archivia which have been in existence for as long as this one accumulate vast quantities of incorruptible parchments that must be stored and sorted in order for any meaningful research on them to be possible. Warehouses with multiple levels stretching for blocks were necessary for this storage.

By this point in his inquiries, Plåk had narrowed the period in which he was interested to a span of about two years. This made locating the relevant documents considerably simpler, although it still left several containers' worth to go through. While he knew more or less what he was looking for, Plåk was not at all certain what form it would take. He hoped to find a log entry or something along those lines that would either confirm or dispute his hypothesis.

No such log surfaced, but eventually he did come across two relevant documents. The first was an invoice in Mybir's name for a specific set of ingredients that matched those needed for a race-change talisman. The second was the internal guild investigator's report on the archmage's unexpected demise. The reason this was relevant is that said demise came less than a full day after the client—almost certainly Philmon Iwo, by the distinctive description—received that finished magic item. Another coincidence? It was becoming increasingly difficult to believe that.

The report said that Mybir had completed roughly two-thirds of the transcending ritual at the time of his death. That was an extraordinary circumstance; a mage undergoing the transcendence process was virtually invulnerable to pathogens or physical infirmity as a result of the 'metabolic cutover' being undertaken. Killing a transcending mage would require a catastrophic event like a volcano eruption. Killing him with an external force, anyway...

Despite the difficulty of doing away with an archmage by employing anything short of a natural disaster, there was one very effective path available to another mage with evil intent and physical access to the transcendent candidate: mistranslation. The model for the transcending process was based largely, albeit unintentionally, on cell biology; specifically on mitosis, or cellular reproduction. Each system and energy pathway of the body was translated into its equivalent in The Slice, one at a time—which is why transcending itself could take years to complete.

There were error-correction mechanisms in place, but their effectiveness was predicated on a set of assumptions, one of them being that the 'source' material; i.e., the mage himself, was by definition error-free. In order to achieve this, the archmage had to create a template—a copy of himself with all germane defects corrected—from which the translation would be conducted. This is critical, because once you've transcended you will be living with the body (and mind) you bring with you for a very, very long time.

In order to create a Slice-compatible template, an archmage casts a suite of spells in serial fashion that capture various aspects of his physical and mental makeup. This is tedious and exacting work, with little tolerance for mistakes. Most archmages who undertake transcendence successfully hole themselves up in a virtually impenetrable stronghold during this period, with only one or a small number of implicitly trusted assistants permitted to enter. While the mage has total control over the spells that create the template itself, the translation process from Primus template to Slice template is very delicate and subject to various types of interference.

Most interruptions result in nothing worse than a translational failure that can be corrected by starting that phase of the process over—vexing, perhaps, but not fatal. Translation as an arcane practice is at the very highest levels of the discipline and rather esoteric; as such the average person could do little to affect it. Another mage with ill intent, however, can prove quite dangerous during this process.

The Mages' Guild internal investigation findings reported that Mybir was discovered unresponsive by a domestic servant who had left a meal in the slot outside the chamber where the transcendence rituals were underway and found it untouched the next day. Concerned, the servant had found the door uncharacteristically unlocked and entered to see the archmage suspended in mid-air in the center of the room, completely lifeless.

The servant immediately fetched Mybir's chamberlain Fesqu, who contacted the Guild and local EE. After extensive questioning along with examination of both Mybir's body and the complex of persistent auras that had built up in the chambers over decades of magical activity, it was determined that a critical step in his translation had not only been interrupted, but the energies involved reflected back into him in such a manner as to be "incompatible with respiration," as the report put it. Someone, in other words, strangled the archmage with his own magic.

Only another mage could have managed this. Employing a mage's personal arcane forces against him was strictly forbidden in all versions of the Code of Ethics for Magical Employment, punishable by expulsion from any Guild affiliations and having all privileges related to resources such as libraries or arcane nodes revoked in perpetuity. It also earned you the enmity of virtually the entire magical community and made you a target. In short, this was a behavior in which one did not indulge lightly.

There was, according to the investigatory report, no sign of a physical struggle and no violent spell had disrupted the area's aura. Nor were there objects of any sort obstructing Mybir's airway. The investigator reached his conclusion based on where the archmage had been in his transcending process and the utter lack of solid evidence of any contributing cause or condition. The signs all pointed to inflicted anoxia as the mechanism of death, but no physical weapon had been employed.

Interviews with the servants and nearby residents established that a bizarre-looking individual with smooth skin and a slim build was the only visitor of Mybir's observed recently. The witnesses were also unanimous that they had not seen him leave the last time he visited, oddly. They all assumed he had slipped out under cover of darkness. There was a goblin of atypical appearance unknown to any of them seen leaving the home the day before the body was discovered, though.

No connection between those occurrences seems to have been established by investigators contemporary to the events, but of course Plåk had the benefit of considerable hindsight and a wealth of information not available to them. He now very much wanted to discover the identity of Mybir's final guest.

Not a lot of Mybir's personal effects, including his journals, were still extant after so many centums. It was highly unlikely anyone who intentionally instigated a mistranslation that put an archmage into suspended animation while he asphyxiated would fail to remove any incriminating evidence from the scene. But there was one trail a mage on Primus could not erase: the imprimatura.

What has come to be known as magic is really just the use of energy drawn from The Slice. The physics governing that particular form of energy differ from 'conventional' energy, which distinction allows magic to accomplish things that would be either impossible or at least very, very difficult on Primus otherwise. In effect magic is a tightly controlled conduit into a higher-dimensional space, the forces emanating from which are regulated and manipulated by the mage to achieve some goal.

The energy mages derive from The Slice is colloquially referred to as 'manna.' The process constitutes more than opening a simple flow, however: it involves nothing less than a matter-to-energy state change. What manifests as arcane energy on Primus is actually more akin to matter in its native environment; it is the fabric from which all physical objects are constructed there. The enormous potential energy stored as matter in the Dark Energetic Continuum is what provides magic its overwhelming utility. The power resulting from this conversion is also why mages must be very thoroughly trained and possess high ethical standards.

Rather than a continuous flow, manna transfers from The Slice to Primus in discrete units called *arcanic capsules*. Every energy transfer leaves behind a very mage-specific fingerprint—the imprimatura—in the matrix of The Slice that persists for tens of millions of years. Those archmages who transcend often learn over time to distinguish among the fine details of these patterns. Plåk realized that he could with patience tease out any magical activity conducted by Mybir during his last days.

When a mage-in-training acquires his first speculum arcanis, that initial filling with manna is initiated by the mentoring mage. However, all subsequent fills are conducted by the new mage. This energy comes from a region of The Slice 'assigned' to that mage at the moment of first contact; future capsules summoned by that mage will derive from this same location in perpetuity. As a result, every practicing mage and magus has a record of his magical activities—his *chancerium*—'burned' into the fundamental fabric of the Dark Energetic Continuum. If Plåk could locate Mybir's chancerium, he could examine that transcript.

The appearance of a chancerium was determined by the level and quantity of magic used by a given mage. Mages-in-training had tiny, inconspicuous chanceria; elderly archmages commanded far larger areas with complex patterns of arcanic impression stamped indelibly into the fundament. Residents of The Slice had a long-standing mutual agreement to treat the area where these records appeared as sacrosanct: a protected preserve, as it were.

There a definite art to reading these imprimatura collections. Time did not exist as such in The Slice; the spell record was not consequently inscribed in a temperolinear fashion. It was more like a multi-dimensional game board. Spells appeared distinct from talismans and phylacteries, as well. Each had a unique imprimatura. While spell energy demands crescendoed and decrescendoed fairly gradually, magic item use showed up as sudden bursts: one-time signals meant phylacteries; repeated identical pulses were diagnostic for talismans. There were, of course, rare exceptions to both cases.

It took Plåk some dedication to locate Mybir's chancerium. He followed it to its distal terminus and examined that activity pattern closely. The record was a bit muddled due to harmonics from nearby chanceria, but finally Plåk was able to identify Mybir's final manna usage. It showed a few trivial spells associated with day-to-day magic operations, followed by a strong burst from what must have been quite a powerful talisman.

The more Plåk studied that last entry, the more confused he grew. Talismans demonstrated a very specific and consistent energy use pattern. This one was perfectly conventional until the end, where it suddenly converted to a form that much more closely resembled a phylactery. Plåk had been an archmage for nine centums but in all that time he had never seen this precise signature. It was unique and therefore fascinating.

He realized he was going to need to establish some base assumptions in order to make any sense of what he was seeing. If Mybir's final companion was indeed Iwo, then the human had come to him for a reason. Given that Iwo was trying to distance himself from his past and Mybir was known for providing magic items that might be useful in that quest, there was nothing surprising to Plåk about having sought the archmage out.

A race-change talisman, which seemed the most logical item for Iwo to be seeking, provided only temporary effects. It would need to recharge between uses because it employed a form of manna flow known as 'pulse coupling' that posed much less risk than the power burst necessary to make the item's effects permanent. Magic at that level was far more demanding and required very careful orchestration under controlled conditions—which is why talismans were never designed to provide more than short-term actions of a few hours or, in unusual cases, a few days.

The signature was consistent with race-alteration magic until the bizarre transition at the end. That was the part Plåk had never seen before. He wondered precisely what Iwo hoped to achieve. The race change effect from a talisman was merely an illusion; it did not alter the physical or genetic reality of the subject. The most common incarnations of that magic item could only provide an illusion of a morphologically similar race, as well: it would not make a troll appear to be a dwarf, for example.

The only two races that were truly compatible with a human in terms of race change illusionary magic would be elf or orc. It suddenly struck Plåk that orcs as a race had been unknown to him on Morianella. He never even heard that word used until some years after he'd 'relocated' to Woklopen. For that matter, would Mybir ever have encountered humans before? They were confined to Morianella and Nusterton. Even the Nusterton colony was on the other side of Esmia from Mybir. The only way the archmage could have seen humans is if he had...

Plåk experienced the curious sensation a transcended archmage feels when a memory that resides totally 'offline' in The Slice is being downloaded into his active consciousness. After a few seconds the indexing was complete and he could access it. Exploring long-unregarded memories in this way was akin to reading an engrossing novel. Mybir had actually been a guest lecturer at the Morianella Arcane Academy! He hosted a series of seminars on enchanting magic items and their use in illusionary magic.

Plåk realized that this explained at one fell swoop how Mybir knew about humans and Iwo about Mybir and his specialty. He came across an even more germane recollection a little further on. In one of his lectures, Mybir had cautioned the students about tampering with the delicately-balanced energy pulses of certain talismans. The reason magic items of this sort provided only temporary effects, he said, is that talisman architecture could not reliably and predictably channel the power necessary for permanence. While it was theoretically possible during the enchanting process to convert the lower-intensity pulses to a single burst that would convey permanence, the energies required would be more than a talisman could handle; the 'side-effects' could potentially be catastrophic and even fatal.

Plåk began to piece together a scenario that made increasing sense as it evolved. Iwo had come to Moqip to commission a talisman to make himself appear as one of the races native to N'plork. He had, either intentionally or otherwise—but probably intentionally—interrupted the enchantment with a spell that all magi, even those at the Incipius level, knew. Timed just right, this break in the spell's normal conduct would interfere with the establishment of the pulsation aspect of the talisman, in effect potentially converting it to a phylactery loaded with much higher energy than was customary or safe.

It occurred to Plåk that combining this interruption, known in magical parlance as an 'interpel,' with a simple focus spell could provide a magic item with a one-time charge approaching artifact levels of power. These two spells were in fact very similar in nature to components of the suite employed to create artifacts. If that sequence had been carried out there should be some evidence of it in Mybir's chancerium even were Iwo the caster, because the enchantment was originated by the elder mage.

Tracking Iwo's chancerium might be of considerable utility, but as a mere Magus Incipius his would be far less obvious than Mybir's. The more Plåk considered the prospect, however, the more plausible it sounded. Finding and analyzing Iwo's magical 'transcript' might provide all sorts of insight into his activities and motivations. It would require, however, a protracted and unavoidably tedious hunt.

There was one thing that might make the quest for Iwo's chancerium slightly less onerous. Since humans were an entirely different species from N'plork natives with alien—albeit mostly equivalent—neural structure, the imprimaturae human magic created in the arcane substratum of The Slice were subtly but consistently separable. Since Plåk and Oloi were, at least to Plåk's knowledge, the only two transcended human archmages in existence (or at least for a few light years in any direction, which amounted to the same thing from a practical perspective), he didn't have a lot of practice spotting human chanceria. To be honest, transcendents really didn't spend much time looking at chanceria, even their own. They were, after all, merely endless holographic matrices of lines and smudges stamped into the walls and really not very riveting. It would be like browsing through your accumulated utility bills for pleasure.

The fact that the unique human magical signature was subtle meant that to have any real chance of picking it out from the kilometers of arcane transcript would require as much knowledge about his overall spell activity as possible. Tracking archmages was relatively straightforward; tracking Magi Incipius not so much. Their arcane records were considerably less extensive, for one thing; additionally, the impression made by their magic activity was much shallower and easier to overlook.

The simplest way to get this done would be, of course, through the use of magic. The problem with employing magic in this particular instance was that since the archive itself was by nature inviolable, the only way to conduct 'data analysis' on it was to create a copy first. He would have to make faithful impressions of large sections of the archive at a time onto manipulable fabric, create a viable search algorithm, and cut the data into pieces to be rearranged accordingly. That was a lot of work.

Thinking about the problem further, Plåk realized that since all he really needed to do was to define and search for some aspect of the arcane signature unique to humans, he could compare a known spell of his own with the same spell cast by a N'plorkian mage—another archmage, preferably, since the correlations would be more one-to-one—and with luck extract that information.

He already knew where to find to Ballop'ril's chancerium, so the bugbear became the obvious candidate. An added complication was that magic performed by a transcended archmage exhibited a different signature from that undertaken on Primus. Plåk had to locate that portion of his own chancerium inscribed before he transcended, which meant tracing his activity back quite a long way.

It took considerable scrutiny, but at last Plåk felt confident he'd identified the human-specific aspects of arcane signatures. Armed with this knowledge, he began moving along the chanceria searching magically for a match. After a few false positives he finally located Iwo's chancerium. It was exceedingly odd.

The first part of the arcane record was quite conventional, chronicling Iwo's development as a mage the way Plåk, or more accurately Dennis Blass, remembered it. There were two obvious regions of disjunction, however, that resembled nothing Plåk had ever before observed. The first was an abrupt shift from purely human to something else: something that more closely resembled goblin. It was slightly preceded by a burst of powerful magic originating outside the chancerial continuum; in other words, a spell not cast by Iwo himself but intimately affecting his arcanic presence. It strongly resembled, although strangely did not match precisely, activity associated with an artifact.

The second anomalous region was much more recent, and far more puzzling. In it, Iwo's unusual but still easily traceable signature suddenly transitioned into what could only be called a 'smear.' While the underlying pattern—the arcanitecture—remained relatively normal, the imprimatura itself went a little crazy. What events it portrayed were a mystery at first reading; it would require carefully teasing out the different concurrent threads to understand fully.

The latter anomaly seemed to have occurred about a centum after the first, based on comparison with the timing of known magical events in adjacent chanceria. It was decidedly odd, and got odder the more closely Plåk examined it. The most important revelation was that at one point in the chancerium the imprimatura stopped showing any human arcane characteristics at all. It degenerated into a confused muddle for a while that finally stabilized as something not quite compatible with any other signature in the N'plorkian archive.

Something had happened to Iwo then, something dramatic. The chancerial record continued unbroken; there was no possibility the latter segment had been generated by some other mage. The unavoidable conclusion was that Iwo had undergone a change so fundamentally transformative that he was no longer human—nor goblin nor any other recognizable species.

As Plåk continued tracing along the chancerium looking for additional clues, he suddenly came across perhaps the most shocking discovery of all: Iwo, or whatever he had become, was still alive and practicing magic. The record was being added to as he stood there watching.

This final revelation was a game-changer for Plåk. This was no longer merely academic arcane historical research, but the ongoing chronicle of something extraordinary. If what he was seeing was correct—and he had every reason to believe it was—a contemporary of his own time on Primus was still alive nine centums later *without having transcended*. What changes Iwo had undergone, and via what mechanisms, suddenly took on extreme and unexpected importance in the archmage's mind. He needed to tell two people immediately: Oloi and Boogla.

Finding Oloi usually wasn't difficult, as transcended archmages could track one another by their arcane presence unless the mage being tracked consciously suppressed it. Oloi was sitting on the dramatic veranda fronting the stately home he'd shaped from the substrate of The Slice, sipping some form of manna-based tea. He watched as Plåk came walking up but made no remark.

"Hello, Oloi. May I talk to you for a bit?"

Oloi nodded. "Pull up a seat. What's on your mind?"

"I finally traced Philmon Iwo, the mage who defaced the *Codex Lapidismotus* in Morianella. I believe he underwent some form of transmorphication in Moqip after fleeing Morianella. There is also evidence he was at least partially responsible for the demise of the human colony north of Jessmirto."

Oloi raised his eyebrows. "There was another human colony besides Morianella?"

"Yes. We launched two lifeboats from the *Isomer*. The comm sync failed during atmosphere penetration; we thought the other ship might have been lost. They apparently made landfall off the Paradiddle Islands, however, and eventually established a settlement on the Esmian mainland. I found the remains of that colony; nearly all of them perished quite suddenly just before Iwo, having fled there from Morianella sometime earlier, took passage to Nar Braylov. He lived in Nar Braylov for a while and then travelled over to Moqip, where it looks as though he encountered archmage Mybir...just before *he* died while transcending."

"Seems to be rather attracted to misfortune, this Iwo," Oloi observed wryly.

"Indeed. While he lacks talent for the magical arts, the same cannot be said for murder."

"Lacks? Present tense?"

"Yes. His chancerium is unbroken from arcanic inception to the present day. Philmon Iwo is still alive, somehow."

"That would make him nine hundred years old and the last genetically intact human on N'plork. You'd think someone would have noticed, transmorphication or not."

"I don't think he's even close to being a genetically intact human any longer. The transmorphication was anomalous. It was talismanic in origin, but the energy flow was abruptly boosted by several orders of magnitude."

"Perhaps an artifact, then? Is there a correspondent bleb?"

"No. Not an artifact. I suspect it was actually a well-timed caesura."

"Ugh. Nasty business, that."

"Yes, well, someone who would murder thousands of people is obviously not constrained by the ethical considerations of magic."

"True enough. How do you theorize he managed to stay

biologically alive all this time?"

"Excellent question. Whatever he did, it shows up rather dramatically in his chancerium. There is a pronounced discontinuity anomaly, following which the arcanic signature resumes with significant alterations. The resumption shows traits of human, goblin, and something else I can't identify."

"That raises other questions. If Iwo is still alive, where is he? Why is the magical community not aware of his presence? Why, for that matter, is he not an archmage by now?"

"He's not an archmage because he doesn't have enough native talent. I worked with him for years on Morianella, but he never made it beyond Incipius for a good reason. As to why we aren't aware of him, I think we actually are. He changed his name somewhere along the way, possibly more than once."

"Indeed? Which one is he using these days?"

"Zizmziz."

Chapter Twenty-One

Boogla was both stunned and intrigued by Plåk's discovery. Intrigued, because it explained why Gumnil Ke-juq's childhood portrayal was so inconsistent: it never happened. At the same time she was deeply disturbed by the clear implication that the highly-respected historian was also a mass murderer. The stunned part came when the archmage told her of his strong suspicion that Philmon Iwo, who had become Gumnil Ke-juq, had taken on yet another name to cover his apparent immortality: Zizmziz, leader of the infamous Umbral mages.

It was no coincidence that Iwo would choose to represent himself with a palindrome. It was entirely in keeping with his deliberate delusion of magical prowess. Palindromic names held special significance for most of the societies on N'plork; they were widely regarded as harboring latent power due to their symmetry. While history granted famous figures palindromic monikers on occasion in recognition of their contributions, adoption of such a name for oneself was considered the height of arrogance and in most cases an ill omen to boot.

Not that any of this mattered to Zizmziz, of course. It was difficult to say how much, if any, of Philmon Iwo remained in the shell he'd built for himself. Although Boogla, Oloi, and Plåk were now aware of his original identity, none of them truly understood the creature he had become. Keeping a human alive for nine hundred years was beyond N'plorkian science or magic, at least insofar as it was known to any of them. Especially puzzling was how a mage who never progressed beyond the lowest 'professional' tier—Magus Incipius—could have pulled off such a feat.

"When I knew Iwo," Plåk said to Oloi as they sat sharing another pot of manna-tea, "He was smart enough to be a good mage, but something about magic never clicked for him."

"What was his occupational specialty on the *Isomer*?" Oloi asked.

"He worked on deck 16 as a life support systems tech, I think. Understand that as a colonization vessel we did not all have rigidly-defined slots the way you guys did in the space services. I was formally designated as a physical sciences officer, but I'd served two hitches in the military before signing on. Not very many of the crew had gone that route."

"I've always meant to ask you about the *Isomer* and its voyage. We knew about the early colonization missions, of course, but we lost contact with most of them. If I remember right yours was one of quite a few in that period classified as 'OU'—Outcome Unknown. What happened, exactly?"

"We were heading for the Reticulum main sequence field; the Trans-Neptunian Observatory reported a cluster of high-probability habitables in that vicinity."

Oloi chuckled. "On one of our missions we actually swung by the optical telescope cluster of the TNO. It was still mostly in working order, even after all that time."

"Not that surprising. They were great instruments. Anyway, we had probably just penetrated the heliopause of the N'plorkian system when there was a global oxygen maintenance generator failure alarm. I'd never seen one of those before, even in training. We all assumed it was a systems fault, because there was no way all of the oxygen generators could fail at once. A shipwide OMG alarm was something you might discuss in the classroom but never seriously plan for, because the odds of it occurring were too low to be credible. There were multiple generators on each deck and they operated semi-autonomously, with three levels of failsafe."

"How was that sort of failure even possible, then?"

"I don't think it was. My guess was some exceedingly unlikely catastrophic alarm unit fault."

"That somehow affected dozens of semi-autonomous subsystems simultaneously? The odds against that are also astronomical."

"If it was a random electrical fault, yes. But not if it was sabotage."

"Sabotage? What purpose would sabotaging oxygen generator failure alarms serve?"

"Not sure. Perhaps to cover some other activity. The decision to launch lifeboats came when the probe halo reported that one of the planets in the current system was habitable. Since we were a colonization mission anyway, the captain felt it prudent to accelerate the schedule."

"What sort of activity would that sabotage reasonably cover?"

"I don't know."

"Who or what do you think might be responsible?"

"At the time I just put it down to exceedingly bad luck. In hindsight I believe there may have been something more sinister in play."

"Do you have a suspect?"

"Isn't it obvious?"

"Iwo?"

"Yes. He had access to the alarm systems and, as we now know, little regard for ethics or morality."

"I'll admit he seems a likely candidate—but what did he hope to gain by panicking an entire crew? Do you think abandoning ship was his intent?"

"I figure the only way we'll ever know for sure is to ask him."

"Tricky."

✳   ✳   ✳   ✳   ✳

The tower Zizmziz had ordered built for himself was really a fortification. Its primary purpose was apparently more aligned with defending against a concerted attack than providing stylish corporate headquarters facilities. Anyone who erects and inhabits a fortress, Tol reasoned, is expecting a war. The Bashers seemed to be of the opinion that they could simply storm the place in their usual fashion and be successful. Tol harbored serious doubts about this strategy, which is why he had detached himself from the invasion force.

At least two archmages had warned Tol about Zizmziz; he was therefore going to regard the subject as armed and extremely dangerous. When approaching perps of that ilk Tol's preferred tactic was stealth, rather than all-out frontal assault. While the combined units of Tantatku EE were massing in the woods across from the Umbral complex, Tol slipped quietly away. The EE officer assigned to watch him tried to follow, but Tol passed momentarily out of his sight behind a large arbor and did not emerge from the other side. The officer walked all the way around the base of the tree twice but found no trace of his Tragacanthan counterpart. He was forced to return to the command post with news that Sir Tol-u-ol had seemingly disappeared.

Tol *had* in fact disappeared, although not with conscious intent. He was aware he was being followed, of course, but not overly concerned about it. He had far more important things to occupy his attention, most of them centered on not getting killed or injured by the maniac of a mage in the fortress in front of him or the maniacs assaulting it. The officer trailing him wasn't particularly good at it; Tol could have ditched him fairly easily. He didn't see any point in that, though. He wasn't concerned with hiding from anyone except Zizmziz.

He was trying to figure out if there was any reasonable way to scale the wall up to a balcony he could see about halfway along one of the four towers surrounding the massive central building. There wasn't much in the way of handholds visible, but maybe where the tower met the curtain wall of the center building he'd have more luck. He was circling around to get a better view while pondering the best approach when there was a sudden flash of light in his brain that literally knocked him down. He regained situational awareness in a dark place surrounded by neatly (and recently) mortared stones. Standing and peering over the edge of a chest-high wall, he realized he was now in fact on that very balcony.

While he probably would never get truly accustomed to this sort of thing, this time Tol wasn't completely disoriented by the unexpected relocation. He figured out where he was fairly quickly and moved on with a resigned shrug. At least he didn't have to scale a potentially slippery stone wall in the early morning gloom.

If Zizmziz was aware of the impending assault, and unlike Akkla Tol believed he was, the mage would probably be in some sort of 'situation room' or command center. That would more than likely be located in the most defensible area of the structure. It would also need to be supplied with lots of wiring leading to data input devices like cameras and alarms, he reasoned. If he could find one of those devices and trace the wires, he might be able to follow them back to the command center.

Tol put one hand into a pocket and found a small leather-covered box nestled in there. Puzzled, he extracted it and realized it was the carrying case for the magic items the forensic mages had given him. He unfolded the attached instruction sheet. *I probably should have looked at this a little earlier*, he thought, *but better late than never*.

There were two items in the box, because he was still wearing the third, an anti-telekinesis ring. He remembered what the forensic mage had told him about not being able to teleport unless the ring had been temporarily overridden and wondered if it actually worked. The fact that he was standing on the stone balcony suggested that it didn't. He scratched behind his ear and decided he would sort that out later. For now he'd investigate the other tools.

One of them was a missile shield amulet. It deflected ballistic projectiles and absorbed energy pulses that impacted the shield cocoon, re-emitting the energy pulses as heat. While that protected the wearer from these types of attacks, it wasn't necessarily good news for anyone, friend or foe, standing nearby. For that reason it came with a large-print warning label to be extremely cautious

275

employing it in a crowd of people you actually like.

The third of the magical protections was supplied in the form of a medallion that could be carried in an overjack pocket or, more effectively, sewed into its lining. This talisman protected the bearer during plummets from high places by exerting a strong upward force whenever it detected free fall. The counteracting force was inversely proportional in strength to the medallion's distance from the planet's surface. It was entertaining simply to hold it out and release, watching its downward progress slow until the medallion touched the floor ever so gently.

Armed thusly and with his trusty boosted disruptor in hand, Tol crept along the balcony until he came to a doorway leading into the tower proper. The door was locked, but the lock didn't look very elaborate and Tol had it defeated in a matter of seconds. Before he actually opened the door, however, he ran his fingers along the inside rim of the door frame, feeling for telltale bumps that might indicate an alarm. His efforts were rewarded by a slight raised area where the anchors for the alarm trigger were embedded in the framing. From his pocket Tol pulled two pieces of metal with a coil of thin wire connecting them and slid the apparatus gently between the door and frame just behind the bump. The metal ends were magnetized and clung to the two halves of the alarm contact while the coil of wire maintained electrical continuity, allowing him to open the door just far enough to squeeze through.

He went through this process a total of four times, at last arriving at the innermost cylinder. This door had a more difficult lock and what he guessed were multiple alarm points. He stood there for a moment wondering what the best strategy for tackling it would be when he heard voices coming along the circular corridor. He ran in the opposite direction and slipped through an open door into a small room, closing and locking the door behind him. He held his breath as the voices passed by.

His sanctuary was a janitorial closet of sorts. It had shelves with assorted cleaning supplies and a few lockers, one of which was not secured. Inside, hanging from a hook, was a loose-fitting jump suit outfitted with a plethora of pockets both large and small. The front and back panels of the jumpsuit bore the black arc and arbor logo of the Umbral mages that he had first encountered in Woklopen. It gave Tol an idea.

The jumpsuit wasn't a perfect fit, especially over his jack, but it was good enough. He had fortunately left his EE helmet in the pram he'd driven to the staging area. Ensuring that the coast was clear, Tol resumed his trek sporting the new camouflage. As he walked, now nodding to rather than avoiding passersby, he felt around in the various pockets. One of them had a particularly curious item in it, which proved on examination to be some form of air filtration mask. Perhaps the staff who wore these clothes were responsible for painting or fumigation.

As he was approaching what appeared to be a major intersection of hallways, two people dressed in jumpsuits similar to Tol's suddenly appeared. As they passed, one of them, a hobgoblin, called out.

"Here, you. Get up to His Magnificence's suite and adjust th' temperature. He's been raisin' a bloody ruckus about it fer th' last half hour. Go on, now!"

Tol shrugged and headed down the hall. The hob yelled after at him.

"Not *that* way. Take the hydrolift!"

Tol decided to play dumb. Well, actually he wasn't playing in this particular instance.

"Uh, I think I lost my, um, access card," he said, hoping that was the right kind of credential here.

The hob gave him an exasperated look and tapped his own jumpsuit pocket. "It's right there wheres it's supposed to be in yer pocket, you heavy-pated clod."

Tol patted the indicated area and gave him a goofy smile. "Bless me. So it is." He turned and walked away in the other direction. The hob shook his head. "I don't know where the staffing office finds these clods, but I wisht they'd look somewheres else."

Tol was pleased he'd managed to stumble across something that would make accessing Zizmziz a little easier than anticipated. True, he didn't know what a 'hydrolift' was precisely, but at least he knew it lay in this general direction. His search for it now carried the additional cachet of 'just following orders.' He marched down one hallway and up another, minimizing contact with others by appearing to be on an urgent mission.

He wound his way along an inwardly-spiraling path until he came at last to a hemispherical bulge with a doorway cut into its face. There were levers on either side of the thin rectangular tracing—next to one was an arrow pointing up; beside the other the arrow pointed down. Tol shrugged and flipped the 'up' lever. Nothing seemed to happen for a few moments, then a whooshing, gurgling noise that suggested a huge toilet flushing came rumbling up the tube. A panel slid open to reveal a cylindrical room big enough for perhaps a dozen adult goblins.

Tol figured out he was supposed to enter the little chamber, but felt strangely reluctant to do so. He could see passersby eyeing him curiously, though, so he took a deep breath and stepped in to allay suspicion. The door closed behind him. He wasn't sure what was supposed to be happening now, but he felt reasonably certain that some sensation of movement would be part of it. He noticed a column of circular indentations running parallel to the door frame, each with a letter embossed on it presumably corresponding to a floor serviced by the lift. He pressed the top one and the little room began to move upward.

The faintly comical gurgling that accompanied this movement suggested that the transport chamber—whatever it was called— was supported on a column of water; hence, 'hydrolift.' Tol started thinking about the water pumps that would be required to raise a box full of people up to the very top of this tower and decided he didn't know enough about engineering or fluid mechanics to make much progress there. It was an interesting idea, at any rate.

The buttons lit up as their corresponding floor was reached; at least, that's the way Tol presumed it worked. There seemed to be more floors than he would have guessed from the outside. Curious. He was between the top floor and the one below it, according to the lights on the panel, when the transporter suddenly stopped. Scant seconds later he heard shouts through the walls and the sounds of running feet, followed by sharp pops and the occasional boom. Something dramatic was going on; Tol guessed the Bashers had begun their assault—in the least stealthy manner possible, to boot. Might as well have announced that an attack was imminent over a public address system out in the woods.

He needed to get out of this little transport capsule, and quickly. He tried to force the doors open, with no success. He'd probably just be faced with a solid wall, anyway, Tol thought. If this thing was floating on water, he definitely didn't want to go through the floor. That left only a ceiling composed of square panels any or all of which could be removable. He pushed on them one by one until a slight upward movement encouraged him to push harder. The panel resisted at first, but eventually slid up and out of the way on top-mounted rails.

Tol felt around the edges of the opening and fingered a bundle of rods and wires that when yanked unrolled into a nifty little ladder. He tested his weight on it and once satisfied it would hold, clambered up into the darkness on top of the transport pod. He kept the location of the access portal firmly in mind at all times in case the pod suddenly started moving again. He didn't want to end up as goblin-flavored paste smeared across the roof of the shaft.

He was only a meter or so below the doorway to the top floor. He wrenched a piece of metal off the walls and employed it to lever apart the sliding doors. Tol squeezed himself through the opening and got to his feet just in time to dodge a knot of people who came running past waving what appeared to be weapons of a form he'd never seen before. They aggressively ignored him; in a few seconds the corridor was deserted save Tol.

He noticed high on a wall a red light flashing: silent but insistent. Twenty meters along there was another. Whatever was going on—and he felt even more certain it involved the Bashers—the building seemed to be in a state of general quarters. He shook his head; that undoubtedly meant that Zizmziz would be hunkered down in some heavily-fortified area and thus much more difficult to access. He hated heavy-handed tactics when subtlety and nuance would have been so much more effective. Nothing he could do about it now.

The design of the tower's inner sanctum was strangely familiar. Tol frowned, wondering where he'd run across this layout before. He passed a computer terminal set into the wall next to a doorway and suddenly it hit him: this was amazingly similar to the Tragacanthan Royal Palace. It could just be coincidence, of course, but the more he saw the more he suspected the same architects were involved. Perhaps he could use the correspondence to his advantage...

Tol pulled up his mental map of the palace and ran through it, hallway by hallway and room by room. He didn't expect there to be a one-to-one match, but he was hoping that the functional resemblance was more than superficial. He picked a door to test his theory. If the correspondence was strong, this one should lead to a 'choke hole:' a windowless room where a pursuing force could be trapped by doors whose locks could only be operated from the outside.

The telltale but easily overlooked external locking module was present; so far, so good. He opened the sliding door and peered inside. Very sparsely furnished, no windows, one other identical door with no interior knob—and two rows of almost invisible 'kill ports' facing each other across the long axis of the rectangular room: it fit the profile precisely.

There should be four of these rooms in total, spaced evenly around the central core like spokes on a wheel. Between them were narrow corridors that led straight into the innermost area, the command center, but sporting vicious traps that were activated when the facility was on battle footing, as it surely must be now. There were only two safe ways into the command center in this situation: an easily-defensible spiral staircase and a hallway with multiple iron doors, each requiring a different access key to open. The corridor itself had at least a dozen cameras along its length, and each door's lock release mechanism could be overridden from the command center if the security chief determined the person using the key was not authorized for entry.

He had no way of knowing if any or all of these measures were in place here, of course. He was simply extrapolating based on the close similarity to the Tragacanthan Palace layout he'd observed so far. Whatever intrusion prevention mechanisms existed, he had to assume they were comprehensive and deadly. Tol sighed. This operation would have been *much* simpler if the Bashers hadn't shown their oversized hand so early.

His only viable tactic at this point was to take full advantage of the status his appropriated clothing afforded and try to bluff his way into the command center and the presence of his quarry. At least, he hoped that's where Zizmziz was. He was making a lot of presumptions here, but he had to start somewhere.

If they had any sense at all they were going to be particularly suspicious of anomalous behavior right now; if he wanted to bluff his way in he was going to have to be quite convincing. Sauntering up to a door and ringing the bell, as it were, probably wasn't going to work. He walked quickly down the corridor to reinforce the illusion he was just an employee attending to some urgent errand while examining every passing detail with his expert tracker's eye.

As he surveilled a group of soldiers came running up. The sergeant barked at him.

"You! We need a maintenance tech in the pit. Come on!"

Tol shrugged. Best to just go with the flow. "Right behind you."

The 'pit,' as it turned out, was the very command center that was his target, located in a recessed circle of floor with terraces of consoles and free-standing instrumentation surrounding it. Tol wasn't sure to what to attribute this run of luck, but he hoped it would be a long-term phenomenon. He was passed into this inner sanctum without even a basic ID check, based solely on the fact that he was wearing the right clothes and in the company of trusted people. You can buy all the locks and security devices you want, he mused, but if you don't implement security in your people you're just whistling in the wind.

They wanted Tol to adjust the temperature, as the hob had said. He peered in the direction one of them pointed and saw the wall-mounted thermostat. Tol was not any sort of engineer, but he knew how to adjust a thermostat. Or, at least *look* like he was. Based on what he'd seen so far, they wouldn't exactly be expecting him to be a genius here. He walked over to the thermostat and they all turned back to what they were doing. Tol pried the case off and started fiddling with wires while he eavesdropped on the proceedings.

It was obvious that the entire crew was on high alert. If the Bashers had begun some sort of assault, that wasn't in the least surprising. Tol surveyed the room. He wondered which one of these jloks was Zizmziz. He had expected some villainous caricature with a black cape and an evil laugh, but no one here even resembled that profile. They were just a bunch of regular-looking people doing their jobs. Maybe this wasn't the true command center, after all. Or maybe Zizmziz just went to the toilet—it was hard to say.

After a few minutes of listening, it became apparent to Tol that Zizmziz himself was not in fact in the room. He heard references to 'the master' that led him to believe that the mage was in 'the bubble,' whatever and wherever that was. He looked for doors and found one curiously-shaped outline in a far wall surrounded by "Authorized Personnel Only" and "Restricted Access" signs. There was obviously *something* in there they wanted to keep private. It was his best bet.

One of the staff walked up. "Got that thing fixed yet? The Master needs you in the Bubble."

Tol tried to hide his shock. "Um, yeah, it's fixed. It will take a little while for the temperature in the room to catch up, though."

"What was wrong with it?"

Tol thought fast, but he was drawing a blank until he heard a familiar voice through bone induction. "It had a, um...misaligned thermocouple. It's back in the right place now." He hoped Petey had given him a reasonable explanation.

The other gob seemed to be fine with it. "Good. Come on. We mustn't keep His Magnificence waiting any longer. He's got a lot on his plate right now, what with the attack and all."

"What is all that about, anyway?" Tol asked.

"You remember the all-hands broadcast yesterday? The one about the misguided puppets of the Tantatku government? They're here now, and they're trying to arrest His Magnificence on some trumped-up charges because they feel threatened by his wisdom."

Tol tried to look a little frightened. "What...are we going to do?"

The gob smiled. "His Magnificence has installed ingenious projectile weapons the likes of which no one has ever before seen. They will repulse these foolish invaders and send them slinking back to the sad halls of government to lick their many wounds."

Tol had the sudden urge to check the floor around this jlok to look for manure running out, because he seemed to be brimming with it. There was some useful information buried in that slopfest, however. Zizmziz had announced *yesterday* that this attack was going to happen. That means he more than likely had some sort of advance warning; a mole in EE's ranks, perhaps? A sprout of doubt sprang up. If Zizmziz knew about the impending attack, did he also know about Tol?

As he followed the gob up a seemingly infinite spiral staircase to the Bubble, Tol could hear sharp popping noises coming from all directions. He'd never heard any sound quite like that before; he wondered if they might be the 'projectile weapons' the gob had mentioned. Although he wasn't a fan of the Bashers' tactics, he hoped they weren't suffering casualties, nonetheless. He needed to put a stop to those weapons as soon as possible.

The Bubble, once they finally reached it, was aptly named. It was a heavily-reinforced dome with twenty centimeter-thick explosive-resistant glass in the windows. At the center of the dome was an elevated chair that could rotate through 360°, surrounded by three levels of consoles and screens. Occupying the seat was... *something* Tol could only presume was Zizmziz. He had a hard time categorizing the person by race. It looked a bit like a hobgoblin or large gnome wearing a goblin skin that had seen its best years when Tol was an infant. He tried not to stare, but it was a real challenge.

"The maintenance tech is here to adjust the temperature, Your Magnificence."

Zizmziz turned to look at them. He stared at Tol intently for a few seconds. Tol did his best to appear awed and respectful.

"I would suggest that you accord my requests a little higher priority next time, Subcommander. I've been sweltering in here for over half an hour."

"Profound apologies, Your Magnificence. The General Quarters alert shut down the hydrolift and the maintenance tech was unable to respond more quickly."

"The General Quarters would not have been an issue had the tech responded in a timely manner to begin with. At any rate, I want a maintenance tech assigned to the command center on a full-time basis henceforward."

"Yes, Your Magnificence. It shall be as you command." The gob headed back down the ladder. "Please get this fixed as quickly as possible," he whispered to Tol as he passed by. Tol gave him a thumbs-up sign and ambled over to the thermostat mounted between two windows. He yanked the cover off and fiddled aimlessly with the wires while he surreptitiously sized up the room. There was only one entrance in evidence: the trapdoor in the floor through which he had come. He didn't buy that, though. Anyone who would build a fortress like this would hardly put his operational headquarters in a place where he'd be trapped if the command center was overrun.

That meant there was another way out. His EE dossier said Zizmziz regarded himself as a great mage, so perhaps the other exit relied somehow on magic. The dossier also implied that he wasn't nearly as good a mage as he styled himself to be, however. Tol wondered just exactly what Zizmziz actually was. His dossier hadn't even seemed all that clear on *who* he was, for that matter.

Now that he'd gained unexpected access to his quarry, Tol just needed to figure out how this was going to work. Even if he did successfully place this jlok under arrest, how was he going to get him past all those loyal employees down there? Well, since the Bashers were obviously committed to their insane assault, he'd just keep an eye on him from here and wait for his more energetic and militant brethren to secure the building before delivering the boss to them. He'd really like to take Zizmziz back to Tragacanth for trial directly, but that would be tantamount to kidnapping from Tantatku's viewpoint, so he'd just have to wait for the diplomats to play their extradition footsies.

Zizmziz had been intent on his screens and apparently ignoring Tol, so when he spoke it took a second for Tol to identify the sound.

"What is your name, maintenance technician?"

Tol's head jerked up; time to think fast.

"Um, Tosh, Your Magnificence," he replied, using a nickname Aspet had given him when they were kids.

Zizmziz grunted. "I find it most peculiar, Tosh, that a lowly maintenance tech should possess an arcane aura. Do you have an explanation for that?"

Tol decided to base his answer on the truth. "People have asked me that before, Your Magnificence. I don't rightly know why I have one. It just...happened one day. I'm not any kind of mage, I promise you."

"Of course you aren't. You would not have been hired into that menial position were you trained in the magical arts. Still, I am disappointed that your aura was not detected in the employment screening process. I shall have to investigate the staffing resources mage who interviewed you. What was his name?"

"I...don't remember, Your Magnificence. I'm only a maintenance tech, after all."

"Yes, yes. Quite so. I've no further time to devote to the puzzle at present, regardless. We are under attack by a pack of witless worms that have no concept of the power at my command, for if they did they would run whimpering into the morning mists."

Tol decided to take advantage of the opening to try a little intelligence-gathering. "Aren't you afraid they might trap us up here?"

Zizmziz laughed. "Ah, no. First, I could destroy their pathetic little force long before they penetrated this far. Second, I have multiple exits from here, even if they did by some chance succeed."

Tol nodded. "I guess someone as smart as you would have, at that."

At this point the popping noises surrounding them suddenly got much louder and more frequent.

"Excuse my ignorance, Your Magnificence, but what is making that sound?" Tol asked, covering his ears.

"That," Zizmziz replied, smiling grimly, "Is why any attack on this fortification has no chance of succeeding. They are known as *rifles*. They propel a dense metallic slug at very high velocity through a barrel that has been grooved in a spiral manner along its inside surface so that the projectile flies true. The popping sound comes from the detonation of my special propellant, which I call 'firepowder'."

Tol suddenly became very concerned about the Bashers. The rifles sounded potentially more deadly than the usual weapons employed by criminals, more so because they would not have adequate defenses against them prepared. He needed more information.

"Where would you even get ammunition for a thing like that?" he asked.

"We make it here, of course," Zizmziz replied, pride evident in his voice. "In the foundry down in the sublevels. The weapons are manufactured there, as well, as is the firepowder. This facility is wholly self-contained, which is why it can never be defeated by their primitive tactics and weaponry."

Scarcely had the final word escaped the mage's mouth when an extremely loud crash accompanied the collapse of part of the bubble's ceiling by a huge irregularly-shaped object. Tol and Zizmziz were both thrown to the floor by the shock wave. Tol stood up and dusted himself off. He surveyed the shattered roof beams, stone, and plaster now occupying most of the chamber.

"Unless, of course, they dropped a huge rock on us," he observed, as Basher commandoes came streaming in through the newly-opened hole. Zizmziz roared with rage and threw up his hands to cast some spell, but two Basher mages counteracted it before it could come to fruition. This enraged Zizmziz even more. He stood there sputtering for a moment before reaching for a pouch on his belt and extracting a small deep-black sphere. One of the Bashers approached him. "Magus Zizmziz, you are hereby placed under order of confinement for crimes against Tantatku and other nations."

The magus smirked. "I think you will find that order rather difficult to carry out," he said, holding the sphere in front of him. Without warning the bubble was filled with an impossibly intense light and a noise that penetrated every pore of their bodies. When he finally regained his senses, Tol found himself alone in the destroyed bubble, having been flung with considerable force against one wall. There was no sign of either Zizmziz or the Bashers. The way Tol had come in was now blocked by debris; he'd need to find one of those other exits. Checking himself for injuries, he noticed that the ring on his finger was glowing a dull red.

Tol climbed over the crumbled stone and twisted steel beams until he found himself at the edge of a rather precipitous dropoff. He was on the very tiptop of the tower, actually *above* it, as the Bubble was located in a column surmounting the main tower by several tens of meters but encased in a semi-permanent cloaking spell that rendered it basically invisible from a distance. That explained the surplus of floors on the hydrolift panel. Tol marveled at what it must have taken to loft that huge rock so far and so precisely, not to mention getting those commandos all the way up here. He hoped they were all right.

No obvious safe path to the ground presented itself even after considerable surveying. Tol was reduced to standing as close to the edge as he dared while waving and shouting. After a full half-hour of this it became obvious to Tol that no one could hear or see him. He pulled his comm and tried to call out. Even with arcane heterodyning he got no signal at all. The shielding must extend down into the radio frequency spectrum. Tol sighed. While he remembered that one of the magic items he carried was supposed to protect him from falling injuries, he hadn't properly tested it beforehand and so wasn't prepared to trust blindly in its efficacy.

He really wasn't left with a lot of options here. He could either wait for a rescue that might never come or try climbing down. The climbing option would be a little more attractive if he had some rope and the surface he needed to be traversing was actually, you know, *visible*. This would be like rock-climbing in absolute darkness— relying solely on feel. He doubted even miss rock-climber Selpla would find that prospect very inviting.

Thinking about Selpla was a mistake, because now he had to face raging hormones as well as roaring acrophobia and rising vertigo. He could close his eyes to fight the latter two, but doing that invariably increased the first. Ordinarily keeping one's eyes open might be considered a definite plus when attempting to descend safely from a precarious height, but given that the uppermost thirty meters or so of said perch was invisible even in good light, it really didn't make a lot of difference.

Tol started feeling around the pinnacle's rocks with his fingers. At first it was difficult to translate what he was perceiving by touch into a mental image that was useful for climbing purposes, but finally he started to understand the pattern in which the stones were laid and thereby to make slow progress in his descent. As he established a rhythm he also learned that concentrating on his own hands to the exclusion of all else minimized the vertigo. As he approached what he estimated to be the halfway point between the bubble and the upper surface of the main building, where the cloaking effect terminated, Tol felt a curious and somewhat disturbing shift in the stones beneath his feet and hands.

It happened again a few seconds later: an abrupt vibration that shook the entire structure. There was a third, more intense movement and then before the undulations from that had died away a loud crunching noise accompanied by a pronounced sway announced the complete breakup of the structure. Fifteen seconds after the first hint of trouble Tol was in free fall.

He flailed around in mid-air, trying to find something to grab that might reduce his velocity or cushion the landing. He found a large block and latched onto it, as much for psychological reassurance as anything. Having something solid in his hands seemed somehow preferable to just...falling. As he struggled to find an orientation that might increase his odds of surviving this, Tol's luck suddenly took a turn for the worse when a huge chunk of stone with reinforcing steel netting embedded in it broke off from a larger fragment and struck the back of his head a glancing blow. As he lost consciousness Tol figured he would never wake up.

The odors of baled grass and freshly-ground grain filled the air. They were smells he knew well, but had not encountered since childhood. They put him in mind of the feed store where he'd worked as a lad. The area beyond his immediate vision was curiously misty and indistinct, but every now and then a shape loomed up from that mist that became something or someone familiar. A number of half-remembered images passed before his eyes in succession before dissolving back into the nebulous ether.

One image that did *not* dissolve was that of a goblin whose facial features gradually clarified into those belonging to his father. Tol knew his father had been deceased for some years, but his appearance in this peculiar place and time did not seem out of the ordinary. His dad stood there regarding him for a long moment with an expression that started out as surprise, perhaps with a soupçon of delight, but soon morphed into concern and finally urgency.

"Tol," the apparition began. The introduction of a soundtrack seemed like a bizarre addition to Tol, who had grown quite comfortable with only the information vision and smell were providing. He shook his head quickly as though to dislodge the irritation of audio. His father seemed not to notice.

"I have to tell you something and we don't have much time, so just listen to me."

Tol nodded in agreement; he wasn't even sure he knew *how* to talk anymore.

"Your sisters were not killed by accident. They were murdered by Zizmziz. Your mother carried a gene for natural magic use that was thought to be passed only from mother to daughter. They call them *wiccalts*. Zizmziz was terrified that your sisters might be able to understand who is really is, and what he did, so he arranged to have them killed. He intended to kill your mother at the same time, but she was spared somehow. We never spoke of that incident because an archmage told us that doing so would endanger her and the entire family. We did not want you and Aspet to have to live your lives in fear, so we erased that event from the family history as well as we were able."

The specter paused, as though collecting its thoughts. "But they were wrong about the genetic transmission. Both of you sons also carry that gene. Aspet's expressed in his supernatural ability to concentrate; to navigate the intricacies of computer networks and programs. It now manifests in his superb statecraft, as well. Yours, on the other hand, lay dormant until Ix activated it. Now you have abilities that no one, even the transcended archmages, can begin to understand. Your destiny likewise is hidden. One thing only do I ask of you: *avenge your sisters.*"

As he spoke these words he began to melt into the background, followed soon by the dissolution of said background itself. Everything went black, but it was a blackness Tol recognized after a time as that which accompanied his eyes being shut. He opened them gingerly, having no idea what to expect, given his most recent waking memories.

He was lying on his back amidst a jumble of broken stones and twisted metal. As his last conscious memories came flooding back he felt along his arms and legs and ribs: nothing seemed to be broken, although his head sported an acutely sore contusion. Odd. There was really no way he should have survived that plummet, especially not intact. Inspecting his chest he came across an unfamiliar lump; suddenly his survival became a little less mysterious. The talisman that was supposed to cushion him in a fall apparently functioned as promised.

He sat up and looked around, trying to suppress the dream or whatever it was on the grounds that he didn't want to think about any of that stuff right now, in the middle of a mission—a mission that had gone very south. His quarry had vanished into thin air, along with everyone else in that room at the time but Tol. Then the room itself had vanished, although the final destination of the components thereof was less mysterious, being scattered all around him now.

Tol got to his feet and began to take stock of the surroundings. He was on the roof of another building, probably the main structure of the erstwhile Umbral command center. There were gaping holes in the tiles through which he could glimpse a chaotic jumble of shattered furniture and twisted load-bearing members, along with the occasional corpse. There was now no doubt in Tol's mind why they were known as "The Bashers." Everything and everyone within his field of vision had been most thoroughly bashed.

The bodies lying here and there were mostly rank and file employees of Zizmziz. Tol couldn't say much of anything good about the Bashers' methods; the collateral damage seemed inexcusably high. The vast majority of these people were just doing their jobs, which were administrative or technical in nature and had little bearing on whatever evil schemes Zizmziz was hatching. While they might be guilty of aiding or abetting in some way, they certainly did not deserve indiscriminate capital punishment.

He spied an odd-looking object caught in the fork of two divergent pieces of reinforcing rod and picked his way through the rubble toward it. It proved to be part of a torso, but not just any torso: this one had belonged to a commando who appeared in the bubble shortly before they and Zizmziz vanished. Tol recognized the distinctive uniform and tactical belt. Something had ripped this particular commando into multiple pieces.

He walked the perimeter of the roof, looking for a way down, but found nothing promising. He dropped through a hole to try his luck on the inside. The interior of the command center building was a scene of utter devastation. There was almost nothing left intact in the entire structure: not furniture, not interior walls, not doors, not even smaller fixtures. Something had incited the Bashers into destroying *everything*. This looked a lot less like an edict enforcement action than total, punitive warfare: efficient and vicious. He was glad the public relations fallout from this devastation wouldn't be his circus.

From Tol's point of view the operation had been an unmitigated disaster. They had caused an enormous amount of property damage and more than likely a sizeable death toll as well without even achieving the principal goal of capturing Zizmziz. Maybe this was the way EE operations were routinely conducted here in Tantatku; if so, it was a miracle there was anyone left alive. He wondered what the penalty was for a parking violation here.

He eventually made his way back to the second floor and found a window through which he could climb down to the ground via a pile of rubble. Back on the ground at last he encountered Basher officers who led him to their field headquarters. The commander, Akkla, seemed quite surprised at Tol's arrival.

"Sir Tol-u-ol! This ees a pleasant happenstance. Ve expected, quite frankly, to find you deceased somewhere in ze building or grounds."

"Yeah. I can see where that would be a reasonable expectation, given that you seem to have blown the living smek out of everything in a kilometer radius."

"Ve like to leave nothing to chance."

"Except that you didn't get Zizmziz."

"Vat? How could you know zat?" Akkla demanded.

"Because I was standing right there when he teleported your commandos to...wherever they ended up. He disappeared too, but I doubt it was to the same place."

"Vat were you doing in the zame room vith Zizmziz? Vy didn't you take him down?"

"I was doing my job, which does *not* involve killing anyone who hasn't threatened me with deadly force. As for 'taking him down,' that would have happened eventually, when the tactical situation allowed. At that point I had no clear egress path with a prisoner. It was better if I didn't tip my hand until I did."

"So, you are responsible for the death of my commandos, then?"

Tol growled. "Look, general calamity, things were going along fine until your collateral damage squad busted in. Zizmziz might have been a little suspicious, but he hadn't yet crossed the line into thinking of me as EE. We have a thing in Tragacanth called *finesse*. I've found over the years that making use of it helps keep unintended consequences to a minimum. I'm truly sorry you lost people in that operation; I know how much that hurts. But don't try pinning that disaster on *me*. You reaped what you sowed."

"If you veren't brozer to ze King of Tragacanth I vould hold you in detention right now for interfering with official EE business."

Tol chuckled darkly. "Funny. What you call 'EE business' here we have another name for back home." He headed for the door.

"Vich is?" Tol turned around, one hand on the door latch.

"Murder."

Chapter Twenty-two

The information supplied by Archmage Blass was radical and game-changing; not all of the elders even believed it. While there was no real consensus reached, there was enough uncertainty introduced that a full commitment could not be justified. Embarking on the Valtir quest as a race would bring untold hardship on them; the rest of the world interpreted any large-scale movement of orcs as a threat. They would wait for the small team they had dispatched earlier to bring back evidence supporting or refuting the validity of said quest before they took that step.

Blass had warned them to expect a visit from the Tragacanthan Royal Consort, but Igra was not prepared for it to occur so soon. Boogla sent a messenger to the Balom enclave asking for a meeting on board a ship moored at the extreme edge of Tragacanth territorial waters, so as to avoid the inevitable protocols and bureaucracy of involving the Galangan government in an international mission. She promised absolute security for the Elder and any staff he chose to bring along.

The orcs had considered goblins their sworn enemies for untold generations. It took every ounce of self-control and diplomacy Igra could muster to accept the invitation and conduct himself gracefully in the presence of so many of them, but he managed it somehow. He was acting for the good of his entire race, he kept reminding himself.

Boogla received him as a visiting diplomat, with the courtesy, respect, and deference she would show any such personage. It took Igra by surprise. He had no prior experience with being treated this way. He was accustomed to abuse and confrontation where other races were concerned; he realized with a start that he had no stock of 'polite' behaviors from which to draw. He would just have to wing it.

"Elder Igra," Boogla began, after all of the formalities had been observed and the orcs were seated comfortably in the command conference room aboard the Tragacanthan naval vessel, "I have asked you here today to begin the long process of reconciliation. As with virtually every non-orc on the planet, I was brought up being told of orc atrocities and insanely aggressive behavior. I was made to memorize the dates and locations of battles and heinous events involving your people centums ago. I took these all as fact; I had no reason not to. However, as Magineer Liaison and Royal Consort of Tragacanth, I began to question the veracity of these claims and went looking for historical proof of them. As you are no doubt aware, there is none. Not a shred. Your entire race has been the victim of a diabolically evil smear campaign that can be traced to one eminent historian nearly nine centums past: Gumnil Ke-juq."

Igra stared at her, imagining Boogla as an orc so that he could frame his response diplomatically. "How can one person be responsible for so much bigotry and hatred? How can millions of people from multiple races across nine centums have accepted such defamatory and inflammatory racist rhetoric as fact without question, without proof?"

Boogla sighed. "That, of course, is the central question here. I cannot explain or excuse past behaviors, but I can do my best to end them and set things as right as they can be set at this late stage. I and others have worked on this problem for some time now, and we've come to the conclusion that Ke-juq was trying to hide something—some act or event that was so heinous that he could not risk anyone ever discovering the truth of it."

"Why would he care what truth was uncovered after he was dead?"

"He did not plan to die. He believed he had discovered a path to virtual immortality, through magic."

"You mean he became an archmage and transcended?"

"Nothing so straightforward. According to archmage Plåk,

whom I believe you know as Dennis Blass, he seems to have perverted a standard magic talisman into changing his race to something resembling goblin permanently. He then used other powerful magic we haven't yet figured out to transfer his entire self into a new goblinesque body periodically. It's all very sick and twisted, not to mention decidedly macabre."

"He wasn't a goblin to begin with?" Igra shook his head in confusion. "Why did he hate orcs so much?"

"The answers to those two questions are closely intertwined. I don't think he hated orcs, per se; rather, he was afraid of what they might be able to do to his reputation. The plan he came up with in his diseased mind was to discredit the orcs as a race so thoroughly that no one would ever believe anything they said. Then even if one of them did figure out that he was responsible for a great crime, those claims would be discounted as unreliable."

"What 'great crime' do you believe incited this profound injustice? What could drive a person to vilify an entire race that way?"

"The destruction of an island civilization *in toto*. The destruction of Morianella."

"We were told that Morianella was destroyed in a great quake brought about by a botched magic spell."

"It was. The spell wasn't botched, though. It was rendered quite faithfully from the *Codex Lapidismotus*. The Codex itself was modified by Ke-juq. Dennis Blass—Plåk—was the archmage who read that Codex and caused the quake, but he did nothing wrong. He recited the substituted incantations with perfect fidelity."

"How did a goblin historian come to be on Morianella?"

"He was neither a goblin nor a historian at the time. He was a resident of Morianella and an aspiring mage; a Magus Incipius, to be more precise. His name then was Philmon Iwo."

"You have said that Ke-juq, or Philmon Iwo, was not a goblin then. What was he?"

"He was your ancestor. He was human. A pre-orc."

This was a lot to swallow, and it took Igra some time to digest. Boogla gave him that time. Finally the old orc lifted his head.

"We were betrayed by a member of our own race? This is grievous news, indeed. But, why would...Philmon Iwo want to doom his entire island and its people? Surely he realized that he would be condemning most of his own species to extinction."

"He was jealous," said a voice behind them. They turned and saw Plåk standing there. "He had tried and failed many times to progress beyond Incipius. I was his mentor and coach; rather than coming to terms with his own lack of talent for magical arts he instead chose to blame me for his failures. He altered the *Codex Lapidismotus* specifically to embarrass me. I don't know whether or not he realized the extent of the damage his actions would cause. It is significant that he chose to leave Morianella prior to the incantation, however. In the end it was his undoing, because there was no one left behind to destroy the evidence of his subterfuge."

Igra was puzzled. "But archmage Blass, surely you would not have been so patient and helpful to someone who showed any signs of being capable of such an act. Did something happen to change him in some radical way?"

Plåk nodded. "Very astute of you, Elder. In fact there was evidence that he was capable of this sort of thing, but I did not put all the pieces of that puzzle together until quite recently. I now believe, based on some research I have been doing, that Iwo may well be responsible for humans, and therefore orcs, even being on this planet."

"How so?"

Plåk sighed. "First, you need to understand that we, and by that I mean your ancestors as well, were on a colonization mission. Our species, humans—known to our own scientists as *Homo sapiens sapiens*—began on a planet on the other side of this galaxy, but by the time my ship left that planet's orbit over a thousand years ago we had already established thriving colonies on at least a dozen other worlds. You don't want to colonize a planet that already hosts one or more sentient species, at least not without their permission, because that's tantamount to invasion and tends to ruffle feathers. You do lots of long-range scans and probes first so that you can rule out any planet that shows evidence of sentient activity. N'plork was not one of our primary destinations. It wasn't even on our maps, if I recall correctly. We just happened to be passing through this system when...the problem occurred. The few scans we had time to conduct showed no evidence of electromagnetic emanations or large-scale industrialization. Even if they had, we didn't have much choice. It was put down here or die in space, or at least we thought so. We did our best not to antagonize any native sentients by finding an uninhabited island and making due, even though it was far from an ideal place to live at first."

"What role does Iwo play in this?" Boogla asked.

"Philmon Iwo had exactly the right access and knowledge base to trigger the otherwise inexplicable simultaneous malfunctions that led us to abandon ship. I now believe there was nothing at all wrong with the life support systems of the *Isomer*. We were panicked into launching the lifeboats by a clever and nefarious false alarm."

"What could he have hoped to gain by this act?" asked Igra.

"That, I haven't figured out yet. I am hoping to ask him."

Igra was a bit incredulous. "*Ask* him? Is Philmon Iwo indeed somehow still alive, then?"

"Not Philmon Iwo, no. Not even Gumnil Ke-juq. But the spirt and intellect that resided in them survives, at least to some extent, as the perversion known as Zizmziz, the tyrannical head of the Umbral mage serpent. He is whatever is left of Iwo after all these years and who knows how many reboots. I doubt he even remembers all that much of being Ke-juq or Iwo, to be honest."

"What makes you think he can answer your question, then?"

Plåk shrugged. "He is the only chance we have of finding out why Iwo did what he did. I have to hope, to believe, that this knowledge is still buried in there somewhere and that we can access it if we approach him in the right way."

Boogla frowned. "Who are *we*, precisely?"

"Myself and Oloi, with the assistance of your brother-in-law."

"Tol? Do you really think he will get near enough to Zizmziz to be of any use?"

"Even as we speak he and Zizmziz are in very close proximity— probably the same building, in fact. I can sense it."

Boogla was concerned at Plåk's revelation, but she realized that any further discussion might reveal details of Tol's mission she didn't feel comfortable sharing under these circumstances. That's not why she was here, at any rate. She turned back to Igra.

"I am going to present the case for vacating the Treaty of Mutual Containment restricting the movements and citizenship of the race of orcs at an international diplomatic symposium in just three weeks. In order to have the best chance for success, I need as much factual information concerning the history and culture of the orcs as possible. I have here the only scholarly paper ever published on orc customs and beliefs and after having met with you I find its contents to be, well, puzzling."

"May I see it?" asked Igra. She handed the monograph over. The Elder studied it for a few moments and began to chuckle.

"Yes, I remember the authors. They hid in the brush near one of our settlements for some time. We felt bad for the hardship they were enduring on our behalf, so in order to give them something to take away we had one of our own bards create an entire mythos and fed it to them piece by piece. They seemed quite pleased by it."

"So, this nothing but a fabrication?"

"Oh my, yes. Our belief system is considerably more... sophisticated than that. Archmage Blass has given us some missing data on our background that will most likely put much of our cultural mores into context once we've incorporated it all into the shared narrative. It may finally help us to understand what the Valtir quest really is and what it means to our race."

Plåk spoke up. "I don't have very long before I must return to The Slice, but I brought you a gift." He held out a digital storage disk. "On this disk is as much of the archive as I could salvage from the lifeboat off the coast of Flam, courtesy of Her Excellency Boogla. I translated it word for word from the human language to Goblish, which you seem to speak and read well enough. It should fill in most all the gaps you reference, and give you a great deal of information on who the orcs really are. For example, it provides documentary evidence for why your race is called 'orcs'."

"Really?" Igra asked, intrigued. "That is not explained in our culture, or rather, it is explained by so many theories that no one explanation holds sway. What is that origin?"

"In summary, there was a book called *America a Prophecy* written thousands of years ago by the human author William Blake. It coins the word 'orc' as an embodiment of the spirit possessed by colonists of the Earth nation America, from which many of your ancestors came. When the goblin/human hybrids were created in Nusterton, the first members of that new race decided to call themselves 'orcs' in tribute to that noble colonial spirit. And with that I must bid you farewell, for now." He sparkled away.

"I, too, must be on my way," said Boogla, "But I wanted you to know that I will do everything in my power to give the orcs a new beginning. Please compile and provide to me an accurate summary of your culture and beliefs so that I can demonstrate to the world that contrary to their impression you are in fact an intelligent, peaceful race with philosophers and deep thinkers. It will not be easy for any of us; both sides have generations of prejudice to overcome. If we take it slowly and work to reassure the nay-sayers from both camps, however, I think it can be accomplished. Make no mistake: it will most assuredly require a supreme diplomatic effort all around and an extended period to be successful. I pledge here and now to make this goal a priority. I would ask that you do the same."

Igra nodded. "I will do this for the sake of my ancestors, my peers, and my descendants. Let none say that the orcs passed up an opportunity so eloquently presented."

Once the orcs had returned to their enclave and Boogla's ship departed, the Elder sat in deep thought for a time. It seemed impossible that the long nightmare of his people might finally be drawing to a close. Could this really be happening, or was it some exceptionally cruel trick of fate or goblin tyranny? He considered the risks and benefits. If he made an error and accepted Boogla's offer as genuine when it was in fact not, it would merely subject the orcs to more ridicule. Conversely, if he rejected her as ingenuous when she was sincere, he might ruin the only chance the orcs ever had of ascending to a place of equality among the races of N'plork. It seemed clear to him that accepting the Royal Consort at face value was the better choice.

On the trip back to Goblinopolis Boogla found herself considering how they got here, historically. A disgruntled and amoral alien saboteur with very different fundamental thought processes correctly gauges the societal naiveté of his adopted planet and leverages that simplicity to blackball his own shipmates to avoid implication in a brace of monstrous crimes. By taking on the visage of a native and engineering himself an influential academic role, he is able to indict and convict an entire race, manufacturing wholly fictional pejorative labels that nevertheless stick indelibly. Even more disturbing, this reprehensible individual has apparently discovered some way to survive as a biological entity for more than nine centums.

Now her brother-in-law was taking him on, at last. Oh, she knew the national EE apparatus of Tantatku was involved as well, but if they were truly capable of taking him down, why hadn't it been accomplished before? Tol was only one goblin, yes, but he was a formidable enemy to have on your tail. He had power that flowed from purity of purpose and a soul unmarred by corruption or base motives. He had a lifetime of successful edict enforcement experience in harsh environments. There was something else in play here, too: something she didn't really understand. She doubted even Tol himself did.

*　　*　　*　　*　　*

There was no sign of Zizmziz. Everyone else in the room was eventually found, scattered randomly in a circle with the former bubble at its center. With the exception of Tol and, presumably, Zizmziz, they were all dead, dismembered violently by the force of whatever magic Zizmziz used combined with the side effects of the Bashers' brute force demolition. Tol spent an entire day walking the area looking for tracks or other evidence, though he knew he wouldn't find anything. The magical aftermath was so strong and complex that sparking brought him very little useable information: just a confused tangle of overlapping signals.

Zizmziz was in hiding now—in a deep dark hole somewhere as Tol had predicted—angry and plotting revenge. He wondered whether the mage had worked out that Tol was EE, or just an unavoidable collateral victim of his escape. Surveying the grim fate of the commandos, he began to wonder why he fell straight down, as it were, rather than being flung tens of meters in some random direction as were the rest of the occupants of the bubble who weren't Zizmziz.

He found his memories of the final moments in the bubble pretty much intact, traumatic event notwithstanding. Zizmziz held a black sphere out and shouted a few words Tol didn't catch, presumably some form of invocation, and then everything blew apart. His best clue came from the fact that one of the commandos had cried out at that moment and drawn Tol's attention. He'd seen the gob turn transparent and sparkly for a split second before disappearing utterly. In fact, now that he thought about it, Tol had seen absolutely no one else falling as he did. Odd, given that there had been a roomful of people at the end. The only logical conclusion was that they ended up somewhere else prior to plummeting.

Tol thought about the talisman that protected him from being killed by the fall and as he did his hand reached unconsciously up to touch it. Something on his finger scraped against the amulet: a ring. He felt that ring with his other hand and realized it was another of the magical guards provided by the forensic mages. It was supposed to prevent teleportation. It was supposed to stop him from being teleported against his will.

It was pretty obvious that Zizmziz teleported himself somewhere; perhaps the sphere teleported everyone in the vicinity—except anyone who happened to be wearing an anti-teleport ring. If that was so, then Zizmziz most likely considered whoever he thought Tol actually was to be similarly deceased. Tol could use that to his advantage, if he were careful about it. He would need to make himself scarce as soon as possible, before any Umbral scouts or spies returned to the area.

Tol sailed back to Tragacanth on the next available ship, trying to keep a low profile to minimize the chances that spies on the docks would notice him and report back to Zizmziz. On the voyage he came to the conclusion that the only way to track a mage in hiding was by magic. For that, he needed a reliable mage of his own. That usually meant Ballop'ril. The archmage was no longer under contract to the Tragacanthan government, unfortunately; Tol couldn't simply ask Aspet to summon him. He decided to try another route.

The morning after his latest reunion with Selpla, as they sat together on her patio sipping greatfruit infusion, Tol set off down that path.

"How's Prond coming along?" he asked.

Selpla shrugged. "Seemed pretty happy last time I spoke to him. His disquisition was accepted. The oral exam is either just passed or coming up soon; I don't remember which. I was talking to Grelm when he called."

"Grelm? Who's that?"

"My brother, silly."

"Wait, you have four? I thought you had three."

"I do have three."

"Grelm isn't one of the names you told me."

"Oh, I see. Yeah, that's the nickname of Fatuhl, my middle brother. When we were kids he had a 'rock titan' costume and whenever he wore it he referred to himself as 'Grelm the Strong.' He didn't like to be called that when he wasn't in costume, so as a dutiful sister I started calling him Grelm all the time. It sort of stuck." She took another sip. "But, why do you ask about Prond?"

"I need an archmage's help, and I figured the best way to Ballop'ril is through his star pupil, who happens to be my girlfriend's ex-coworker."

Selpla got a look in her eyes Tol had come to recognize as 'caution: slippery slope ahead.' He instinctively went on his guard.

"You know," she began, moving her finger lightly across his arm, "I might be more motivated to make that case to him if we were...in a more committed relationship."

Tol grunted. "More committed? I haven't so much as spoken to another female except in the line of duty—or socially, at your insistence—since we started dating. I don't see how I could be any more committed to you."

"So, you're saying you don't intend to look elsewhere, ever?"

Tol opened his mouth to respond but then stopped and took her hands in his.

"Selpla, I need to bring the people responsible for the Palace attack in before I can concentrate on us. You can help that happen, which would then free me up for...other things. How about it?"

Selpla sighed. "All right, I'll contact Prond and see what I can arrange."

Tol kissed her. "Thanks, babe. I gotta run."

"Come back to me safe and sound, Tol."

He grinned back at her over his shoulder. "That's the plan."

Selpla watched him walk out her door. "So *close*," she said, wrinkling her nose and pumping her fist.

Ballop'ril was, as always, cordial and willing to assist wherever possible. He translocated himself right into Tol's office, in fact.

"I have considerable difficulty in tracking Zizmziz," Ballop'ril said in response to Tol's question. "He is not an archmage and his magic use is...unconventional."

"I would have thought unconventional magic would stand out," Tol observed.

"Not an unreasonable presumption, but the reason his does not is that it employs an abomination of his own devising he calls the *rete arcanis*. In effect, he seems to 'borrow' manna streams from multiple other mages and uses them to power his own spells. The only unique signature that sort of magical employment exhibits is simultaneity— and that is exceedingly difficult to see as it is happening because there are a great number of active mages at the lower levels." He lowered his voice and spoke as if confidentially. "To be perfectly honest, I'm not entirely convinced the rete actually exists."

"I see. So, you can't really help me find Zizmziz, then?"

"*I* can," said a voice behind them. They turned and saw Plåk standing there.

Tol shook his head. "You seem to show up at just the right time quite often, archmage. Do you just sit around up there in The Slice and monitor people's conversations? Is that like your hobby or something? If I gave you the perfect lead-in while I was sitting on the toilet would you materialize in my bathroom?"

Plåk chuckled. "I probably would, at that. Being semi-corporeal means I can't smell anything. That would be a definite deal-breaker otherwise in your case."

"Ha, ha. Petey, you takin' notes? So, archmage Plåk, how can you help me find Zizmziz? And what's in it for you?"

"You've found his chancerium?" Ballop'ril interjected.

"Yes. And the imprimatura is still actively being written. To answer your second question, Tol, what's in it for me is closure and justice. Zizmziz sabotaged my ship in an earlier incarnation, not to mention causing me to be the instrument for destroying an entire island and its people. I'm quite keen to see him held accountable for those transgressions."

"Why don't you just zap him with some archmage spell? It's not like I can arrest you or anything." Tol said. "I tried that; it didn't work."

"Believe it or not, Sir Tol-u-ol, I do have some respect for the rule of law. Yes, I could probably take care of Zizmziz myself, although it would require some careful planning due to the fact that I'm transcended, but I'd prefer to see him put on trial and judged by a jury of his peers. Vigilantism isn't really any more acceptable to mages than it is to the rest of society."

Tol nodded. "Glad to hear you say that, archmage. So, how can you help?"

"I can't actually track him directly from his chancerium, but I can make some logical deductions from the clues his magical activity provides. As Ballop'ril has told you, Zizmziz has only a Magus Incipius level of earned magical prowess. His higher magic relies solely on either magic items like phylacteries—of which he reportedly has a sizeable collection—or the use of the rete arcanis. Each leaves an identifiable signature behind. Tracing rete spells can be even more problematic because they don't necessarily involve the same network of mages every time, but the last significant magic employed by Zizmziz was a powerful and unique talisman known to the archmage community as an 'orb of defense.' It generates a hostile telekinesis area of effect spell that violently flings everyone except the caster along random vectors with enough force to cause great bodily harm and even dismemberment."

Tol nodded again. "Yep. That's exactly what happened to those Basher commandos. Chewed up and spit out in all directions. Zizmziz had this shiny black sphere."

"If you were there to witness that," Ballop'ril asked, "Why are you here to tell us about it?"

Tol grabbed his talisman and held up a hand to show off his ring. "Got my own magic gewgaws."

"Ah. So telekinesis and falling don't bother you, then."

"I wouldn't say they don't bother me. I still get pretty dizzy.

They apparently are not quite so fatal as all that, though."

"Well, we are all grateful to whoever provided you with these items. Without them the likelihood that you would be talking to us today is quite remote," replied the bugbear.

"Assuredly," Plåk agreed, "Although I'm not surprised you had them. At any rate, the use of that powerful item left tendrils of arcanic essence that I was able to follow because I was, fortuitously, staring at his imprimatura as it was being written. I traced the tendrils to a spot on N'plork where I believe Zizmziz is now hiding. I have spoken with Oloi on this and we are prepared to assist you in the containment of this rogue mage. It is Oloi's belief that your status as a naïf may well be connected in some way with this final confrontation."

Tol sighed. "Sounds like that 'chosen one' stuff again. I don't suppose I'm ever going to escape that, am I?"

"Not while you live, I'm afraid. But cheer up. You'll be able to collar more dangerous criminals more easily. You'll be like a superhero," Plåk said brightly.

Tol frowned. "What's a...superhero?"

Plåk chuckled. "No, I guess you wouldn't know about them, would you? It just means a very good person with powers beyond those normally encountered."

"I'm just a cop," Tol replied, shaking his head.

"Of course you are," said Ballop'ril, "And we are just mages who want to help a simple cop get his gob—or whatever Zizmziz has become."

"I appreciate that. Where is he, then?"

"He has apparently returned to the scene of the crime, as criminals from my planet are wont to do."

"That doesn't narrow it down much with Zizmziz," Tol replied with a smirk.

"I mean his greatest single crime on N'plork: Morianella."

"Is he sitting on a ship out in the middle of the Ustrad, then?" asked Ballop'ril.

"Possibly, but I don't think so. I think he may have reconstituted the Morianella Academy's Portum Arcanum."

Ballop'ril displayed his 'surprised and skeptical' expression. "After nine hundred years? Surely there can't be enough of the structure left to regenerate the stasis envelope."

"What the smek is a...Portum Arcanum?" Tol asked.

"Every magical academy has a specially-enchanted chamber where mage students learn the intricacies of teleportation and translocation," Ballop'ril explained, "It acts as a sort of 'fail-safe' haven where the mage and/or the subject of his teleport will return automatically if anything goes wrong with the spell's casting mechanics. They are quite robust and contain a lot of magical wards because they have to be able to deal with a wide range of potential mistakes while ensuring the safety of the students who make them. Teleportation magic is not at all trivial to get right, you see."

Tol grunted ironically to himself. Ballop'ril heard him. "Unless, of course, you happen to be a naïf, but those aren't exactly common. You are, in fact," he added, looking at Tol pointedly, "The only one I've ever encountered personally."

"He's the only one I've ever encountered, as well," Plåk added.

Tol shook his head again, more emphatically. "Smek. *Enough* about me. Getting back to Zizmziz: so, what, he's sitting in the middle of a ruin on the ocean floor? What's he doing for breathing? Or staying warm, for that matter? They told us in schola that's it really cold down there. It wasn't exactly balmy at sixty meters."

"I don't think he's in a ruin, per se," Plåk replied. "I think he's regenerated the magical envelope—the coelom—in which the Portum was embedded and he's taken refuge there. For breathing he probably used a more sophisticated version of the spell that Prond employed to allow you to explore the lifeboat off Flam. That oxygen exchange mechanism can be established more or less in perpetuity if a reliable manna stream is available. The temperature can be regulated in much the same way, by heat exchange."

"I guess he would feel pretty safe there, all right," Tol nodded. "How *do* we approach him in a place like that? Teleport?"

"Teleportation into a Portum is tricky," said Ballop'ril. "Because of the way they are constructed, they block all but a very narrow range of what you might think of as 'magical frequencies.' Effectively, the only way to guarantee you'll make it into a Portum is to duplicate the arcane resonance pattern that was used in its creation, as Zizmziz undoubtedly did. That's a bit problematic if you're not familiar with the Portum, however, because it's not possible to determine the pattern externally."

"Fortunately, I think I can find the location in my own chancerium where I first used the Portum to effect a teleportation return," said Plåk, "It will have stored the pattern as an overlay. Faint, but hopefully still readable."

"Excellent," replied Ballop'ril, "You go gather that information and I will prepare some containment and disabling spells for our use in the operation."

Tol was puzzled. "*Our?*"

The wizened old bugbear smiled benevolently at him. "Of course, Sir Tol-u-ol. You did not think we would abandon you to face this mad perversion of a mage alone, did you? Zizmziz poses the gravest of threats to the magical community of N'plork and it is in all our best interests that he be neutralized. Plåk can be of great assistance to you in this, but his transcendent condition imposes limitations on what he can accomplish here on Primus. You will need an archmage with 'boots on the ground,' as I believe the expression goes, in order to have the best chance of success. I am happy to serve in that capacity."

Tol exhaled audibly. "I don't know what to say, archmage. I suppose 'thanks' is the best I can manage for now."

Ballop'ril laughed. "No more eloquent response could be forthcoming, I assure you." His face took on a serious cast. "Before we go any further, what, if I may be so bold as to inquire, has Oloi told you about being a naïf?"

Tol sat down heavily in a nearby armchair. "More than I wanted to hear."

Chapter Twenty-three

Zizmziz crouched in his protective magical capsule and surveyed the room. It appeared almost completely intact, even after a catastrophic quake and nine hundred years underwater. Morianella's buildings had slid down a long, shallow slope created by the collapse of one side of the seamount on whose summit they were located. Most had their structural integrity disrupted by the movement and had disintegrated, but a few, like the Portum, were magically reinforced and so survived relatively unscathed.

The Portum, embedded in what was left of its superstructure, came to rest at about three hundred meters depth because the Arcane Academy was situated in the highlands of the northeastern reaches of the island, on the upslope side of the fissure that precipitated the collapse. The remains of the southernmost buildings, in contrast, were scattered down as far as a thousand meters below the tossing waves.

After nine centums, of course, the unprotected wooden components had been thoroughly devoured by cellulose-loving invertebrates. The exposed iron had likewise long since rusted away. The Portum was steel-reinforced stone; moreover it was encapsulated by a magical force barrier that kept anything larger than a microorganism from entering. A few fungi had managed to grow on the walls, as well as colonies of some species of opportunistic marine bracken, but for the most part the Portum was considerably more pristine than one might expect considering its violent history.

Zizmziz positioned himself in the center of the Portum and began to expand his bubble. When the capsule came into contact with the Portum's protective shell it would bind to it and close off any leaks; these cracks and openings would glow violet for a while to show that a seal had been effected. Once he felt confident of the Portum's integrity he transferred the oxygen and heat exchange spells to the Portum envelope. He now had a more or less permanent refuge protected from discovery by both nature and arcane cloaking. Time to get to work.

His project for today was revenge. For years he and the Tantatku authorities had been operating under an unofficial and sometimes uneasy truce, but the Bashers' violent attack on his headquarters had changed everything. Now they were his sworn foes, and before the end he would make them rue the day they had cultivated enmity with the great and terrible Zizmziz. The commandos who had arrogantly assumed they could simply take him by force had paid the ultimate penalty for their miscomprehension, but they were merely foot soldiers in this war. He wanted the elites—the leadership who planned that grave insult of an operation. He would crush them like the insects they were.

Thinking back on the assault, his recollection ran across Tol and stopped dead. That *aura*. It was totally unlike any he had ever before encountered. What *was* he, exactly? A goblin spy? A mage who had somehow infiltrated the ranks of the Umbrals? If so, his vetting process had serious flaws that must be corrected by whatever means necessary. No immediate concern, though: he was undoubtedly deceased now, whoever he had been. That orb, magnified by the rete arcanis, was too powerful magically to leave survivors, especially from such a great height.

He was no longer content merely to operate with virtual impunity—the goal that drove him now was to obliterate the Bashers utterly, starting with their own headquarters in Dollo. Let them see how *they* liked it. To accomplish this he would call upon the entirety of the vast resources at his disposal, chief among them the rete arcanis, his most glorious achievement.

But, how best to go about this destruction? Fire? Explosives? He alone on N'plork knew the secrets to dynamite, TNT, and gunpowder, after all. He had taken great pains to keep those revolutionary formulas secret. The bunker deep beneath his ruined headquarters where the raw materials were stored was magically sealed when he left the vicinity. No one could force their way in without tripping the self-destruct traps, which would ignite the powder stores and leave a crater tens of meters deep. It would also reduce anyone in the blast radius to very small fragments of bone and tissue. The mental visualization of that event left Zizmziz breathing more rapidly and with elevated pulse. He may even have wet himself a little.

His first order of business, now that his undersea safe haven was secure and functional, was to establish lines of communication with subordinates who would put his plans for retaliation into action.Something about orchestrating the entire operation from the site of an extinct civilization appealed to him. He did not regard the fact that he was largely responsible for its extinction as germane. That was another life, another person. His recollections of that place and time were indistinct at best.

After a great deal of thought, he decided to make use of an obscure magical principle known as 'cumulative vibrational harmonics' to strike at his enemies. He would use a special form of remote scrying to establish the frequencies and patterns that characterized the natural arcane vibrations of the Basher headquarters building. Once he had accurate characterizations of those patterns, he would create a series of persistent spells tuned to their precise vibrational rates and overlay them.

After they had become incorporated into the arcane environment of the building, he would modify their frequency to create a destructive resonance that would gradually destabilize the entire structure. At the proper moment he would then inject a strong force pulse that should simultaneously disrupt every load-bearing member and reduce the headquarters to rubble almost instantaneously. Timed properly, there would be no warning and no chance for escape for anyone in the building.

This would only represent the first step in his revenge, however. His intelligence operatives would give him a list of names and assignments for every surviving Basher who had participated in the outrage perpetrated in Zuum. Zizmziz would eliminate them all, one by one, in the most unpleasant manner he could manage. Subtlety and finesse, never major components of his repertoire, no longer applied at all.

As he paced and plotted the demise of the Bashers, Zizmziz felt rage welling up at all the insults he had imagined himself—or that grain of self that persisted across his various incarnations—to have undergone for the past nine centums. At length he decided that *everyone* would suffer as a result. There was a sealed glass tube in a secure laboratory deep beneath the ruined headquarters building in Zuum that he had kept safe for nearly a millennium. In it were tiny organisms too small to be seen with even a good magnifying glass that could spell doom for all sentience on N'plork.

They were synthetic viroids that acted as minute manufacturing facilities for proteins known as prions. These prions clumped together in the brain and prevented neurons from connecting with one another. Over time they reduced any sentient organism, no matter how originally intelligent, to little better than a vegetable. Along the way, however, they passed through various stages of violence and other primitive behaviors.

The prion viroids were the last remnants of an experimental protocol on board the *Isomer* designed to study the remarkable resistance of these particular prion clumps to denaturation by chemical or physical means, to which normal proteins are susceptible. The research goal was to elucidate the means by which this resistance was achieved so that the mechanism might be put to use to protect other protein-based applications, mostly coatings and enzymes, from degradation. Prion-based diseases had long since been eliminated in human society by the development of vaccines that allowed the body's own immune system to reverse the pathological mis-folding and return the affected proteins to their normal conformations.

Zizmziz knew that no such defense existed here on N'plork,

because prions of this sort were unknown. He had also come up with a diabolically clever means of infection: *pizorum*, or infusion liquor. Infusions were the cultural element that tied all of the races of N'plork together. Based on leaves, beans, or pods, infusions were consumed by everyone. Stankabru beans, greatfruit pods, Semialeaf, and a hundred other plant products were steamed to release their oils and flavors. All of them, however, used the same substance to consolidate and prepare the results before the water was added: pizorum.

Pizorum was a protein-based combination of emulsifiers and enzymes that rendered the molecular products of steaming suitable for dissolution in water during the infusion process. It brought the characteristic flavors and odors of the targets of the infusion to the forefront in a way no other process could. Put simply, without pizorum infusions were just water with a weird taste.

As a result of its universal utility, pizorum was the single most widely-purchased commodity of its kind worldwide. Absolutely everyone kept a flask or two in their pantries. It had an exceptionally long shelf life—not that anyone ever tested those limits, its popularity being what it was. It was also the perfect vector for introducing a prionogen that could be absorbed through soft tissues in the mouth and nose into the general population.

With the help of a computer program developed for calculating the spread of a fungal infection common among goblins and hobgoblins, primarily, Zizmziz had calculated the optimal route for distributing his prions to as much of the planet's sentient population as possible. He couldn't get everyone—at least not at first—but if things went well he would succeed in reducing most of the world's leaders to simpering, violent idiots in a few months' time. Once that was accomplished he would be the undisputed ruler over everything and everyone. He would then exact additional vengeance on every person associated with the Bashers: one at a time and personally. Only then would the insult he had suffered be sufficiently assuaged.

The tube containing the prions was even now being retrieved

from the secret bunker by a trusted associate, who would teleport it directly here. Zizmziz would carefully divide the prion matrix into four portions, to be introduced into the four major manufacturing facilities that among them produced almost all of the world's pizorum. These prions were actually produced by genetically-engineered viruses that could live on the walls of any vessel indefinitely. As with all viruses, they injected their genetic material into cells of the host organism; these, however, then cranked out prions in huge numbers.

Once in circulation in the general population, the propagation of prions across society would be virtually unstoppable. Nearly everyone on the planet drank infusions of one sort or another on a daily basis, and all of those used pizorum. Since prions were unknown as disease components in N'plorkian biology, there would be no defense against them. The scholars who might be able to understand and fight the infections would be too adversely affected by them to make any difference. Zizmziz would surely win this battle sooner or late. He could afford to wait.

*   *   *   *   *

Ballop'ril sat in his private conference room at the Arcanium, across a gleaming glonkwood table from Tol. They were going over some strategy notes while waiting for Oloi and Plåk to appear.

"Despite the fact that he's been practicing the arcane arts for close to nine centums, from all appearances Zizmziz really isn't terribly proficient at magic. He relies on magic items and his 'rete arcanis' for any significant magical activity." Ballop'ril said.

Tol frowned. "What, exactly, is this rete arcanis thing, and how did Zizmziz come to have one if he's not that great at being a mage?"

"The rete arcanis is putatively a coordinated network of mages—mostly Incipius and Arcanis—who contribute manna and some baseline magical impetus to Zizmziz. They can't provide him

316

with spells he's not capable of casting, but they can greatly magnify the power he's able to bring to bear on the ones he can."

"I'm not very tuned in to magic, admittedly, but I've never heard of that before. How common is a rete arcanis?"

"It is unique to Zizmziz and the Umbrals, as far as we're aware. No one other than Zizmziz knows for certain how it works, in fact. As I've said before, I'm not entirely certain it truly exists in that form. At any rate, it's not a technique that's taught in any academy. What we do know is that it gives Zizmziz raw power that exceeds any other mage on N'plork, at least for the magic he's able to cast."

"How did he convince all those other mages to cooperate? What's in it for them?"

"Those are really good questions, Tol. We don't know the answer to either. It could be that Zizmziz has control over something or someone dear to them, essentially extorting their complicity. Or, he might have somehow parasitized them, with or without their knowledge. It's not very likely that they are lending their manna to him of their own free will, however. While the occasional less-than-moral mage can't be ruled out, an entire network of them is extraordinarily improbable."

"So, an extraordinarily improbable network of mages is helping an evil underachiever along the path to ruling the world?" Tol summarized.

Ballop'ril chuckled. "Yes, I suppose you could put it that way. While we don't really understand Zizmziz's ultimate intent, domination of one or more social arenas is not an unrealistic supposition."

At this point Oloi shimmered into existence in the room there with them.

"I believe Zizmziz has as his final goal nothing short of control over all magical activities on N'plork."

Tol rolled his eyes. "Smek. Not again. What is with these jokers?"

Oloi laughed. "I think Zizmziz is coming from a slightly different angle than Namni, but I see your point. Magic is an extremely potent force; it isn't really surprising those with aspirations to autocracy seek to control it."

"I like him," Tol heard Petey declare through bone induction.

"You're just a sucker for vocabulary," Tol replied as quietly as he could.

"Guilty, as charged."

"I beg your pardon?" replied Ballop'ril.

"Uh, nothing," Tol responded, a little embarrassed, "Just... talking to myself."

The bugbear smirked ever so slightly. "To continue, then, it seems to me that the most viable strategy here is to contain Zizmziz both physically and magically, and to do this absolutely as soon as possible after contact is made. We can't afford to give him any opportunity to employ the rete arcanis...whatever it is."

"Have we any concrete idea what sort of facility he's in currently?" asked Oloi.

"Archmage Plåk said the Portum was just a room, similar to this one in most respects. It had the usual range of precautionary magical protections cast on it."

"Speaking of Plåk, where is he?" interjected Tol.

"I don't know," Oloi admitted, "He said he would meet us."

"He's a difficult one to predict or track, that's for sure," agreed Ballop'ril.

"We can't afford to wait around for him," said Oloi, "Every minute we spend here is one more minute Zizmziz might be using to gain momentum in his inevitable counterattack. You said the Tantatku edict enforcement agency did considerable damage to his building..."

"They smekking-near *levelled* it. Worse, there were *dozens* of civilian casualties. Unconscionable, in my view," Tol said emphatically.

"All the more reason he will be out for revenge. He is a

cornered animal now, and those are among the most dangerous of creatures. This will be what you might call a 'hazardous duty' assignment."

Tol sighed. "Ain't they all?"

"Plåk has provided me with the Morianella Portum's ingress key," said Ballop'ril, "That will allow Tol and me to gain access via teleportation. There is no reason to think that the fate which befell the island has changed the ingress coordinates, so long as the Portum is still intact. Were it otherwise, Zizmziz could not have used it as a refuge."

The word 'teleportation' spurred something in Tol's memory. He suddenly remembered what it was.

"Uh, I have this ring thingy here that keeps me from being teleported." He held up his finger. "I'm supposed to deactivate it."

Ballop'ril examined it. "Yes. You just need to concentrate. Tell the ring not to interfere, as it were."

Oloi shook his head. "It's just a piece of jewelry on you."

Both Ballop'ril and Tol looked at him with surprise.

"What do you mean?" asked the bugbear.

"Yeah," added Tol. "It probably saved my life when Zizmziz used his orb back there."

"The ring had nothing to do with that," Oloi persisted, "You are no longer subject to any external magic that manipulates your relationship with The Slice. Take the ring off and I will demonstrate."

Tol shrugged and turned it one way, then the other before sliding it off his finger.

"Now," Oloi continued, "Archmage, please teleport Tol-u-ol and the chair in which he is seated across the room."

Ballop'ril shrugged in turn and gestured towards Tol. There was a flash of harsh light accompanied by a strange crackling noise and suddenly Tol found himself falling backwards. He leapt up and forward to avoid hitting the ground. The chair he'd been sitting on was now situated near the far wall. Ballop'ril's eye ridge shot up.

"Interesting. This is connected with his being a naïf,

presumably."

"Yes. Tol is more than just a naïf, it turns out," Oloi replied, "He is for all practical purposes an incarnate: an *Elementalis Primus*."

Tol shook his head. "I'm a *what*?"

"Do you remember when I told you about the arcane elementals?" Oloi explained, "They were the creatures that came down to N'plork and taught the parasciencers how to use magic and become the first mages? They are formally known as *Elementalis Nativus*. In other words, they were elementals who were native to The Slice. An Elementalis Primus is an elemental who is native to the Prime plane; in this case, the planet N'plork."

"I keep tellin' anybody who will listen—and that seems to be just about nobody lately—that I'm *no* kind of magic-user," Tol complained.

"We know that now, Tol," agreed Ballop'ril. "Until now we thought you were a naïf: a mage who acquires magical powers through some agency other than skill and practice. If what Oloi says is true, and I certainly have no reason to doubt him, you are not that at all. An Elementalis Primus does not use magic: he in effect is *composed* of it." He saw Tol bristle. "Before you start sputtering, hear me out. I don't mean you are no longer a goblin or anything of that radical nature. What I mean is that you and magic have a completely different relationship than the one I and other traditional mages enjoy. For me to perform magic, I must draw manna from The Slice and manipulate that energy using a set of ritualized neuromuscular actions we refer to collectively as *directives*—what the outside world knows as *spells*. For you, however, magic simply happens. You employ it unconsciously in much the same way you use your senses or...perspire. It simply is part of you. That's not to say that you have no control over it at all, but that control will need to be cultivated and exercised actively in order to be effective. It also means that magic items such as your ring and talisman are useless. They work by interfering with or modulating the external flow of manna from The Slice to the user. Your manna is self-generated, essentially, and so there is no external flow to control any longer. You cannot be the subject of telekinesis or any other conventional spell because all manna directed at you is simply absorbed into your matrix. It's a bit like trying to put out a grease fire with more grease."

Tol grimaced. "So I'm a grease fire now. Lovely."

Oloi rolled his eyes. "That was figurative and you know it. What he's trying to get across to you is that you're not some kind of victim. On the contrary, you have been given an inestimable gift; one that is most likely unique on N'plork and possibly simply unique, period."

"Yeah? If I'm unique, how come you have a term for my kind, then?"

"Touché," said his pocket.

"Elementalis Primus is just a theoretical possibility, or at least it was until now," answered Ballop'ril, "We have a term for it because we are scholars and we have terms for virtually everything we can envision, whether or not we've actually encountered it."

"Fine. I guess that means I'll give these magical doohickeys back to the forensics mages, then." Tol started to remove the talisman from around his neck.

"Keep them on, at least for now" said Oloi, "They may not help you, but they won't hurt, either. And they are worth quite a lot. Such tokens are not trivial to create, either in terms of effort or time necessary for their enchantment."

"We can wait for archmage Plåk no longer," Ballop'ril announced, "We must move quickly. I will translocate to the Portum, but I am concerned about precisely how we are to get Sir Tol-u-ol in position, given his resistance to magic."

"Tol will get himself there with no problem," said Oloi.

Tol grunted, "I guess I can just swim. Apparently that goes pretty fast for me, or at least it did on the way to Flam last time."

Oloi chuckled. "I heard about that little episode. In fact, that's exactly how you will get to the Portum—but swimming won't be involved. I will show you pictures of where the Portum is and what, according to Plåk, it looks like and you will simply will yourself there."

"Is that so?" Tol replied, "I didn't realize moving around would be so easy now. That will put a real crimp in my frequent traveler rewards program. Any advice on how, exactly, I do that? I mean, 'simply will myself there' doesn't sound very helpful in terms of concrete step-by-step instruction."

"We talked about this before," Oloi said, patiently, "You have the ability to make things happen just by imagining them. See that chair that you were sitting in, that is now on the other side of the room? You want to be sitting in it right now. You really do. Sit in it."

Tol shrugged and started forward.

"No. Don't walk over there. Just sit in it."

Tol looked confused, but then closed his eyes and concentrated. When he opened them he was sitting in the chair. He looked around in even more confusion.

"There. That was easy, wasn't it?" Oloi beamed.

Tol stood up. "Yeah. But that's just a few meters. Morianella is a whole lot further away."

"Doesn't matter a bit. From the perspective of The Slice, through which you travel whenever you use your abilities for translocation, there's no difference in going five meters or five light years. A wormhole is a wormhole."

"What the smek is a wormhole? What the smek is a worm, for that matter?"

"A wormhole is a tunnel that connects two locations in space through another set of dimensions. A worm is a little invertebrate. I can explain more fully some other time, if you really want."

Tol shook his head. "No, I don't think you can, or should. I'm fine with 'what' and 'where;' I don't really need 'how'."

"I will explain it for you later," Petey said from his pocket.

Tol started to make some sarcastic reply, but stopped himself.

"Thanks," he whispered.

Ballop'ril walked over to a wall that glowed with soft backlit radiance as he approached. With his fingers he traced lines on the board that appeared in various colors, according to their purpose.

"The architectural plans supplied by Plåk, derived from his archived memories of the location, show the Portum to be shaped in this manner, with furniture in approximately this configuration presuming Zizmziz has not altered it drastically. Because the area is under at least three hundred meters of water, the only way in or out is via teleportation. A Portum, as I told you earlier, is designed explicitly to control teleportation activity, but we have the key that will allow us, or rather me, to bypass those protections."

"What about me?" Tol asked.

"As archmage Oloi indicated, you cannot be teleported, per se. You will have to reposition yourself. You've done it before on several occasions, as I understand. This will be no different."

Tol was getting agitated. "Yes, it *will* be different. I did not *do* any of those things. They just *happened*. I don't know how to make them happen on command—especially to a specific spot three hundred meters below the Ustrad sea in a sealed room. What if I materialize on the *outside*?"

"You can't," replied Oloi. "Even if you are not aware of it, your brain surveys the final destination carefully and drops you in just the perfect spot."

"So, bobbing out in the middle of the Noorprid was 'the perfect spot'? I must have unconsciously wanted to be fish bait."

"That was more than likely just bad math. You intended to drop onto the deck of a ship and forgot to account for the fact that it was moving, probably at flank speed."

Tol considered this. "I guess that's possible. Sounds like something I would do."

"Indubitably," agreed Petey.

"Not helping," Tol growled back at him.

While Oloi and Tol were conversing, Ballop'ril had been filling in details on his magic board. He finished drawing and turned back to the others.

"I'm going to aim for this point," he said, pointing to a spot in the room, "Tol, if you can manage it, I think the best place for you strategically will be right about here. We don't know precisely where in the room Zizmziz will be, of course, but materializing here and here will give us more or less full coverage. Oloi and, hopefully, Plåk will round out the squad, as it were. They will be unable to manipulate objects, but they can still use magic. You and I, Tol, will have to handle the physical confrontation aspects. Zizmziz knows who I am, but I don't think he knows much about you."

Tol grunted. "He knows I was in the room when he blasted the Basher commandos to bits. I was dressed as an Umbral tech at the time. He could see my aura and was somewhat suspicious of me, although I don't think he'd worked out that I was EE. I suspect he believes me dead now. I would, in his shoes."

Oloi had disappeared briefly and suddenly returned. He walked over to Tol and held up one hand, palm forward.

"Concentrate on my hand, Tol," he said, "And I will give you the exact layout of the Portum. I was just there. Ballop'ril's depiction is quite accurate...and Zizmziz is indeed present."

Tol stared at Oloi's palm and a nicely-rendered three-dimensional representation of the Portum appeared in his head.

Ballop'ril frowned. "I hope you did not tip him off to our intentions."

Oloi shook his head. "I remained outside the arcanic envelope; he is not advanced enough as a mage to have detected my presence."

"Well done, then. All right, everyone. Are we ready? Tol, do you have a plan for the takedown?"

"I have this null-magic doohickey here that we use for arresting magic-using perps back in Tragacanth. Once we get them back to the precinct the forensic mages have some sort of room they keep them in that's supposed to keep them contained. I don't know how, but it does seem to work. Not that we arrest actual mages very often. Most of the time it's just some jlok who got hold of a magic ring or something and is using it to pull off robberies or extortion."

Oloi nodded. "A null-magic generator should work fine on an Incipius. It would be of limited use for any higher-level mage, though."

Tol cocked his head. "Other than the one who broke the RPC—and I'll get him eventually—I honestly don't remember ever being asked to arrest a mage at that level or higher." He grinned. "Of course, no mage worth anything at all would be caught dead in Sebacea."

Ballop'ril raised his arms. "I will translocate in now. I'm going to cast a personal stealth field as well, to try to postpone detection by Zizmziz long enough for you and Oloi to get there. Please don't tarry. This will be a difficult encounter for all of us, I expect." He dropped his hands and shimmered away.

"Let's go, Tol. You just concentrate with everything you've got on that place I showed you. I'll help you as much as I can."

Tol closed his eyes and called up the memory of the Portum. It was much clearer than he expected: virtually perfect, as though he were watching a vid, rather than remembering something. He willed himself into it by a process he was not at all sure of and suddenly an entirely new set of odors surrounded him. He opened his eyes and saw a medium-sized room, the walls of which were hung with odd-looking panels of some shiny silver material. Oloi's translucent figure wavered off to his left. Further in the room he could just make out the insubstantial outline of Ballop'ril's stealth field. On the far end of the central table, with his back to them, was Zizmziz. He turned slowly around in his chair and grinned at them.

Chapter Twenty-four

"Welcome, gentlegoblins. Oh, and bugbear; my apologies. I'm dreadfully sorry our meeting has to take place in such a dreary locale, but fate will do as it wishes. Won't you all be seated?"

No one moved. No one spoke. They stared at one another across the table. The awkwardness built to a fever pitch. Finally Ballop'ril's stealth field wore off and he cleared his throat.

"We have come to address a rather serious issue, Magus Zizmziz. The Council of Mages and Engineers and the Society of Sages and Mages have designated me as their official representative in this matter."

"Certainly, archmage. What issue could possibly bring two archmages and a..." he peered intently at Tol in some puzzlement, "...goblin who apparently is not, after all, in my employ to the center of the southern Ustrad Sea? Three hundred meters beneath said sea, in fact?"

Tol had been patient long enough. "I can't speak for anyone else, but *I'm* here to see that you answer to a huge list of criminal allegations. Smek me, I don't think I've *ever* seen a rap sheet quite this long before." He unfolded a stack of papers he'd pulled from his overjack pocket.

Zizmziz lost his pleasant countenance, much to everyone's relief. It was creepy and disconcerting.

"So you're an EE officer, then. I should have realized that in Zuum. I don't know how you managed to survive that encounter, officer, but there are two salient facts here that you need to consider. One, you're *way* out of *any* country's jurisdiction here, and two, any attempt at arresting me would be tantamount to suicide on your part."

"You're an arrogant one, Incipius," replied Ballop'ril, "And you should know that SagMag is considering arcane sanctions against you, up to and including total manna embargo."

Zizmziz broke out in gales of laughter. He wiped the tears from his eyes and glared at the bugbear. "My manna supply is not subject to embargo of any sort by your ragtag band of hedge wizards, Archmage Ballop'ril. Don't call me 'Incipius' again, either. That is a misleading title bestowed by an organization that lost any relevance it might once have had decans ago. I have long since surpassed the level of any of your mages."

Oloi rolled his eyes and with a wave of one hand the chair slid forward and away from underneath Zizmziz. He fell heavily to the floor and jumped up angrily.

"What was that ridiculous display?" he growled, wiping the dust from his cape.

Oloi regarded him calmly. "That was a simple component of one of the preliminary trials for Magus Arcanis. A candidate ready to test for that rank would have seen the dweomer for that telekinesis burst and countered it without thinking. You are properly categorized as no higher than Magus Incipius."

"Absurd. Look at my aura. Archmage or beyond."

"Your aura," Ballop'ril said, "Is an abomination. It is a disturbing mishmash that contains a superficial glimmer of archmage, yes, but the harmonics don't come near to matching your native vibratory framework. It looks almost as though you ripped it from a true archmage upon his death and somehow incorporated the residuals into your own. In fact," he continued, staring intently at Zizmziz, "I believe I recognize it."

Zizmziz drew back in alarm. "This is my natural aura, generated by long years of study and arcane accomplishment. Your jealousy at my power and influence reflect poorly upon you, Archmage. Go back to your little academy and pontificate to your small-minded student body. The world needs more hedge wizards to weed gardens and strip molds from the wall, doubtless."

"Philmon, you've taken the wrong path," said a voice from behind Zizmziz. He whirled around to see Plåk standing there. "You were perhaps an honorable man once, although I'm not certain of that. Be that as it may, I now finally understand what you did on the *Isomer*. What I don't understand is why."

Zizmziz stared wordlessly at the newcomer for a long moment, mouth agape, as though struggling to access a long-dormant memory. Finally he spoke: slowly, tentatively.

"D...Dennis? Dennis Blass? You...you're *alive?*"

"I transcended centums ago, but yes, I'm still alive. No thanks to you, I might add. I call you Philmon," he added after a moment's pause, "But I'm not entirely convinced there's any of him left in you, other than a few stray memories. He was human; you're... something else."

"He is something like a spirit golem," Oloi said, "He's using a system similar to a chancerium to transfer his memories and intellect to a new body each time the current one gets too old and feeble to be of use."

Tol frowned. "What happens to the person already occupying that body?"

"Discarded," Oloi replied flatly, "Like a used wrapper. All of the existing neural connections are wiped clean when the new personality is introduced."

"Forgive my ignorance, but how is that even possible?" asked Tol.

"I'm not sure," Oloi replied, "Let's ask the developer."

"I have no idea what sort of sick fantasy you are prattling on about," said Zizmziz. "I underwent a talismanic species change over eight centums ago and I've kept the same body since then."

"You want us to believe that body is eight hundred years old?" asked Ballop'ril.

"I dunno. Looks about right to me," Tol responded, wryly.

"I don't care what you believe," Zizmziz answered haughtily, "It is of no consequence to me. To show you that I am indeed 'honorable,' I will give all of you one chance to leave me to my own affairs."

"Honorable people don't flee from prosecution," Tol said, reaching for his disruptor, "They face their accusers and prove their innocence—where applicable. Zizmziz, on the basis of an international warrant, I hereby place you under confinement in accordance with edict." He moved toward the mage and was propelled with considerable force against a wall when Zizmziz flicked his wrist. Ballop'ril cast his own wall of force spell but it was halted a meter short of Zizmziz like a wave crashing against a sturdy sea wall.

"Idiots," Zizmziz growled, "Do you think I am without defensive capability? Do you think I quail in fear at the sight of the mighty archmages here present? I have arcane power that they can only dream of. And you," he said in the direction of Tol, who was sitting on the floor rubbing a respectable knot on the back of his head resulting from his collision with the wall, "Your unusual aura does not impress me. Do not meddle in the affairs of mages, or it will spell your doom." He turned back to the others.

"Transcendents are of no consequence. Ballop'ril, I caution you against taking any further action. I have no wish to destroy you, but I will not hesitate to defend myself vigorously if attacked. Again, leave now and we will put this ugly episode behind us. Stay and I will do what I must."

Ballop'ril balled one of his hands into a fist and punched outwards. The heavy conference table slammed with terrific force into Zizmziz's abdomen, pinning him against the far wall. He brought his own hands together and then pulled them apart abruptly. The table exploded into thousands of tiny wooden splinters. He and Ballop'ril struggled with opposing spells; where they met sparks flew and small flames flickered violently. Ballop'ril had far superior magical ability, but Zizmziz possessed the rete arcanis. With each second his power seemed to grow.

Oloi and Plåk had been communicating in The Slice, out of hearing of anyone on Primus, and now began a concerted attack on Zizmziz as well. They heated up the room in his immediate vicinity until it became quite hard to breathe. The spell was simple but very difficult to combat if done correctly. With two archmages driving it, the temperature increase was almost impossible to reverse, rete arcanis notwithstanding. Zizmziz had no choice but to divert most of his manna into deflecting the heat.

He struggled against the thermal attack for a while, growing visibly angrier as he did do, until finally he let out a loud exclamation and pulled a dark orb from his pocket. Tol recognized it.

"He's got that teleport sphere. Watch out!"

"It will not work in here," Petey told him through bone induction, "Unless it is tuned to the specific arcane frequency of the Portum and that's highly improbable."

Ballop'ril threw a greenish cocoon of radiance around himself. The orb pulsed once: a deep crimson that bathed the entire room in dark red for a moment. Nothing seemed to happen until Tol noticed that Oloi and Plåk were both frozen in place. Zizmziz was now dangerously angry and he advanced on Tol and the bugbear with hands blazing in reddish fire. Ballop'ril yelled for Tol to duck as he launched a barrage of fuzzy silver energy spheres on an intercept trajectory with Zizmziz.

The Umbral mage swept one arm across in front of him and the silver balls scattered like sapon bubbles in a strong breeze. With the other hand he called forth a hail of small, sharp projectiles that darted toward Ballop'ril in a lethal swarm. Ballop'ril raised a shield to ward them off and then launched his own return fire.

These back-and-forth volleys continued for some time. Tol decided that discretion was the better part of valor and sequestered himself under a smaller table for cover. He figured Ballop'ril would eventually tire Zizmziz out and Tol could get off a decent shot at him with the disruptor then. He wondered what had happened to the transcended mages. They had not spoken or moved a centimeter since the red flash.

Finally Zizmziz collapsed under a pile of conjured force blocks, giving Ballop'ril the opportunity to catch his breath. Tol crawled over to where he was recuperating.

"What do you suppose is going on with Oloi and Plåk?" he whispered.

"I don't know. It appears to be some form of stasis, but I'm not aware of any magic that could affect a transcendent in that manner. It's almost as though their carrotes—the semi-corporeal bodies they inhabit on Primus—have been 'disconnected' from The Slice."

"Seemed to have something to do with that red flash from the orb thing," Tol replied.

"Yes," Ballop'ril agreed. "And you say this is the same object Zizmziz used for the offensive teleport action?"

"Far as I can tell, yeah. The flash was white that time, though, or at least the reflection was whitish; I was actually looking at one of the Bashers when it happened."

"Not strictly an orb of defense, then. They only have one function, which is to repel attackers through telekinetic expulsion. This may be more of a multipurpose version, although if so it would represent a new incarnation of that enchantment. I have never before encountered any magic originating on Primus that could have such an effect on transcended mages, however."

"It is not magic," Petey said, audibly, "It is quantum physics. Specifically, that sphere is somehow altering the spacetime fabric by a mechanism I cannot elucidate. It almost certainly came from the Terran starship and is thus beyond our means to analyze meaningfully."

"Altering the spacetime fabric?" Tol said, "What the smek does that mean? Sounds like it came from a science fiction vid."

"It means," Ballop'ril interjected, "That we are dealing with something of much greater and less predictable power than I had surmised. This is not merely a talisman or orb; it is an artifact—and one of alien origin. We must find some way to neutralize it. At the very least we must prevent Zizmziz from using it again."

A sudden movement from the other side of the room diverted their attention. It was Zizmziz, rising from a pile of debris. He shook himself and held up the orb.

"This farce has gone on long enough. Archmages or not, I will prevail." He grip on the orb tightened. "The predatory fish will find whatever is left of you quite tasty, of that I have little doubt."

"No, Zizmziz!" Ballop'ril shouted, "Do not use the telekinetics here! The Portum capsule will destabilize!"

"All that matters is that you'll all be taken care of," Zizmziz growled.

Ballop'ril threw up his most powerful spatial stasis enchantment. The faint bluish radiance enveloped him and Tol momentarily, but that portion of it covering the goblin sloughed off like a scuttleworm shedding its skin. A blinding white flash burst from the orb and the frozen figures of Oloi and Plåk vanished.

When the telekinesis pulse came into contact with Ballop'ril's shield a violent, swirling mass of sparks and crackling erupted. The pulse passed straight through Tol with no apparent effect— as though he weren't even present. After the fireworks subsided Ballop'ril looked beaten down, but he was still there and intact. The same could not be said for the Portum, however. Cracks were appearing in numerous locations in all four walls, the floor, and the ceiling. It was obvious their underwater refuge would cease to be a refuge in short order. The attendant noise was considerable, and growing.

Ballop'ril closed his eyes for a few seconds, then shook his head and shouted at Tol over the din.

"Tol you must listen to me. The orb has modified the teleportal access key for this Portum; I can no longer activate it. I could find the new one eventually through trial and error, but we haven't got the time for that. I know Oloi has given you some instruction in arcane meditation. You *must* concentrate all of your thought on destroying that orb, and you must do it now, before this entire structure implodes. Do you understand what I'm asking?"

Tol nodded. "I think so." He sat cross-legged on the floor and thought back to the exercises he'd learned from Oloi. Ordinarily there was no way he could concentrate on something esoteric when the tactical situation around him was going to smek so vigorously, but Oloi had helped him cultivate a meditation trigger that he accessed now. It was an arbor. He started at the crown, with sunlight sparkling on the leaves and picked a branch that he then followed down to a bough, a limb, and the trunk. By the time he reached the roots the outside world ceased to impinge and he was perfectly focused.

Tol visualized the orb from his clearest memories and then imagined a giant hand squeezing it tighter, ever tighter, until at last it shattered and was ground into powder. There was a tremendous rushing and rumbling and groaning in the background, but Tol did not allow it to disrupt his vision. He concentrated on his father's ghost saying, "Avenge your sisters." He called up his last memory of them while crying out, "For Resu and Vesu!" Finally he heard Ballop'ril's voice and felt himself being shaken by the shoulders. He eased up out of the meditative state and was very confused by what he saw: in front of him, beach; behind him, mountains.

The air was fresh and salty. Innumerable rivers, streams, and rivulets ran down the hillsides, as though an unfathomable amount of water had been dropped on them recently and was in the process of running off. Strangely, there was no vegetation at all except for a few patches of what he would call coral if he didn't know better. He looked around in growing bewilderment until he saw Ballop'ril making his way down a muddy path.

The bugbear waited until he was within comfortable range of Tol before speaking.

"Congratulations, Sir Tol-u-ol. That was the most astonishing display of magic I've ever witnessed."

A whole host of questions were jostling for priority in Tol's head. They were making such a clamor that he couldn't decide which one to ask first. He looked at Ballop'ril helplessly, with wide eyes.

"Where...is this?" he finally managed to squeak out, choosing the most immediate one.

"My best guess is that we are exactly where we were, except at a little over three hundred meters greater altitude. This is still the middle of the southern Ustrad Sea."

"So, what island is this, then?"

The answer came from his overjack pocket.

"Morianella."

Tol was still discombobulated from recent events, but his detective sensibilities were beginning to reemerge. He looked around at the bare, rock-strewn ground.

"This? This thing we're standing on is Morianella? You mean not all of it sank into the ocean nine hundred years ago?"

"No, it all sank," replied Petey, "But you raised it back to the surface."

Tol rolled his eyes. "*I* raised it. Me. Can you even begin to explain how I would go about such a thing?"

"Only proximately. In effect, you cancelled out Plåk's spell."

"How can you 'cancel out' a major quake?" He looked around again. "And even if I had somehow managed that, where are all the buildings? Plåk said this was a thriving city-state. There should be the remains of buildings, cobblestone roads, piers, docks...stuff like that."

"I do not have all of the answers you seek, unfortunately. You seem to stand astride the intersection between magic and exotic physics now—one foot in each realm, as it were—in a place where there simply is not much baseline data from which to extrapolate. When you destroyed the orb, you changed something fundamental to local spacetime. I simply do not possess the sensors necessary to provide you with any further analysis."

"I actually destroyed the orb? How can you be sure of that?"

"Its signature temperospatial deformation is no longer detectable. Whether or not you literally destroyed it is open for debate, but at any rate it has ceased to impinge on spacetime in the same way."

Ballop'ril chuckled. "Oh, it is quite destroyed. Pulverized, in point of fact. Well done, Tol."

Tol frowned. "Where is Zizmziz?"

The bugbear stared off into the middle distance for a few seconds before replying.

"Magus Incipius Zizmziz now resides in a rather peculiar place. He is in what I can best describe as an 'alternate time line' of which he is the sole occupant. I believe the transcendents might be able to elaborate more fully."

"Are they still...with us, then?" Tol asked, a little uncertainly.

"Thanks to you, yes, we are," said a disembodied voice that became less thoroughly disembodied after a few moments. It was Oloi.

"We were prisoners of the orb, in a manner of speaking. Had you not destroyed it, we might have ceased to exist for all practical purposes when our manna reserves ran out."

Tol shook his head. "I won't even pretend to understand what's goin' on here."

Plåk shimmered into sight. Oloi gestured to him. "I think Plåk has more of it worked out than I at this point."

Plåk looked at Tol, over at Oloi, and then back at Tol again. He took what would have been a deep breath had he still possessed lungs.

"I just now put all of these pieces together, so bear with me if it's still not as coherent as I'd like."

Tol chuckled. "It's not likely to be coherent to me no matter how long you work on it, so no problem."

Plåk laughed in turn. "Oh, I think you're smarter than you give yourself credit for. Regardless, the explanation requires a bit of backstory. Remember I told you that Oloi and I are aliens? We both came here in spaceships, although several hundred years apart. My ship, the TCV *Isomer*, was a colonizing vessel designed to support several generations of people on a one-way trip to set up settlements on other worlds. When you build a floating city that you'll never see again, you put a lot of your best technology on there in hopes it will help the people on board to survive. There are so many little things that have to be monitored and controlled on a ship that size that a sophisticated computer is pretty much essential. Our computer system had a thing called 'predictive analytics' programmed into it that allowed the artificial intelligence to make predictions about the values of tens of thousands of parameters involving the ship's systems and resources at any given point in the future. We used it to ensure everything was going the way it was supposed to be."

"Sounds pretty slick," Tol said.

"It was. This next part gets kind of tricky. The distances involved in interstellar travel are quite frankly very, very difficult to convey or comprehend at any deep level. The light you see all around you, that comes from your two stars, travels at the ridiculously fast speed of just under three hundred million meters per second. That's three hundred *thousand* kilometers each *second*. That means light could completely encircle this planet five times in one second. I tell you all this to give you some idea of scale. The planet I started from, Terra, is roughly ninety thousand light years from here, on the other side of this galaxy. That means that traveling at the speed I just said it would take you almost a hundred thousand years to get there. It's not possible to travel faster than that, as light's velocity is the 'speed limit' of the normal universe. That means that moving from star to star takes many, many years in normal space. The only way to make interstellar travel practical, therefore, was to come up with some means to taking 'shortcuts.' The way we do that is to take advantage of the fact that space can be thought of as a fabric. The heavier an object is, or more accurately the more massive, the more it bends space around it like a metal ball resting on a piece of stretchy cloth. If you get something massive enough, you can pull two sides of the fabric together to where they almost touch. If you then make a little tunnel connecting those points, you can travel between them in far less time than it would take if you followed the warp of the fabric itself. Are you still with me?"

Tol nodded. "Yeah, it sounds a little weird, but I can follow it."

"Good. All right, those little tunnels between points are called *wormholes* and they're created, or at least were on my ship, by generating tiny black holes in a truly mind-bending device called a SHAM drive, after Schwarzschild-Hawking-Ansari-Misakawa, the last names of the four scholars whose discoveries were most instrumental in its development. A black hole, by the way, is an object that is so dense that not even light can escape it. Since it can neither generate nor reflect any light at all back at your eye, it exhibits by definition the most absolute blackness obtainable, hence the name."

"How do you go about creating a 'black hole' on board a spaceship?" Tol asked.

"Essentially it involves blasting a tiny ball of atoms with so much energy that they break down into their most basic building blocks, called quarks. If you make enough of these quarks and keep them separated until you reach a certain critical number before mixing them together, you get a tiny black hole that lasts for a few millionths of a second before it evaporates. That's not much time, but in tandem with another technology called 'local temperostatic resonance' it's long enough to create a singularity, blow it up into a wormhole big enough for the ship, and zip through before it collapses. If you keep doing this over and over, you can travel at many times the speed of light, relative to normal space. None of that really matters for my story, though. What does matter is that there is a relationship between time and velocity known as time dilation that doesn't become apparent until you're almost at the speed of light. The closer you get to that speed, the faster time appears to be passing for someone watching you from some external location. From your perspective time seems normal. That means that while I might only have experienced a year's worth of aging going from one star to another, for the people living on planets circling those stars thousands of years might have passed. You can see how that might put a crimp in things like interstellar commerce and passenger movements. Not much point in sending goods to a customer or trying to visit a friend or family member if they, or you, won't arrive for a millennium or two, is there?"

Tol thought about it. "No, I guess there wouldn't be."

"Now, imagine what happens if you're travelling at dozens of times the speed of light. Actually, time dilation sort of breaks down past the speed of light because that is what's known as an asymptote, meaning it's a mathematical line you can't ever cross. But obviously you *do* cross it in what we call superluminal space, so you have to modify the equation to account for that. What happens is that once you get in the superluminal realm you start going *back* in time very rapidly."

He stopped and took another (simulated) deep breath.

"Here's where things get seriously screwed up. Ready?"

Tol shrugged. "You mean they haven't yet? Let 'er rip. Petey will explain it all to me later, no doubt."

"I'm not certain I have enough battery life for that," the pen replied, "My power supply is only rated for about one and a half centums."

Tol sighed. "Your comedy module needs to be replaced. Or better yet, removed."

"Comedy? There was no comedy there."

"Moving on," Plåk continued, "In order for trips between stars to be useful for those people not on the starship itself, there has to be some way to make time behave, as it were. We accomplished this by creating a thing called a tHIM—which stands for *'t Hooft Isotemperon Modulator*—that allowed the ship to traverse space through wormholes without going back in time. Most of the universe is t-invariant, meaning that the direction time is flowing does not affect the way physical laws manifest. The decay of a group of elementary particles called K-mesons, however, exhibits t-variance, meaning essentially that time only flows forward for them. One of the oddities associated with this t-variance is that in the presence of decaying K-mesons spinning neutrons generate an electric field that can in turn be used to contain those mesons. If you feed this entire process back into a modified version of the wormhole generator you can create a self-perpetuating system where K-mesons decay and reconstitute themselves forever. The decay itself is t-variant, so it can be used as a sort of 'clock' to keep the flow of time always going forward. Once that flow has been measured the system can be reset and started again with the flow direction sensors inactivated. The upshot is that by using this system you can keep track of where time appears to be for external observers and adjust the shipboard time such that to them your journey only takes, well, whatever you want. We usually set ours to a year of external future for every ten thousand light years traveled. Did any of that make sense?"

Tol smirked. "Not a bit. But, as I said, Petey will explain it to me if I need to know. So, how does Zizmziz fit in to all of this?"

"The tHIM is the thing that Zizmziz, or Philmon Iwo back then, removed from the primary wormhole generator. I don't know why; knowing him he probably had some kind of scheme worked up involving it. At any rate, when he removed the tHIM, the SHAM drive stopped working right, or rather, the drive actually still worked just fine, but our ability to manipulate the exochronic environment—that's how much time appears to pass when we're at superluminal—was disabled. Remember that predictive analytics function of the ship's computer? It used the exochronometer function of the tHIM to calculate how long a lot of different resources would last. One of these was breathing air. Without the tHIM it would take thousands of years, from an external observer's viewpoint, to get to our destination. Since the computer used that time, not relative shipboard time, for its calculations, it decided we would not have enough air to get to our destination and set off the alarms. The ship's senior officers did not understand the origin of the alarms, as no one had ever removed the tHIM before, and having no reason to doubt the computer, they ordered us to abandon ship to be safe. When Philmon left he brought the tHIM with him. That is the origin of the black orb."

Ballop'ril nodded appreciatively. "You seem very well versed in all of this quite esoteric knowledge. What did you do on board the *Isomer*?"

"My official position was physical sciences officer, but mostly I was a graduate student working on my doctorate in Quantum Teleportation Physics," Plåk replied.

"Fine. The black sphere controls time or whatever," Tol said, trying to get past what he regarded as the gobbledygook to something more salient, "How does that allow it to blast commandos into bits and teleport people?"

"I'm still working on that," Plåk admitted.

"It was a synergistic merging," Oloi said, "Between the tHIM and a standard translocation amulet. Zizmziz probably didn't even perform it intentionally, at least not at first. The tHIM's quantum footprint has what one might term 'lobes' or 'spikes' and when one of those mathematical extrusions happens to overlay with a certain degree of precision on the pattern exhibited by a talismanic enchantment, the results can be devastatingly powerful. Zizmziz probably stumbled over this and decided to put it to use. The fact that he understood neither the physics nor the magic involved to any deep extent is quite apparent."

"Fascinating hypothesis," Ballop'ril replied, "What brought you to that conclusion?"

"Plåk showed me where his chancerium was and I started monitoring it. I noticed that every time he used the orb there were two distinct, initially parallel, spell signatures that overlapped periodically in a pattern that repeated if you followed it long enough. It was a classic synergy except that one of the components was unexpectedly t-variant. Once I figured that out the puzzle solved itself."

"How can you discern t-variance in a chancerium record?" Plåk asked.

"Temporal asynchrony. If you move retrograde along the chancerium the quantum overlay actually flips into its linear enantiomer. That of course cannot happen with normal t-invariant energy dispersal patterns."

Ballop'ril's eye ridge went up. "Fascinating. What happened to you two down there?"

"I think I've gotten that mostly worked out now, also," answered Oloi. "When a mage transcends and then returns to Primus for a visit, he constructs what is essentially an umbilical cord back to The Slice through which the manna that supports his life force on Primus flows. That umbilical cord is actually a form of wormhole, governed by physical laws that exhibit t-invariance. The orb disrupted that t-invariance and caused the persistent wormhole to collapse, trapping us here on Primus with only the manna currently in 'circulation,' if you like, to sustain us. We were both nearing the end of our visitation periods and had low manna reserves as a result. We realized that something was very wrong and retreated along the wormhole path to the discontinuity point, attempting to repair it before we ran out of manna entirely and were trapped here on Primus as powerless and invisible astral specters."

"Has that ever happened to anyone?" asked Tol.

"Good question. If it has, at least on this planet, it probably wasn't the result of the same mechanism. Isotemperon Modulators are hard to come by on N'plork. It would be rather difficult to detect such entities if they do exist."

"All right," Tol said, "Now for the big one: how is this island we're standing on here, and how did we get on it?"

Ballop'ril and Oloi both looked at Plåk. He composed his thoughts for a moment and then began.

"When I cast the spell from the book that Zizmziz modified, the resultant quake was centered on a substantial fault that ran beneath the island. The quake opened a rift along that fault fracture and Morianella slid down an embankment more or less intact over a period of a few hours. When the orb disintegrated, it warped the local spacetime fabric into which it was anchored and fired off a dying pulse of t-variance. Temporal causation was interrupted and the end result was that the timeline for Morianella got 'reset' to some point before our lifeboat landed here. That's why the island is back in place but the buildings and people are not. The vegetation's causality vectors were not tied to that of the geological substrate and so what you see around you in that regard is more or less what was present before the island re-emerged."

"Were you aware of the fault beforehand?" asked Ballop'ril.

"No. Had I known about it I would have refused to go along with the request to accelerate the process and stuck to the modest relocation spells I initially proposed."

Tol scratched behind his left ear. "If time got reset, why are you still around? Shouldn't you still be out in space or something?"

Plåk nodded. "Perfectly logical question. The answer is that t-variant quantum causality doesn't work that way. A timeline is not a set of inextricably-interwoven events and objects. It's a matrix of causality vectors that exist independent of one another. You can, under certain circumstances, tease them apart. This is one of those cases. Morianella was still colonized by humans and destroyed nine centums ago. From the point of view of an uniformed observer, the island just mysteriously reemerged today. Anyone examining the quantum energy patterns in this immediate area would notice a definite anomaly, however."

Tol shrugged. "Whatever you say, your mageness." He was fiddling with something in his lower overjack pocket. He pulled it out. It was the null-magic device.

"Oops. Guess I forgot all about this."

"It would have made no difference back there," Ballop'ril said. "The magical forces in play were too intense for such a device to function without a great deal more power than could be carried in something that small."

Tol looked closely at the object and chuckled. "Especially since I forgot to put in a battery."

Chapter Twenty-five

Zizmziz was apparently dealt with, but that left Weekax. He was, after all, the reason Tol had gotten interested in the Umbrals in the first place. There were still questions concerning precisely how he was able to dismantle RPC security in the Palace—and of course Weekax had not yet answered to Tragacanthan authorities for his actions.

Now that the Umbral mage organization was disrupted and its members scattered, tracking him might be a little more problematic. Tol sat in his office in Justice Hall idly flipping a charcoal stylus over and over, tapping it on the desk with each spin. His informants had suggested that Weekax was in Zuum before the Basher attack. The casualty list from that disastrous operation had not listed anyone by that name, but these shadow mages often had one or more aliases, so it was hard to be certain.

The Bashers seemed to think their assault on the Umbral headquarters coupled with the putative downfall of Zizmziz meant that the Umbral mages had ceased to exist, or at least were neutralized as a source of annoyance. Tol never made assumptions. They were dangerous and misleading. Until he had personally laid eyes on a corpse he could positively identify as belonging to Weekax, Tol was going to consider him alive, fugitive, and dangerous.

Ballop'ril was Tol's best contact in the magical community, and when Tol asked him for help in tracking Weekax he in turn assigned the newly-minted Dr. Prond to assist. Prond was fascinated by Tol's anomalous elemental status now, and readily agreed. He arrived at Tol's office just before lunchtime and they began their business transaction in a restaurant across the plaza from Justice Hall.

"So, the last intell I had on Weekax was that he had traveled from Tragacanth to Zuum in Tantatku," began Tol, munching on bumber shoots in spicy leggen-nut oil. "That trail has gone cold since the attack on Umbral headquarters. It could be that Weekax got snuffed by the Bashers, but my gut tells me that's not the case."

Prond nodded. "Your gut's gotten you through a lot of tight situations, Sir Tol. I'd be inclined to trust it. How can I help?"

"My forensic mages tell me this guy has a pretty unconventional way of using magic that leaves a specific trail I was hoping you could help me follow."

"Unconventional, in what way?"

"I am told his spells, like his aura, were too perfect. They lacked any of the small variances exhibited by normal mages. He was, in the words of a senior forensic mage, like a computer model of a mage, rather than the real thing."

"Hmm. Interesting. That will only help us if we can find mages who have witnessed his spells or seen him personally, though. Did they mention how this attribute was supposed to assist us in tracking him?"

"Not as such. But, I had a thought. It seems to me that there's a pretty good chance he was part of that rete thing that Zizmziz had going. I read a report issued by CoME that whenever the rete was in use, it could be detected by other mages who happened to be near one of the rete's members. It also said that each member of that network left a slightly different 'residual energy signature' behind on something it called the..." He pulled a crumpled piece of parchment out of his pocket and referred to it. "...*arcanic isofluctuary halo.* Any idea what that is?"

Prond exhaled. "It's not universally accepted as existing, just like the rete itself. Essentially the AIH is a sort of envelope that pinches off from The Slice and surrounds planets embedded in it. It responds to any use of manna in a way that is unique to each mage. An expert can even tell what skill level a mage is at by examining the signature."

"Sounds useful. Why do you say it isn't universally accepted?" Tol asked.

"Not every researcher who tries to investigate its properties can detect it. The Halo seems to be rather selective in who it allows to examine it, in other words. Those mages who can't see it tend to dismiss it as a product of the imagination and disregard any research done on it. Science relies on reproducibility; if it isn't there investigators are correct in being skeptical. As a result, we really don't know that much about it."

"How about you? Can you see it?"

"Yeah, it's pretty clear to me. It's a lot fainter than mages' auras, but still visible."

"Great. So, here." He unfolded another parchment sheet and handed it to Prond. It was the analysis CoME had provided of Weekax's profile. "If I take you to places where we think Weekax might have engaged in magic, can you verify it?"

Prond considered. "Yes, most likely—provided it's within the past fortnight or so. The Halo tends to get 'overwritten' after a while. In places where not much magic happens it may last a fairly long time, but there's no guarantee of that."

Tol nodded and pulled a metallic-looking page from a folder. "My mages also said you'd know what to do with this."

Prond studied the characters. "This is a translocation template for Koppra in Azlymosh. Do you have reason to believe Weekax is there?"

"His halo signature thing was reported by mages in Blostt coming from a cruise ship headed for Koppra just two days ago. The ship is docked there right now. If we can get there today we should be able to confirm whether or not he's in the area."

"And if he is?"

Tol waved a packet of parchments. "I have an international writ of detention right here. Since the ship sailed from Hagfar, Rublosqi law applies and we have an extradition treaty with them."

"What if he leaves the ship and seeks asylum in Koppra? That's why most people head to Azlymosh, you know. Not much other reason to go there. Really not very hospitable."

"Yeah, tell me about it. He's traveling under a false name; Rublosqi EE think he's just on holiday and plans to stay on the ship all the way around to Tebmol. The cruise circumnavigates Turmia almost entirely. I wouldn't mind taking it myself someday, actually."

"Sounds nice: all those exotic ports in Tantatku and Solemadrina, especially. Anyway, this template has a recent validation stamp on it, so it's probably going to be safe to use without testing first."

"How do you test a teleport template?" Tol asked, puzzled.

"This is actually a translocation template, although the difference is not important in this case. The way we test them is with one of these." He produced a small object with rounded corners from a pocket of his robe. "This is called a quest cube. It contains sensors for all of the major environmental attributes we associate with life compatibility, as well as exact position. It has a short-delay homing talisman embedded in it so that it will return to its starting point within ten minutes automatically. We send it to the template coordinates and it comes back to us having recorded all the relevant data points to demonstrate whether or not the template takes you where it's supposed to."

"Huh. Well, ready to go?"

"Yep. Get right next to me. All right, walk forward one pace and then another, in time with my step. Go!"

Tol concentrated on allowing the translocation to affect him, as he'd been practicing. An indistinct view of The Slice appeared around them for a brief moment and then they were standing on a windswept beach a hundred meters from a pier moored to which sat an impressively massive cruise ship. Prond put his finger over a small circle on one corner of the template and the area glowed dull orange for a moment. Tol raised his eye ridge.

"Just confirming that the template is valid," Prond explained. "It has a built-in log that records who last validated it and when. That way the next mage who wants to use it will know how likely it is to be trustworthy."

Tol grunted. "Good system. So, if Weekax is aboard that ship, how close do we need to get for you to be able to confirm that?"

"Depends on how active he's been magically. Spells and magic items vary in the intensity of signature they leave behind. Of course, if he's still actively embedded in the Halo, that should stick out like a sore thumb, so to speak. Let me take a look."

Prond sat down abruptly on the sand and crossed his legs. He spread his hands out, palms down, and held them parallel to the ground. He closed his eyes and his breathing slowed. Suddenly he made a sharp intake of air and his head rocked back. Tol grabbed Prond's shoulder in alarm.

"You all right?"

Prond nodded in the affirmative and took a few deep breaths before standing up. "Your perp is definitely on board that ship right now. I need to get back to Ballop'ril as soon as possible. Can I leave you here?"

"Sure. I can get home on my own. What's the emergency?"

"The rete, or whatever it is, has destabilized dramatically. It appears to be breaking down; the results could be catastrophic if the matrix is allowed to fragment uncontrolled. I have to inform the archmage."

"All right kid, take off. You've done what I needed you to do, anyway. Good luck and...thanks."

Prond waved goodbye and shimmered away, leaving Tol standing there staring at the cruise ship in thought. If this one was anything like the *Avvolli* it had a small brig, but putting mages in detention was not always a straightforward proposition. They had a tendency to disappear without warning.

He had spent some time in the EE archives pulling background info on Weekax. What he found was somewhat unsettling. The mage had been accused of a dozen or so crimes in three different countries, but none of them had come to trial. In two cases the trial date had actually been set, but both times the witnesses suddenly refused to testify. When questioned, they claimed to have no recollection of the incident. Confronting them with their earlier signed statements elicited genuine confusion and even anger from what they perceived to be fabrications at their expense. Whoever this jlok really was, he had a solid system going.

Tol had alerted what passed for EE in Koppra, but as he'd discovered earlier, Azlymosh wasn't particularly interested in helping the international community corral its fugitives. He would be on his own. That was fine. Tol liked it that way. Fewer complications; fewer 'tactical incompatibilities.' He strolled over to the Port Authority office and checked the embarkation schedules posted in a glass-fronted bulletin board. This ship was the passenger liner *Burkil*, home port Hagfar, Rublosq.

Confident that he'd found the right boat, Tol pulled out yet another piece of parchment with a photo of his quarry on it, taken from the RPC personnel data store. He studied the face closely. The first thing that struck him was the absence of any readable emotion in his facial features. It may just have been the circumstances under which the photo was made—sitting in a security office staring at a little red dot above a camera wasn't exactly stimulating—but Tol's instinct told him this was just the way the guy looked normally. He must be one wicked cartes player.

He needed a way to seal off the only exit from the *Burkil*. If Prond had been correct, the odds were high that Weekax was still on board, as he hadn't seen anyone come down the ramp. He could have teleported, but if you're going to go zapping around, why spend money on a cruise ship ticket? Chasing the smekker around on the ship would be hard enough, but if he were to disappear into Koppra that would hose things up dramatically. Koppra was a town in which disappearing was quite a simple matter, in point of fact. Almost, one might say, *designed* with that goal in mind.

Thinking about disappearing led Tol to another potential complication: that annoying habit mages had of vanishing into thin air. How was he going to neutralize that escape route? As he pondered, Tol idly twisted the ring on his finger. The ring he'd been given by the RPC mage. The anti-telekinesis ring...

Perhaps the most disturbing aspect of his new, quite unwanted, magical abilities was the sudden appearance in his head of fully-formed thoughts that he quite definitely did not originate. He knew he did not originate them because they spoke in what to him was pure gibberish. One of these cogitations plopped into his neocortex at that moment and began to spout said gobbledygook.

If you can cohere the talisman's output from area of affect to discrete stream and align it at the critical angle with the vector of Weekax's manna pipe, you might be able to induce a destructive feedback loop if he tries to translocate.

Tol rolled his eyes. "Yeah, let's do that. Let me know how it turns out." He didn't even know who he was talking to now. It was like some nerd had taken over part of his brain and was trying to bore him into a coma with gobbledygook. He had flashbacks of listening to his brother attempting to explain electronics to him when they were kids. He also remembered how much he had secretly wanted to be able to grasp what Aspet was saying.

He paused at the bottom of the embarkation ramp to consider how best to present himself to the Purser's Mate controlling access to the ship. If he flashed his EE creds the mate would undoubtedly arrange an escort; that would effectively nix any element of surprise. If he told them he was visiting someone on board, he would have to get a visitor's badge and more than likely they would expect him to wait in the lounge while someone went to fetch the person he was visiting.

"Hey Petey, can you access the passenger list for this boat?" He said into his overjack pocket. There was a pause for a few seconds before Petey's somewhat muffled voice replied.

"I found it, but I shall have to break the encryption first. If I can negotiate a route back to the EE cloud in Tragacanth I will have a lot more processing power available. Hang on."

"Too bad we don't have telecommunications satellites to bounce off of," Tol mused.

Even though Petey did not reply immediately, that pause contained an almost palpable air of incredulity.

"Did you just suggest satellites orbiting the planet for the purposes of radio frequency relay?" Tol shrugged. "I guess. It's something Oloi told me about. The planet he was from had a huge number of them up there for centums. They bounced an incredible amount of signals around from all over the place."

"How would you track an orbiting object like that?" Petey asked.

"You don't have to. Apparently there's a sweet spot where the satellite orbits at exactly the same speed as the planet rotates. It stays put relative to the ground all the time."

"Stationary orbit. Interesting. How did they get the radio reflectors up there in the first place?"

"I dunno. Some kinda motor with a lot of power, I guess."

"It would need to be *very* powerful to overcome gravity." Another pause. "All right, I have defeated the encryption. There is no one by the name of 'Weekax' on the passenger manifest, but of course you knew there would not be."

"Yeah, I did. The gob's no fool. He knows we're lookin' for him. Can you cross-reference to the aliases repository for me, please?"

"Already done. I only see two that directly correlate to 'Weekax.' One is 'Gulmat,' used some time ago to register at an inn, the debt for which stay was later paid by Weekax's credit account. The other, which has a positive match in the passenger list, is 'Cluzzo'. He shows up as a tier two passenger on the Alta deck."

"Not exactly a common name. That's probably him. In the cheap seats, eh? He's smart enough not to draw attention to himself. That makes him doubly dangerous. Gotta figure some way to catch him alone to minimize the possibility of collateral damage. There's been enough of that already. Can you see if Cluzzo's been takin' advantage of any onboard services that would leave a record behind?"

"Scanning. It appears he has been very careful in that respect, with one exception. He has filed an onshore excursion notice for... today, in fact."

"Today? What time?"

"In about an hour," Petey replied.

"Looks like he's going to have an escort," Tol grinned.

A little under an hour later Tol was sitting at a table in a dark corner of a small bistro with an unobstructed view of the *Burkil*'s embarkation ramp. He clipped Petey unobtrusively on his overjack lapel and spoke quietly to him.

"I'd like you to help me keep track of Weekax in case he tries any magical hooey."

"*Hooey?*" Petey asked, "Is that a type of magic you possess as a naïf?"

Toll rolled his eyes. "You know what I mean. In case he tries to teleport or go invisible or some kinda nonsense like that."

"You want me to monitor his position in both physical and arcane space to minimize the likelihood of avoiding capture."

"Yeah. But can you really imagine me saying it that way?" Tol grunted.

"I am not equipped with what you could term an 'imagination,' but I would indeed find such phrasing out of character."

Just then a dray pulled up and two figures wearing robes Tol recognized as Juji'i walked up the ramp. They returned two minutes later in the company of a third of a slimmer build.

"Cluzzo is on the move," Petey reported.

Tol pushed back his chair and strolled nonchalantly in the general direction of his rented pram. This was a game he'd played many, many times. He didn't have even a small fraction of the encyclopedic knowledge of Koppra's geography he possessed for his native city, of course, but he had Petey and that was almost as effective.

They wound their way through the narrow, dusty streets of the port city for longer than Tol would have thought possible given its apparent size, but appearances can be deceiving. Koppra was an ancient city, a port that had been in constant use since before Tragacanth was even colonized. There were layers upon layers upon layers that radiated out like pond ripples in a rough semicircle from the port facilities until they died away among the towering sand dunes and caliche hills to the west.

At last the dray came to a halt in front of a sprawling single-story building of the warehouse variety, although its actual function was not immediately obvious. Tol parked around the corner and continued his surveillance on foot, relying on Petey to guide him.

"What is this place?" he whispered.

"The city tax registrar's office shows it to be a *Wo'hala*: a storage and distribution depot for commodities earmarked for tribal dispersal. In effect, this is where the various tribes warehouse supplies they have purchased. According to the cultural briefings database, supply convoys arrive at irregular intervals throughout the year to transport the stored goods back to their tribal areas."

"Interesting. Wonder what business Weekax has here?"

"Insufficient data. Were I capable of speculation, however, I might suggest that a correlation could be made with something Aqyiar told you in Hiffa."

"Aqyiar? Oh, yeah. That chieftain. What did he say?"

"He told you that a senior member of the Umbral mages was close to one of his immediate family, and that made the Umbrals a *Pomos* or auxiliary house to his tribe. There is a reasonable probability that Weekax is that connection. If so, he may owe some measure of allegiance to the Juji'i."

"So they brought him here to do...what? Save on freight charges?"

"Unclear. It does not seem likely his presence will be connected with transport of goods, however. The supply convoys make a number of stops along their routes and are considered integral to the social continuity of the tribes. The journey, in other words, is at least as important as the delivery process itself. Logic suggests rather that Weekax will be asked to assist with some other problem, the solution to which involves the use of magic."

"I guess we'll just have to get in a little closer and see for ourselves," Tol said.

As he was making his surreptitious approach to look for another way into the building, a new vehicle pulled up. It was a small cargo dray with no windows in the back that reminded Tol of paddy wagons back home. The rear door swung open; two bound and hooded figures were led into the warehouse by armed tribals. Tol's interest was piqued. Looked almost like a kidnapping in progress.

"Any idea who those two were?" he asked Petey.

"One was a goblin, the other of indeterminate mixed race. We are on the very edge of the range of my physiological sensors, but their subdermal hydration state suggests non-natives. Those born to the desert have more efficient water-processing as a result of their environmental influences and thus exhibit a different hydrological distribution profile."

"They don't sweat as much, in other words."

"Correct, at least partially."

"Can you access the blueprints for this building?"

There was a pause. "Not as such. However, I can see the utility tunnels beneath it. There appears to be an access point in the northeastern alleyway that could be employed to gain entrance."

Tol shrugged. "Works for me. Lead on."

The alleyway was stacked with disused shipping crates and barrels of various sizes. Petey guided Tol unerringly to the spot his map indicated, but there was a large pile of quite ancient-looking debris there. Tol kicked at it.

"Some of this smek looks like it hasn't been moved in years. I'm thinking this is not a critically-important utility access point."

"Difficult to assess. The record-keeping practices of the locals are not compliant with international standards."

Tol chuckled. "Not much here is, including the government itself. Mostly they collect taxes and defuse disagreements between tribes. The infrastructure is, um, minimal." He knelt down and started heaving junk aside. He stopped only once, as a dray rolled up and the driver gave Tol a quizzical glance. Tol responded with his 'hey, I'm just doing my job' shrug and the dray moved on.

After forty-five minutes of grunting, lifting, and shoving, Tol finally uncovered a metal hatch cover with rust heaps where the hinges should be. After taking a breather he squatted down and with a great outpouring of brute strength pulled the recalcitrant cover open, a few centimeters with each mighty tug. When at last the opening was wide enough for a goblin to squeeze through, he dragged some crates back to cover his excavation efforts as well as he could and slid down into the darkness.

Tol was no stranger to sliding into darkness. He'd done it a number of times during his career. He'd slid into sewers, cargo holds, basements, cellars, caves, ditches, and even a crevasse caused by an active geologic fault. Every time one slides into a dark place there is an element of danger because, well, it's dark and who knows what sorts of creepy-crawlers might be living down there. He took that sort of thing in stride; risk was, after all, what he got paid to face on a daily basis.

The ladder leading down was rickety, but held his weight. The total drop from street level was perhaps five or six meters. He pulled his torch and shone it around. He expected a concrete or stone-lined tunnel with pipes for water or power bolted to the walls, with possibly a sewage or storm drain trench running down the middle of the floor. That was not at all what he got.

This tunnel was smooth—and here and there, even in the dim light of his torch, glinted with a definite yellow hue. Tol wiped away a layer of grime and took an involuntary step back as the brilliant metallic luster of the surface came popping out. He held Petey up to it.

"Can you analyze that material?"

Petey hesitated, as though even an AI might be awestruck. "It is within fifty-six parts per million of being pure gold. Not even an alloy: the balance is oxides and trace impurities from the smelting process."

Tol whistled under his breath. He shone his light up and down the hallway. The yellow glint patches seem to go on into the distance in both directions.

"If this entire place is lined with gold, it must be worth a smekking fortune. How could something this valuable be apparently forgotten?"

"Given the perpetually depressed economy of Azlymosh, that question is even more significant. This section of hallway alone could be used to finance a range of badly-needed social and infrastructural improvements that would benefit the entire nation."

"Where did they *get* all this smekking gold? Is Azlymosh known for gold mines? That wasn't part of the cultural briefing *I* got."

"No, it is not. The nearest documented gold mines are near Venpralo in Solemadrina. Interestingly, there are no large-scale precious metal movement records whatever for gold mined anywhere on N'plork destined for Azlymosh. That most likely means this structure was built before such records began to be obligatory, approximately twenty-three centums ago."

Tol was silent for a while, pondering the unexpected turn this operation had taken. Finally he shook himself. "Gold or not, I still have a job to do. This is obviously not in fact a utility tunnel. Is there any way to get into that warehouse from here?"

"The gold somehow interferes with my sensors, although by what mechanism I do not comprehend. You need to explore; hopefully I will be able to detect any vertically-oriented discontinuity that might indicate an entrance when we get closer to it. I shall attempt to synthesize some useful data from existing sensor readings in the meantime."

Tol tried to forget about the fact that he was traversing an almost unimaginable treasure trove and concentrate on the task at hand, but it wasn't a trivial undertaking. Flashes of yellow brilliance from his torch light kept reminding him. The tunnel was not straight. It curved and twisted like a frantic serpent. Without Petey's constant flawless positional feedback, Tol would quickly have gotten hopelessly lost.

"Are you sure we're still under that warehouse?" Tol asked after a quarter hour of winding around in the auric labyrinth.

"Yes. We are currently beneath the southwest corner. Ah. Walk another six paces and look straight up."

It took a few seconds for Tol to process this last command. He shrugged and followed Petey's instructions. There, in the darkness above him, the roof of the tunnel curved outward. Dead center of the resultant bulge he could just discern a circular outline. He stared at it for a bit, then began looking around the floor and walls beneath it.

"What are you doing?" Petey inquired.

"Looking for a way to reach that hatchway up there. Not much point in building a door if you don't provide some way to get to it."

"Perhaps the ladder was stored above after each use. It is very unlikely that it still exists, since that building has been in place less than a centum. Whatever structure existed there when these tunnels were constructed is long demolished. It is quite possible, in fact, that the portal above us has foundation poured over it and thus leads nowhere at all."

Tol grunted in triumph and yanked a metal ring set into the floor. As he pulled, a curious collapsed mechanism expanded into a neat helix. Handles set in the base allowed Tol to continue pushing the assembly up into the roof space until it met a frame of some sort and locked into place. A spiral stairway now ascended to the hatch above them. Tol examined it; the stairway seemed structurally sound despite its obvious antiquity. "Up we go," he said, and started climbing.

At the top there were six buttons in a two-by-three grid set into the ceiling adjacent to the hatch, beneath a rounded iron stub mounted at the end of a deep groove. He pushed against the metal cover but it was solidly immovable. He held Petey up to the grid.

"Is this some kind of lock?"

"Yes. The correct order, according to the wear patterns in the cylinders, is 5,6,3,1,4,2, with one being in the upper left and two the upper right."

Tol's tongue peeked from the corner of his mouth in concentration as he pressed the keys in the indicated pattern. There was a deep thunk and the iron stub shifted slightly to the right. Tol pushed it along the groove with some difficulty. He suspected no one had done this for a very long time.

When he reached the far end of the slot, a halo of dust descended from the perimeter of the hatch. Something had been released up there somewhere. Tol took a deep breath and pushed against the metal circle with all his might. It gave way—slowly, grindingly at first, but then with more fluidity as the gap widened. A dim illumination flooded the passage, gone pitch dark now that Tol was using his hands for something besides holding a torch.

Tol stuck his head up through the newly-created portal and saw that he was in a small room completely enclosed by bricks. There were no windows and—more importantly—no doors. What little light there was streamed through a few narrow cracks in one wall. He lifted himself up the rest of the way and stood. The room was perhaps two meters on one side and no more than a meter on the other. Examining the walls more closely, Tol realized that one of the longer ones was actually a false partition, probably at the end of a hallway. He'd discovered a secret room in the warehouse. Shining his torch on the floor he could see that no one else had walked in here for many decans—perhaps even centums.

As he pondered this latest unexpected development, Tol heard voices coming from the other side of the false wall. He listened carefully. He thought he recognized three of them: Aqyiar was one, but the other two seemed really unlikely to him. He held Petey up to a crack in the mortar between bricks. "Petey, can you identify those voices?" he whispered.

"I can identify three: Aqyiar, chieftain of the Juji'i tribe of Azlymosh, Hinyak of Terimpu, and Jovsox of Correq."

"That's what I thought. Why would those smekkers be here? What connection could a couple of Marine deserters have with the chieftain of a desert tribe?"

"It sounds," Petey replied, "As though they are being sentenced to something called a...*kevi'i patun*, which translates roughly to 'sacrifice of atonement.' There is very little about that ritual in my database, but it does seem to be lethal."

"Huh. Must've really pissed Aqyiar off somehow. Is that 'kevi'i' thing legal here?"

"Azlymosh has, for all practical purposes, no national code of edicts. The tribes set and enforce their own standards of conduct more or less autonomously. Aqyiar being the head of state for his tribe, one would have to say it is legal. From the standpoint of the international community the burden of evidence for conviction is lacking considerably; in essence all that is required is a unilateral decision by a chieftain. No right to counsel exists, nor is there any formal appeals process in place."

"You piss off the chieftain, you're hosed."

"Correct, if unnecessarily colloquial."

"When, from your perspective, is colloquial necessary?"

"It is *never* necessary. It is, however, an unavoidable component of your speech. I call it unnecessary when there is one or more ways to express the same thought without additional or, relative to the speaker, difficult verbiage."

Tol rolled his eyes and changed the subject. "I need to get in touch with Oloi, but I never got the summoning amulet back. Any ideas?"

"I recorded the energy flows surrounding your use of that amulet, as well as during the anomalous teleport episode. It should be possible to simulate the amulet's function using your acquired arcane abilities."

"So, how would I go about doing that?"

"You just need to concentrate on contacting Oloi—only contacting him. Do not imagine him actually here, or you could well drag him here again. An irate archmage may not be a reliable or cooperative ally."

"Agreed. Here goes."

Tol closed his eyes and imagined himself talking to Oloi in The Slice, as though he had established a video comm connection. After a few seconds he heard the archmage's voice.

"Welcome, Sir Tol. What a pleasant surprise. Thank you for making the trip yourself this time."

Tol's eyes snapped open. He was in The Slice, sitting in what appeared to be a drawing room made from clouds, light rays, and colored...gelatin? He took a deep breath and tried to control his runaway pulse.

"I think you overshot a bit," said Petey's voice through bone induction.

"I...I need to ask you something," Tol finally managed to squeak out once he'd regained minimal composure. He would never get used to this sort of thing. "I stumbled across something very strange in Azlymosh and you're the only person I can think of who might have some clue what it is."

Oloi was drinking something a lot like infusion from a small ceramic container. He called it 'tea' and offered some to Tol, who declined.

"I will help if I can. What did you encounter?"

"An underground tunnel completely lined with almost pure gold. Not a small tunnel, either. It twists and turns and goes on for, well, for a long way. I don't really know *how* far."

Oloi was intrigued. "Fascinating. And what makes you think I would know the origin of this golden tunnel?"

"Remember when we had that discussion about the dark energy continuum and all the strange things you'd encountered in that starship of yours? You mentioned a creature that could live in outer space and ate light elements, pooping out heavier ones like a miniature nova?"

The archmage rocked back and stared at the ceiling. "Ah, yes. The so-called 'starworms.' They're only theoretical, though. None of our scientists—scholars—had any solid evidence of their existence, only anecdotes and anomalous sightings. Do you really think the tunnels were made by a starworm?"

"I don't have any idea. But according to Petey the gold coating the walls is purer than we know how to make on N'plork, not to mention the fact the tunnel probably contains more gold than the entire output of all the smelters on the planet for the past centum. I've been thinking about where this thing could have come from, and every one of those thoughts ran smack dab into 'somewhere else'."

Oloi was silent for a few moments. "Tol-u-ol, from time to time I have tended to underestimate you, even though I knew early on that your destiny was beyond that of normal goblins, but once again you have reminded me that you are extraordinary in many ways. The odds are in fact good that you are correct about the starworm, but that you could have reached such an astounding conclusion employing the very, *very* limited evidence with which you were presented is simply beyond belief. I salute you, my friend."

Tol grimaced in annoyance and embarrassment. "Look, I came here for information, not admiration. I mean, I appreciate it and all, but that kinda talk really isn't my thing, you know?"

Oloi chuckled. "No, it obviously isn't. Very well. Starworms, if they exist, are manifestations of a primordial matter/energy field called an *extrino cloud* that is not gravitationally bound to any other body in the universe." He stood. "You have piqued my interest in this phenomenon. Shall we go take a closer look?"

Tol shrugged. "Sure. How do you want to get there?"

Oloi pointed at the air behind Tol. "We'll simply follow your trail back."

Less than a minute later they were standing in the pitch black tunnel. Tol pulled out his torch and Oloi conjured some additional illumination. The archmage magically wiped the dust and grime from a section of the golden wall and waved a little metal rectangle over it. He moved his thumb across the instrument in a crisscrossing pattern.

"According to my little multispectrometer, the isotope ratios in this gold are all wrong for interstellar dust. In other words, this gold was not made in the heart of an exploding star like virtually all of the other gold in the universe. You can't just mix hydrogen and helium in a test tube and make gold, or any element for that matter. It doesn't work that way. Everything in the universe that isn't hydrogen was made in the unimaginably hot and pressurized center of a star, either during its lifetime or when it runs out of stable fuel at the end and explodes in a nova or supernova. The only way to manufacture gold—or any other element—is by transmutation: you can either split apart the nuclei of larger elements or mash smaller ones together until they have the right number of subatomic particles to be gold. On my own planet there were people who called themselves alchemists who searched for many, many years to find some method for turning other, more common elements into gold, but they did not have the ability to do either fission or fusion and so failed. The starworms, however, reportedly *can* do fusion. They carry little fusion reactors in their bodies and excrete heavy elements depending on the proportions of lighter elements in their food. Gold is only one of several dozen possible excretion products, I should add. In this case, it appears to be almost pure, which means that it is no accident. Someone did the math and gave this worm precisely the right combination and volume of lighter elements to produce gold and only gold as the excreta."

Tol frowned. "Which means, presumably, that whoever did that wanted the gold for himself. Why is it still here?"

"How much of these tunnels have you explored?"

"Not a lot," Tol admitted, "Maybe a couple dozen meters."

"It is quite possible that the starworm's keeper did in fact harvest all the gold he needed at the time. He could have left the rest intact as the easiest storage method. Once you get a worm going, it probably continues to produce excreta more or less forever, so long as you feed it right."

"So, what happens to the starworm eventually?"

"Eventually the extrino cloud to which the starworm is attached will drift far enough away that the connection can no longer be maintained. The worm will either dissipate or translate to a new home."

"How did the worm get here in the first place? More importantly, who was feeding it?"

"I don't even know if those questions can be answered," Oloi admitted, "The tunnels could have been here for a very long time indeed: thousands of centums, even. They could easily predate the aboriginal peoples. The extrino clouds are very difficult to track, even for an advanced spacefaring race, because they are composed of matter and energy that lack normal telltale signatures. Conventional sensors that measure energetic or gravitational wave fluxes can't see them. We have to rely on subtle effects of the clouds on surrounding cosmological structures to detect their passing. It's possible, although extraordinarily unlikely, that the gold excreta was simply an accident—whatever combination of lighter elements that caused this worm to produce gold as a fusion byproduct happened to be present naturally. If the worm was being fed, whoever did so was probably not a native of this planet, for the simple reason that the technology and knowledge needed to accomplish such a feat is considerably beyond even your current state of civilization here on N'plork. Indeed, I think even the scholars on board my starship would have found such a task daunting. Given the apparent antiquity of these tunnels, I would tend to believe that some very ancient sentience was responsible, or..." He paused for a moment. "Or, temporal dilation was involved."

"What the smek is 'temporal dilation,' again?" Tol asked.

"Time travel," Petey replied, audibly.

"*Time* travel?" Tol shook his head. "How much more implausible is this going to get?"

"Time travel is all around you, Tol." replied Oloi, "When

you look up in the sky at night, you are going hundreds or even thousands of years into the past. The light from those stars started out a long, long time ago."

"Well, yeah, but I'm not an active participant in that journey. I'm just passively observing light that has made the trip. You can't just move backward in time the way you can in space."

"Time and space are not separate entities. They are both components of a singular construction known as spacetime. There is nothing intrinsically directional about time. Physical laws work equally well going either way. The reason time appears always to be going 'forward' has more to do with thermodynamics than anything else. All I have to do to move backward in time is create a wormhole that allows me to traverse between two points in space at an apparent velocity in excess of the speed of light. In effect, if I get from point A to B before a photon would, I've traveled back in time. From the perspective of someone watching me travel through the wormhole I would appear to exit from it before I entered it."

Tol grimaced. "That's just too weird for me to grasp. Can we skip the explanations and just focus on what I can actually see and comprehend, please?"

"Fair enough," Oloi chuckled. "The bottom line is that this worm might have been manipulated by an alien or by someone from N'plork's own future. If I had a spectrochronometer—that's an instrument which measures aberrations in the local flow of time—I might be able to narrow things down, but I don't. The one thing that seems clearest to me is that no one else in Azlymosh, or most likely the entire planet, knows about these tunnels."

"Yeah, that's pretty certain. Otherwise there wouldn't be any gold left and somebody would be filthy rich. Thanks, archmage. You've answered my question about as well as it can be answered."

Oloi nodded. "Good fortune to you, Tol-u-ol," he said, and sparkled away.

"Talking to archmages," he muttered, "Is like trying to learn a foreign language. Backwards."

Chapter Twenty-six

Tol quietly ascended the ladder and closed the hatch behind him. The lid fit so perfectly into the floor that it was almost impossible to see.

"Mark this spot for me, Petey. I'm not sure I can find it again otherwise."

"Marked."

He crept over and peered out through a crack. In the dim light he saw two figures apparently chained to a wall. In front of them there was some sort of pedestal or, he realized after a moment, an altar. Four or five other figures were standing in the shadows beyond the altar. The voices were faint and the reverberations from the concrete and brick muddled their meaning. Petey was able to filter out most of the interference and translated for Tol.

"Aqyiar is reading a list of charges. They seemed to be centered on planning a sexual assault of someone named *Iloni'i*, presumably the chieftain's daughter, by his aggressive demeanor. Jovsox and Hinyak are denying the charges and in fact claiming not to know of even the existence of this Iloni'i."

"This sacrifice thing. I presume it is fatal?" Tol asked, quietly.

"Unknown in this specific case, but as I indicated earlier, generally any activity described with the word 'sacrifice' entails lethality."

"They aren't guilty," Tol said flatly.

"How can you be certain of that? They are assuredly guilty of your attempted murder on two separate occasions, not to mention desertion, armed robbery, sentient slavery, and a litany of other offenses."

"Yeah. They will stand trial for those, too. But not if these jloks knock them off first. This particular charge, however, is a setup. I can feel it. I've seen too many of them. Somebody wants them dead, or at least on the wrong side of Aqyiar."

"Logic suggests it may be connected with their desertion, then."

"Yeah. Somebody either tracked them to Azlymosh or they just ran into the wrong person here. Seems like pretty steep odds, but fate has a way of arranging these things."

"Your perception of a metaphysical entity orchestrating certain events is fascinating but completely without rational basis. It verges on a violation of entropy, in point of fact."

Tol shrugged. "I call 'em like I see 'em. I've seen improbable meetings and things that lined up perfectly create a situation that really had very little objective possibility of taking place. That's happened too many times to be random chance. *Something's* going on, that's for sure."

"It has been my observation that biological sentients tend to filter out data that does not conform to their preconceptions."

"By that I suppose you mean I only notice when things work out right?"

"Correct. Succinctly phrased."

Tol shrugged. "Suit yourself. Right now I need to get to the other side of this wall and stop the sacrifice."

"How do you propose to accomplish that?"

Tol sighed. "I'm just going to wish real hard."

"For anyone else on N'plork," Petey answered, "I would deem that course of action irrational and pointless. For you, however, it may well be effective."

Tol closed his eyes and visualized being in the room with Aqyiar. A startled exclamation made him open them again. He was standing next to the altar. The chieftain regained his composure in a commendably short time. Two of his companions drew their weapons and positioned themselves between Tol and the chieftain, but Aqyiar waved them aside.

"Sir Tol-u-ol. What an unexpected but not unpleasant surprise. For the moment we shall set aside 'how' and simply ask 'why' you have chosen to visit."

Tol took a deep breath. "Great Chieftain, though it pains me to do so, I have come to plead for the lives of these two...miscreants." He gestured toward the completely flabbergasted pair chained to the wall in front of them.

"In our society, Sir Tol, leniency can be bought, but it would require a great treasure indeed to purchase freedom for ones such as these. They have committed a very grave sin against the daughter of a chieftain, which according to our customs is punishable by sacrifice. Why would you, of all people, wish to save them from condemnation? We are aware of their attack upon you in the deep desert, and we know something also of other crimes they have committed. It seems to me that this action would correspond to justice from your own perspective, as well."

Tol decided to skip over his 'they're being framed' assessment as being unnecessarily confrontational and therefore counterproductive.

"Great Chieftain, I do not for a moment suggest that these two deserve less than what you have planned for them. However, I am a sworn edict enforcement officer and a knight. The oath I have taken requires me to deliver them up for trial by a jury of their peers. I will do everything I can with the constraints of local edict and custom to accomplish that. I have no other choice."

Aqyiar was silent for a moment. "Very well, what geld do you offer to compensate my tribe for their crimes?"

"Great chieftain, what would you say if I told you of a system of tunnels lined with purest gold?"

Aqyiar and his tribals laughed. "I would say," the chieftain replied, "That you have been reading books written to amuse our children. There is a myth deeply rooted in our culture of a great sorcerer named Azlym—he after whom this entire nation is named, in fact—who conjured a serpent that shed purest gold wheresoever it burrowed. This sorcerer lived so far in the past that he preceded even the parasciencers by centums. This is how we know this story

369

to be pure fable."

Tol stood his ground. "I don't know anything about Azlym or his serpent, but I do know for a fact that the tunnels of gold are real. I've walked through them quite recently."

"Were this true, Sir Tol, why would you not simply take the gold for yourself? You are a goblin with access to magic, as evidenced by your sudden appearance here in this hidden and highly secure chamber. You could simply transport the gold to your own demesne and be wealthy."

It was Tol's turn to laugh. "Two reasons, Great Chieftain: first, I have more money than I'll ever use already and second, the gold is not mine to claim. It belongs, as far as I can tell, to the people of Azlymosh."

Aqyiar stared into Tol's eyes for a few pregnant seconds before looking away. "You are being truthful. Very well, if you will lead us to this fabled gold I will give the prisoners into your custody."

Tol nodded. "I do have one condition, or rather, a request: that you use the immense wealth to better the lives of all the people of Azlymosh. Hospitals, roads, telecommunications, food—that sort of thing. I don't honestly know how much gold is down there, but I suspect it's enough to improve life for every single person in the nation. Come to think of it, there's probably enough to flood the precious metals market, so you'll probably want to be careful how much you spend at once."

Aqyiar smiled. "If this treasure be as great as you say, rest assured we will be most circumspect in its disposition. And all will benefit equally; this I swear on the tombs of my ancestors." He motioned to one of his companions, who released the prisoners from the wall and led them, still chained, to stand by Aqyiar. He turned back to Tol.

"Here are the condemned whose lives you have bought. They are, by our customs and tribal edicts, now your property. Show us the gold for your side of this bargain."

Tol walked over to the brick wall marking the dead end of a

short hallway leading from the room. He pointed at it. "Knock this wall down."

Aqyiar nodded to one of his lieutenants, who disappeared into the darkness and returned thirty seconds later with a stout maul. It took no more than a half-dozen swings to create a hole big enough for their passage. Once inside, Tol whispered to Petey. "Guide me back to the hatch, please."

Following the pen's instructions Tol walked to a spot on the floor and knelt down. He ran his fingers over the smooth stone until he encountered a barely-perceptible joint. He spread his hands apart and pushed down on both sides of the invisible panel at once. The lid popped just enough for him to get two fingers under each side. After a fair amount of grunting and heaving, the rusty hinges finally gave way and the metal hatch swung up.

They all crowded around and stared into the pitch-black opening. Tol snapped on his torch and revealed the spiral staircase that was still in place. "I've only explored maybe thirty or forty meters total of the tunnels. I have no idea how far they go, or what might be in them further along."

Aqyiar sent one of his minions down with instructions to bring back some gold. He was gone perhaps two minutes and then clambered back up the stairway. From the pocket of his jack he extracted several slabs of gleaming gold he had knocked down with the butt of his disruptor. Aqyiar examined them closely. "And the walls are truly lined with this?" The gob nodded in assent. "For as far as I could see in either direction, Saheer."

The chieftain turned to Tol. "Then our bargain is sealed, Sir Tol. You have bought the lives of these miserable wretches, but they must leave Azlymosh forever. If I see them here again there will be no further discussion. The sentence of sacrifice stands; you have but purchased a one-time postponement." He addressed Hinyak and Jovsox. "You are perhaps the most fortunate individuals I have ever encountered, that a Knight of the Crimson would trade an unimaginable fortune for your otherwise worthless lives. Do not waste this extravagant gesture. You have exactly one chance to see old age."

Back in his rented pram, with Hinyak and Jovsox cuffed and sitting in the back seat, Tol drove in silence toward the docks. Finally Jovsox spoke up. "How did you know where we were?"

Tol looked back at them. "I didn't. I was lookin' for somebody else and just came across you."

"Are you really a knight?"

"Yeah. I am."

"I ain't never met a knight before." Hinyak elbowed him to shut up.

"Neither had I, before I became one."

Jovsox wasn't through asking questions yet.

"Who were you lookin' for?"

"A mage named Weekax. Slippery smekker."

Jovsox started snickering. Hinyak elbowed him again, harder.

"Ow!"

"What's so funny?" Tol asked.

Hinyak practically threw himself at Jovsox, but the goblin wasn't deterred.

"He was standin' right there in that room."

Tol slammed on the brakes and pulled over.

"What do you mean, 'he was standing there'?" he growled.

"I mean some kinda magic stuff was part of the sacrifice. He was supposed to be doin' that part. I overheard Aqyiar tellin' him it was his duty to the tribe, or something like that."

"Will you just shut up?" Hinyak bit the words off.

Tol sat there trying to figure out what to do now when he heard Petey through bone induction.

"Although the lighting was rather suboptimal, with some digital correction I have managed to generate a useable portrait of everyone in that room. There's an 82% chance that I have identified Weekax, even though he has made some attempt to alter his physical appearance through magical means. His arcane aura cannot be similarly altered; only two occupants other than you possessed such an aura, and one of them was almost certainly the result of a magical item sequestered on his person."

He turned the pram around. "Since there ain't any incarceration facilities here, you boys get to ride around with me."

Jovsox started to reply, but the look in Hinyak's eyes dissuaded him. He relaxed and sat back. Tol wasn't interested, either way. He was calculating. If Weekax had to be reminded of his 'duty,' then he probably wasn't a willing participant. That meant that more than likely once the sacrifice was cancelled he would be on his way. As a mage he could just translocate somewhere, of course, but Tol had a hunch that still wasn't his plan at present. Weekax undoubtedly knew he was being hunted, especially now that he'd seen Tol here. With Tol seemingly on the way back to Tragacanth with his prisoners, Koppra and its utter lack of any organized arcane guilds or EE was probably looking like a pretty safe place to hole up for a while. Tol was counting on this, in fact.

As he became more familiar and comfortable with his magical faculties, Tol was beginning to grasp if not their actual mechanism, at least the effects of same. With a little concentration he could see mages' auras—and not just those in his line of sight. He could actually observe them through walls and across considerable distances, especially if he knew what he was looking for specifically. He backtracked toward the warehouse, on the lookout for auras.

Jovsox still seemed fascinated by Tol. "What kinda mage are you, exactly?" he asked. Hinyak kicked him on the ankle.

"Stop hitting me!" Jovsox complained.

"What did I tell you about talking to cops?" Hinyak replied through gritted teeth.

"It don't make no difference now," said Jovsox quietly, "Besides, he just saved our skins."

"I ain't no kinda mage," Tol answered. "I'm just a cop. I..." The rest was cut short by Tol suddenly swerving hard. "Found the smekker!" he said, screeching to a halt. He turned around to his prisoners.

"I saved your lives once. I won't do it again. If you are not in this pram when I get back, I will contact Aqyiar immediately. I doubt you will survive to see either sunset. At least with me you'll get a fair trial. Your choice." He slid out of the pram and took off at a trot around the corner.

"Scoot over," Hinyak said, "Give me some room so I can swivel around to work the door handle."

"Are you crazy?" replied Jovsox. "I ain't getting outta this pram. Those tribal smekkers will cut us up like they was butcherin' grazers."

"I told you a long time ago that if you stuck with me I'd take care of you. I'm tellin' you, we need to take off. We'll head straight for the docks and blow this place."

"Even if we make it to a boat alive, where we gonna go?"

"I got family in Bivil, Ovinis. Laidback town. We can chill, maybe head up into the mountains on the border with Asmagon. Nobody will ever find us there."

"I got a bad feelin' about this."

"Have I ever led you wrong before?" Jovsox took a breath to reply but Hinyak cut him off. "No, I haven't. Let's blow."

He had managed to get the door open even with manacled wrists. They bumped and slid their way out of the pram and stood next to it for a moment. "We have to get these cuffs off," Hinyak said. He looked around at the sparse industrial streets of the warehouse district. Something caught his eye. "This way!" They started walking as quickly as they could without drawing undue attention to the fact that their hands were fastened behind their backs.

They crossed the narrow street and ducked into an alleyway.

"Whatta we doin' back here?" Jovsox rasped, trying to catch his breath.

"The storefront's sign said this is a ship's chain and anchor seller," Hinyak explained, "The trash bin ought to have old chain

cutting heads or something else we can use. Help me get this open."
They backed up to the lip of the bin. Hinyak leaned forward and
lifted the lid far enough for Jovsox to get his head under it and force
it up further with his shoulders. Hinyak then balanced on one leg
and used the other to push the lid the rest of the way open.

They rummaged awkwardly for a few minutes until Jovsox
suddenly yelped. "Ow! Smek, that thing's *sharp*." Hinyak looked
up with interest. "Yeah? Can you get it out?" The goblin grimaced.
"I...I think so." He swung his arms as far to the right as they would
go and then bent forward to bring them and the prize out of the
bin. He turned around and faced away from Hinyak to give him a
better view.

"Perfect!" Hinyak exclaimed. "Just what I was hoping to find.
Hand it to me." He nodded in the direction of the nearby structure.
"Go stretch your cuffs across the corner of that building and stand
as far out of the way as you can." Jovsox did as he was told. Hinyak
followed him over and once the goblin was in position struck the
chain repeatedly with the cutting head fragment until it snapped.
Jovsox laughed with boyish glee and did the same for him.

They returned to the bin and rummaged around until Hinyak
found a hefty nail he could use to pop open the lock on their cuffs.

"You're pretty good at that," Jovsox observed.

"I've had a little practice," Hinyak replied with a grin.

Free of their restraints, the pair now headed for the docks,
about six blocks away. They tried to make their way as quickly as
possible without overly appearing to be fleeing and thus drawing
attention to themselves. Something that had been eating at Jovsox
now bubbled to the surface again.

"Who do you think set us up with that chieftain's daughter?"
he asked as they walked.

"I'm not sure," Hinyak replied, "But it must have been
someone we pissed off in the past. I don't know how they found us
here, though."

"That cop did."

"That was just a coincidence. He wouldn't even have known we were around if we hadn't wrecked his pram."

Jovsox sighed. "*Someone we pissed off in the past* don't narrow it down a lot."

"No, I guess it don't."

*　　*　　*　　*　　*

Tol ran down the street and then cut over one block. "Do you truly believe," Petey asked as he ran, "That those two will still be in the pram when you return?"

Tol snorted, "Of course not. They're probably already halfway to the docks by now."

"How then do you propose to recapture them?"

"That will take care of itself," Tol responded, somewhat cryptically.

"You are an enigma."

"But a likeable one."

The pen seemed to consider this. "Granted," it replied at length.

Tol suddenly slowed and dropped behind a row of planters lining the approach to what looked to be an inn. Two figures were conversing just on the other side.

"I did as you asked. Now I expect the other half of the payment."

"I told you payment would be rendered when I had the deserters in my custody."

"The fact that your plan did not produce the results you intended is not my problem. I played the role we agreed upon."

While his companion was more animated, the first one to speak seemed totally calm, detached, and...*mechanical*, for want of a more accurate descriptor. Tol realized it was Weekax himself. The other person he could not identify. The conversation now took on a more strident tone.

"Where are the deserters, then?" demanded the one who wasn't Weekax.

"Chieftain Aqyiar rescinded the sentence of sacrifice and a goblin edict enforcement officer from Tragacanth took them away."

"*Tragacanth*? What is a cop from Tragacanth doing in Bazgush?"

"Arresting two criminals."

Although the pair were not in Tol's direct line of sight, the exasperation of the first was palpable.

"I meant, what business does a cop from another country have arresting people here? This is far out of his jurisdiction. Azlymosh doesn't even *have* a formal national EE force."

"You answered your own question. If you really insist on gaining access to the criminals, you have only two choices: go to the government of Tragacanth through international channels, or waylay the EE officer before or during the voyage back. I strongly discourage you from attempting the latter."

"Explain to me again why you were involved in the 'sacrifice' to begin with."

"I owe you no such explanation, but I will offer it nonetheless in the spirit of goodwill. After I conveyed your fabrications to the chieftain, he became enraged and demanded that I assist in the capture of the two whom you caused to be accused. I did so because I am obligated by close social ties to do the chieftain's bidding. It became apparent that the punishment for the crimes you pinned on them was to be more extreme than you planned, but there was nothing I could do to mitigate that once the wheels had been set in motion. Because the sacrificial ritual has an arcane component, I was required to participate in that, as well. Given that the final result was to be their deaths, it seemed to me that justice as you see it would have been fulfilled. I do not, therefore, understand why you were so distraught at that prospect."

"Because I wanted them brought to trial for desertion back in Frespiola. Dying in some foreign country is not an effective deterrent. I wanted others to see up close and personal what happens to Marines who disregard their oaths and duties. Also, I wanted to see them incarcerated so that I could feel...less violated by Hinyak's treachery."

"You blame him for ending your career? I think you discount your own contribution to that event."

Petey interrupted via bone induction. "Proximate analysis indicates that the aggrieved speaker is Senior Petty Officer Ekkot, Frespiolan Marines, retired. He was the recruiter who was discredited after Sergeant of the Sextant Hinyak failed to report for his officer candidacy hearing. He apparently has been trying to bring Hinyak and Jovsox to trial in Frespiola for desertion for some years now."

Tol nodded. "Makes sense," he whispered.

Ekkot's reaction to Weekax's flat statement seemed disproportionate.

"I'm not going to stand here and listen to a...golem tell me how to live my life. If you want the rest of your fee, bring me Hinyak and Jovsox."

"Or, I could simply take it."

Tol heard a crackling noise and decided it was time to intervene. He stood up and came around the end of the line of concrete and foliage to a troubling sight. Weekax had encased Ekkot in some manner of fiery electrical cocoon. He was suspended a meter or so off the sidewalk, writhing and thrashing in obvious distress. Weekax stood there regarding him mildly, clinically. He saw Tol and appeared startled for a moment, but regained his mechanical countenance quickly.

"Let him go," Tol growled.

"I think not," Weekax replied, "We have unfinished business, to which you are not a party. Be on your way."

"My way," Tol replied, "Is arresting you for high treason against the Crown of Tragacanth. Release him and surrender peacefully."

Weekax looked puzzled for a moment, "I...don't remember..." then he laughed; more of a hollow rattle than true laughter. "I see by your aura that you carry one or more magic items, goblin. That will offer you scant protection against my powers, I'm afraid." He flung a sudden burst of bluish energy from his palm in Tol's direction.

Tol dodged it and shook his head. "Another egomaniac mage. How trite."

He drew his disruptor and advanced on Weekax, who threw up a yellow-tinged shield around himself. The magical barrier disrupted the flow of energy holding Ekkot and he fell to the pavement gasping. "Get out of here," Tol yelled at him. Ekkot did not need to be told twice. He struggled to his feet and limped off down the sidewalk. Tol knew his disruptor wouldn't be able to penetrate the shield, but he also knew that bleeding off the weapon's charge would use up some of Weekax's manna. He set it on 'pulverize' and started blasting. The yellow shield glowed with angry greenish violence where Tol's blue energy bolts hit it.

"Be careful," Petey suddenly said, "There is something not right about Weekax."

Toll rolled his eyes. "You mean, besides being a murderous maniac?"

"I mean, his life energy readings are atypical. He is not a true goblin."

"At this point I don't really care what he is, other than trying to kill me."

Weekax deduced Tol's strategy after a minute or so and changed tactics abruptly. He made a clenching motion with both arms outstretched, his face a grimace of extreme concentration. A dome of silver metal appearance formed around Tol and the concrete beneath his feet dissolved into a viscous soup, trapping his feet and legs. He found it increasingly difficult to breathe. Tol closed his eyes and twisted his facial muscles into a knot.

He heard a 'thump' followed by a 'whoosh' and opened his eyes to something quite unexpected. In fact, everything that happened as a result of his own magic was unexpected because he had no idea what he was doing. The inn, the sidewalk, the planters and Koppra itself were no longer in view. In their place were a whole lot of stars and really not much atmosphere. Tol flinched and floundered as he began to asphyxiate. A protective capsule appeared around him after a few seconds of respiratory panic. He could breathe now, at least. Where, exactly, he was doing that breathing was not a question for which any answer seemed forthcoming.

Chapter Twenty-seven

Tol was floating freely in...space, as far as he could tell. He could twist along all axes without hindrance. Gravity definitely seemed to be taking a break for the moment. He looked around and saw something large, round, and covered with blue, green, brown, and white mottling. He had no idea what it was. In the other direction he saw a huge floating metallic building with three gigantic semicircular convex bays, one on top and two below, lined with windows. It sailed majestically, silently, past him and he could see that it tapered to a long rounded rectangle, widening again at the far end. As it passed he could see that the rearmost section sported four huge nozzles. It was some kind of ship, by all appearances. Even the largest naval vessels on N'plork would look like dinghies next to this behemoth. He couldn't help but gape.

There was no sound whatever coming from outside his bubble. He could hear his own breathing, but nothing else. "Petey," he said, suddenly remembering the pen, "Where exactly are we?"

"Good question," the pen replied, "My positional sensors indicate that on the latitude and longitude grid we are still one point four kilometers from the docks in Koppra, but our altitude is now... unmeasurable. Given that we were in an almost absolute vacuum for a few hundred milliseconds prior to the instantiation of your protective capsule, I would have to speculate that we are in orbit around the planet N'plork. The odds against this are tremendously large, of course, but I quite honestly have no better explanation."

While Petey was speaking Tol had been surveying the scene. Other than the colossus of metal and glass now receding into the distance, he saw absolutely nothing else around them. If that was indeed N'plork, it was very pretty from this vantage point. The continents of Bazgush and Turmia seemed vast to him on the ground, but they were insubstantial blobs in a limitless expanse of green and blue from up here. The landscape was littered with swirling white and grey patterns which he realized after a few moments' consideration must be clouds.

"So," he said toward his pocket, "What happens now?"

"You got us here; you can get us back," came the reply, "And I wouldn't tarry on that; the ionizing radiation level has increased dramatically. Your bubble will protect us for now, but I do not think it prudent to rely on that shielding for any extended period."

"I guess I'll need to figure out what I did and try to reverse it," Tol sighed. He floated there for some time with his eyes closed, trying to recreate his last moments confronting Weekax, but he wasn't getting very far. It was though something was blocking any attempt to reconstruct that memory in detail. It was probably his own dislike for magic—and more importantly for his having been saddled with it against his will—at the root of that failure, he realized.

His bubble came into contact with something with a jolt. Tol opened his eyes and found himself staring at what was apparently a body, unlikely though that seemed. Tol drew back in surprise and shock. The body was disfigured but somehow artificial: more like a mannequin than something that had once been alive. There was also a familiarity about it. He couldn't actually touch the creature because of his protective sheath, but with some wriggling he managed to bump into it enough to start it slowly tumbling so that he could see more aspects. It was Weekax, or at least it *looked* like Weekax.

Tol blinked. "Petey, what is going on? How did he get here? What *is* he?"

The pen was silent for a moment. "It would appear," it answered finally, "That the anomalous readings I was getting from Weekax before were being generated by his having been a golem, rather than a fully biological organism. Petty Officer Ekkot was accurate in his assessment. We appear to have been teleported above the planet by some defensive magical reflex on your part.

The question of whether Weekax was included intentionally or as a collateral action is answerable only by you."

"Me? I don't even know what I did, or how I did it. I didn't mean to kill him; just arrest him."

"It does not matter, morally speaking. This Weekax was never alive to begin with, so your actions did not result in his death. I strongly suspect he is now merely out of range of whoever or whatever was controlling him and so appears lifeless."

Tol puzzled over this series of unexpected occurrences until his head started hurting, at which point he got frustrated. "I could use some smekking help from Oloi right about n..." He involuntarily clapped one hand over his mouth when it sank in what he just done, but it was too late. There was a pause of a few seconds, and then suddenly Oloi was thrashing around next to him.

"What are you and I doing up here, Tol?" he asked via telepathic projection because there was no air to conduct sound unless he wanted to invade Tol's capsule. As an ethereal energy blob he didn't need oxygen himself.

Tol looked at him and shrugged. "Floating, mostly."

Oloi ignored this. "How did you get here in the first place? Who is that?" He gestured at the motionless body there alongside them.

"Not sure how I got here. Magic, I expect. That's the gob I was trying to arrest in Koppra, except Petey tells me he's actually a golem. His name is, or I guess was, Weekax."

Oloi shook his head. "And why am *I* here, precisely?"

"I was hoping you could help me get, you know, *down*. Also, do you have any idea what that is?" He pointed over Oloi's shoulder. The archmage turned around and gasped in shock at the huge shape approaching them, although the effect was a little muted when expressed telepathically by a being with no actual lungs. He spun back to Tol. "I'll be right back. Don't go anywhere." He disappeared in a shower of sparkles that instead of wafting to the ground and dissipating as they usually did formed a little shimmery nebula. Rather fetching.

"*Don't go anywhere*? Well, smek. That didn't accomplish much," he muttered.

"You summoned a transcended archmage against his will from the Dark Energy Continuum to a free-floating orbit around the planet. There are few instances in which that could reasonably be considered not accomplishing much," replied Petey. "Granted, it may not have accomplished the goal you intended. Even that outcome, however, is not yet decided."

"What the smek are you jabbering about?"

Suddenly, space, the stars, and the mostly blue orb beneath them dissolved smoothly into an interior scene appointed with gadgetry the likes of which Tol had never even imagined. Standing beside him were both Oloi and Plåk.

"This," Petey answered, without missing a beat.

"Two for one sale, eh?" Tol said, once he was able to talk again. He couldn't come up with anything actually clever at the moment.

The archmages ignored him. Plåk was looking around with his mouth hanging open. Finally he turned back to Oloi and spoke in English.

"It *is* the *Isomer*. There's no doubt. How is this possible?"

Oloi shrugged. "You got me, dude. I guess the orbit didn't decay, after all."

"After nine hundred years? We left it in a low parking orbit. It shouldn't have lasted more than a few weeks, at best."

They had walked over to a viewing port while they talked. Oloi studied the scene for a few seconds.

"About that parking orbit. Take a look."

Plåk stared down at the planet. "Geostationary. That's way higher than we left it. I don't understand."

Oloi pointed straight down. "Not only is it geostationary, look at what it's parked over."

Plåk oriented himself with coastlines and land masses peeking

384

through the clouds.

"Looks like Northern Tantatku or maybe Azlymosh."

"North-central Tantatku. Zuum, to be more precise. Umbral mage headquarters."

"Iwo! But...how did he get back up here in time to change the orbit? He and I launched in the same lifeboat. That's how we both ended up on Morianella."

"I think we may have been underestimating Philmon Iwo all this time," Oloi replied. "Let's go check out the ship's AI and telemetry." He turned to Tol and switched back to Goblish.

"We're going to go snooping around. You're welcome to come with us."

"Where the smek are we?"

"This is the Terran Colonization Vessel *Isomer*. The starship that brought Plåk, Zizmziz, and the orcs to N'plork nine hundred plus years ago."

Tol was trying hard not to show how completely flabbergasted he was at the moment. "Huh. I got the impression from Plåk it had been destroyed."

"We both thought that. We're headed off to see if the ship's computers can shed any light on how that fate got avoided."

Tol shrugged. "May as well tag along. It's not like I'm going to be doing a lot of detective work on my own in this situation."

"You might be surprised. There are always leads to follow."

With Plåk, or rather Science Officer Blass, taking point, they entered the lift. Blass stood there for a moment trying to remember how this worked. He slid open a panel and swiped a screen to bring up a three-dimensional map that floated serenely in the air before them. Studying it for a while, he at length spoke in the direction of the wall panel.

"Alpha Delta One One Six; Go."

The map disappeared and they felt a subtle movement of the lift car. Tol grinned.

"Wish our lifts were this smooth."

"We're traveling at quite a high rate of speed right now, too. There are inertial dampeners in the lift itself that keep the G-forces from being too obvious. Otherwise we'd be plastered against the floor, ceilings, or walls most of the trip."

"The walls?" Tol asked, puzzled.

"Yeah. When you have a ship as large and complex as this your lifts need to be able to move along all three spatial axes, not just up and down."

"How the smek do you manage that? What kind of insanely complicated track does that take?"

"It's just a bunch of tubes. The real trick is to put your lift in a spherical capsule that rolls around like a giant pet wrat's ball. Gyroscopic stabilizers keep the passenger compartment parallel to the local floor."

"Whatta you mean, 'the local floor'?" asked Tol.

"In space 'up' and 'down' are completely arbitrary." Oloi responded, "The artificial gravity can be adjusted so that any surface in a given space feels like the floor. If we made the walls transparent and you could watch the crew of a big ship like this walking around, you'd see that 'down' changes in different areas, depending on architecture and function. One interesting result of this is that in places you can walk from the uppermost to the lowermost decks while traveling in what feels like a straight line: no stairs or lifts involved."

Tol shook his head. "I'm not even going down that road. My capacity for mind-blowing events isn't very big, and we hit that limit half an hour ago."

Oloi chuckled. "Understandable. We're going to switch back to our native language now, because Goblish hasn't got some of the technical terms we need to use. I'm sure Petey can translate if you like."

Tol give his customary shrug. "I'll just follow along and try not to get any more overwhelmed," he replied without much conviction.

The Computational Services bay was locked, but fortunately

the authentication scanner still recognized Blass even in his wraith-like state and allowed them to enter. Plåk wasted no time finding and accessing the various telemetry feeds he needed to figure out what was going on. He pointed to another console. "That's the power routing panel. Take a look and see what you can find out," he said to Oloi. "I'll work on the nav systems." Oloi nodded and went to work.

By the time the archmages needed to return to The Slice, they had made some interesting discoveries. Tol wanted to know about them.

"We have to go recharge now," Oloi explained. "You can wait here or come with us. I'd advise the latter, because an operational starship is a bit of a hazardous place for anyone who hasn't been trained properly to be wandering around unescorted."

"Come with you? I thought I wasn't supposed to hang around in The Slice for very long."

"That no longer applies to you, Tol. You can think of yourself as a 'dual citizen' of Primus and The Slice now. The changes you've undergone have rendered you immune to acclimatization; or rather, they've pushed that process to its logical conclusion and beyond. In fact, we can teach you to be able to visit any time you like."

Tol thought about it. "Maybe. We'll see. All right, I'll tag along. I want to hear what you've found out."

Thirty seconds later they were standing in Oloi's 'parlor' in The Slice. They sat at a table and began to compare notes. Oloi and Plåk spoke in English with Petey translating for Tol. He realized that this was the first time he'd seen both archmages together when they weren't translucent.

"He boosted the orbit and maintains it by rerouting most of the ship's propulsion systems to the maneuvering thrusters," Oloi began, "There's enough raw fuel to keep the ship here for at least ten thousand more years that way. I have no idea why, though."

"I do," replied Plåk grimly. "He's done a clever hack of the chronocompensators that, as far as I can tell, turns the long range comm array into a sort of isochronic reflector, aimed right at Zuum. I don't believe that 'arcane net' thing exists at all."

Oloi rocked back. "Yes...he just layers aligned temporal loops one atop the other to magnify his low-level spells. There's a limit to that, though: entropy is additive. At some point the latent entropic component will get large enough to start creating bizarre harmonics. Still, it explains how he can produce such powerful magic as an Incipius. The rete arcanis is just a cover."

"I found something much more disturbing than that, though," Plåk continued, "I noticed some anomalies in the power distribution and traced them to a bank of impulse modulators."

"Wait, I thought TCVs weren't armed..."

"They aren't, at least not formally. But we had some impulse modulators to take care of asteroids or other rocky debris we might encounter coming out of superrelativistic space. Remember, we didn't have a functional wormhole drive: that's why it took several generations to get anywhere. Our top speed was no more than 1.5c."

"Right. I forgot about that. I'm amazed you were able to get going that fast, to be honest. The power requirements must have been colossal."

"Well, yeah, they were. Not to mention the inertial dampening needed. Those huge coils on the top and sides of the ship converted a lot of that into heat and then released it when went superluminal. The temperature in the 'hot spot' about ten kilometers behind us could reach over a million degrees Kelvin. Even with all that it took us almost a year of shipboard time to reach c. When we came back into normal space it's not like we had radar or something that could look ahead of us: that's just not practical when you're going that fast. We had to power up the modulators and hope we didn't materialize somewhere problematic, like inside a planet or on top of another vessel. Mapping missions took an extreme importance, as you can imagine."

"I have a lot of respect for you guys. By the time I came along we didn't have to worry about any of that. The wormhole drive allowed us to saunter along at sublight and still go from one side of the galaxy to another in, oh, about a shipboard day all told. We still had to make sure we were in one of the sectors designated as jump points to minimize any potential unpleasant effects on nearby planets or deep space outposts. You don't want to reenter Euclidean space within an AU of a planet, because the 'shock wave' of particles that builds up in front of the ship will pulverize pretty much anything. And of course as a line ship we had some pretty impressive defensive weaponry, of which one component was that shock wave itself."

"Did you ever have to use it?"

"Not during my time on board, other than drills and exercises. In the academy we learned about a few previous scuffles, though. Most of them were just misunderstandings or saber rattling."

Tol interrupted in Goblish. "Sorry to be a bother, but what does '1.5c' mean?"

"It means point five units beyond the speed of light. Not one and a half times the speed of light, though. Once you pass c— light speed—the number changes from a liner multiplier to what was known to us as the Dirac scale. It's sort of complicated, but basically that number represents the value a waveform would have if you collapsed it at that energy level. How fast you're actually going depends on several parameters like the resting mass of the ship and some other stuff involving energy source and dispersion characteristics. For the *Isomer*, that meant our top velocity was generally around twenty-two times the speed of light, although measuring absolute velocity past C is tricky because, as I implied back there, time and space are not separate entities but a waveform. In other words, you can't just click a stopwatch at point A and again at point B and get a useful number."

Tol gave them his blankest look. "I don't pretend to understand absolutely *any* of that except for the last bit. Why can't you use a stopwatch to figure out your speed?"

"Because," Oloi chimed in, "Velocity is distance over time and time is not flowing at the same rate for your stopwatch as it is for the ship. The underlying units aren't even the same. It would be like trying to measure how far it is from your house to the grocer using units of volume."

Tol nodded. "Right. I'm not going to ask any more questions because the answers are actually increasing my ignorance, not decreasing it."

"Also remember that a lot of what we're talking about doesn't translate to Goblish very well. I'm sure Petey's doing the best job possible, but most of this relativistic stuff is based on physics not known to N'plorkian scholars. For example, I don't think anyone on N'plork has actually measured the speed of light. Do you have any idea how fast that is?"

"You mentioned it earlier, but the number was too big so I forgot."

"299,792 kilometers per second."

"I'm sorry guys, but I can't really comprehend anything going that fast. Thanks for trying, though."

Oloi chuckled. "Understood. I'm not really sure I comprehend it at any deep level, either. To me it's just mathematics." He turned back to Plåk. "Why do you think he was boosting the impulse modulators, then?"

"It looks like he intended to use them as offensive weapons. They were aimed at several principal cities of N'plork including," he looked at Tol, "the Tragacanthan Royal Complex."

Tol blinked. "So, what does that mean? What kind of damage are we talking about here?"

"That ship is capable of going more than six million kilometers per second. It's bigger than any vessel ever built on N'plork: the size of a medium N'plorkian city, in fact. Even without any higher mathematics background, I think you can see how much energy this thing can put out. Now imagine most of that energy focused in a beam about the diameter of this room. A single full-power pulse would not only utterly vaporize any building and people it hit, it would drill a crater at least a hundred meters deep beneath it. In a second or two the Tragacanthan central government would effectively cease to exist."

Tol got serious. "That has to be prevented, at any cost. What can we do?"

"I tried to shut off the power supply to those things, but he has it routed in such a way that doing so would probably require more time and effort than I might be able to put in even with maximum manna storage. It's very difficult for us to manipulate objects on Primus, as you've no doubt noticed."

"If we can't turn it off we'll need to destroy the ship," Oloi said, "Easiest way to do that is de-orbit."

"Ordinarily I would volunteer to do it for you, but of course in this case that would be a guaranteed recipe for failure," Tol said.

"We will need your help, in fact. But don't worry. All you have to do is follow simple instructions. You don't have to understand the technology involved."

"You just described my whole life."

Given the size and complexity of the *Isomer*, they decided that it would be best to destroy it as soon as possible. While they had reason to believe that Zizmziz was out of commission, he could have set the weapons to fire on some sort of timer, not to mention that they might be activated accidentally. Too many lives were at stake to take chances. They returned to the ship and met in a conference room near the flight deck.

"We just need to calculate the de-orbit burn such that frictional contact is maximized," Plåk said, "That should reduce the ship to pieces no larger than a pram. Then we engineer the reentry so that those pieces fall somewhere harmless. On N'plork that's not hard to do, as it's mostly water and the vessel-to-ocean area ratio is very, very small."

"Agreed. Do you know how to access the nav systems to get this done?"

"It won't be that easy. A lot of those control systems were

disabled prior to launching the lifeboats per Colonization Authority policy—and most of the rest have been taken over by Iwo for whatever his ultimate purposes were. We'll have to set the thruster profiles manually and start the burn sequence from the propulsion console."

"That means we'll definitely need Tol for at least the final burn initiation. Even with manna loading we won't have enough time to get all of that accomplished." Oloi turned to Tol. "Hear that? We're going to need you to push some buttons for us."

"Pushing buttons I can do. So long as I know which buttons to push, of course."

"We'll make that very clear."

Plåk had to consult the ship's internal map to find Propulsion Systems Control. He'd only been there a few times and that was, of course, over nine hundred years ago. With Oloi and Tol in tow he headed off. On the way they explained to Tol what they were going to do and what his role would be.

"Once we set the thrusters, you'll need to get to the propulsion console, which we'll show you on the way, and press areas on three different control surface—they aren't actually 'buttons,' per se—to initiate the burn sequence that will drive the ship to progressively lower orbits until it starts to burn up in the atmosphere," Plåk said.

Tol was a little skeptical. "So, this gigantic thing is somehow going to be reduced to pieces no bigger than a pram? You gonna blow it up, or what?"

Oloi answered. "Have you ever looked up at night and seen shooting stars?"

"Sure. I even saw a couple of them turn into huge fireballs. Entertaining, to say the least."

"Those fireballs were probably dray-sized chunks of rock burning up in the atmosphere. Objects like asteroids hit the blanket of air surrounding the planet at tens of thousands of kilometers per hour. Hitting the air molecules is like running over sandpaper. The friction causes a lot of heat. The temperature eventually gets high enough to break down the structure of the rock and vaporize the smaller, lighter components completely. The result can be a fireball that is visible from a considerable distance, depending on the altitude and angle of entry."

"Do...asteroids the size of this ship ever hit here?"

"Very rarely. Once every two or three million years, probably. One the size of the *Isomer* could in theory wipe out all or at least most life on N'plork if it hit just right, though. Not to worry, though, because we're going make certain that virtually all of the ship is vaporized high in the atmosphere. What few chunks do make it down we're going to aim at the open ocean. The odds that any of them will hit people or vessels are extremely tiny indeed."

"That's, um, comforting, I guess. Are you sure you know what you're doing?"

"I know it's difficult to digest," Plåk replied, "But both Oloi and I lived on ships like this for years before we became mages or even knew of the existence of magic. We know a lot about them and how they work. Anything we don't know, or remember, we can get from the ship's AI because my officer's access credentials are still active in the authentication system."

Tol's security sense got the better of him. "Is it normal for them to be active for so long?"

"Not usually," Oloi answered, "But since this is a multi-generation colonization ship, the rules are a little different."

"Also," added Plåk, "We left in rather a hurry and the security protocols weren't initiated because we thought the ship would be destroyed within a couple of weeks. If we'd even suspected it would still be here 900 years later I think we might have been more conscientious in that regard."

"Why *is* it still here?" Tol asked. It seemed like the giant grazing quadruped in the room.

"We don't know," Oloi said after a few seconds of silence. "Somehow Philmon Iwo either set all this up before he evacuated, which seems unlikely, or found a way back up after evacuating but before the orbit decayed, which seems even more unlikely."

Tol had a thought. "You guys are always talking about gallivantin' back and forth through time. What if he just came back in time after he was a mage?"

The archmages stared at Tol, and then at one another. Plåk cocked his head. "Temporal displacement through magic? Is that... possible?"

Oloi shrugged. "Translocation involves wormholes. Why not? The power requirements don't change much as you increase either the spatial or temporal vector components. There's a manuscript in my library on theoretical time travel. Let's have a look." He teleported the book to the table and they flipped through it.

The monograph in question was heavy on speculation and light on actual magic, but it did seem to confirm that translocation was the key to any travel through time via magical means. Retrograde temporal displacement is fraught with complications, as anyone who has given the subject any thought will be aware. The myriad pitfalls are of sufficient magnitude, in fact, that mages tend to shy away from any real experimentation along those lines.

A major snag in the hypothesis that Iwo used this means to realize his goals was that manipulation of translocation magic is simply beyond the skill level of a Magus Incipius. An Incipius could use a preexisting template to travel between locations well enough, but understanding of the mechanics of the spell itself required at a very minimum a Magus Arcanis. The kind of research necessary for such a radical departure from the established practice really moved the project into archmage territory, in point of fact. Whatever Zizmziz had been, he was no archmage.

The only realistic way this could have been accomplished, therefore, was with considerable assistance from a higher-level mage. So long as Zizmziz presented his interest as purely academic, or at least hid any malicious intent, such cooperation was neither unreasonable nor proscribed. In the end, though, it didn't matter how he did it. What mattered right now was preventing the improvised weapons from ever firing.

They took Tol to his position first. Plåk waved a finger in the air over the propulsion panel and blue numerals appeared floating above the three areas of the touchscreen. "See this little light right here?" he asked Tol, pointing to a tiny red pinprick at the top of the panel. "When this turns green, touch these actuator panels in this order. If you've done it right, this entire vertical bar over here will light up."

"And then what happens?"

"Then the ship will be nudged downward until it begins to disintegrate in N'plork's atmosphere. It will, in other words, spiral in to its doom."

"And how long will I have to get off from that point?"

"Plenty of time. Well over an hour before things get dicey. We'll come down and make sure you've made it off."

"Thanks. This isn't exactly my idea of the perfect way to kick off, being incinerated in a crashing spacecraft. Come to think of it, this isn't a way I've ever even considered. Until recently I thought of spaceships as something that, if they really existed at all (no offense to either of you), flitted back and forth a long, long way from here."

"I think it's rather a stirring end, flaming across the sky like a meteor," said Oloi, smiling.

"You're welcome to it," replied Tol, "Except of course all you would do is return to The Slice, I suppose. I won't have that luxury."

"Not entirely true," said Plåk. "Come on, Oloi, let's get up to the nav station."

With not much else to occupy him while he waited for the little light to turn green, Tol wondered what Plåk meant by 'not entirely true,' but eventually decided it wasn't worth the mental effort.

At last, the light glowed green. Even though Tol was staring at that spot, it took a couple of seconds for the change to register. When it did he reached over and touched the glass surface in the order and areas indicated and waited. The column lit up as promised. He'd done his job—now it was time to scoot off this doomed behemoth.

He walked away.

"Where are you going?" he heard Petey ask, "You are supposed to wait here for the archmages."

"I'm just going to wait for them in the hallway to save some time."

"What if they come in from another direction?"

Tol gestured with his hand in a sweeping arc. "You see any other doors into this room? Because I don't."

"They could teleport."

"Then I'll stand in the hallway where I can see this spot," Tol replied with some exasperation.

"I do not believe relocating to be necessary or prudent," insisted the pen.

Tol frowned, "Why are you making a big deal out of this?" Outside the huge vessel at that moment, four dish antennas rotated smoothly back into their stowed positions in bays set into the underside of the superstructure as the power to their guidance systems was shut down. The signals they were transmitting, however, were not terminated because the stow failsafes had been disabled. In their default orientation all four were aimed at precisely the same spot on the interior of the ship.

Tol stood in the doorway of the propulsion deck for a few minutes, but the nervous energy built up and he began to pace.

"Now what are you doing?" Petey demanded.

"Just walking back and forth to work off some of this tension."

"Again: not a good idea."

"Stuff it, will ya?"

Tol reversed direction and took a single step, then stopped. The walls were...buzzing. He figured it was something to do with the orbit decaying and kept walking. For some reason he was suddenly feeling very fatigued and his leg muscles were sore. Weird. Without warning the floor beneath him began to glow red hot and then fall away, taking the air in the vicinity with it. Tol flailed and grabbed a structural spar, instinctively wrapping himself in the protective cocoon at the same time. Everything around him was disintegrating. He heard explosions going off all over the ship.

"What the smek happened to 'well over an hour'?" he yelled at Petey. As the last word left his mouth Tol felt a strange dizziness that quickly escalated to an inability to think or even move without great difficulty. The integrity of the outer hull had been compromised; all the atmosphere was gone. He was still wrapped around the spar; it took every last gram of his concentration and effort to maintain that grip. Meanwhile the *Isomer* plunged ever downward, its entire outer surface now trailing great clouds of fire and vapor.

The archmages finished their reconfiguration and headed immediately for Tol. The nav computer would extrapolate their course changes and see that the ship was being de-orbited. It would inform the AI, which would then shut down all unnecessary power and prepare for optimal insertion. They had selected the option that would keep certain subsystems like the lifts operational until the end. This ship, unlike most, was designed with this specific endpoint in mind.

When they got to the propulsion console they could see that Tol had done his job. He was nowhere in sight, however. "Odd," Oloi said, "Where would he have gone?"

"We did tell him to stay here and wait for us, right?" Plåk replied.

"Yes. Quite definitely."

They searched for an hour and ten minutes with increasing urgency. "He's here; I can feel his arcanic presence!" Oloi yelled over the steadily growing noise of a starship falling apart around them, "Why can't we see him?"

"Some kind of fold or pocket in the fabric," Plåk yelled back. "I don't know where it came from."

"Can we assume he will get back to N'plork of his own accord?"

The remaining structure fell away, leaving them floating in space above a huge fireball that continually birthed smaller ones.

"I don't think what we assume matters any longer."

As Tol fell he began to lose consciousness. Even though Tol's protective capsule had re-formed when the oxygen levels dropped, Petey realized they were both doomed if something was not done very, very quickly as it would not prevent them from being incinerated. He rerouted his backup power cells to the surface of his housing and gave Tol the strongest jolt he could. It brought him awake, but not really cognitive. Petey told him with full volume bone induction to teleport them back to Goblinopolis. Tol responded a little bit, but Petey could tell by his brainwaves that there was a lack of comprehension. He tried one last ploy.

Through the thick haze that enveloped his brain, Tol heard a voice as though from a dream. It was somehow familiar and somehow...important. He focused every tiny grain of attention he could muster on making it out.

"Come back to me safe and sound, Tol."

As the words became clear, Tol realized his clothes were beginning to flame up as the protective capsule failed. He suddenly wanted desperately to see Selpla one more time. He closed his eyes to think of her and after a few moments realized the heat and buffeting had ceased. The air smelled like...Selpla's bedroom. He opened his eyes once more and saw that there was an excellent reason for that.

"Welcome home, Tol-u-ol," he heard Petey say, "I need to shut down for a while now in order to recharge."

Tol tried to reply but nothing coherent came out so he just grunted in affirmation. He looked down at his burnt clothing and blackened skin and figured he should clean up, but he was so tired. He made it as far as the living room sofa and then collapsed utterly.

Chapter Twenty-eight

Selpla came home that evening to a house that smelled faintly of smoke. She was understandably concerned and headed for the kitchen to investigate, but only got as far as the living room. The sofa, to be more precise. She almost panicked as it was not apparent who was lying there in the burnt clothing at first, but as she crept closer she realized it was only Tol. The panic was replaced by worry. She sat next to him and assessed the situation. His overjack was mostly burned away, as were his boots and the bottom half of his pants. His skin in those areas, as well as his arms, was charred, but he didn't seem seriously injured regardless. Goblin skin was not only extremely tough, it healed very quickly when abraded or burned.

She gently undressed him, cleaned the soot off, and covered him with a blanket. When he finally awoke she was sitting in a nearby chair with a pot of infusion.

"Hi, sleepy head. Your spare clothes are on the bed. Rough case?"

Tol sat up and rubbed his eyes. "Yeah, I guess you could say that." He looked down at his cleaned and bandaged arms and legs. "I guess it wasn't a dream, after all. That's good. If I start havin' dreams like that I'm goin' to the shrink."

Selpla knew better than to start in with questions too soon. Tol would tell her in his own time. She decided to change the subject.

"Did you catch that amazing shooting star last night? I've never seen anything like it. It was huge and bright and pieces of it kept breaking off or something."

Tol chuckled grimly. "Yeah, I was...aware of it."

He took the day off from work to recuperate and other things which were centered on the fact that Selpla also took a vacation day. A little before midday he got a voice message on his comm; by the alert tone he recognized it as coming from Aspet. During a lull in activities he listened to it and turned to Selpla grinning widely. "I'm gonna be 'uncle Tol'." She hugged him. "That's fantastic news! I'm so happy for Aspet and Boogla. I wonder if it will be a boy or girl?"

"Dunno. Our family has always been sorta male-heavy, but all I've ever heard about from Boogla are her sisters and mom. She's never mentioned her father, or any brothers. That's a little weird, now that I think about it."

Selpla got a far-away look in her eye. "I wonder what it's like to be a mom?" She returned from her reverie to see Tol drop (gingerly) to one knee. He fished around in the remains of his overjack in a secret sub-pocket sewn into the same pocket where he kept Petey. Opening it with two fingers, he extracted a beautiful gold ring set with tiny diamonds and emeralds. He held it up.

"If you'd really like to find out about the 'mom' thing, I'd be happy to assist in that effort. I've been thinkin' about this for a while now and I think it's time to take this relationship to the next level, as they say in the videoz. Will you marry me?"

Selpla sat there, stunned, for a few seconds before she started crying. She kept trying to say 'yes' but all that came out was incoherent blubbering. Finally she gave up and just nodded. As they hugged, Tol suddenly thought of something. "Now, understand this isn't one of those high society games you told me about. I really mean it." Selpla looked at him and the waterworks started up again. "So do I, Tol," she said between sobs, "For the first time, so do I."

They were at Eske's enjoying a celebratory lunch when his comm buzzed to tell him that a voice message he'd received some hours earlier marked 'important' had not yet been listened to. He noticed the circuit number was from work. He sighed and put the thing to his ear. Thirty seconds later he stuffed it back in his pocket and shook his head.

"I will never get used to this smek."

Selpla touched him on the arm. "What's the matter?"

"Two perps I rescued, arrested, and then left on the street in Koppra when I...went to meet with Oloi and Plåk are now somehow in a holding cell in Sebacea. The desk sergeant said they just appeared there. Neither of them seems to have any idea how that happened. One of them mentioned my name, so they called to find out what I knew. I guess I'll head down there later and write up the charges. I suspect Frespiola will want in on that action, too."

Selpla's eye ridge went up. "How *did* that happen?"

Tol shrugged. "Because I wanted it too, I guess."

Petey suddenly powering back up interrupted the discussion, to Tol's relief.

"Welcome back," Tol said into his pocket. Selpla looked puzzled for a second, then laughed.

"People are going to think you're strange if you keep doing that," she said.

It was Tol's turn to laugh. "Nothing new there."

Petey calibrated his voice circuits for a moment before replying.

"I have worked out what happened to us back there, if you want to hear it."

Tol shrugged. "Selpla hasn't really been briefed yet, but go ahead. I'll fill her in later. We are in a public place, though, so keep that in mind."

"I do not believe any uninformed listeners would be able to comprehend much of this. It borders on the irrational, as has become quite the norm for activities in which you are involved. The ship did not actually disintegrate suddenly. It in fact followed the schedule indicated by Plåk and Oloi quite closely."

"How is that possible?" Tol asked, "They said it would be over an hour. It was more like two minutes."

"One hour and twelve minutes, in point of fact. The reason it seemed like two minutes is that we were embedded in a temporal loop that resulted, as far as I can estimate, when the transmitting and focusing mechanism for the isochronic modulator streams aimed at N'plork returned to their stowed positions without their signal input being terminated. They apparently all aimed at the same spot, which just happened to be one we traversed as a result of your insistence on pacing back and forth. I did warn you not to do that, incidentally. We walked the same six point eight meters a total of eight hundred and forty three times, by my count."

"Isochronic modulator? Temporal loop?" Selpla cut in, "What are they?"

"Some kinda spaceship smek," Tol replied, rolling his eyes.

"*Spaceship*? Did you get hit on the head during any of this, Tol?" She felt his forehead to see if he was running a fever.

"I wish the explanation was that simple. I need to talk to Oloi about this, I guess, but not right now. Right now is all about us." He took her hands across the table.

Later in the afternoon Tol called Aspet and relayed his own good news. Aspet confided in him that they'd already had tests done and the baby was a girl; her name was going to be Leitha.

"Nice," Tol replied, "I woulda figured another Boogla, though, to be honest."

"This is highly confidential, but my wife's name is not actually Boogla: it's Kanitha. The name she goes by is actually the title for the head of her secret society, the Sisters of the Code. She became 'the Boogla' on her mother's death. If Leitha decides to follow in her mother's footsteps, she will one day more than likely be 'the Boogla,' too."

"Wow," Tol said, blinking, "That's, um, actually sorta nifty."

"Please consider all of that stuff about Boogla state secret, at least for now."

"You got it, boss."

While he didn't relay any of the Boogla secrets, he did tell Selpla about the baby.

"Leitha. That's a very pretty name," she said, snuggling next to her new fiancé on the sofa.

"Yeah, it is. And something tells me," Tol replied, "That she's going to make history."

402

Epilogue

Orcs: a New Beginning

The Valtir quest was ultimately successful. Boogla and Plåk compiled and presented all of the information from the *Isomer* lifeboat off Flam to Igra, while Boogla arranged for the Abbess of Eithmorg and Igra to meet for the first time, thus joining the two parallel orc social lines at last. The Valtir proved, of course, to be the "data vault" on board the Flam lifeboat that chronicled the history of humans and their transformation to orcs in some detail. In time the orcs worked out just what the Round Table ritual really was and where it came from.

Plåk, with Oloi's assistance, created an English language training course in Goblish and led an entire generation of orcs back to their native tongue, which they found easier to handle than Goblish or Higglin because unlike the N'plorkian languages English was designed for the human vocal apparatus. Other human languages had been spoken on board the *Isomer*, of course, but neither of the archmages had been fluent polyglots so the best they could do was translate the English portions of the existing manuals in case the orcs wanted to study them.

True to her word, Boogla presented a proposal to vacate the Treaty of Mutual Containment at the international diplomatic symposium in Zilond, Spleroste. She accompanied it with not only several hundred pages of documentation, but testimony from Dr. Reoksa and three additional well-known history and sociology scholars. Finally, she showcased a selected number of never-before-seen poems, literary works, and objets d'art that strongly contradicted the prevailing notion of orcs as racially primitive and insane.

A non-binding vote taken at the symposium at Boogla's request resulted in a slight majority for vacating. This was in fact a huge victory for her, because going in the odds that anyone at all would have voted that way were essentially zero. It would take considerable time and diplomatic effort, but on the way back to Goblinopolis she already knew her final triumph was inevitable. After nearly a thousand years of undeserved bondage, the orcs would at last take their place as equal players on the stage of N'plork.